STAY ON THE BLUE GRASS

Ronald K. Myers

STAY ON THE BLUE GRASS

DOUBLE DRAGON

CHAPTER 1

It was a rare day. The sky was clear. Usually a dirty-orange dome of filth hovered over Blue Town.

Here, the town's hero, Sergeant John McQueen, stood high on a plastic podium. Before him a sea of puffy-faced people were giving him a big sendoff. He was getting ready to go after his five-hundredth infected Dinky. And he wouldn't be using a squirt gun. Squirt guns had been outlawed.

Throughout the crowd, Humpty-Dumpty-shaped people with faces like pigs, joined hands and shouted out cheers of encouragement; but living in one of the few remaining livable places on earth and a fear of the green grass virus, forced these well-wishers to stay in the confinement of the sterile blue grass. McQueen's speech could not be watched on TV. Debris from satellite wars had clogged broadcast signals.

Each time McQueen waved to the pink-faced people, phony smiles beamed up at him; and even though hope radiated from their swine-like eyes, in their hearts they wanted to know when the danger would end. They wanted to know when they would be free to venture off the blue grass. But until they were freed, they chose to be entertained.

Having been partially brainwashed, McQueen didn't know if he was providing productive or destructive entertainment. If he couldn't capture the escaped Dinky, he would have to do something he had never done before. He would have to shoot a Dinky.

Years ago, an electronic magnetic pulse wiped out all computers, cell phones, and devices that ran on magnetic strips or disks. Now, some of the old technology of the twentieth century was slowly being revived. If the broadcast signals could be tuned in on one of the ancient, picture-tube TVs, these bored, pudgy people of Blue Town would spend an exciting evening stuffing food into their mouths and watching their hero kill on TV.

McQueen looked beyond the crowd. The green virus-infected land outside the boundaries of the safe blue grass was deserted. Warrior guards marched within the confines of the blue grass; and even though it wasn't necessary, they waved their arms in the empty air and shouted, "Stay away! Stay on the blue grass!"

The people of Blue Town usually didn't go near the orange warning signs; but this day, a few chub-faced rebellious youth became brave. They moved toward the dangerous green grass. But their bravery didn't last. Like all the other pig people, they didn't want to mutate. If they touched the green grass or non-approved water they would mutate and shrink to little, big-eyed, floppy-eared Dinkies. Then, they would be forced to live out the rest of their days working in the green, virus-filled, agricultural fields.

One by one, the young pig people waddled away from the green danger and crammed their ballooned bodies into the mumbling huddle of other pig people waiting on the parade field of blue grass.

In the distance, gray loudspeakers, on tall steel poles, screeched and clicked. All heads turned toward the sound. The sergeant of the guard's voice blared into the sun-filled day: "Stay on the blue grass!"

Holding his opened palm up, Sergeant John McQueen reached skyward. He held a salute to a higher being and posed to be photographed for a propaganda poster. Throughout the crowd, the pig people nodded their pink heads and grunted with approval. Just before the camera snapped, Corporal Burke pushed against McQueen and stuck his ugly face into the picture. In the mirror reflection of the camera lens, McQueen could see what would be the finished picture. In it, Burke's face was unshaven; and he was forcing his ugly cheese-face smile. Even though he wore an extra tight fitting uniform, it was wrinkled. And his corporal stripes were dull and old; they announced the shame of not being promoted in years. His appearance broadcasted laziness. Next to McQueen's perfect military appearance, Burke stood out like an imbecilic leech.

The spindly cameraman placed his hand on the tripod and looked up from behind the camera. "Corporal Burke," he said, and waved the back of his hand in a sweeping motion. "Sergeant McQueen is the hero today. Step down please."

With an expression of a man who had just been caught with his fly down, Burke touched his receding chin and blew air out of his thin-lipped mouth. With bitter reluctance, he stepped down off the podium.

Sergeant McQueen stood alone and watched himself in the camera monitor. He was dressed in his white warrior uniform. Various colors of medals lined the left side of his chest. His coal-black hair hung smooth and sleek down his straight back. When he lowered his arm, his three gold sergeant stripes shimmered in the silver sun; and his jet-black eyes leveled a lingering gaze at the people in the crowd.

The cameraman snapped the picture and mechanically folded the tripod. Then without emotion, he slung it over his skinny shoulder and walked away.

Corporal Burke jumped back up onto the podium and announced, "Augur, the hero of the mutant Dinkies, has been spotted."

A reporter with a gray beard yelled out from the crowd. "How can that be? Augur is a myth."

Burke shook his head. "Augur is no myth. He's an escaped Dinky. He's been infected with a new strain of virus. He's wanted dead or alive. If Sergeant McQueen can catch him, he'll capture the all-time record."

Waving his hand and bobbing his red-haired head like a scarlet beacon, a little freckled-faced kid in the crowd yelled up at Burke. "Corporal Burke, I thought you had the all-time record."

Burke assumed a posture of superiority and looked toward the little kid, but he did not make eye contact. "No son," he said as if he were trying to convince the crowd. "I told you, 'I hope to have the record some day.'"

The kid put his hand over his mouth and his eyes narrowed with suspicion. Burke turned his back to the kid and pointed to Sergeant John McQueen. "If you reporters will step forward." He motioned with his hand. "Sergeant McQueen will answer your questions."

As the reporters waded through the crowd, Burke leaned over and whispered in McQueen's ear, "Why should the corporation give you the right

8

to reproduce?"

"It's the law," McQueen said. "If you capture five hundred Dinkies you will have earned that right, too."

"If you catch the Dinky," Burke said, and his lips curled into a self-important smile. "Why don't you use some of those reward money credits and buy something to bulk up that puny body of yours?"

"I like my body the way it is," McQueen said, and tensed for the reporter's onslaught. Highly excited, the news reporters pushed and shoved their way up the four little steel steps and rushed up to stand on the plastic podium. McQueen reached out to shake their healthy left hands, but they didn't acknowledge his friendly gesture. They lifted their right hands and pointed their camera-implanted cam-fingers at his face. The questions flowed.

"Sergeant McQueen, how are you going to do it this time?"

"If you capture Augur alive, will you ask him where all the Dinkies are going?"

"What if he throws virus water on you?"

"What will you do if he hits you with a piece of wood?"

"Augur is the champion of the Dinkies. Will you have to kill him?"

McQueen turned and smiled at the cam-finger pointing reporters. "I'm a warrior for the Chief Earth Officer. Until advances in science make it possible for us to go off the blue grass, I will continue to take orders from him."

A reporter, with only one middle finger on his hand, pointed his cam-finger in front of McQueen's face. "Did Chief Earth Officer Nelson order you to

9

pursue your five-hundredth Dinky if it runs off the blue grass?"

McQueen didn't answer.

Another reporter, with a full set of fingers, pointed his little cam-finger at him. "The world knows you were exposed to the wood-virus when you were a boy. Will that virus affect you in the future?

"I'm not a prophet, McQueen said. "Don't ask me about things that haven't happened yet." He looked down. Even though charged particles striking the earth's magnetic field played havoc with the all communications signals, a reporter standing next to the podium was trying to get a picture on one of the few working TV monitors. For a brief second, the dark screen fluttered and came in clear. A side view of McQueen appeared. Under his smooth-fitting uniform, the symmetric muscles on his strong arms moved with the sinuous grace of a dancer and then the screen blinked black.

Another reporter, with a two-fingered hand, flashed his cam-finger at McQueen. "Why do you call it a chase when it is a battle against the virus?"

McQueen didn't answer.

Another reporter's voice rang out. "How much longer do we have to stay on the blue grass?"

McQueen smiled a big white-toothed smile in the reporter's direction. "After I capture my five-hundredth Dinky, all your questions will be answered."

The reporters swarmed around him; and reading pre-prepared reports, they talked into their cam-fingers.

Corporal Burke wormed his way through the

reporters and stood at the front of the podium. When he raised his hand, all heads in the crowd turned toward him. "Escaped virus-carrying Dinkies are still a danger to the world." He raised his clinched fist above his head. "They must be shot with the antidote."

Waves of murmurs flowed from the crowd. Burke made a T sign with his hands. With enough menace in his voice to make the people comply, he yelled out, "Time out!"

Quiet cloaked the crowd and he continued. "Sergeant McQueen has done his job before. He will do it again. Let him pass and get on with it."

McQueen looked at the route he would have to take to get to the OvalCar. A hoard of pig people bunched together and blocked his way. He whispered to Burke. "That's a lot of people to wade through."

Burke nudged McQueen's elbow. "They're not people. They're pigs."

Even though the pig people had the characteristics of pigs, deep in his heart, McQueen knew they were human beings with fragile feelings. The more Burke disrespected them, the more McQueen didn't like it. He flashed a disapproving look in Burk's direction and stepped off the podium. A wall of well-wishers surrounded him. Somewhere behind him, a voice called out. "Sergeant McQueen!"

McQueen looked back over his shoulder and watched through the open space below the elbow of a reporter's lifted arm. The little freckled-faced kid's red head was bobbing through the crowd and getting close.

The crowd was too bunched up for the kid to get to McQueen. After a brief struggle with an extra-large fat lady with a butt that stuck out so far that it looked like a shelf, the kid turned and ran up to Burke. Burke acted as if the kid wasn't there, but the kid persisted. When Burke finally looked down, the kid presented him a piece of plastic paper. "Can I have your autograph, sir?"

Burke took the plastic paper and signed it. "Here!" He pushed it into the kid's chest. "You little son of a bitch."

For a moment the kid's eyes filled with tears, but in a flash, the despair in his freckled-face fill with hate. He gave Burke a dirty look and threw the paper on the ground. McQueen wanted to go over and comfort the kid, but the crowd parted and he walked toward the waiting vehicle.

In the center of the crowd, a lumpish lady waved a red hat in the air and shrieked, "Don't let them hit you with the virus-water. You'll turn into a Dinky."

A man's voice from the right side of the crowd rang out. "Be careful. We don't need another dead mutant like your father."

McQueen cast a mean glare to where the remark had come from. All advice stopped.

So what if he happened to get exposed to the water-virus, he had been exposed before and it had not affected him. The antidote they gave his father didn't work and he died. He was okay before they touched him. But it may have been because the water-virus has different strengths.

A reporter, with reddish-brown hair falling over his eyes, blocked McQueen's path. When

12

McQueen was close, the reporter lifted his hand and stuck his cam-finger in front of McQueen's face. "Is he right?" he asked; and with his other hand, he pushed his hair from his green eyes. "Were you exposed?"

McQueen talked into the reporter's single cam-finger. "I've never been exposed to—" he said, but stopped.

He turned away from the cam-finger and continued toward the waiting OvalCar. The last time he had talked to that reporter he had had two fingers. Apparently, the reporter had gotten another one chopped off for reporting facts.

In the past, when McQueen didn't know the answers to the reporter's questions he had not answered. He wondered why he was trying to do it now. His father had said, "Don't be like those chopped-off-fingered reporters that make up questions about things that haven't happened yet. They're trained to report what the Chief Earth Officer wants. If they don't report what he wants, they get a finger chopped off until they do."

McQueen felt as if he had been running a long race, and he was about to cross the finish line, a winner. All he had to do was catch just one more Dinky. Then he would have the right to move onto an estate protected on all sides with fields of beautiful blue grass. Then he wouldn't have to live in the acrid blue grass of the common pig people and answer any of those reporter's stupid questions. But until that happened, he would have to play their little games.

He turned back to the cam-fingered reporter. "If I answered questions about something that hasn't happened yet, I would be foolish."

The reporter's reddish-brown hair fell over his eyes, again. Pushing it out of his eyes, he revealed a flash of anger. "But the people deserve answers."

While he held back his feelings, McQueen's intolerance oozed into his heart. "Until those things happen," he said and smiled faintly. "Those kinds of questions don't need answers."

The reporter persisted. McQueen quit talking, turned his back to him, and made his way to the waiting egg-shaped OvalCar. When he stopped at the edge of the blue street, he turned to the crowd and lifted his arm in salute. As the people cheered, a woman driver dressed in a black uniform that clung to her shapely body flipped up the silver-glass of the OvalCar's door and held it open. McQueen stepped in and leaned back into the body-forming seat. The driver strapped him in and flipped a switch on the dashboard. The seat molded to the contours of his back and the LED in the dashboard flashed. The old scratchy computer voice stated, "Warrior safe to transport." The driver placed her hands on the steering wheel and sat back in the driver's seat. McQueen felt the skinny plastic wheels beneath the OvalCar spin for an instant. When they caught on the blue asphalt, the OvalCar lurched forward on its way to where the Dinky had been spotted.

Driving down the road, the driver looked in the rearview mirror. McQueen maintained eye contact for only a brief moment, but it was long enough that he felt messages of mutual interest.

Smiling, the driver said, "I don't know if I'll be permitted to drive you around when they proclaim

14

you a prince of peace."

McQueen studied the driver's reflection in the mirror. When she turned, her long black hair flowed over her perfect breasts like a satin waterfall. Something seemed familiar about her, but he couldn't figure out what it was. "I don't remember you driving me before," he said. "What's your name?"

The driver tilted her cute head to one side and talked back over her shoulder. "Danielle," she said. "May I ask you what you will do when the Friends of the Earth Corporation give you your own house?"

Even though he was only a few hours away from the good life, McQueen had suppress the thought of a new virus-free life for so long that he was afraid if he dwelled on it too long the Friends of The Earth Corporation would up the Dinky count to six hundred or more. "I haven't thought of it much," he said and shrugged. "Maybe I'll raise a family."

Danielle smiled a warm motherly smile. "That would be nice. You and your family could live inside the safety of the blue grass."

"It is a beautiful dream. But until I actually catch the Dinky, I don't like to think about it."

A small tree branch with green leaves sat alongside the blue road. A brief look of agitation formed on Danielle's brow. She gracefully turned the wheel. The splash of green foliage whizzed past the side window. Her look of agitation softened. "Is it true that you will be the first warrior granted the right to reproduce?"

As the sight of the threatening virus-laden tree

branch vanished in the rearview mirror, McQueen answered. "Yes, and I'll have to choose a mate."

Danielle's face glowed like a flickering flame about to flare. "Do you have anyone in mind?"

He studied her face and her long black hair. She was beautiful, but a nervous heartbeat thumped in his chest. "No," he said, and swallowed. "But I'll be looking."

At the side of the road, the OvalCar wheels crunched on fine blue gravel. Danielle's cheery face turned toward McQueen. "We're here," she purred, and stopped the car.

McQueen stepped out of the OvalCar and looked across a safe, blue grass meadow. Uncut green grass framed it, and orange signs, on metal sticks, stood out like neon lights.

CAUTION, they read, STAY ON THE BLUE GRASS. WOOD AND WATER VIRUS BEYOND THIS POINT, DINKY MUTATION EMINET.

McQueen looked between two orange signs. The targeted Dinky stood there and didn't move. He was a little more than a meter high with a little pudgy belly, but his short legs looked powerful.

If the Dinky ran off into the green forest, McQueen couldn't chase him into the woods. Wood-virus would fall off the tree branches and onto his head. If he chased the Dinky into the tall wet grass, the water-virus would wrap around his legs and infect them. He would be condemned to the life of a mutant Dinky. He wanted to capture this Dinky alive; but if he stepped off the blue grass, McQueen would have to shoot him. The antidote-bullets were supposed to stun and cure Dinkies with an advanced stage of mutation, but every Dinky he had seen shot had died.

McQueen walked into the meadow. Unlike Blue Town's air that was rampant with pig people's obnoxious odors, this air was fresh and clean. It made him feel good. He stopped and watched the little Dinky. Like a happy drunk, it was jumping up and down, and waving its little hands at McQueen.

Even though it was his sworn duty, McQueen didn't understand why he should have to shoot this little Dinky. Even though they were small, they were a valuable energy source. The corporation preferred that they be taken alive, but when they escaped, it frowned upon warriors who failed to shoot them.

Walking toward McQueen, the little Dinky stuck his thumbs in his stumpy ears and waved his fingers. "Come on, you big dummy," he yelled, and ran toward an orange warning sign.

McQueen smiled inwardly. He had never had to shoot one yet. But the way this little guy was running, he didn't look like was infected with anything. For a five-hundredth capture, he looked too easy. In a few minutes, McQueen would have him in his hands. If the signals got through, he would be on TV tonight. The Chief Earth Officer would be placing the Medal of Honor around his neck. With the big credit bonus that went with it, McQueen would be able to buy enough water to take a real shower. He wouldn't have to use dry clay to bathe his body. If he was awarded enough money credits, he would buy his own OvalCar, complete with a paid driver. Then, he would scout around and find the perfect reproduction mate.

Fifty meters away, the captain of the warriors

stood at the side of the road and talked into an amplified wrist bullhorn. His orders raced across the blue meadow and barked into McQueen's ears. "Sergeant McQueen! Check your weapon."

McQueen clicked the antidote-bullet-clip into his sidearm, returned it to his holster, and snapped to attention. "Sir, weapon ready to fire."

Looking at McQueen and pointing to the little Dinky, the captain walked ten meters onto the safe blue grass and yelled, "Warrior, complete your obligation."

McQueen stretched out his arm and held his palm toward the sky. "For the good of the corporation," he said, and walked to the edge of the blue grass.

The little Dinky stopped running and leaned his back against the post of an orange warning sign. McQueen walked toward him. But the Dinky didn't seem to care. He crossed his legs as if he were waiting for an OvalBus and stared at McQueen. Twenty meters from him, McQueen stopped walking. With his two pointer fingers together, he waved them up and down and gave the universal signal for the Dinky to bow down and wait to be inspected, searched, or captured. If the Dinky failed to obey the signal, any warrior had the right to shoot him.

The little Dinky bowed his head and waited.

Although McQueen was still disappointed that he didn't have to chase the Dinky, he continued walking. The capture wasn't going to look very good on TV tonight. But a capture was a capture.

When he was ten meters away, the little Dinky's floppy hat fell off his little round head and landed on the grass.

"Dinky," McQueen barked, "pick up your cover."

The little Dinky uncrossed his legs, bent over, and stepped toward his hat. Just as it was at the tips of his fingers, he kicked it with his little leather-shoed-foot. The hat skidded across the grass. The little Dinky stood up and grinned at McQueen.

McQueen stepped closer and repeated, "Dinky, pick up your cover."

Again, the Dinky bent over and kicked his hat just before the tips of his fingers touched it.

McQueen stepped closer and yelled at the Dinky. "Dinky, you know the laws. No aspect of a Dinky's time is to be left to chance or left to its own discretion."

The Dinky picked up his hat and pushed it down onto his big head until the tops of his big ears bent downward. Then, he lifted his head and looked directly into McQueen's face.

"Dinky, you—" McQueen shrieked, but stopped in mid-sentence. Suddenly, he recognized the little Dinky. It was Tommy, the mutant Dinky he had known on his father's farm. They had practically grown up together. McQueen smiled. Tommy was deliberately trying to make him laugh. But he couldn't laugh. He was on function status. And laughing or not, McQueen still had to catch the Dinky. Pleadingly, he whispered, "Tommy, let me catch you."

Tommy smiled a mischievous smile. "Sorry, Johnny." He wagged his little round head around in a wobbly circle. "You have shoot me."

McQueen reached for his weapon. "Come on,

Tommy, quit fooling around. They'll only question you."

"Doze days over."

McQueen wrinkled his brow in puzzlement. "Tommy, you know how to talk. Why are you using that broken mutant language?"

Tommy turned his back to McQueen. "You no catch-a me when I go on green water-virus grass."

"Don't do it, Tommy. I'll have to shoot."

"Maybe I see you at water house." Tommy took off running.

The voice of the captain boomed across the blue grass. "Sergeant McQueen, complete your obligation."

McQueen ran after his little Dinky friend and chased him along the edge of the virus-free blue grass. Tommy hopped into the green grass and stopped. He put his hands on his hips and tapped his little foot. McQueen stopped in his blue tracks and looked down. A meter away from the toes of his warrior boots, the silvery virus-filled liquid clung onto the green grass.

McQueen knew if he touched the water-virus he would have to be decontaminated. He would have only a short time to be given the antidote, and it didn't always work. There was always the chance that the virus would kill him or cause him to mutate into a Dinky.

He looked back over his shoulder. A line of OvalCars drove to the edge of the road and stopped. Reporters jumped out and raised their arms. Being careful to stand on the safe blue gravel, they aimed their cam-fingers toward him.

McQueen looked back at Tommy. Tommy ran

across the green grass, jumped into the tall green weeds, and ducked under a low tree branch. He went out of sight for a moment then popped back up and hopped over a small stream of flowing water. On the other side of the stream, he turned and motioned for McQueen to follow.

McQueen didn't move.

Tommy just stood there, waiting.

The captain's voice boomed again. "Sergeant McQueen! You are on function status. Complete your obligation."

McQueen lifted his weapon and took aim. Like he had done when they were boys, Tommy made those crazy faces. He rolled his big, round, black-dotted eyes, and stuck out his little pink tongue. McQueen pulled on the weapon's trigger, but an uncontrollable burst of laughter erupted from his lips. The gun jerked. Whap! It fired. The antidote slug went wide and missed Tommy's head by a centimeter. Tommy stuck out this pink tongue again, then turned and disappeared into the thick green bushes beyond the tall trees.

The captain rushed up to McQueen. "Stand at attention, Warrior."

McQueen replaced his sidearm to his holster and stood at attention. The captain stood in front of him. With the tip of his nose next to McQueen's, he yelled loud enough for the reporters to hear. "Sergeant McQueen! What are you trying to do? Entice other soul-less Dinkies to escape and spread a new virus?"

McQueen stiffened to a stone state. "No, sir."

Blasting bad breath into his face, the captain kept his nose next to McQueen's. "Do you know

21

that warriors do not keep escaped Dinkies under control they will spread a new virus that will mutate all the people of the world?"

McQueen looked straightforward. "Yes, sir." He did not move a muscle, twitch an eyelash, take a shallow breath of air, or create any movement that would give the captain a reason to reprimand him more.

Even though the air in the meadow was fresh and clean, as he yelled, the captain's rotten breath intensified. "Warrior do you know it is your obligation to marshal the collective energy of the Dinkies and keep an ordered social universe?"

This captain made McQueen want to throw up. He tried not to breathe. The captain was an idiot. He acted like his ignorance came from his upbringing. His parents were probably idiots, too. McQueen figured he might be able to impress the captain with a little knowledge.

"Yes, sir!" he said. "I understand that if the Dinkies are permitted to roam free it will cause a steady deterioration of our delicate ecological system. Then we would have an inevitable and steady deterioration of our system. And also suffer the loss of usable energy. Blue Town's strength and well-being depends on usable energy. If we lose it, our standard of living will be lost. We cannot let that happen, sir!"

The captain stepped back and shook his electrified crop in McQueen's face. As if he were going to strike McQueen in the face, he lifted it. McQueen tensed for the pain, but the captain smiled with satisfaction and slammed the black crop into the palm of his black-leather-gloved hand.

"Warrior McQueen, recite your orders."

McQueen took a much-needed breath of good air and looked straightforward. He talked like a machine. "Sir, the work of every Dinky is fully planned by the Chief Earth Officer. Each day, every Dinky receives complete written instructions. These instructions describe every detail of the task the Dinky is to accomplish, as well as the means to be used in doing the work."

The captain turned to one side and methodically pounded his palm with the electric crop stick. "Warrior, continue."

McQueen breathed a little easier. "The written instructions of the task specify not only what is to be done, but how it is to be done and the exact time allowed for doing it."

The captain turned his back to McQueen. "Warrior, you have complete knowledge of your obligation. No aspect of a Dinky's time is to be left to chance or to be left to a Dinky's discretion."

McQueen wanted to say, "He's not just a Dinky, he's my friend." But he could not argue with any superior officer. He stood tall and clinched his teeth until his jaw hurt.

The captain turned and thrust his finger at McQueen's stone face. "You have failed to perform your obligation. Do you know the procedure you must now follow?"

"Yes, sir. I must return to the barracks and report my failure to the Chief Earth Officer. At my request, the Chief Earth Officer may grant me twenty-one hours to correct the situation."

The captain turned his back to McQueen. "Warrior Dismissed."

Sergeant John McQueen saluted the back of the captain's head and did a perfect about-face. As he walked toward the waiting OvalCar, the captain cussed under his breath. McQueen's ears perked up and he listened. "Decorated warrior my ass, he's a decorated joke."

CHAPTER 2

McQueen stopped at the edge of the blue grass and lowered his head. The agony of shame spread all over his body. Trying to hide his face, he slouched his shoulders, stepped onto the fine blue gravel, and walked toward the waiting OvalCar.

He had never killed a Dinky. And now because he had let Tommy go free, Nelson, the great chief earth officer, would order him to kill Tommy. No matter what had happened, Tommy was still his friend, and he didn't want to kill him.

Before the virus had come, Tommy and he had worked and played together on his father's farm. Tommy didn't look any different now than he had then, and he didn't have a single sign of a new virus. But being friends with a Dinky was illegal.

McQueen looked ahead. Danielle stood next to the OvalCar door, waiting. Thinking about what had just happened, McQueen squared his shoulders and walked toward the car and Danielle.

At the youth camp he had been trained to put all his feelings aside and complete his sworn obligation to the Friends of The Earth Corporation. The teachings at the youth camp claimed that Dinkies had no souls and that they were not one of God's creations. It was more than okay to kill them. He had, had a clear shot at Tommy and he had missed.

In front of his foot, a brown stone lay on the blue pavement. Like other misplaced pieces of the past, it stood out and struggled to regain its rightful place on the man-altered earth. He kicked it. It flew off the side of the road and into the green virus-filled grass.

McQueen may not have had enough courage to shoot Tommy, but he couldn't help it. Tommy was still his friend. He had a soul, and he was more human than all of the warriors McQueen had trained with. But he couldn't understand why Tommy didn't he let him catch him? Maybe he escaped when he was working the fields. If he did, the corporation could claim he had created a new virus. Then, anybody had the legal right to kill him and collect the reward.

McQueen looked for another stone to kick. There was none. He hastened his stride.

People who had mutated into Dinkies were the only ones that could harvest the food from the green virus-causing plants, but Tommy's value as a crop gather wouldn't keep other warriors from shooting him. McQueen would have to capture him before some gun-happy warrior shot him and then argue his value before the Chief Operating Officer. If McQueen could capture Tommy alive, he could say that it was for the good of the corporation. As a warrior, it was his duty to enforce the conservation law that stated: All energy, especially the Dinkies' slave energy, should not be destroyed. Therefore, whenever possible, the warrior's duty is to direct all energy to where it will do the most good.

But it didn't matter what the law stated, Tommy's slave energy would be erased if he were dead. McQueen only had twenty-one hours to save him and the energy he represented.

Danielle opened the door to the OvalCar. Holding his hand over his shame-filled face, McQueen stepped into the car and leaned forward.

Danielle reached up and gently pushed him into the body-forming seat. She wrapped the constraint bars around him. For a fleeting moment, their eyes met. He felt an attraction to her, but his mind depressed it. He focused on Tommy. If he could have just killed him, everything would have changed. Right now, he would be getting ready to live a grandiose life on the beautiful blue grass.

He looked directly ahead. Leaning over his body, Danielle pulled on the seat belt. "This strap is jammed."

The sound of her voice brought back memories of the songbird's lyrical twittering on his father's farm. It took his heart back to a better time. Danielle struggled with the strap and pushed against his body with hers. He felt her semi-soft body against his and the smell of her hair drew him to her. A strange yearning cried from his heart. It was new to him. They were face-to-face. His eyes fixed on hers.

This woman was different. No other woman had ever made him feel like this. It was like he'd known her all his life. He wanted to ask her out, but he was a failure. He couldn't even hint that he cared about her.

He cast his eyes downward and showed no emotion. She looked away and settled into the driver's seat.

On the way back to the main base, he looked out the OvalCar's window. Safe patches of blue spruce trees and blue grass flitted past. He remembered what it was like before the water-virus had contaminated the green vegetation of the earth. Dreams of Tommy and him walking on the green grass and swimming in the water of the off-limits lakes should have made him happy, but they did not. In the back of his mind he searched for the reason why it didn't.

Driving down the road, Danielle constantly looked in the rearview mirror.

McQueen figured the electronic, rear seat monitoring screen was broken again. He put his head in his hands and wondered about Danielle. She knew he had just failed to capture his five-hundredth Dinky. She probably knew that he could have shot him, too. And she was probably thinking he was the worst warrior on earth. Maybe she kept watching him because she wanted to see what a coward looked like.

At the main entrance to the barracks, Danielle leaned her beautiful body against him, again and released him from the body-forming seat. He felt her presence, and a warm feeling glowed inside his chest.

She had energy. He had just felt it. But he couldn't focus on her. Those reporters were going to want a good reason why he didn't shoot Tommy. He didn't know what to tell them. He hoped he could just slip past their pointing cam-fingers.

He stepped out of the OvalCar and stood up. A bull-necked reporter with a crew-cut jumped up from behind the car and jammed his cam-finger in front of McQueen's face. "You were trained by the corporation to be a hunter and killer of disease carrying Dinkies." He shook the cam-finger. "Why didn't you shoot that Dinky?"

McQueen rubbed his chin and hesitated. Suddenly, he felt he had the textbook answer. So,

28

like a textbook soldier, he crossed his arms behind his back, stood at parade rest; and from memory, he recited the manual. "Every human being ever born and all the things that have been built, represents energy. That energy must be transformed from one state to another."

The bull-necked reporter pulled his cam-finger back and talked into it. "Answer the question, Sergeant McQueen." He pushed the cam-finger back in front of McQueen's face.

"It's a warrior's sworn oath," McQueen continued. "A warrior must ensure Dinkies' slave energy is always preserved and transformed for the good of the pig people of the world."

The bull-necked reporter persisted. "Get to the point, Sergeant McQueen. That Dinky could be carrying a new virus. Why didn't you shoot it?"

"Dinkies are disappearing every day. If Dinky slave energy is not preserved, it will be lost. It is in the best interest of the Friends of the Earth Corporation to capture Dinkies alive."

The bull-necked reporter slouched back against the OvalCar. Holding his cam-fingered hand out and running his other hand through his short-bristled hair, he asked, "Will the blue grass still be safe if that Dinky has spread a new virus?"

"I don't have time to answer your questions now," McQueen said, and shut up.

CHAPTER 3

Nudging the reporters aside, McQueen stepped away from the OvalCar and looked toward the entrance to the barracks. If he had captured Tommy, his five-hundredth capture record would have stood for years. If he had captured Tommy, fellow warriors and officers would have been lined up, saluting him at the front of the base. But they were not.

He wasn't too disappointed because he figured his old buddies would greet him anyway. But when he walked to the front of the barracks, no fanfare or fellow warriors were waiting.

His former warrior friend, Corporal Burke, stood at the entrance with a big cheese-face-smile on his face. "Too bad you missed that little Dinky," he said in a loud obnoxious voice.

"Don't get your hopes up, Burke," McQueen snapped back. "You're not getting my stripes. I still have the sergeant slot and I'm not giving it up."

A triumphant smile beamed on Burke's face. "I think you're wrong this time, Johnny." He reached out to touch McQueen's stripes.

McQueen jerked his arm away from Burke's probing fingers. "You've been trying to weasel me out of my stripes for years."

Burke stepped back, lifted his head in an arrogant manner, and pointed to the stripes on McQueen's arm. "Now, those stripes are mine."

Burk's remark caused McQueen to dislike him even more than usual. "Oh really?" he said and tilted his head to one side. "What are you trying to pull off this time?"

Burke wiggled his fingers in front of his face in a mocking manner. "You'll find out soon enough."

"Why don't you just quit the baby crap, Burke? Doesn't it matter that I helped you get through warrior school? Why do you still want my stripes?"

Burke leaned his back against the stone barracks wall. "Because I know I can have them." He grinned and rubbed his fingertips across his massive chest. "After today no one will object."

McQueen's fellow warriors usually supported him. Now that Burk was trying to steal his stripes again, and the fact that no warriors, who were supposed to be his friends, had greeted him, he felt like a single animal fighting for survival. "That's no reason to steal my stripes," he said, trying to suppress his true feelings. "You could have your own slot if you worked for it."

"Why should I work, when I can get ignorant people like you to do it for me?"

McQueen sighed. He knew it was useless to try and help Burke help himself. "You know, Burke," he said, with a disgusted tone to his voice," I wish I hadn't helped you at all."

"You don't really mean that, do you? Old buddy?"

Shaking his head, McQueen said, "I wish I didn't mean it, but your actions show me that you just don't have what it takes to make a good warrior."

"You're crazy, McQueen. I'm made of the same thing you're made of." He paused and stared at McQueen. "You've handled a lot of mutants." His usual big cheese-face smile spread across his face. "The way you're shaking your head, it looks like one of them transferred the virus to your brain."

"Even if one did infect my brain, mine still has something yours doesn't have."

"Like what?"

"The quintessence of what a warrior stands for."

"You can't say anything to rile me," Burke said, and waved his hand as if he were waving off McQueen's remark. "By the way, thanks for helping me make you look like an idiot."

McQueen felt an involuntary shiver but shook it off. "You've been trying to make me look like an idiot ever since we got out of warrior school. Why do you always have to show everyone that you're the scum of the barracks?"

Burke pointed to his own chest with his thumb. "Don't worry about me," he said, and jerked his finger at McQueen. "Worry about how you're going to get out of what I got you into."

"You've said that before, and nothing happened."

"But it's different this time."

McQueen intentionally turned his back to Burke. Walking away, and making crazy signs by waving his hands in circles next to his ears, he said, "I don't want to hear it."

When McQueen got to the main barracks, he stood outside glass doors while the computer scanned his body. After a moment, its voice announced, "Warrior recognized. Please advance to next stage."

McQueen opened the first door and stepped inside the recognition cell. He placed his eye in front of a scanner and placed his ear next to a reflection recognition lock. "Warrior cleared to enter."

He opened the next door and entered. An iron box slid out from the side of the wall. The computer announced, "Please deposit sidearm in lock box."

He placed his sidearm in the lock box, walked into the decontamination chamber, and pulled the lever. The laser's excited violet-glow activated and sent purple light waves over his body. All traces of viruses that may have clung to his uniform or his body were being eliminated. He looked out the glass door. Outside, leaning on the hall wall, Burke stood with his feet crossed and his arms folded across his chest.

McQueen watched Burke's face. That frozen expression, as if he were smelling something rotten, was still there. McQueen looked at Burke's body. Stacked muscle layers shingled his frame, but because he was too lazy to develop his mind, he was a blockhead. McQueen was sorry he had shown him how to jump the steroid ray. It only took a few seconds a day to read the required current events screen, but Burk wouldn't do it. He had muscles in his head that have never been used. If he had to work for his physique instead of relying on steroids, all he would have would be a jelly belly and toothpick arms.

The "virus contained" light flashed, and the computer voice spoke. "Warrior clear to continue to live and fight for the Chief Earth Officer."

Automatically the decontamination chamber's glass door opened. Burke was still leaning on the hall wall.

McQueen figured Burke would continue what he tried to start outside. Tearing people down always made him happy. Cringing, McQueen stepped out of the chamber and waited for Burk's usual cut downs. But they didn't come. With a contrived look on his face, Burke just stood there. His disdainful facial expression and gesture projected arrogance.

McQueen didn't acknowledge his presence. He hated Burke's extra tight fitting uniform. He hated his constant strutting and posturing, and he hated when he howled out hideous orders as if he were reading from a TelePrompTer. Just the sight of him was enough to make a person sick. McQueen walked on by, but he was afraid that Burke might have finally found something to use against him. When they were going through warrior school, McQueen had told him about his father's farm and the little Dinky, Tommy. McQueen outranked Burke, and Burke always got a kick out of using people who were superior to him.

Like a little kid's voice tattling to the teacher, Burke's mocking voice echoed down the hallway. "Johnny," he cried. "Nelson wants to see you?"

McQueen kept on walking. That slime probably told Chief Earth Officer Nelson about Tommy. Walking with his back to Burke, he lifted his right hand next to the side of his face and flashed him the middle finger.

"Nelson still wants to see you," Burke repeated.

McQueen looked forward and snapped back at Burke, "Corporal Burke, don't be ignorant all your life. Show the proper warrior respect. It's Chief Earth Officer, Nelson."

Burke ignored McQueen's rebuke. "Nelson still wants to see you," he said, and snickered.

McQueen turned and was going to reprimand Burke. After all, he outranked him; but he only had a short time to see the chief earth officer and get permission to catch Tommy. He continued walking.

McQueen stopped at the entrance to his cadre room. On his door was taped a sign:

Move over little coward.

Big warrior moving in.

He recognized the grade school writing. It was Burke trying to germinate a rotten seed in his mind. He reached up, ripped the paper sign off the door, and threw it on the floor. The automatic vacuum cleaner system came out of the wall and sucked up the trash.

He went into his room, lay on his bunk, and thought about what he would tell the chief earth officer. Why had Tommy run? He was always welcomed everywhere he went. His little antics had always made everyone laugh. That was why he had gotten away with so many things that other Dinky's would have been shot for doing.

He couldn't believe Tommy had a new virus. Maybe he just went too far, pushed some new warrior to the limit. Maybe the corporation only wanted to tell him to slow his comedy down around certain warriors. But Tommy would have told him if he was in some trivial trouble. The question of why didn't Tommy let him catch him, kept running through his mind. Tommy knew his place. He had always known his place. Sons of Dinky workers were automatically conscripted to farms and filled the ranks of civil service. Tommy's father had taught him well.

But then again, a lot of Dinkies were disappearing. They were going somewhere. Their population was so diminished that the remaining numbers were insufficient to rev up agricultural production. Many virus-free, red, purple, and blue food-fields were dying from neglect. McQueen figured that maybe Tommy was helping the other Dinkies escape, or maybe he knew where they were hiding. If Burke told Chief Earth Officer Nelson he was Tommy's friend, then Nelson knew why he didn't shoot him.

McQueen stood up, changed into his dress-blue uniform, adjusted the medals on his chest, and walked toward the chief earth officer's office. For a moment he thought he could be all wrong. CEO Nelson was the head of the corporation. If he didn't have some compassion for the Dinkies, he wouldn't be in the preferable position he was in.

McQueen stood in front of the chief earth officer's door. To insure a clean tight wrinkle-free fit, he pressed his open hand down the front of his uniform. He took a deep breath and knocked his code knocks on the door — one short with three longs. It was the old Morse code — dit-dah-dah-dah — his father had taught Tommy and him when they were just kids. The chief earth officer and the other warriors didn't know how the codes were formed, and McQueen never bothered to tell them. His father had said that it might come in handy some day. Who would have ever thought that the first letter of his name, J, tapped out in Morse code, would be a code to gain access to one of the most powerful men on earth? It was like his father had said. "Sometimes the simplest codes are the hardest to break."

Dah-dah-dah, Dah-dit-dah, Dah-dah, tapped back from the other side of the door meant OK, M, or Okay McQueen. He put his eye to the pupil scanner. The door opened.

The chief earth officer's bodyguard came forward and scanned McQueen with a handheld scanner. "Never can be too safe," his old warrior friend, Judd, said to him.

Judd had always been a regular guy, and he owed McQueen for saving him from the virus-water during his three hundredth capture. If the water had hit Judd, today he would be a mutant working in the fields. He had said he could never thank McQueen enough. But this was no time for amities and friends to chat about old times. Being Chief Earth Officer Nelson's bodyguard, Judd would stick to business. He would stay on military function status. Standing straight and tall, he lifted his arm and pointed to the table. "Proceed."

McQueen stepped to the end of the long marble table and stood at attention. The seamless wall at the other end of the table cracked open. The seated chief earth officer rotated around on a half-moon platform and stopped at a height just high enough that McQueen had to look up at him.

McQueen was surprised that a man with a CEO's power would resort to such childlike games as the old, higher than your opponent makes him feel inferior game. Maybe this CEO wasn't a smart as everyone thought he was.

For a moment, Chief Earth Officer Nelson leaned back in his plush swivel chair and tented his fingertips. Then he picked up a metal wand and pointed it at McQueen. "Warrior! State your business."

Standing rigid as a statue, McQueen stared straight ahead. "Chief Earth Officer Nelson. Sergeant McQueen requests permission to speak."

With a pained look in his pale eyes, Nelson waved his wand. "Speak."

"In accordance with the laws of the corporation and the Soldier's Code of Conduct, I am requesting permission to have twenty-one hours to capture an escaped Dinky."

Nelson tapped the metal wand on the table and looked at Judd. Judd opened a wall safe and took out a gold plate. A velvet blue ribbon attached to The Medal of Honor sat on the plate. When Judd placed the plate on the table, the plate's shine dulled compared to brightness of The Medal of Honor.

Nelson pointed to the medal with his wand. "You were to have captured your five-hundredth Dinky today. If you had performed your function, I would be placing this medal around your neck."

He slapped the metal wand on the marble table. The sharp sound smacked into McQueen's ears and made them ring with high-pitched pain.

Nelson raised his voice. "Why did you fail to complete your obligation?"

McQueen shook his head. The ringing stopped. He looked at the medal. Arranged in a semicircle, the velvet blue ribbon enhanced the bright-platinum medal and caused it to glow like a precious jewel.

McQueen thought about what that medal would have meant. He would never have to salute any officer again. He would be guaranteed a wonderful life.

Whap! Nelson slammed his wand on the table, again. "Well?"

McQueen startled to a more rigid attention. "Chief Earth Officer Nelson," he said. "I thought it would be advantageous to the corporation if I captured the Dinky alive."

Nelson tilted his head as if he were listening to something, then he raised his voice. "Warrior, why do you even think to say that?"

"Chief Earth Officer Nelson, the average corporation member's energy diet is equivalent to having fifty-eight energy producing mutants working continuously twenty-four hours a day. We need every live Dinky we can get."

Nelson blinked with surprise and jerked his head as if he were trying to shake what McQueen had just stated from his mind. "Just who do you think you are? Your kind knows nothing. You're not even a successful warrior."

"I believe you're mistaken, Chief Earth Officer, I have medals." McQueen pointed to the medals on his chest. "For the good of the corporation I have broken all the capture records."

Nelson turned his head down and didn't look at the medals. "You didn't capture one Dinky today." He stood up. "All corporation life requires energy and sufficient power to maintain the lifestyle you and I are accustomed to. It is a struggle for survival. The fittest only win when warriors do their jobs."

McQueen didn't understand why Nelson was putting his accomplishments down. Four hundred and ninety-nine Dinkies was a feat no one else had ever come close to. He looked to Judd for some sort of facial expression to help ease the uneasy situation. Judd gave him a blank look. A heavy silence filled the room.

The thought that any chief earth officer could be as uncaring and as unfair as Nelson had never entered McQueen's mind. He stood in semi-shock until Judd cleared his throat. Then, awaken form his temporary speechlessness, he spoke. "Chief Earth Officer Nelson," he muttered and then raised his voice. "My record shows that I do my job."

Nelson continued as if McQueen had said nothing. "On this virus infected earth we are in competition with many other species that have no souls. We must destroy useless virus carrying mutant energy and capture useful mutant energy to secure its continued flow through our superior corporate living systems."

"I understand, Chief Earth Officer Nelson."

"Look," Nelson said. "If you understood anything, you would have stopped a new virus from spreading throughout the land. You would have shot your Dinky friend."

Now, McQueen knew Burke had told Nelson about Tommy and him being friends. He never realized anyone's former best friend would go so far.

"But, Chief Earth Officer," he pleaded. "The Dinky did not appear to have a new virus."

"I can't believe you're that ignorant," Nelson said with a smug look on his face. "If you would have brought your little friend in, we could have checked him for a new virus."

McQueen didn't answer. He only looked at the

floor.

Nelson lifted the wand.

McQueen knew he was about to be dismissed. "I have no Dinky friends, Chief Earth Officer Nelson," he lied. "Give me the twenty-one hours. I will bring the Dinky back."

Nelson dropped the wand on the marble table. "I'll give you nineteen hours. You have already wasted two."

McQueen held his palm up in a saluting gesture. "Thank you, Chief Earth Officer Nelson. I will complete my obligation."

Nelson turned his back and spoke to Judd. "It will be a pleasure to see this one get recycled. Get that half-breed out of here."

Judd did what a bodyguard was expected to do. He continued the chief earth officer's cruelty. He yelled at McQueen. "Warrior dismissed."

McQueen dropped the salute and went out the door. With only nineteen hours left he would have to work fast. But he couldn't leave until after the TV interview. And that would take up another hour. He decided to change into his hunting uniform. That was what the TV reporters wanted anyway. And with his uniform on he could leave right after the interview.

In his room, he clinched the last belt on his blue-spruce-blue hunting uniform. Then he checked his face with the face scanner and instantly cured any blemish that might show up on TV. When he stepped to the programmed hair dryer, his hair was blown into perfect place. He would look good for the TV interview, and he still had a chance to catch Tommy. When he caught him, he would receive

41

The Medal of Honor, he would not get recycled; and he would consider Danielle for a reproduction mate. If she accepted, he would sweep her off her feet and carry her to a blanket of blue grass.

A Morse code signal thumped on his door. Tommy's tricks for memorizing the code jumped into McQueen's cluttered mind. "Di-dah-da-dit," sounded like, the hell with it. That was the Morse code letter L. He wondered what was going on. Then more thumps: "Dit-it," sounded like, did it." That was the letter I. Then one more thump: "Dit." That was the letter E. Someone had just tapped out the word LIE!

He opened the door. No one was there.

Something had to be wrong. Judd was the only warrior in the barracks who would tap out a message. He was trying to warn him, but friend or no friend, if he got caught, they would both be recycled.

He stepped back into the room and closed the door behind him. When he stepped to his bunk, pounding echoed through his door. He walked over and opened it, just a crack, and looked out. Three armed guards and a smiling-faced Burke stood in the hallway.

Burke stepped forward and put his hand on the door handle. "Sergeant McQueen, you are now in lock down."

"You can't do this to me. I have to go on TV in thirty minutes."

Burk's lips tightened into a thin smile. "No you don't," he said, and Bam! He jerked the door shut and let out a loud horselaugh. After he quit laughing, he talked through the door. "I'm taking your place," he said and snickered through his nose. "Nelson ordered it."

McQueen wanted to pound on the door. He lifted his fist, but lowered it and asked, "Why?"

"He thinks you have been infected with the mutant virus and can no longer function as a warrior."

"What about my nineteen hours?"

"You get more than nineteen hours." Burke paused as if he were catching his breath from laughing. "They will be right in your room."

McQueen stared at the closed door. It seemed to turn red. "You can't do this to me." He clinched his fist to control his temper. "You owe me."

"Yeah, I know. Pay back can be wonderful. I'm giving you the opportunity to help another warrior when you're recycled."

"Burke, you're a lowbred son of a bitch."

Burke giggled through the door. "Come on out. We'll talk about it."

McQueen wanted to jerk the door lock free and grab Burke by his obnoxious neck. He put his hand on the metal handle. A quick electric shock surged through his hand and flew out the top of his head. Before he knew what had happened, the high voltage shock had thrown him across the room.

Burke's mocking laugh echoed through the barracks hall. Still laughing, he tapped on the door. "Hey, Johnny, how do you like me now?"

McQueen sat on the floor and tried to shake the pain from his shocked hand. "If I ever get out of here," he said, and stopped.

Burke laughed again. "You'll like me even more when Nelson rips your medals off your chest right on national TV."

McQueen got up off the floor and sat on the end of his bunk. If he lost his medals, all the money credits he had built up over the years would be deleted. He would have no money to spend. He wouldn't even have a warrior pension. He will be forced to start his warrior training all over. He would be at the bottom of the warrior chain, right back where he had started seven years ago.

Not one recycled warrior had ever lived through the first week. If he managed to make it to the sixth day, those in charge would inject him with the virus. He would mutate into a Dinky or die. He knew he could never live through warrior training again. Any order to be recycled was a sentence of mutation or death. Something was definitely wrong here. Tommy must know something or the corporation wouldn't want him dead. Whatever he knew, he didn't know Burke would kill him. McQueen had to get out of his room. He had to get out of the barracks. He had to warn Tommy.

Thirty minutes later, as if he were talking to a toddler, Burke was talking through the door. "Hey, Johnny, I'm going to the TV reporters now. I just thought I'd stop by and let you know that Nelson ordered me to report that you have been killed by the wood virus."

McQueen wanted to cry. He wanted to bust right through that door and rip Burke's rotten head off his steroidal swollen neck. But, he didn't. He stood up and paced to the window. He couldn't go out the window. It was laser protected. No one could go in or out without getting his brain fried with microwaves. McQueen pounded his fist into his palm and talked to himself. "Think, dummy, think! Tommy always pulled some kind of prank, made them laugh. He always escaped. If he were here, what would he do?"

Burke shouted through the door. "Johnny, did you hear me?" I'm going to the reporters now."

McQueen tried to figure out Burke wanted more than anything else. Then it dawned on him: His stripes. Burk had wanted his sergeant stripes since he beat him in the warrior dual. McQueen shouted through the door, "Hey, Burke, you still there?"

"Burke chuckled and pounded on the door. "Yeah, I'm still here, Johnny. Do you have a problem?"

"No, but when you show up without my sergeant stripes, you'll have a big problem."

"I already have new stripes. I'll just say they're yours. Those stupid reporters won't know the difference."

"Yes they will."

"Burke hesitated before he answered. "How do you know?"

"Check out the picture of me getting my four hundredth capture."

"What are you talking about?"

"My stripes were stained with brown virus water. The decontamination killed the virus, but the stain was deliberately left there."

"You're crazy. You're so picky, you'd never wear stained stripes."

"It wasn't my idea. It is a visual reminder, to warn other warriors of just how close I came to mutating into a Dinky."

45

"Sorry, Johnny, I don't believe you. I never heard of such a thing."

"You would have if you had kept up on your current events like all warriors have pledged to do."

"So what, I'll just stain the stripes I already have."

"Maybe you could, but you have to be on TV in a few minutes. I have my stripes right in my hand."

"I'll just get the guards and come in and take them off you."

"You feel froggy, jump."

"Don't talk your mutant Dinky language to me. Get those stripes ready, Private McQueen. I'll be back."

McQueen pulled out the bottom drawer to his locker. Making sure the door was still closed, he reached up under a metal ledge and flicked open his secret panel. He reached in and felt around. It was still there: the plastic canteen full of fake, brown, wood-virus water. He pulled it out, stood up, and unscrewed the cap. A rotten-wood odor rose up from the dark liquid.

He figured it might work. Not only would Burke see the dark color, he would smell the wood, too.

Burke didn't knock. Bam! He kicked the door open.

McQueen jerked with surprise and almost dropped the opened canteen, but managed to slip it behind his back.

Burke paused in the open doorway. Then, with two security guards at his sides, he entered the room and stretched out his hand toward McQueen. "Hand over the stripes."

Still holding the opened canteen behind his back, McQueen smiled. "They're right here, behind my back. Try to take them."

Burke stepped closer. McQueen swung his hand from around his back and jerked the canteen in front of Burke. Brown water splashed up into Burke's face and on the guard's face.

The guard grabbed his own face with his hands and stepped back. He looked at the brown water on his hands. A look of horror flooded his face. Turning to one side, he shrieked, "Virus-water!" and ran out the door.

McQueen jerked the can to the right. Brown liquid splashed on the other guard's face and shoulder.

Burke barked at the guard, "Don't move."

The guard froze.

Burke turned and grabbed the front of the remaining guard's uniform; and using it as if it were a towel, he rubbed the brown, dripping water from his face. The guard pushed him so hard that Burk tumbled backwards and landed on the floor. The guard turned and ran down the hall toward the decontamination chamber.

When McQueen stepped past Burke, he noticed that he still had his worn corporal stripes on his arm. He paused for a moment and then swished out the door and locked it shut. He would have to act fast. After the guards decontaminated themselves they would sound the alarm.

CHAPTER 4

Driving her OvalCar toward an intersection, Danielle Fairchild looked up at the traffic light. It was red. She lifted her foot from the accelerator, touched the brake, and stopped. The driver in the OvalCar behind her honked the horn and demanded immediate attention.

Wondering what the driver wanted, Danielle looked into the rearview mirror. Honking the horn with erratic little honks, the driver stuck her head out the window. "Move it," she yelled and pointed to the light. "It's red."

"Damn!" Danielle said out loud. "I just stopped for a green light." I'll never get used to stopping for a green light. Just because no one is allowed on the green grass the corporation didn't have to change the whole traffic light system and reverse red for green.

The light turned red. She drove through the intersection and looked into her rearview mirror. The horn-honking driver turned right and was gone. In the distance, another OvalCar was coming down the road. Danielle pulled off to the side of the road and stopped just beyond the barrack's main gate.

Stretching her long slender legs, she leaned back and ran her finger down the illuminated pickup log on the screen. It went black; it wouldn't work. She lifted the microphone to talk to the driver of the other car. The microphone didn't work either.

She slammed the microphone onto the dash. "Damn, sunspots and space junk. They're zapping the screen frequencies again."

There would be no decent TV until there was a

48

full moon to lift the junk up. Then it would be low tide; the radio waves wouldn't travel worth a damn.

The other OvalCar drove closer. Danielle reached under her seat, pulled out her plastic backup log, and read the name of the next scheduled pickup: Corporal Burke. She sighed and looked at her watch. "Almost time for a shift change."

The other OvalCar, pulled behind her and stopped. She turned around in her seat and waved. The driver stepped out or her OvalCar and walked up to Danielle's window. "Hey, Danielle." The driver smiled. "Too bad it isn't time for a shift change." She pushed her auburn hair out of her green eyes. "You have just enough time to pick up Burke."

Danielle shrugged. "Sally, if you were a really good friend, you would relieve me early, and pick him up."

Sally's smile vanished and her face distorted. "Euuck!" she said with a deep voice. "No one wants to transfer that creep. I wouldn't wish that on anyone."

"Maybe he'll be late," Danielle said with a sly grin. "Then he'll be your headache."

"But, Danielle," Sally teased, "don't you want to be seen with that big strong warrior?"

"All he has is phony steroidal strength."

Sally bent over and leaned her elbows on the ledge of Danielle's window. "What type of a warrior are you looking for?"

"I'm not looking, but if I were, my type of warrior, my ideal of masculine beauty, would have to have slender gracefulness."

Imitating Burke, Sally wagged her head around

49

like an imbecile. "Burke has none of that. But he has a remarkably slender intelligence."

Danielle laughed and nodded her head in agreement.

"Maybe you could send him to obedience school," Sally burst into a laugh. "They could train him like a dog."

"He'd probably flunk," Danielle said. "I don't know how that half-wit ever became a warrior."

"Cheer up. You only have to take him to the TV station. I have to stick around and bring him back."

"Yes, you do. But just think, Sally, you'll get a chance to watch his cheesy smile."

Sally made a face at the thought. "What makes it worse," she said, "he actually believes those looks are seductive."

"Someone should tell him the truth," Danielle said. "He looks like he just crapped his pants, and enjoyed it, too."

A look of horror came over Sally's face. "When did he do that?"

Danielle giggled, and a sly look gleamed on her face. "Yesterday."

"I wouldn't doubt it," Sally said and laughed. "When I pick him up, if I don't look at his ugly face, I'll have to listen to his bragging. And after he tells his usual lies on TV, he'll think he's a big hero."

"Get ready for the big come-on," Danielle said. "He thinks there's not a woman in the world who wouldn't jump at the chance to be with him.'

"I can see it now," Sally said, and shuddered. "He'll put on his cheese face and ask me to go out with him."

"And I know you're going to say, 'Yes,' because you're really in love with him."

Sally stuck her finger in her mouth and pretended to throw up.

Danielle looked at her watch. "I've got to get to the barracks and pick up your boyfriend."

Sally shook her head as if she were trying to get rid of a bad taste in her mouth. "My boyfriend? You'll see him first. If you haven't been sick today..." She paused and let out a little twittering bird laugh. "Here's your big chance."

"I know it's the chance of a lifetime," Danielle said. "But because you're such a good friend, I'm going to let you have him. I'll tell him you'll be waiting for him."

Sally stepped away from the window. "I don't want to take you man." She gave a casual salute. "Go get him, honey." Giggling, she ran back to her OvalCar.

Danielle wished it would rain. Then all OvalCars would have to be decontaminated before they could be put back in service. Then she wouldn't have to pick up Burke. But better yet, maybe she could pick him up and somehow make a sharp turn and cause a freak accident where he would be thrown from the OvalCar and into a puddle of water virus; but then again, when he mutated into a Dinky, he would more headaches for the Dinkies; and they already had enough problems.

Danielle took one last look at the sky. There were no rain clouds. She sighed, pulled onto the road, drove to the front of the barracks, and parked. TV reporters mobbed around the front entrance.

They were doing interviews with themselves and answering stupid questions about things that hadn't happened and things that might not happen.

A balding, chunky reporter, with a long nose, rushed over to Danielle's OvalCar and tapped on the window. "Driver, who are you picking up?"

Danielle kept the protective window up, turned the switch, and talked through the microphone that transferred her voice to the outside speaker. "I'm not at liberty to divulge that information."

"Looking down his long nose, the reporter lifted his hand and pointed his cam-finger to the window. "If you can't tell us who it is, then you are here to pick up someone important. Isn't that right?"

A little, almond-eyed reporter, with a nose like a pig, ducked under the reporter's outstretched arm and popped up next to the window. "When Sergeant McQueen captures his five-hundredth Dinky, are you the one he has picked to reproduce with?"

Suddenly her heart jumped with an uncontrollable pleasant fantasy. The best privilege a hero warrior could be granted was the right to choose a mate and reproduce. Only people from the Friends of The Earth Corporation were granted the privilege. It was every woman's dream to be chosen. If John McQueen would ever ask, she would have to give his request top priority. But she didn't need some little, pig-nosed reporter putting ideas into her head. If he started a rumor that he had picked her, it would ruin her future chances with anyone who would ever consider her.

She cast a stern look through the window.

"Don't put words in my microphone. If the corporation wants you to know something, they'll tell you."

A skinny reporter rushed over to the window and pushed the little pig-nosed reporter aside. "We know you're here to pick up Warrior McQueen." He breathed in deep to catch his breath. "Did he get the twenty-one hours?"

Like pigs at a trough, at feeding time, more and more reporters wallowed around Danielle's OvalCar. A reporter at the outside edge of the swine-like group motioned to the group of reporters who were milling around the entrance to the barracks and shouted. "This driver's here to pick up McQueen."

The group turned in unison, rushed to the OvalCar, and encircled it, more. In no order and with everyone talking at once, questions and comments avalanched into the window's microphone and invaded Danielle's sanity.

"What time is Warrior McQueen scheduled to be transported?"

"Do you know where Augur the Dinky is hiding?"

"Did the chief earth officer order you here?"

"What do you think will happen if McQueen doesn't capture the Dinky?"

"Were they going to throw virus water on him?"

"Did you actually see the Dinky?"

"Was it Augur or Tommy?"

Danielle waved her hand and mouthed the words, shut up!

For a moment they quit throwing questions at

her and looked toward the barracks. A reporter put his cam-finger in front of another reporter. "If that Dinky's Tommy, McQueen will never get him."

"That's right another reporter said. "Tommy's too little and he's too smart."

They turned back to Danielle, and the questions started, again.

"Did the Dinky have a new virus?"

"Was McQueen exposed again?"

"Will he die like his farther?"

Danielle turned up the speaker on the window and spoke. "I'm only going to tell you reporters once. "I'm here to pick up a warrior, no more, no less. It is my job. If the warrior does not get here on time, the next shift driver will take over."

Danielle shut off the microphoned window. She could see the reporters' mouths asking questions, but now she did not have to listen. She tapped her fingers on the steering wheel. She wondered where dumb-ass Burke was. Late, as usual. Five more minutes and she wouldn't have to pick him up. "Keep screwing around, cheese-face," she said out loud. "You'll make my day."

Four and one-half minutes later, as if they had been shocked, the reporters bounced away from the OvalCar. Danielle watched them rush toward the barracks entrance. John McQueen bolted out the doors and started toward the OvalCar. With the horde of reporters sticking their cam-fingers in his face, he stopped. Danielle caught glimpses of him trying to look over the waving arms and pointing cam-fingers. His dark circled eyes had the look of a sleep deprived man about to cry.

She was struck by a horrible thought. Maybe

McQueen didn't get the twenty-one hours. Maybe he got recycled. He jerked his head from side to side. He looked like he was searching for something.

He stepped out in front of the reporters. For a few moments, Danielle saw him clearly. Like uncut grass blowing in the wind, his dark black hair splashed over his wrinkled forehead.

Those reporters could be a pain in anyone's life, but in fifteen more seconds she'd be off function status. She'd leave butt-kissing-Burke here. Her shift relief would have to take over, but that was John McQueen out there. What would it hurt if she stuck around a few seconds? She just wanted to see his face again. She had only transported him a few times. His uniform really looked good on his slender body. Now that he was standing in his blue-spruce blue hunting uniform, she realized something she hadn't realized before. McQueen was a handsome man.

The reporters mobbed around him and blocked her view. She struggled and squirmed abound in her seat, but she still couldn't see him. Stretching her neck toward the front windshield, she managed to see him. His chest wasn't like other warrior's chests. It didn't stick out like some kind of a monument to steroid use. It wasn't stacked with mountains of unnecessary muscle. It was perfectly formed, and it was in balance with the rest of his swimmer's type body.

McQueen held up his hand in a salute. His smooth deltoid muscles formed a sinuous curve and accented the many metals that were embroidered across the major pectoral muscle of his chest.

Walking through the reporters and toward Danielle's OvalCar, his long strong legs stepped with the precision of a majestic prince. A single eagle feather, with a white tip, caught the light, reflected a brown-purple sheen, and stood upright at the back of his head. Danielle had never seen that before. She let her gaze slide down his body. This warrior was uniquely attractive, and his confident walk gave him a look of controlled power.

The time clock in her OvalCar clicked shut. She was now off function status. Right on time, Sally pulled her relief OvalCar in behind her.

"Time to go," Danielle said to herself. "But where is McQueen going? He isn't scheduled to be picked up. Maybe he's taking Burke's place."

McQueen fought his way through the mass of reporters and stood outside the window of her car. Danielle let her eyes scan his conditioned body and travel up to his face. His lips moved, and his arms flapped like a scared wide-eyed animal that had just escaped from its cage.

She wondered what he wanted. He looked like he was in a hurry, cute though. She figured he would walk right past her OvalCar, but he didn't. He stood there next to her, and she could almost feel the expression in his dark eyes change to a questioning wonder.

She felt his eyes on her, slowly sweeping from her head to her toes. As she felt weak-kneed, a strange flip-flopping sensation flared in the pit of her stomach. She wondered what was going on here. All these feelings were new. For the first time in her life, she was attracted to a man. And McQueen was not just any man. He's was a warrior. Her father warned her against warriors. He had said they could be big trouble. But this one was a hero. Maybe after she checked back in to the motor pool, she could come back and pick him up. It won't hurt to go somewhere and just talk. She would see.

She opened the microphone. McQueen spoke fast and furious. "Please let me in. I only have eighteen hours. Get me away from these reporters."

"I can't. I just went off function status."

"Don't lock me in the seat. They'll never know?"

Danielle jerked her head as if she had been struck with a bolt of knowledge. "Why didn't I think of that?"

"Okay," she said. "But you'll have to keep those reporters back. I don't want them taking over my car."

McQueen turned to the reporters and held his palm up in salute. "Let me pass. I must complete my obligation."

The reporters cleared a path and mumbled amongst themselves:

"We're the lifeblood of information."

"We should have first dibs at this story."

Danielle knew she shouldn't speak on behalf of any warrior. It was her professional obligation to always stay completely neutral. Her only job was to transport. She was not an ambassador for any warrior. For the first time in her life, she turned up the speaker and spoke up in someone's defense. "Sergeant McQueen has eighteen hours to capture the mutant. He has no time to talk to you wonderful reporters."

She pulled the latch. The door opened. McQueen jumped in and sat in the seat.

Danielle closed the door and bent over him.

"No time to form fit me," he said. "Let's get out of here."

Danielle was not accustomed to taking orders from any seated warrior. Once they were in the seat, for their own safety, she had full control. Then, the only orders she was permitted to obey had to come from motor pool command.

She was beginning to think she had made a mistake. Maybe this guy was just another cheese-face-Burke-type warrior who had tricked her into letting him into her OvalCar. "Well, hello to you, too," she snapped back.

"I'm sorry," McQueen said. "I don't mean to order you around. But you don't understand. They're trying to kill me. Please drive me away."

"Those reporters aren't that desperate for a news flash. Maybe you should get in the other car."

"I'll never live long enough to transfer."

Danielle had heard pickup stories before. The warriors were experts, regarded pickup escapades as a sport; but somehow this didn't sound like one. Maybe this guy was telling the truth. "I'll have to secure your seat before we can leave."

McQueen leaned forward and pointed to the dashboard. "There is no time. Jump it."

She wondered how McQueen knew she could jump the circuit. Had he been watching her every movement all these months? And there was that something when their eyes had met. Maybe this was the type of man her father told her she would meet someday. If she got caught transporting an unscheduled passenger she could lose her driving position; but for some reason, she didn't care.

She barked orders at McQueen. "Sit back. It will be safer if I secure you." She stepped close to secure him, but jerked back. A small splotch of brown water was on his thigh.

The "Warrior not safe to transport!" light flashed on. Avoiding contact with his wet thigh, she bent over and jumped the kill switch with her metallic coated fingernail. She straightened up and adjusted the body-forming seat. For the second time, they leaned their faces together. The spark of love struck deep in her heart. She shook it off and looked down at his lap. "Is that wood-virus water on your thigh?"

"No."

"You know if it is, you must have the antidote or you'll mutate into a Dinky."

"We all know that. But believe me, it's not real virus-water."

"Are you sure?"

McQueen tilted his head down and talked low. "One hundred percent. But if I had the virus, I'm not sure I would take the antidote."

She jerked her head forward to better hear him. "What?"

McQueen shook his head and mumbled, "Nothing, please get me out of here."

Danielle jumped into the driver's seat. "I don't know why, but I'll take your word for it."

She turned the car around, headed away from blue-metallic haze of the setting sun, and drove away from the main base.

McQueen leaned back in the body-forming seat

and wiped the brown water off the back of his hand with his dry dough-like cleaning sponge.

Danielle figured if McQueen were a phony, the radio would inform her. She reached over and thumbed the dial. The radio scratched, but no intelligible signal came through; and it would be dark in a few minutes. A sickening feeling of mutating into a Dinky climbed into her mind. She scooted her body as far away from McQueen as she could manage. Looking at him in the rear view mirror, she asked, "Do you know you can die from virus water?"

McQueen smiled. "It's not virus water. It's safe bottled water. I colored it."

"It smells like wood virus to me."

"I'm glad it does. I gave it the false aroma of wood. As a weapon, it works very well." He chuckled. "If I would have had a squirt gun, I would have gotten away sooner."

"Squirt guns are deadly weapons. That's why they are illegal."

McQueen held up his hand. "I know, I know. It just would have been easier."

Doubt flooded Danielle's mind. Everyone on earth was afraid of the brown wood-virus water. It was the most powerful virus in the mutant strain. It usually killed the person before the sun set. A person with a squirt gun full of brown wood-virus water could maim or kill a lot of people, in a matter of a few minutes."

McQueen pulled out his canteen and unscrewed it. He squinted one eye and peeked inside. "I still have a half a canteen. Would you like some?"

"You have to be crazy." She turned and faced

him. "I'm letting you out, right now." As she lifted her foot to stop the car, the announcement screen in the silver dashboard stayed black, but a scratchy radio transmission came on. "Attention drivers. Chief Earth Officer Nelson has just reported that Sergeant John McQueen, the record holder of many Dinky captures, and savior of the world, has just died from the wood-virus. If the atmosphere clears up, Warrior Burke will be giving a TV press conference in ten minutes."

McQueen pulled his back away from the back of the forming seat. "Damn, they didn't even wait for Burke. Nelson already has me dead."

Danielle put her foot back on the accelerator. "Didn't Chief Earth Officer Nelson give you eighteen hours?"

"Yes, he did. But he lied out of that. They were going to kill me and blame it on the wood-virus."

"Why would anyone do that? You're a decorated hero."

"I'm not sure why they did what they did." He leaned forward. "But I think it's because Corporal Burke wants my sergeant slot. If I wouldn't have escaped, he would have gotten my stripes and spoken at the news conference."

Danielle sped up the car and turned down a side road, but one word he had just said jumped up like a vicious animal and grabbed her by the heart. "What do you mean he would have gotten your stripes and spoke at the news conference?" With her heart pounding, she hesitated and looked in his direction. "Did you kill him?"

"I didn't kill anyone. In fact, there is nothing

wrong with him or the other two guards." He shook the canteen in his hand. "I threw this fake virus-water on him and his cronies. Then I got away. Burke's probably still in the decontamination chamber, scared to death."

Danielle imagined how wound up Burke must have been trying to wipe fake water off his big puffed-up body. He probably cried like a little baby. McQueen's escape with the fake water seemed comical. A warm friendly feeling emulated from his body. She was no longer afraid. For the first time in months she smiled at a man. "Okay, hero, where do you want me to take you?"

McQueen looked out the front window, his eyes wide and searching. "I have to find that Dinky."

"Do you have any idea where he'll be?"

"He might be at my father's old farm. But that's the first place they'll look for me."

"You want me to drop you off close to the farm?"

"You could," he said and hesitated. "But if Burke and the other warriors are there, the Dinky won't be."

Danielle thumbed the TV's tuning wheels. "Before I pulled into the base, there was a scratchy report. All I could make out was something about a Dinky dancing around Forbidden Lake."

"Dancing?" McQueen said. "That will just have to be Tommy. He's still up to his old tricks."

Danielle pulled onto the back road that wound alongside Forbidden Lake. "Maybe you can capture him in the dark. You can go back to the chief earth officer and straighten things out."

Hope filled McQueen's face. "Maybe you're right. If I get him back within the twenty-one hours, maybe they'll erase the whole incident."

Danielle slowed the car and stopped in front of a big orange and black sign. It read:

DANGER

MUTANT WATER VIRUIS — MUTANT WOOD VIRUS

Do Not Drink Or Come in Contact With.

To Avoid Death or Mutating Dinky Virus

Stay on Safe Blue Road.

Danielle peered across the slick darkness of the deep lake. From out of the black, a single green flash of light blinked.

McQueen lurched forward. "Open the door!"

She pulled the lever. The door of the OvalCar clicked open and swung upward toward the silver stars in the black sky. McQueen jumped out and waved at the green light. "Tommy, is that you?"

No answer.

Danielle stepped out of the OvalCar and stood next to McQueen.

McQueen called again, "Tommy?"

The green light flashed long and short Morse code flashes. A happy expression flowed from McQueen's face. "It's him!"

McQueen turned toward Danielle and put his hand on her shoulder. She felt excitement for him. As if he were going to say, "Thank you," he looked into her eyes. She leaned forward. Their lips drew close. Danielle closed her eyes.

Suddenly, from the side of the lake, Tommy flashed the little green light and yelled, "Come on, you big dummy."

McQueen jerked away from Danielle and ran toward the green light.

When he was ten meters away from Tommy, searchlights flashed on his back. Next to the shoreline, OvalCars flooded the road.

Burke jumped form a military OvalCar and yelled at McQueen. "We got you now, Johnny. There's no way you'll survive a walk through that mutant water."

Tommy jumped into the water and splashed toward the center until he was chest deep. A meter away from the water, McQueen stood on shore. Tommy swung his arm in a come-here motion. "Come on, you big dummy."

Burke pointed his sidearm at McQueen and yelled, "McQueen, we're taking you in. Pack it in, or we'll shoot."

McQueen stepped toward the water.

A chill crawled over Danielle's body. "Come back, John," she cried, and quickly covered her mouth with her hand.

McQueen snapped his head around and glanced at her. A hurt look loomed in his face. He turned. He looked as if he were going to dive headfirst into the virus water.

Danielle wondered what was going on. She felt like she was about to lose her best friend. She knew she must stay professional, but she had just called him John. She could not let her emotions take over. She wasn't sure what Burke's motives were. Was he really trying to kill McQueen? Or was he merely acting on orders from Chief Earth Officer Nelson?

It didn't really matter. If McQueen dove into the mutant water, she would never see him again.

But what if the water was safe? McQueen had said the water in his canteen was fake, but what if it wasn't. But then again, if his thigh was covered with brown wood-virus water when he got into her OvalCar, he should be dying. But he didn't even look sick. The law guarantees him twenty-one hours to catch the mutant, but they didn't give him the twenty-one hours. They did not go by the law. Something was wrong here?

She dropped her hand from her mouth and rushed toward McQueen.

CHAPTER 5

From out of the black night, bright lights from the military OvalCars flashed on McQueen. He shielded his eyes with one hand and lifted his other hand into the air in a questionable surrender gesture. He looked toward Danielle. She was rushing toward him. Behind him, a few meters offshore, something splashed. McQueen turned toward the sound. Tommy sloshed his little head up out of the water, waved to him, and yelled, "Are you coming, you big dummy?" Then he slipped back under the dark water.

Without warning, Burke and his fellow warriors opened fire. Antidote-bullets flew through the night and chopped the top of the water where Tommy had been. Danielle put her hands over her ears, ran to the far side of her OvalCar, and squatted behind the protection of the back wheel. McQueen stood in the line of fire and tried to protect Tommy. Antidote-bullets whizzed around his head. None hit him.

McQueen knew these warriors had never been in a combat situation, and a warrior's first combat experience usually creates an unwanted reaction: The stress and immediacy of the moment causes most warriors to fire high. Was it that unwanted reaction? Or they were deliberately missing him. He didn't have time to take a chance and find out which one it was. Danielle was right. He raised his hands over his head. He was going to give up.

Danielle stood up, took a few steps away from the safety of her OvalCar, and stopped. The warriors glared in her direction, but they stopped firing. Like a traffic cop, she held up her hand and walked toward the warriors. "Don't shoot!" she begged. "He's going to surrender."

McQueen's fellow warriors lowered their sidearms. McQueen dropped his hands to waist level and looked at Danielle. She didn't know Nelson, but he did. Nelson had a habit of not playing fair, and Burke would make sure he didn't break that habit. McQueen's knew his warrior days were over. His only hope to stay alive was to follow Tommy. Maybe he could guide him through the forest and take him to the hidden cave. But he couldn't tell Danielle that. She couldn't get involved.

He stepped toward her to say good-by. "Don't!" she screamed, jerked her arm up, and pointed at Burke.

Burke held his sidearm with both hands and aimed at McQueen. Jerking on the trigger, he looked in the direction of his warriors. "Shoot!" he whined. "He's got the virus from his father."

McQueen stood in awe, almost hypnotized. He never thought his old warrior school friend would actually shoot him.

Burke slammed the weapon against his own powerful thigh and turned toward the other warriors. "What are you waiting on?" he shouted. "Shoot him before he spreads the virus."

McQueen breathed a slight sigh of relief. This time Burk's laziness was a gift. He never cleaned his weapon. It was jammed. But any second, he'd have it ready to fire. He wanted McQueen's sergeant slot so bad, he probably had poison in his antidote bullets. But if McQueen dove into that virus-water, he would mutate or die.

Looking down, Burke fumbled with his sidearm. He lifted his head for a second and barked at his warriors. "I told you to shoot."

The warriors raised their weapons and aimed, but they did not fire.

McQueen looked back to the deadly water. He had to make a quick decision. Instead, he hesitated. He had been in water before. It had been on his father's farm. But just after they couldn't save his father, the housing authority had saved McQueen with the antidote. Maybe the water was safe. Before the virus came, Tommy and he swam in it for years, and neither one ever got sick and McQueen never turned into a Dinky.

Burke was still fumbling with his sidearm. Danielle stepped between him and McQueen. McQueen shook his head and signaled for her not to come any closer. Like the professional driver she was, she stopped and stood in a military posture.

Movement glinted into the corner of McQueen's eye. He stepped toward the edge of the water and looked back. Burke lifted his sidearm and squinted his weasel-like eyes. McQueen turned toward the lake, flexed his legs, and dove headfirst into the dark mutant-causing water. He closed his eyes, held his breath, and felt his body glide through the water. When he began to slow, he swam just like Tommy and he had done when they were having contests to see who could swim the farthest under water. He had always won. Tommy had said that because he was twice as long he always had a head start.

With a long stroke of his arms, he powered through the water, opened his eyes and looked up.

On the dark water above his head, spotlight beams danced like laughing demons; and like gigantic raindrops, antidote bullets spla-ploomed the surface. He stretched his arms out in front of his head and cupped his hands. With a long powerful stroke, he pulled his slender body deeper and toward the center of the lake.

He wasn't encouraged by the thought that he would have to swim to where Tommy was standing. If he could make it, it would be the longest underwater swim of his life; and that was a long way.

Panic pains crept around his chest. Already, his body was pleading for air. His glide through the water slowed. Ignoring his body's begging for air, he forced himself to take another stroke. He cut through the deep dark water in front of him.

What if he had, somehow in the excitement, gotten turned around and was swimming in the wrong direction. He'd done that before. Tommy always thought it was funny. It wouldn't be funny now. He was out of air. He had to swim for the surface.

He stabbed both hands in front of him and pulled. Plunking antidote bullets cut the spotlighted water above his head. He dove back down and stroked toward where he thought Tommy was. When he thrust his legs into a powerful frog kick a zinging bullets disturbed the water just in front of his right knee. He kicked faster.

Deep-water pressure pushed on his eardrums. He swallowed to clear them and his head hit something, hard. He reached out and felt it. It was an old sunken tree limb. "Wood-virus", flashed in his oxygen-deprived mind. Scrambling over the limb, he scraped his belly against the rough bark. It stopped him. He put his foot on the limb and pushed. He surged upward, but slowed. Reaching high over his head, he cupped his hands, and pulled. This time faster. He was definitely out of air.

He told himself that just three more strokes would get him to the surface and air. He pulled three quick strokes. But he wasn't near the surface. There was a good chance that he would drown. But he couldn't panic. He couldn't get excited. He would eventually come up.

It's like Tommy always said, "Dead bodies eventually float to the surface."

He tried to think of something funny, tried to think of anything but air; and he tried not to get excited.

When his knee touched the stone ledge of an underwater drop off, he bent over, placed his feet on the ledge. Then he crouched down. Taking one last desperate stroke, he pushed off. Up he went.

When his ears lost their equalization, he knew he was almost there.

One more pull. He broke the surface, gasping for air.

Tommy treaded water next to him. "Take it easy, you big dummy."

"I can't," McQueen said. "My boots are pulling me down."

"Well kick them off."

"I would, but I'm not ready to drown," he said, kicked his legs, and pushed down with his cupped hands. Staying afloat and huffing between breaths, he asked Tommy, "What are you running from?"

Tommy splashed a playful splash toward him. "What are you running from?"

"I'm not sure."

"I didn't mean to dissuade you from your course of action," Tommy said. "But if you would have come in when I told you, they wouldn't have gotten near you."

McQueen treaded water and breathed deep until his heart slowed. "You ..." he said, and coughed. "You can still talk normal?"

"No kidding?"

With a jerk of his head, McQueen flipped the water from his face. "I thought maybe that mutant virus had affected your brain, made you talk like a dumb Dinky."

"There is no such thing as a dumb Dinky."

"What?"

"I'll tell you about it after we get out of here. You stayed under too long, they'll think you've drown. They'll be breaking out the boat and laser draggin' for your body."

McQueen followed Tommy into waist deep water. They waded up to shore next to a big log. McQueen stopped in his muddy tracks. "Tommy, are you crazy? That old log is loaded with wood-virus."

Tommy jumped up onto the log, sat down, and motioned to McQueen. "Come on, you big dummy." He chuckled. "Just walk around that dark green patch on the ground. You'll be just fine."

McQueen turned and faced the forbidden lake. Lights from the dragging boat beamed across the water. "I can't go back now." He jerked his head from side to side. "But if I step on that log, I'll surely die or mutate. Oh, well." He shrugged and stepped up on the log.

Tommy pointed to the log. "Make yourself comfortable. Have a seat and take your boots off."

McQueen stepped back from the log. "Are you nuts? I need them."

"You need to live more than you need to wear your boots. Take them off and throw them on the shore. Your so-called buddies will think you knew you were going to drown and gave up your boots and they washed to shore."

Taking off his boots was the last thing a warrior did before he knew he was about to die, but it wasn't common knowledge. McQueen suspiciously stared at Tommy. "How did you know that?"

Tommy looked at McQueen's boots. "Maybe I can read your mind." He looked up and smiled a compassionate smile.

McQueen took off his boots and tossed them onto the shore. Tommy handed him a pair of Dinkies' one-size-fits-all leather moccasins. "Try these on for size. The Dinky ID marks have been stripped out."

McQueen took the moccasins from Tommy's outstretched hand. "Where did you get these?"

"Out of my pocket."

"I suppose you always carry around a spare pair of moccasins."

"Not really, but I knew you'd need them."

Before today, McQueen hadn't seen or talked to Tommy for years. Tommy's knowledge that he would need the moccasins bothered him. "You know something I don't know, don't you?"

Tommy tilted his round head and shrugged one

shoulder. "I might." He pointed to the moccasins in McQueen's hand. "Get those things on."

McQueen watched the strong searchlight on the drag-boat scan the opposite shore. "Those warriors who were supposed to be my friends didn't even give me a warning. They just shot."

"You noticed that?" Tommy joked, and the boat's light scanned the shore to their right. "That boat's getting closer."

"They'll give up pretty soon," McQueen said. "After a magnetic force or something wiped out all the computers, they haven't figured out how to make new laser dragging beams. They're afraid long use will break them. So they only use them for short periods of time."

Tommy stretched his little arms over his head and yawned. "Even if they had computers, those half-wits wouldn't have enough sense to use them anyway."

Slipping the leather moccasins onto his feet, McQueen asked, "I never thought you would do anything that would get you shot. What did you do to get those warriors so mad at you?"

Tommy laughed. "Oh that? I'll have to tell you about it sometime."

Something in McQueen's mind seemed to click. It appeared for a moment, but vanished. He looked at Tommy's smiling face. "Somehow I knew you'd say that." He jumped off the other side of the log.

The small thin moccasins he was wearing were not like the hybrid, spider-web, reinforced boots he had just tossed aside. The rough ground indented into the bottoms of his feet. He stood for a moment and breathed in the surroundings. The soft scent of the lake's water and the dew-covered green grass enveloped his senses and brought back a forgotten happiness. It reminded him of when he was a kid, running barefooted with Tommy, in the forbidden forest.

Up ahead, Tommy ran into the forest. McQueen thought he was running away and he wouldn't see him again. But Tommy stopped and parted the thick branches, clearing a way for his old friend.

McQueen ducked his head under a low hanging tree limb and duck-walked under a thick stand of low hanging thorn bushes. Tommy walked next to him. "Do you think you could get used to walking like that?"

"I guess I could." He stopped walking. From his crouched position, he looked around. "It gives me a Dinky view of the world."

On the other side of the thorn bushes, a clearing of green grass and tall trees silhouetted against the night sky. McQueen stood up and stepped onto the grass of the clearing. "Is this blue grass?"

"It doesn't matter what kind of grass it is," Tommy said. "It just doesn't matter."

"It might not matter to you, but I don't want to mutate into a Dinky."

Tommy stopped walking, looked back and smiled his big wide-mouthed smile. "What's the matter with being a Dinky?"

McQueen started to answer, but Tommy butted in. "If you don't quit stopping," he said and continued walking. "I'll leave you here for those idiots to shoot you."

McQueen jerked to a slow walk. "I'll move as fast as you want." He hastened his step. "Just show me the way to my father's old water house"

"I could, but not tonight."

"Why not?"

The other Dinkies are all around us. I can't take you there until I talk to them."

Searching for Dinkies that could be lurking along the dark path, McQueen turned his head from side to side. "So what am I supposed to do, sleep all night on this water-virus grass?"

"I may be a Dinky," Tommy said. "But I'm not that inconsiderate."

A warm familiar feeling of trust that had been suppressed beamed in McQueen's brain. Somehow he knew Tommy could be trusted. "I know you're not inconsiderate," he said, "but where am I going to hide?"

"Remember that old tree house we built, when we were kids?"

"I'll never forget that."

"It's still there."

McQueen gently pushed on Tommy's shoulder. "Let's go. When daylight comes, those housing authority hunters will come in their protective suits and masks. They'll be looking for us."

Tommy led the way through the semi-dark. McQueen tried to follow; but at a dark spot, he wandered off the little footpath and crashed through jagger bushes where long, spine-filled canes wrapped around his legs and slowed him down. He kicked his feet free and kept on going until he had worked his way back onto the path. A few meters later, he continued to follow Tommy. They jumped over little water streams and waded through a shallow river.

Up and over a goldenrod-covered hill, they walked past the burnt out remains of his father's log house and the collapsed wooden gray barn. In the distance, the green-vine-covered water house jutted out from the side of a hill.

"Let's get into the water house," McQueen said. "It's right there."

"No way," Tommy said. "If you go in there tonight, you'll never live to see the light of day."

"It looks safe to me."

Tommy pulled on McQueen's elbow. "Come on, that's the first place the housing authority will look for you."

"They'll never find us in the secret cave."

Tommy nudged McQueen toward the path to the forest. "The cave isn't so secret anymore. Do you remember the way to the tree house from here?"

"I'm not sure. The forest doesn't look familiar."

"Maybe it will come back to you. I can't be seen with you here."

The moon slipped out from behind a cloud. McQueen stopped at the edge of the path that led to into the forest and the tree house. He reached over and pulled a branch away from a partially concealed orange sign. The light of the moon revealed big bold black letters.

FORBIDDEN FOREST
CHIEF EARTH OFFICER NELSON
HAS DECLARED THIS FOREST
OFF LIMITS

WOOD AND WATER-VIRUS ZONE
EMINENT DANGER OF MUTATION OR DEATH

McQueen looked into the forest and talked with his back to Tommy. "Here's another one of Nelson's zones. And this sign's been here a while."

Tommy looked up at the sign and then at McQueen. "They put it up right after your father died."

"I wonder how many more places Nelson is going to put off limits."

"He'll probably put them up until he has control of the whole world and all the people in it."

"You would think that with all the technology in the world the scientists would have come up with a vaccine that would make all the water and plants safe."

"It is rumored that Augur has a vaccine."

"I sure could use that vaccine," McQueen said, and looked at his hands. "When will I start showing signs of the virus?"

Tommy winked in his direction. "You'll be surprised."

CHAPTER 6

Tommy tramped through the tall dew-covered grass and searched the darkness for signs of warriors. After they had shot at him at the lake, and without warning, he knew they had no intentions of catching him alive.

Walking out of the tall grass, he stepped onto the beaten path. To his right, tops of the grass tussled. He tensed and prepared to run. The grass stopped moving. His eyes searched the darkness. Close to the ground, golden eyes glowed. He stepped back. A little gray possum scampered out and ran down the path, its wet fur glistening in the night.

Tommy chuckled. On a night like this, two barrel-chested warriors had lumbered into the dark forest to hunt for Dinkies. For protection against water virus exposure, they had pulled translucent plastic shields down over their faces. But his friend, Freddy, had pulled a thin, white sheet over his head and hid behind the trunk of a tree.

Tommy had climbed the tree, crawled out onto a limb that hung out over the dark path, and waited.

When the white-suited warriors walked under the limb, Freddy placed the bright end of a lit flashlight into his mouth. Under the thin sheet, his face glowed eerie red. Like a ghost, he jumped out from behind the tree. The warriors stopped as if they had been paralyzed. All their attention focused on Freddy's phantasm. Above their heads, Tommy sucked in a cheek expanding mouth full of water. Then he hung by his feet, reached down, lifted up the warrior's shields, and ripped their facemasks off. When the warriors reached up to pull him down, he squeezed his cheeks and blew. A burst of water spritzed into their faces. They dropped their flashlights, grabbed their wet faces, and ran out of the forest yelling, "Virus water! Get us to the decontamination chamber!"

And since that time, even though those warriors still wore their stupid white suits and full facemasks, Tommy hadn't seen any of them brave enough to come into the forest and hunt for Dinkies at night. He was pretty sure that none of them would come in after him.

He looked up at the silent sky. It was nice to be out and about and not have to worry about the housing authority or some dumb ass warrior trying to catch him.

He stepped out of a curtain of tall grass and onto the dirt road that led to McQueen's father's old burnt down farmhouse. No lights could be seen in the distance. Only a little light from the stars lit his way, but it was enough. He had grown up on the farm with McQueen. If he had to, he could walk there with his eyes shut.

At the bottom of a tall hill, the stone waterhouse loomed up in front of him like a safety shadow. At the entrance, a stick leaned against the doorframe. He picked it up and swished the green, three-leafed vines away from the steel door. He opened it, walked in, and stopped in front of a little stone wall. Water from an artisan well gushed out a pipe, cascaded over a series of wooden boards, and splashed into a deep pool as big as an OvalCar. Tommy stepped up to the pipe, tilted a wooden handle, just a little bit, and took a long drink. He

79

wiped his mouth and kicked some brown dirt into the clear spring water pool. A brownish stain tainted the pool. "There's some more wood-virus water for the idiots." He dove into the water.

He swam down into the pool. When it narrowed into a round stone-lined well, he swam deeper. When he felt a small round opening, he pulled himself along a long, skinny water tunnel. In the darkness, he felt for, and grabbed pull-slots that had been carved in the stone lining. He pulled again and then again. At the end of the tunnel, he entered the bottom of another deep pool. From above, hazy orange lantern light glowed on the surface. He placed his feet on the solid stones at the side of the tunnel, kicked off, and glided to the light.

When his head popped up out of the water, he was in the secret cave that McQueen's father had dreamed about, but never finished.

He looked toward the orange light. Next to the hidden alarm system, Freddy sat on the edge of the cot. He was eating a green apple reading a science book. Tommy splashed a handful of water in his direction. Freddy looked up. As his thick glasses flashed a soft glow of orange, he snapped the book shut, put it on the cot, and stood up. "What say, Thomas?"

Tommy pulled himself up out of the pool. "All's quiet outside, Freddy. The evening dew took care of that."

"Good," he said, and swallowed the last of the apple. "I got to sneak into town and get some bicarbonate of soda."

Tommy shook the water from his face. "Those green apples always give you a stomachache. Why

80

do you keep eating them?"

"I could wait until they're red, but I guess I like to eat them green because the pig people are too ignorant to eat them."

Tommy flashed a playful grin. "Who's ignorant? You're the one who has an upset stomach."

"I might have a stomachache now, but after I take the bicarbonate of soda it will be gone, but those Pig people will still be ignorant."

Tommy gestured toward the cot with his hand. "If you want to lie down for a while, I'll go into town for you."

Freddy took the last bite of his apple. "No way." He swallowed. "You're a wanted Dinky." He walked to the pool's edge. "I have to get out and move around, been working all day."

With water dripping from his wet shirtsleeve, Tommy pointed to the pool of water. "You feel froggy, jump."

"Very funny, Thomas. Too bad we couldn't find a way to get in and out without getting wet."

Tommy bent at the waist and wiggled out of his wet shirt. "We probably could. But if we make another exit and someone's there waiting for us, and we're not wet, they won't run for their lives."

"Yeah," Freddy said, "it's a good thing they're afraid of water."

Freddy bent over and flexed his legs to dive.

Tommy held up his hand. "Wait!"

Freddy turned toward Tommy. "What?"

Tommy pointed to Freddy's face. "Take off your glasses."

Taking off his glasses, Freddy said, "Did they

catch McQueen?"

"Almost, I waved him into Forbidden Lake."

Freddy put his glasses in his side pocket. "How did you do that?"

"Didn't you know? McQueen and I grew up together right here on his father's farm."

"You mean his father was the one the housing authority got rid of and burnt down his house?"

"He's the one. It was McQueen's father's idea to build this secret cave and search for the old hand-and-knee coal mines.

"Why didn't his son finish what he started?"

"Me and McQueen were going to, and we had a pretty good start on it before they came and took him away."

Freddy nodded in understanding. "Too bad they brainwashed him in that youth camp."

"They might have brainwashed him, but when he didn't shoot me, he knew I was using our phony Dinky language. Maybe his brain washing is washing off."

Freddy flashed Tommy a sad look. "He might have been your friend, but no one has ever recovered from those camps."

Tommy twisted his wet shirt into a tight spiral. Water dripped onto the dirt floor. "If McQueen's like his father, he'll be okay."

"Are you sure he isn't just faking it so he can get another capture?"

"I don't think so. On the way here he could have caught me anytime he wanted." Tommy shook his semi-dry shirt out of the spiral and glanced around the cave. "Too bad his father didn't live to see this place finished."

"Does McQueen know about it?"

"He only knows about the little secret cave we dug before they took him away. He doesn't know about the mineshafts or other tunnels."

"Maybe he told two-faced Nelson about it for a promotion, and he's coming back here to spy on us."

"I don't know. But I do know he could have killed me and he didn't. I would have been his five-hundredth capture."

"When was the last time you saw him before today?"

"I saw him all the time, but I never went up to him."

"But you said you two were old buddies?"

"We were, but after I saw what the housing authority did to his father, I could never take a chance and tell him. I just don't know how bad that youth school affected his mind."

Freddy's eyes fixed on Tommy's with a concerned glare. "Is he propagandized or just loony?"

Tommy hated the thought that McQueen might be crazy. He shuddered and pushed the unwanted feeling out of his mind. "He might be brainwashed," he said and paused. "But so far, he seems okay. But I just can't tell."

Tommy stepped to the cot. Next to it was the hidden alarm system that was connected to the pipe that stuck up above the pool of water of the artisan well in the water house. "I have guard function status tonight. The warriors will be looking for McQueen."

"Will they find him?"

"No way. I had him throw his combat boots on the shore of Forbidden Lake. They'll think he drowned."

"Those are good boots," Freddy said.

"Tomorrow I'll circle back through the green grass and get them."

"You think they'll still be there?"

"The housing authority will be afraid to touch them. They're soaking wet. The water-virus will be too hot for them to handle."

Freddy stood beside the pool. Getting ready to dive, he breathed deep, looked at Tommy, and smiled big. "Their ignorance," he said, and sucked breath between phrases. "Never . . . ends . . . but do you know . . . where McQueen is?"

"He's hiding in our old tree house. By the time you get back my shift will be over."

"Are you going to tell the others?"

"I'll call a meeting."

Freddy lifted his hand and made an okay sign with his thumb and fingers. "I'll do all I can to help." He rubbed his stomach. "But I've got to get to town first."

"Thanks. If I can convince the others, I might bring McQueen here. Maybe he can help us like his father did."

Freddy stepped up on the stone edge of the pool. "We need all the help we can get." He bent over and put his little hand into the water. "This stuff's always cold. You sure no warriors are hanging around outside?"

"I didn't see any. But be careful. They're shooting without warning."

"I'm not afraid," Freddy said with a

mischievous grin. "I can always put my flashlight in my mouth."

Tommy pursed his lips like he was spitting water. "Water would be better."

Freddy smiled and flexed his knees for the dive. Tommy picked up the little air mask that was connected to the hand compressor and offered it to the Freddy. "You need this?"

"No way. I'll catch you later."

"Until that time," Tommy said.

Freddy dove headfirst into the deep pool and was gone.

Tommy lay on the cot and thought about what he would say at the meeting he was about to start. He wanted his old friend, Johnny McQueen, to be with him again. But if he showed McQueen the tunnel complex, and the brainwashing had erased his moral or ethical strength, it would be the end to all that his father and the Dinkies had worked for. He closed his eyes and fell into a semi-sleep.

* * *

Plonk! The alarm lever went off next to the cot. Tommy jerked up off the cot and stood up. Freddy was coming back. He waited next to the pool until Freddy surfaced. When he did, in his hand he held a watertight yellow box of bicarbonate of soda. "I'm glad the water-virus scare makes the corporation waterproof things," he said, and the secret stone door to the tunnel complex slid to the side.

Tommy's relief guard walked in. "You're relieved, Tommy. Go get some rest."

No rest tonight," Tommy said. "I'm calling a meeting."

The relief guard walked to the cot and sat down. "Knock yourself out. I'll listen through the wall."

Tommy and wet Freddy walked through the secret door and closed it behind them.

Tommy walked to the meeting room and stood behind a big wooden water barrel. He picked up a heavy, wooden club and banged on the side of the barrel.

As the banging thumped throughout the tunnels, sleepy-eyed Dinkies straggled out of their rooms and flowed into the meeting room.

They gathered in a semicircle and sat down on the dirt floor. Tilting their little floppy-hatted heads to one side, they grumbled and talked amongst themselves. Tommy used his fist as a gavel and pounded on the barrel's smooth top. When all was quiet, he spoke loud and clear. "This emergency meeting will come to order."

Sludge, the outspoken Dinky, who wanted to take Tommy's leadership position, raised his muscular fist in the air and yelled up at Tommy. "We have to work in the morning. You better have a damn good reason for waking us up."

Sludge had thin reddish-blond hair and he was not handsome, not one bit. When he talked, his mouth looked like it had a fat night-crawler hanging down the side of his mustached mouth that moved and jerked with each word. His skin broadcasted age lines that were records of the many years he had spent drinking and fighting, and the top of his muscular back was bowed from a life of picking and shoveling in the mines. His eyes were watery-brown, set in a face that had worn out many a combatant's fists.

In spite of his apparent lack of education, Sludge was a highly respected member of the work crew. When there was a cave in and someone had been buried, Sludge was always the first to start digging and the last to quit. Even though he had a bad foot that he dragged when he stood on it too much, he had worked on his hands and knees and pulled many a Dinky from what would have been a dark grave.

Tommy didn't want the meeting to turn into a senseless argument about how Sludge should be in power. He kept his calm and spoke. "You all have no doubt heard about John McQueen and his failure to capture his five-hundredth Dinky."

"He's the scum of the earth," Sludge yelled. "Trap him in the water tunnel and let him drown."

A few other Dinkies mumbled and nodded their heads in agreement.

"I would agree with you," Tommy said, "but the very ground you stand on actually belongs to John McQueen."

Sludge stood up. His little, muscular chest heaved with heavy breathing. "What kind of crap are you trying to pull? We spent years digging this tunnel system so we could have a safe place to live."

Another Dinky jumped up. "That's right. Why would you want to bring a pig person into our sacred home?"

Someone in the back yelled out, "And a warrior to boot."

Sludge took a few steps forward and spoke directly at Tommy. "That's right, answer that,

Mister Know-it-all."

A few of Sludge's followers raised their arms in the air and chanted. "Know-it-all! Know-it-all!"

Tommy banged his fist on the top of the barrel. "Hold on," he yelled over their chants. "We're not working for the corporation down here."

The Dinkies quit chanting. Tommy continued. "Let's keep this meeting civilized."

The old Dinky, sitting next to the wall, waved his hand toward Tommy. "Go ahead, Tommy, answer the question. Why would you want to risk all we have?"

"He don't have no answer," Sludge said, and looked to the old Dinky.

The old Dinky lowered his left shoulder and tensed his right arm as if he were getting ready to give Sludge a good punch in the chest.

Sludge's eyes focused on the old Dinky's hand. The old Dinky rolled his fingers into a fist, wrinkled his forehead, and glared at Sludge.

Sludge was strong and could have beaten the old Dinky in any fight. But the old Dinky was one of a few who had had the courage to plan and carry out escapes from slavery. If it weren't for his bravery and the Dinkies that had died at his side, many would still be in irons. The Dinkies owed him. Not a one would disrespect him.

Sludge threw a sideways glance at the old Dinky's face and sat down.

"I shouldn't have to remind you," Tommy said. "But you all know McQueen's father was the pig person who dug the secret cave."

Sludge objected, "Anybody can dig a cave."

"Not anybody can design a water tunnel with

an alarm system and a tunnel that traps invaders."

"So what? We found the mine shafts."

"Without McQueen's father's knowledge, we wouldn't have known they existed."

"Back up a minute," Sludge said. "You said McQueen's father was a pig person. How can McQueen be a pig person?" He's got reddish-dark skin."

"His ancestors were Indians," Tommy said. "What's wrong with that?"

"You can't work with dark people," Sludge said. "They ain't normal."

"How would you know that?"

Sludge turned toward the crowd of all white Dinkies behind him. "Did you ever see a black Dinky?"

"Come on Sludge," Tommy said. "We all know how you feel about people of different skin, but Warrior John McQueen, his father, and I, worked together on the secret cave and the water tunnel."

"See, I told you. You can't work with dark people," Sludge said, and sat on a rock next to the barrel.

"What do you mean?"

Sludge looked up at Tommy. "They never got it done."

The crowd giggled.

Tommy held up his hand. They stopped giggling. "It wasn't our fault."

Sludge pointed to the room's stone ceiling. "Yeah, I know. With those tall pig people you gotta make the cave twice as high." He lowered his arm. "It's twice as much work, and it takes twice as much time."

"We had only completed the first small section of the secret cave when the housing authority came."

And that shows how dumb those pig people are," Sludge said. "These old hand-and-knee coal mines were just only a few feet away and they couldn't find them."

"If McQueen's father had had more time, he would have found them. But the housing authority burned down his house and took little McQueen away."

Sludge looked toward the crowd. "John McQueen is no longer the son of his father. He's been prop, propa—"

"Propagandized," Tommy corrected. "Brainwashed."

Sludge vigorously nodded his head. "Yeah, yeah, yeah, that's what they did to him at the youth camp. They brainwashed him."

"I grew up with McQueen," Tommy said. "I don't think that brainwashing took."

The old Dinky raised his hand. All the Dinkies looked toward him. "Can you guarantee us that he is not just trying to get amongst us to get his five-hundredth capture on a grand scale?"

"That's right," Sludge said and banged his fist into his opened hand. "If he tricks us all, and we all get caught, that dumb ass, Nelson's gonna give him the right to pick a girl and reproduce. His blood line will live on."

"So, what is your point?" Tommy wanted to know. "I'm sure he wouldn't pick your girlfriend."

The Dinkies held their mouths and giggled.

"That's not funny," Sludge said. "We don't need McQueen reproducing pig people. They'll grow up to be just like him. We don't need his kids catching our kids."

The old Dinky raised his hand again. "Well, Tommy, for the sake of a friendship that may not be what it used to be, are you willing to sacrifice all that we have slaved for?"

Tommy lowered his head and shook it from side to side in deep thought. He looked up. "I can't be sure, but John McQueen was my best friend. I have to at least give him the benefit of the doubt."

Sludge stood back up. "You can give him all the benefit of your doubt. But you ain't givin' him none of ours. You bring him here, we'll drown him."

"A chant rose out of the crowd. "Drown him! Drown him!"

Tommy picked up the club and banged on the barrel. The chanting stopped. "I'll go outside and see if McQueen has suffered the effects of that youth camp."

"Don't waste your time." Sludge said. "He's brainwashed." And like a footnote to the argument, he added: "And he's too tall for the tunnel. If he don't stoop over all the time, he'll scrape dirt off the roof. Who's gonna shovel that dirt?"

Tommy shook his head in disgust and blew out a long lingering breath of air. "Let's not start imagining things before they actually happen. I was only with Sergeant McQueen a short time. You may be right. He may be brainwashed."

Sludge jerked his finger at Tommy. "Quit stalling. We got to get some sleep. You know he's brainwashed."

Tommy waved his hand at Sludge; and shaking his head, he said, "If I discover that McQueen has been propagandized and has not recovered, I'll bring him back to the water tunnel."

Sludge swung his hand up and smiled. "Now you're talkin'. You get him to dive in and swim into the water tunnel. I'll be waitin' on the other side with my hand on that trap door lever."

Tommy paused. He didn't want to drown his best friend in the tunnel, but he had no choice.

"It is agreed then," he said. "If I find that McQueen is propagandized, I will bring him to the water house. I will trick him into swimming into the tunnel." He looked toward Sludge. "I will give you the signal from the drinking pipe." Tommy lowered his head. "You can trap him in the water tunnel until he dies."

"That's right!" a mutant said from the back of the crowd. "We'll give him some real water-virus."

CHAPTER 7

Like fabulous fireworks, falling pieces of space junk trailed across the night sky. Their fluttering light blinked down and changed the blue-gray forest into various shades of virus-green. When the sparkling tails began to fade, a multiple mix of marvelous colors flared outward sending a kaleidoscope of friendly colors high above McQueen's head.

"Tommy, look at that," he said, and turned around. But Tommy had gone into the night.

The light fluttered and went black. McQueen stood on the path and waited for his eyes to readjust to the dark. When he could see again, he started down the path.

If he slept in the wood-virus tree house, and he didn't die, he'd probably be a Dinky by morning. But what was the difference? He had swum in the virus-water that would kill him. And to make matters worse, he was swishing through green virus-leaves, walking on green virus-grass; and wisps of green virus-weeds whipped at his boot-less ankles. Everything in the green forest that touched his body would speed his mutation. Now, it was irreversible. He wondered how long he had left to live; and if he didn't die, he wondered how long it would be before he shrank to the size of a Dinky. Tommy probably left him standing there and went back to prepare the Dinky colony for a new member: Dinky McQueen.

He put the Dinky thoughts out of his mind and continued walking. Dense tree shadows crawled over the path and blocked the illuminating beams of the moon. When darkness turned to hopeless black, he couldn't see. Inching along, he remembered his old boyhood skill. He moved his eyes in quick jerks and did not look directly at any one thing. These rapid eye movements improved his night vision, but the tall trees and short foliage were not familiar. He looked back over his shoulder and listened. The subtle snap of a twig traveled to his ears. Thinking it was probably some mutant animal scavenging for food, he ignored it; but he knew Burke liked to ambush people; and it would be just like him to be lurking behind a tree with thirty other warriors backing him up.

McQueen slowed to a crawl. Taking careful steps and stopping after each step, he listened. Dissecting every sound that entered his ear; he constantly had to decide if it was something he had to defend against. Fear and uncertainty invaded his mind and spread to his body. He tensed for what might be ahead and stepped down the angry purple path.

The silent swish of something moving alerted his defenses. It sounded like a housing authority hunter, in a plastic suit, walking through a stand of grass. He stopped walking. The sound stopped. He wondered what was the matter with himself. When he walked, the swishing sound was his own pants legs rubbing against each other. He knew he was getting too excited. Those idiots wouldn't be out here at night. They would too busy getting soused at the Dance Box. He hastened his step and continued walking.

The familiar sound of water cascading over a small series of rocks, tinkled somewhere in the deep dark. He stopped and peered into the familiar forest. He felt his heart speed up. He looked behind himself and in front of himself. The night shine of a small crick of blue-black water ran right in front of his one-size-fits-all, Dinky-moccasin-covered feet. Something in his mind cleared. Old memories crowed his brain and spread out into comprehension. He knew the old tree house was near.

Taking big confident steps, he stepped into the thick brush, rustled through last year's tree leaves, and stopped in the shadow of a tall oak tree. When he gazed skyward, a plank-sided triangle shaped box, overgrown with branches and semi-concealed with thick leaves, silhouetted against the dark sky. He had made it to the tree house.

Pervasive odors of acorns and light-brown oak leaves, stirred his senses. He remembered the hundreds of times Tommy and he had climbed up into that tree house. But now the tree house was different. Branches had grown around the boards and embraced them tight against their strong branches. Slices of the soft moonlit sky shone through the half roof and out the single window, making the tree house appear lighted and inviting.

He stepped to the bottom of the tree and looked at its enormous trunk. The little board steps Tommy and he had nailed to the side of the tree were gone. The tree house was too high for him to jump up, grab a branch, and swing over; and the trunk was too wide for him to wrap his arms around and climb up.

Thunder rumbled in the distance.

It could have been heat lightning, but he didn't

want to say outside in a shower of virus-filled rain. He looked at a skinny tree that stood next to the tree house. Maybe he could climb it and swing over; but when he walked up to it and looked up, he could see that it was too far away from the tree house. If he'd climb up, he wouldn't be able to reach over far enough to get in.

Another memory flashed into his mind. "That's it!" he told himself, reached up, grabbed the first branch on the skinny tree, and began climbing. After a few pulls and a few leg wraparounds, he was close to the top.

Looking down at the tree house roof, he judged where he would land on it. He reached up, grabbed the top of the main section of the tree, and swung his feet out toward the tree house. The skinny tree bent over and lowered him toward the roof. When he was five meters from the top, and just when he was about to release his grip and let the skinny tree top fly back up into the night without him . . . Whap! The tree cracked loud and sharp. Hanging on, he sailed down. His Dinky-moccasined feet hit top of the roof with a loud painful thump. Like flat petals of rain, little leaves swished all around him. A blue-gray haze of the slender tree's top flew past his face, fell into his lap, and bounced up about a meter. Then it twisted in midair, causing a leaf-laden branch to whoosh past his head, catch on the edge of the roof, and quiver to a stop.

In a semi state of shock, he sat on the top of the roof. Green leaves and dark branches surround him. The tree's broken top sat conveniently over his thighs, not hurting a thing.

"I should have known better," he said. Those chokecherry trees always broke. Tommy and he had broken enough chokecherry trees to fill a house with firewood for a year. Now his feet hurt. He shouldn't have left his warrior boots on the shore. Maybe Burke had them sitting like trophies on his cadre-room mantel. McQueen sighed. At least he didn't get hurt and better yet, he was here and Burk wasn't.

McQueen slipped his legs out from under the broken branch and dropped down into the tree house. A thick layer of old brown leaves covered the floor. He bent over and scooped them up to make a bed. Something sharp jagged into his hand.

"Snake!" registered in his brain.

He jerked his hands back and kicked at the leaves. His foot hit something hard. A long trail of movement rushed beneath the leaves and, Voof! It stopped at the wall of the tree house. He relaxed and smiled. It was the rake Tommy and he had used to rake up big piles of leaves and jump into them from the lower branches. He picked up the rusty rake and raked the leaves into the shape of a nice comfortable bed. Then he put the rake into the corner, lay down on the leaves, and watched the sky through the opening in the roof until he fell asleep.

* * *

The faint sound of the broken chokecherry tree, bouncing against the tree house, entered his ears. He sat up with a start. Morning light gleamed into his sleepy eyes. He blinked and turned toward the sound. A knock on the tree house roof echoed down from the ceiling.

"Is anybody home?"

97

It was Tommy. He was up to his old tricks again. McQueen stood up and smiled. "The door's open. Come on in."

Tommy let his little short legs hang down and hopped into the tree house. "How'd you sleep last night, you big dummy?"

McQueen thought it was too early in the morning to be calling anyone names. Shaking his head, he looked down at Tommy. "Why do you keep calling me a big dummy?"

Tommy pointed toward the tree house roof. "That was a chokecherry tree you rode down."

McQueen nodded his head in disgust. "I remembered after it broke."

"How could you forget? We broke enough chokecherry trees to fill a barn."

"And then some," McQueen added. "How did it go with the other Dinkies?"

"They all think you've been propagandized at that youth camp. They said it was up to me to find out if you're in your right mind."

McQueen reached for the handle on the rake in the corner and leaned on it. "I can't say here forever. I've been exposed to a lot of virus. I'll die or mutate into a Dinky, and soon." He lifted his hand and checked it for a virus rash. There was none. He breathed a sigh of relief. "You think you can change their minds?"

"I might, but Sludge wants to take over my leadership job by opposing everything I try to do. He'll be hard to budge."

"You mean for once in your life you don't have any tricks up your sleeve?"

Tommy put his hand on the rake handle next to

McQueen's hand. "Maybe," he said and paused. "I could make him an assistant leader or something."

"Did you bring any food?"

"Just some water and your boots. They're up on the roof."

A rumble on the roof shook the tree house. McQueen jerked back away from the window. "What's that?"

"Tommy smiled. "Don't get excited. It's just that chokecherry tree shifting."

"It shouldn't shift that much."

Tommy jumped up and grabbed the edge of the roof. He held on with one strong little hand and reached up onto the tree house roof. He felt around, grabbed the boots and a wooden canteen of water. He dropped down to the tree house floor and looked up at McQueen. "There is only a little branch at the bottom keeping that chokecherry tree from rolling off the roof. It's a wonder it didn't fall off during the night."

McQueen looked down at the boots and drew back. "They have water and wood-virus all over them."

"So?"

McQueen shrugged, sat down, took off the mutant moccasins and put his boots on.

When he stood up, Tommy thrust the wooden canteen of water into McQueen's chest. "How about this?"

McQueen drew back. "That's wood-virus water. What are you trying to do to me?"

"There is no more wood-virus water in this canteen than there is in that canteen you have on your belt."

McQueen relaxed. "You had the same idea I did, fake virus-water?"

"Sure, it is," Tommy said and shook his head with a negative jerk. A twig cracked outside of the tree house wall. Tommy looked out the side window.

Bam! He jerked his head back with such surprise and force that he banged it on the wood wall of the tree house.

"What are you, nuts?" McQueen said, and looked out the window. To his surprise, a white-plastic-suited housing authority hunter, with a full facemask, stood on a ladder.

McQueen looked to Tommy. "Now we know what that noise was."

Tommy reached for the end of the ladder. The hunter grabbed his little hand and twisted it back. McQueen stepped back, reached into the tree house and grabbed the rake. He swished its rusty teethed end at the hunter. The rake's teeth ripped the hunter's thin protective suite.

McQueen was thankful that Nelson was too cheap to buy good suits, and he was thankful the hunters weren't warriors. If they were, right now, Tommy and he would be dodging antidote bullets.

The hunter released Tommy's hand and grabbed at the tear in his suit. McQueen swung the rake at him again. The hunter balanced on the ladder, reached up, grabbed the end of the rake handle and hung on. McQueen pushed the rake out as far as he could stretch. The ladder, the hunter, and the rake sailed backwards. The hunter windmilled his arms, but managed to stay on the ladder. McQueen leaned out the window and pushed the rake, more. The ladder increased its backward momentum. The rake handle flew from McQueen's hands. Three meters from the tree house, the ladder caught on a small tree and the balancing hunter wrapped both arms abound the ladder's sides and hung on. The rake fell. McQueen looked down toward the ground. Two more hunters grabbed the ladder. Muffled voices escaped out their facemasks and sounded like they were coming from a long tunnel. "We got you, McQueen. Come on down."

The hunter on the ladder started to climb down.

Tommy jumped up and grabbed the edge of the tree house roof. "They'll be back up here in a few seconds. Get up here on the roof."

McQueen boosted Tommy up on the roof and pulled himself up on top. He looked at Tommy. "Now what?"

"Just like the old days. We'll walk down this tree you broke."

Tommy jumped up on the tree and took the first step toward the bottom.

McQueen put one foot on the tree and stopped. Tommy looked back. "Now what's the matter?"

"I don't think I can balance on this thing. It's too skinny."

"For crying out loud," Tommy said. "Don't you remember anything? We did it a thousand times when we ran over that fallen tree over the big gully behind the barn."

McQueen blinked and memories of Tommy and himself playing on that skinny tree they used for a bridge flashed in his mind. It was high above the gully, and he wasn't afraid then. "That right," he said. "What's the matter with me?"

Tommy looked back over his shoulder and toward the ground. "They got the ladder back up. If you don't get moving, there's going to be plenty the matter with you."

McQueen stepped onto the fallen tree and walked with more confidence than a tightrope walker. "Get moving," he told Tommy. "All three of them are in the tree house."

McQueen looked back. The half-fallen tree, they were walking on, groaned. The little branch on the ground that was holding the tree snapped like a delayed firecracker. The tree rolled a full turn. Tommy's feet flew into the air. McQueen's feet slipped off the round tree. His knees hit on the rough rolling bark. They both dropped down, crashing through tree limbs and thick leaves. Near the ground, they both managed to grab onto a skinny branch. It snapped off. They sailed toward the sticks and leaves below. When Tommy's feet hit, he fell sideways. McQueen's feet touched down and flew out from under him. Tumbling backwards, he watched Tommy's head thunk on the hardwood rake handle.

McQueen rolled over in the brown leaves, got up, and offered his hand to Tommy. "Come on. Let's go."

Tommy didn't move. McQueen looked toward the tree house. The warriors were coming down the ladder.

McQueen shook Tommy. "Are you all right?"

Tommy didn't move.

McQueen couldn't leave Tommy there. Maybe he could surrender and claim him as his five-hundredth capture. He shook his head and forced the inhumane thought from his mind. Tommy was McQueen's friend. He decided to carry him.

He bent over and picked up Tommy. Tommy opened his eyes and looked a McQueen's warrior uniformed chest. He swung his fist and caught McQueen in the mouth. Surprised, McQueen dropped Tommy onto the ground. Tommy rolled over and looked up. The three hunters surrounded them.

McQueen stepped on the toothed end of the rake. The handle flipped up. He caught it in the palm of his hand, swung it around, and held it as if it were a fanged baseball bat. "Get back. I'll rip those suits."

Behind a facemask, a hunter's muffled voice said, "Go ahead. There's no water here."

McQueen swung the rake. It made a glancing blow, but its teeth ripped one hunter's suit and stuck in the boot of the other. McQueen jerked on the rake for another swing. The rake's teeth stayed in the boot and the skinny rake handle pulled from his hands. As vicious smiles beamed behind the hunter's facemasks, Tommy sat up and laughed at them.

One hunter pulled the rake's teeth out of the thick sole of his boot and pointed the rake's handle at Tommy. "I'll shove this rake up your little laughing ass."

"Take it easy," the other hunter said. "We got them."

Jerking the rake at Tommy, the hunter spat out, "That's the little son-of-a-bitch that jumped on our backs back and wrapped that see-through green plastic around our heads."

Tommy smiled and reached for his wooden canteen of wood virus-water.

McQueen suddenly knew Tommy was the one that had led that bunch of Dinkies who jumped on a gang of hunter's back's and taped green see-through plastic around their heads. When they rushed back to the blue grass those hunters had panicked. They thought the whole world had turned into green virus. Some ended up in therapy for a long time. No wonder they were mad at him.

The hunter on McQueen's right, reached for him with an antidote-syringed-finger.

Tommy yelled, "Don't let him touch you with that finger."

McQueen faked a flying back-fist, dropped his hand, swung his combat-booted foot around, and whacked the syringed finger. The antidote sprayed into the air.

Tommy opened his canteen and jerked water toward the hunter. The hunter laughed behind his mask. The hunter on his left jumped back in surprise, looked at the clear water, and laughed too. "You can't scare us. That's clear water. It won't go through the second layer in our suits."

The third hunter jumped behind McQueen and grabbed him around the waist. "McQueen, we're taking you back to quarantine."

The second hunter grabbed Tommy by the neck and held him secure.

The first hunter reached over and held McQueen's wrist with one hand. "You'll die on national TV." He reached behind his back for the hybrid-spider-web arrest bands.

The hunter who had McQueen by the waist, talked in his ear. "Nelson will show the world what happens to people who trespass into off limits forests and live in wooden houses."

Holding McQueen's wrist, the other guard fumbled with the arrest bands; but he couldn't get them out of his back pocket.

McQueen wished he had given up and taken his chances. He was already caught. If he went on TV with the five-hundredth Dinky, maybe everything would be okay. He shook the thought from his head and wondered what was wrong with his mind. Nelson has already lied to him. He couldn't trust him. Even if he went back, they would make an example of Tommy.

He lifted his free hand in front of the hunter's face. "Wait!"

The hunter stopped and held the constraint bands over McQueen's wrist. McQueen continued. "You three hunters look like pretty smart guys. You know the virus out here is so bad that every second you stay here you are closer to dying."

"Our suits will protect us," the hunter in front of McQueen said.

Looking at the hunter's hand, McQueen snuck his hand to his belt and twisted the cap of his half-filled wood-virus canteen. "You're mutating in to a Dinky as we speak," he said. "Just look at your hands."

The hunter in front of McQueen looked at his hands. "I don't see anything. I have gloves on."

McQueen unscrewed the cap on the canteen and pointed to the hunter's stomach. "Look at that. You got brown wood virus all over your stomach."

The hunter behind McQueen tightened his grip on McQueen's waist. "You dirty Dinky lover. If squirt guns were still legal, I'd squirt you to death."

McQueen pushed back into the hunter that was holding him. Then he lifted his feet off the ground, reached behind his own head, and ripped the facemask from the hunter behind him. The other hunter charged toward him. McQueen kicked at his facemask. His foot hit a glancing blow and knocked the facemask halfway off the hunter's face. McQueen grabbed his opened canteen from his belt and threw the brown water in the hunter's face. The hunter fell backwards onto the other hunter that was holding Tommy. Tommy rolled out of the hunters grip, reached up, and pulled that hunter's facemask off. The hunter screamed in fright. McQueen threw brown water in the hunter's face behind him. Then he turned and tossed the last splash onto the hunter's face who was just getting up off the ground. Tommy jumped up and dashed out of reach.

Clutching their faces in horror, the mask-less hunters rushed down the path. In the distance, one yelled, "Don't stop until we get to the decontamination truck."

Tommy patted McQueen on the back. "Way to go, you big dummy."

"Why are you calling me dummy, again?"

"Now that we have been seen together, you will never be allowed to go back. You are now an official traitor to the corporation."

CHAPTER 8

Walking on the path back to the water house, Tommy looked back over his shoulder. "McQueen, you don't look so good. Can you make it to the water house?"

McQueen rubbed the side of his head. "I can make it, but for some reason, my mind's in a big tangle."

Tommy stopped walking. "Those housing authority morons won't be back for a while, you want to stop and take a break?"

"That's okay," McQueen said, and paused. "Keep walking. I'll try to sort it out."

Tommy turned and continued walking. Behind him, McQueen walked and talked. "People exposed to wood virus that haven't already turned into Dinkies have always died at sundown." He looked toward the sky. Tree leaves blocked his view. He couldn't see where the sun was. "I was exposed after sundown. Do you think it's too late for the antidote?"

"As far as I'm concerned, it's always too late," Tommy said, and his words hung in the air.

Like a fatal reminder, Tommy's words caused McQueen to feel sick and helpless. "I can't win," he said." If I live, I'll mutate into a Dinky."

"So?"

"I'll no longer belong with the superior pig people."

Tommy raised his hands in the air and rotated them in little circles. "What makes you think they're superior?"

"For one thing, they don't have to work in the

fields."

"That's true, but they don't have to stay on the blue grass."

McQueen looked at the beauty of the forest. It was all around him. The various shades of greens made him feel peaceful, and his eyes didn't ache like they did when he stayed in the barracks and worked under the bright blue lights. "They do have more freedom," he said, and a sparrow swept across the path in front of him. Although it was small and insignificant, he marveled at its ability to maneuver its tiny body between the tree branches. It made him wonder what it would be like if he lived and shrank to the size of a Dinky. Then he could be like Tommy. When the warriors chased him, he could duck and hide in the tall grass. If he were brave, he could maneuver around and between them. He would enjoy agitating Burke. He smiled at the thought and looked at Tommy. "Pig people might not be superior after all."

Tommy dropped his hands. "You think you can adopt the values of us low-class Dinkies?"

McQueen reached out and placed his hand on Tommy's shoulder. "Hey, wait a minute, Tommy. I don't think you're low-class."

Tommy paused for a moment. "Thanks." He kept on walking.

McQueen's mind seemed to be functioning like a broken crutch. "I feel like I've been gone a long time," he said, and tried to clear the incoming memories that were flooding his mind. "And I can't figure out why I put my life in the corporation's hands."

"You seem to have a lot of blanks."

"I'm trying to fill them in. Sometimes you tell me things we did together and I can't remember them."

Tommy kept walking and put his little hands into his pockets. "Do you remember your father's parable about the man who believed in the stones of life, but was killed because he trusted mankind?"

McQueen paused and looked skyward. Words came from his mouth, but he didn't know where they were coming from. "When a time comes when people cannot trust their fellow man, civilization is doomed."

"That's right," Tommy said. "Do you remember more?"

"Without belief in the stones of life, a man's trust is used against him for the other's gain."

Tommy encouragingly held his palms up. "Do you know what that means?"

McQueen shuddered, and a strange chill ran up his spine. "I have no idea. I don't even know why I remember it."

"Can't you think for yourself? Can't you just try?"

"I am trying, but I feel like some kind of machine built for the good of the corporation."

"I think you're brainwashed."

"I don't know if I would call it that," McQueen said, and the part of his military disciplined brain barked in his head. "If I don't function as I was trained to do, I will be eliminated."

Tommy shook his head and didn't say anything.

They walked down the overgrown path, and the thoughts in McQueen's head began to untangle. He slowed his pace, and Tommy walked ahead of him.

Next to the orange sign at the entrance to Forbidden Forest, McQueen stopped and looked at the entrance to the water house. Tommy stood there waving and yelling, "Come on, you big dummy."

McQueen was going to die at sundown. If Tommy and he were such good friends, why did he keep calling him a big dummy?

He walked away from the sign and quickened his steps. When he got to the entrance to the water house he stopped and stared at Tommy.

"What's the matter?" Tommy asked.

McQueen's eyes shifted to the big, gray, stone blocks. "I missed this place," he said. "I dreamed about it, always wanted to come back here."

"Why didn't you?"

"I was always afraid of the water-virus." He put his hand on the steel door and felt the doorknob. "I know where I am." He wiggled the doorknob. "And this feels familiar. But now that I'm here, I can't remember why this place is so important."

Tommy looked up at McQueen. His mouth twisted downward and it was if a shield of sadness covered his face. He turned his back to McQueen and looked at the steel door.

"What's the matter?" McQueen asked.

"I wish you would remember," Tommy said, and pushed McQueen's hand from the doorknob.

"Remember what?"

Tommy didn't answer. He turned the knob and pushed. A squawk vibrated from the rusting hinges. The door swung open. A green vine, covered with green leaves of three's, dropped down and swung in front of his face. He ducked and the vine swung

110

past his head. He turned back toward McQueen. "Don't let that vine touch you."

"I know," McQueen said. "It's the wood-virus plant. It must be really powerful. It's really dark-green." He swung his head out of the way of the swinging vine. "I don't know why I ducked. If I live, I'm going to mutate into a Dinky anyway."

Tommy looked at the wooden lever next to the water pipe that would trap McQueen in the water tunnel. "I don't think you're going to mutate into anything."

McQueen turned and caught the vine in his hand.

"What are you doing?" Tommy asked.

McQueen held the vine and studied it. "It feels pretty good not to be afraid of this."

Tommy spoke loud and forceful. "Are you a brainwashed? Don't you remember the havoc that vine wreaked on you that summer? It's poison ivy?"

McQueen let the vine drop, but he didn't answer.

Tommy dragged his feet and stepped to the drinking pipe. He stopped and put his hand on the wooden lever.

McQueen felt something click in his mind. He grabbed the sides of his head with both hands and opened his eyes wide. He stood for a moment, took it all in, and covered his face with his hands. Suddenly, he dropped his hands from his face, ran over to Tommy, and hugged him. "Tommy," he said. "I just saw a flash. Everything came back to me. It was bits and pieces before. But now, I remember everything we did."

Tommy took his hand off the lever and slumped until his knees bent. "It's about time."

McQueen stepped back and looked at Tommy as if he had just seen him for the first time in years. He smiled big, grabbed him again, hugged him, and patted him on the back. "Damn, I must have been brainwashed like we used to talk about."

McQueen released him and stepped back again.

"McQueen, your eyes are watering," Tommy said. "I think your brain washing just got washed away."

"Yeah." McQueen wiped the tears of joy from his face. "Who would have ever thought poison ivy would cure me."

"Yeah," Tommy said, and smiled. "Who would have ever thunk it."

"I remember, thunk it. You said, 'Who could have ever thunk it would be such a terrible case.' It's a good thing we knew about baking soda. Pasted that stuff on day and night and it finally went away."

McQueen stepped to the corner of the water house and pulled a little square stone from the wall. "Who would have ever thunk it. The secret powder to cure it is still here."

"We keep it here for Dinkies that go out," Tommy said. "Got to keep it fresh or it won't work. When they swim through the tunnel, it washes off."

"Does it get that bad?"

Tommy pointed to the poison ivy vine curled around the top of the doorframe. "When the carbon dioxide builds up in the air that stuff gets powerful."

Something is wrong here," McQueen said. "Nelson keeps a poison ivy plant right on his desk.

112

Sometimes Nelson lets the warriors handle it. I wonder why they don't get poison ivy."

"Most warriors don't get it because of the steroid rays they use. If Nelson gives them fake rays, they'll get poison ivy. He'll say it's the virus. It gives him an excuse to get rid of troublemakers."

"That plant helped the housing authority get rid of your father."

McQueen looked at the poison ivy vine hanging next to the steel door of the water house. "It was wrapped around an old piece of wood. "Just before he died my father had poison ivy and the wood-virus all over his face and hands."

"Your father didn't die from wood-virus. The antidote killed him."

"I know, they didn't get to him soon enough."

Tommy violently shook his head. "Have you ever heard of anyone living after they received the antidote?"

"No, but I'm sure there are many of them out there."

"Would you take the antidote if I could get it?"

"I would, but it's too late."

"Even if it means you'll turn into a Dinky?"

"It's better than being dead."

"What if I tell you we have a cure?"

McQueen figured Tommy was trying to spare his feelings. "You don't have to lie to me just to make me feel good," he said. "I have accepted the fact that I will die or become a Dinky."

"Talk about accepting something," Tommy said with a dismissive wave of his little hand. "I might have to make up something to get the other Dinkies to accept you."

113

McQueen shook his head and felt his right eyebrow wrinkle. "After all the Dinkies I have captured, they have a few reasons not to trust me."

"After we go through the tunnel, we'll just have to play it by ear."

"Makes sense to me."

"Good, now I'll show you the new, old secret cave."

McQueen swung his arm down. His hand slapped into the water. Cool fresh water splashed onto his face. He ignored the water dripping off his face and smiled. "Damn, Tommy, it's nice not to be afraid of water anymore."

"It sure is," Tommy said. "We have a lot to talk about."

Tommy went to the drinking pipe and put his hand on the wooden lever. "We sure do. We can do it right inside."

McQueen stood next to the pool of water and hesitated. "Are you sure we'll fit. We're not little kids anymore. The secret cave will be a little cramped."

"Tommy put his hand on the wooden lever. "I think we'll fit," he said, put his little mouth to the drinking pipe, and took a long cool drink.

Bang! The steel door to the water house flew open. Tommy jerked his mouth away from the drinking pipe. Water ran down his little chin. Burke and three warriors walked in. TV reporters oozed in behind him with their cam-fingers pointing. McQueen jumped back and held his back against the stone wall.

"Take it easy, McQueen," Burke said, and folded his arms across his chest.

114

Tommy nudged McQueen on the elbow and whispered, "Jump in."

Burke raised his voice. "Yeah, McQueen, jump into that virus water. He motioned to the TV reporters with his arm. "Come on over, boys. Record the great hero, Sergeant John McQueen, committing suicide."

The reporters held out their cam-fingers as if the pool were radioactive and warily walked toward McQueen.

One reporter looked at Tommy wiping the water from his chin and asked, "Sergeant McQueen, did that Dinky trick you into drinking the virus water?"

McQueen didn't answer.

The second reporter pointed his cam-finger at McQueen's wet hand, scanned it up his body, and stopped at his wet face. "Are you going to die for us on TV?"

McQueen jerked his head to the right. Drops of water flew from his face. The reporters jumped back. He ran his hand down the front of his chest, looked around the room, and searched for a way out.

Burke flexed his biceps toward the cam-fingers and turned until he was sure McQueen had a clear view of his upper arm. "Answer the reporter's questions," Burke said.

McQueen didn't answer. His eyes fixated on Burke's arm. Sergeant strips were there. Nelson had given him his stripes.

Burke bent his head down and looked at his own arm. The new sergeant stripes glowed gold in the dim light. He puffed up his massive chest and turned to the reporters. "We are going to let ex-sergeant McQueen play his little game."

McQueen snapped his head right and then snapped it left. Seeing no way out, he spoke. "I'm not playing a game. I'm trying to stay alive."

"If you wanted to live," Burke said, "you would not have associated with the Dinkies."

The reporters stepped closer to McQueen and warily held out their cam-fingers.

Burke stood back and spoke with authority. "Sergeant McQueen, we are recording your association with the Dinkies. You will be on TV. We will transfer this evidence of your traitor actions to the corporation's hall of shame. It will serve as a reminder. It will show your hero-worshiping pig people that the virus is real."

Burke stepped closer to the cam-fingers. "Yes, Friends of the Earth Corporation," he announced in his arrogant voice, "this ignorant act of Sergeant McQueen's will serve as a lesson to other warriors who choose to associate with infected Dinkies."

A reporter pointed his cam-finger to the cascading water. "Is that water flowing over wood?"

"Yes it is," Burke said. "This entire pool of virus-water is also infected with wood-virus."

The reporter jerked his cam-finger back and pointed it at McQueen. "Sergeant McQueen, do you plan to drink this water? Do you plant to commit suicide?"

McQueen figured he was going to mutate anyway. But right now, he had to do something to get away. He looked at the two warriors on his right. If he could jump right between them, he could run out the door. He stepped toward the drinking pipe and flexed his knees to leap. Before he could spring free, three warriors jumped in front of him. His escape was blocked.

He un-flexed his knees, held his palm up, and held a salute. "Yes, I'll commit suicide," he said into the cam-finger. "Warriors, step away from the well."

The warriors looked at Burke. Burke motioned with a slow tilt of his head. "Let the fool pass."

McQueen took Tommy by the arm and they stepped to the drinking pipe. Tommy looked into the deep pool. "I'll go first," he whispered, "you follow."

"Hey, Dinky!" Burke shouted. "Do you have something to say?"

Tommy stiffened his little body. "No, sir."

"Then keep your ugly mouth shut."

Tommy put his face to the drinking pipe and looked up at the reporters. Waving the back of his little hand, he said, "Stand back unless you want splashed."

The reporters dropped their cam-fingered hands to their sides and jumped back. Tommy took a big mouth full of water and stepped up onto the edge of the pool wall. McQueen knew he was ready to dive in. He held his mouth over the drinking pipe and flexed his knees to follow Tommy.

One brave reporter ran up to McQueen and thrust his cam-finger into his face. "Sergeant McQueen is about to drink from a fountain full of mutating wood-virus water," he announced. "He is about to commit suicide."

Burke stepped in front of the other cam-fingers

and flashed his cheese-face smile. "This warrior is suffering from the effects of his exposure to wood-virus. You can see by his death defying actions that he has brain damage."

"How would you know that, Sergeant Burke?" a reporter asked.

"Sergeant McQueen and I went through warrior training together. It's a shame that a great warrior's brain has been crippled with the water-virus. Now he is about to further expose himself to the wood-virus."

"How long does Sergeant McQueen have to live?"

"After he drinks the wood-virus water, Sergeant McQueen will be dead before the sun sets."

A reporter held his cam-finger to his own face and talked into it. "Sergeant John McQueen, the hero of the pig people and the Friends of the Earth Corporation, is about to mysteriously drink from a pool of deadly wood virus-water."

McQueen bent over and put his mouth to the drinking pipe. He was still afraid of the virus. He didn't want to drink. The water flowed over his closed mouth. He opened it, sucked in, but didn't swallow. He looked up with the cheek expanding mouth full. The reporters held their breath and kept their cam-fingers focused on him.

One warrior spoke up and talked fast. "Don't swallow it, McQueen. You can go back. You can take the antidote. You can get recycled. You'll live."

"Burke stared at the warrior. The warrior snapped to attention. "Sorry, Sergeant Burke," the warrior whined. "I was out of line."

118

"Let him swallow," Burke said. "That Dinky standing next to him is his kid brother."

The reporters jerked their cam-fingers away from McQueen and pointed them at Burke. "What?"

Tommy looked up and spit a stream of water out of his mouth. It flowed into air. The reporters jumped back like they were on the end of a cracking whip. Tommy looked to McQueen. "Let's go!" He dove into the deep pool.

McQueen turned to spray water out of his mouth. Burke ran up and sneak punched him in the chest. McQueen gulped in surprise and swallowed. He needed a big breath of air for the dive. Burke's punch had done something to his chest. He couldn't breathe in. The warriors reached for him. There was no time to recover and breathe. He dove in after Tommy. Down they sank into the dark water.

McQueen felt for the old opening that lead to the tunnel. He couldn't find it. Tommy grabbed him by the hand and pulled. McQueen glided to the opening. Tommy went in first. McQueen was right on his feet and followed him into the skinny secret water tunnel. When McQueen's shoulders scraped the sides of the narrow tunnel, he was already out of breath.

If he got stuck he would drown. Big-shouldered warriors would never fit through this narrow tunnel. He was glad he didn't jump the laser steroid beam and load his body with excess muscle. He never knew why he preferred a swimmer's body. Now it was saving a life. It was his.

But he needed air. He didn't remember the tunnel being so long. If only Burke hadn't punched

119

him in the chest he could swim through with ease.

He felt a grab-hold on the side of the round tunnel wall. He grabbed it and pulled. He sailed out the tunnel and rushed for the surface. His head broke through the top of the water. He breathed in deep breaths and sucked in much needed air.

Inside the secret cave, Tommy treaded water and looked at McQueen. "You're really out of shape."

Freddy, the mutant guard, bent over the pool of water. "Tommy, you and McQueen have to go back out."

Tommy grabbed the side of the pool wall. "What?"

McQueen breathed slower and listened.

Freddy waved his little hands. "If you stay here, they'll think you drowned. They'll bring in the laser dragger and drag the well. They'll find the tunnel."

"That's right," Tommy said, and tipped his head toward McQueen. "You ready to go back out?"

McQueen rubbed his chest. "I'm not sure. Burke punched me in the chest, knocked the wind out of me. I need a few minutes break."

"You don't have a few minutes," Freddy said.

"Give him the facemask," Tommy said.

Freddy ran to the bunk, scooped up the facemask, and threw it at McQueen. "Here, put it on and get out of here. And don't come back up."

"Tommy filled his lungs with air and looked at McQueen. "When we get to the other side, come up nice and smooth, like we used to when we tried to scare your father."

"What if Burke's still there?"

Start splashing them with water. That should give us enough time to get out of the water house."

The solution seemed so simple. McQueen wanted to ask Tommy why they didn't think of that before, but Freddy leaned over the pool. "Don't forget," he said. "There's no one on the other side to pull the handle and signal me. If you come back through, I won't know who it is. I'll have to shut the tunnel gates and drown anyone that's in there."

Tommy looked toward the little pump handle on the air compressor. "Start pumping. We're on our way."

McQueen put the mask on his face, surface dove to the tunnel entrance, and entered. Tommy swam behind him and pushed at his heels. McQueen breathed in. The facemask had no air coming into it. Tommy pushed at his heels again. The air flowed into the mask. McQueen breathed in deep. At the end of the tunnel, he took off the mask and grabbed onto Tommy's hand. Then they ascended to the surface, slow and easy.

Their heads eased through the top of the water without a sound. McQueen looked toward the steel door of the water house. Burke and the warriors were gone. A lone reporter stood outside the opened door talking into his cam-finger.

"We could sneak right past him," Tommy whispered.

"If we do, then they'll drag the pool."

"That reporter has to know we're still alive. Let's scare him a little."

CHAPTER 9

Trying to get a signal on the TV in the dashboard, Danielle sat back in her OvalCar and thumbed the tuning dials. The Friends of The Earth Corporation had given many reasons why radios and TV's seldom worked. First, they claimed it was high tides. Then they blamed it on sun flares. Next they said the earth's magnetic field had caused the interference. She didn't understand any of the reasons. She only knew her TV wasn't working. She banged on the dashboard. The screen sputtered, fizzed, and sound came from the speakers.

The picture came in clear and the audio could be understood. Danielle sat up in her seat and watched. The recording of McQueen and Tommy committing suicide was being aired.

When McQueen dove into the pool an uncontrollable sadness swelled inside her heart, and tears formed in the corners of her eyes.

A call came over her radio. "Driver Fairchild, proceed to the water house. Pick up, Warrior Burke."

She banged herself in the forehead. "Just what I need, more grief." She wiped the tears from her eyes, turned the car around, and headed for the water house.

On the way, she thought of the things McQueen and she could have done. She would have kissed his high cheekbones. She would have held his face in both her hands and took in its strong features. His kiss would have had the taste of expensive wine. Many nights she would have nuzzled against his neck and breathed in his happy aroma of fresh air and clean virus-free water. But now there would be no kisses or smells in her dreams. Now, John McQueen was dead. She wiped her face, but the tears still flowed.

The TV scratched. An impatient voice beamed over the speaker. "Driver Fairchild! Proceed to your destination!"

Danielle miserably nodded her head and clicked the microphone to signal that she was on her way. She allowed herself one more fabulous thought. If Sergeant McQueen had been granted the privilege to reproduce and picked her, they would have lived on the blue grass. They would have had enough kids to line up like baby bluebirds on a wire.

She stopped in front of the water house, waited in the car, and watched. Outside the water house, Burke waved his hands and took positions of importance. He turned, and looking into the cam-finger's reflective lenses, he swaggered, posed at different angles, and showed off the new sergeant stripes on his arms.

Danielle knew he wasn't fit to be lowly private let alone a sergeant. She cussed under her breath and talked out loud. "Go ahead, Burke. Flash that ugly cheese face and show off those stripes you stole."

A short thin reporter with narrow shoulders walked up, stopped next to a portly reporter, and nudged him. They pointed their cam-fingers at each other. Expecting to hear some breaking news, Danielle powered her window down.

Talking to the thin reporter, the portly reporter talked into his pudgy cam-finger. "How did it happen, Frank?"

Frank put his skinny cam-finger to his own face. "Worst thing I ever saw, George. They just joined hands and committed suicide."

George breathed in a deep breath, and his bloated stomach heaved like he had just finished running a race. "Did you see any reason for them to do such a terrible act?"

Frank looked at George's heaving stomach; and as if he were trying not to talk about the stomach, he twisted his lips to the side, looked away from George, and said, "Irregularities have been brought to our attention."

"A big mistake was made," George said, and pointed to the water house. "Right in there, Sergeant John McQueen and a Dinky committed suicide today."

Frank jumped between the cam-finger and the water house, blocking George's view. "McQueen's been called gay," he said and flinched. George had tramped on his toe. He ignored the pain, jerked his foot out from under George's foot; and as if nothing had happened, he talked into the cam-finger. "Do we have more information on this?"

George's lips formed a satisfied grin. "Rumor has it that McQueen lived with a gay Dinky."

The thought of McQueen being branded as gay infuriated Danielle. Looking like clowns getting ready to join a sideshow of lies, the reporters had no right to say such a thing. She wondered how many more backdoor denial, underhanded statements those idiots were going to make and tear a good man down. They probably had bags of phony information they could pull out and make any good story great. Those stupid reporters always jived it

124

up and made up sources that didn't exist. When they didn't have any new news, they performed made-up conversations to increase their own worth.

She threw herself back into the seat, shifted her gaze away from the reporters, and tapped her foot on the car floor. The two reporters continued their show saying:

"No one's suggesting warrior McQueen's suicide is a good thing. But who knows what kind of super virus he may have created by befriending that mutant."

"Not all hero warriors are weird."

Danielle wished the reporters would tell it like it was. They were saying McQueen was weird. And nothing could be further from the truth.

The door to the water house was open. She leaned over the window of the OvalCar and looked inside. Behind a cub reporter standing next to the door, two figures ease up out of the pool and slosh to the door. She couldn't see them very well in the darkened water house, but one was the size of a Dinky and the other one was as tall as McQueen. She got out of the car and walked toward the water house.

The cub reporter turned toward the two figures. With excessive excitement and glee, he lifted his little cam-finger to his own face. "It's McQueen and the Dinky," he yelled. "Sergeant McQueen's alive." In an attempt to block their exit, he spread his arms out wide and stood in the doorway.

Tommy walked up to the cub reporter, put his wet fingers in front of his face, and flicked them. Water flecked onto the cub reporter. With drops of water dotting on his face, the cub reporter stood in

125

fright. He didn't move.

Danielle shouted at him, "That's virus water. Your face has just been splashed with virus water."

The reporter jumped back, pulled out a handkerchief, and began to wipe the water from his face. The other reporters stuck out their cam-fingers and rushed toward the water house. McQueen and Tommy sidestepped past the stunned cub reporter and ran toward the forbidden forest. The skinny reporter ran after them, and the portly reporter waddled behind. When they came to the orange off-limits sign, they both came to a sudden stop.

When McQueen and Tommy disappeared into the green of the forest, Danielle's heart filled with glee. McQueen did not die in the pool. He was alive. But without the antidote, he would be dead before night fell.

She walked back to her car and stood beside the opened door. She wondered why she had shouted at that reporter. She had never done that with anyone else, ever. She wanted to know what this McQueen guy all about, but she couldn't get involved. It was the corporation's business. It was her obligation to drive. If she interfered, she would get recycled. She would be better off if she just forgot all about John McQueen. She would have to stay professional and not let her emotions take over. She must not get attached to him. After all, he did fail to catch the Dinky. And now he was covered with virus-water, and was running around with the Dinky he couldn't catch. She didn't want to do it, but if she saw him again, she would have to call in his position. She wouldn't get involved. She couldn't.

She opened the door to her OvalCar and hesitated. Something didn't seem right. With her own eyes, she had watched McQueen dive into the virus water of Forbidden Lake and he was still alive. Didn't someone say the virus-water was fake? Maybe the whole damn lake was filled with fake virus-water.

She stepped into her OvalCar and slid behind the wheel. She knew she shouldn't do it, but after she got rid of pain-in-the-ass, Burke, she planned to drive to the lake. McQueen and that little Dinky were there before. Maybe they'll show up there again. If they did, she would try to talk McQueen into giving up. He could go back to the barracks. He could take the antidote and live. No matter what Burke said, McQueen was still a hero. The pig people loved him. They would never let the corporation mistreat him. There was no reason he couldn't surrender and be given the antidote right in front of the TV reporters.

As Danielle drove Burke back to the base, he flashed his ugly cheese-face looks and was his usual obnoxious self. She answered his smart remarks with one-word answers, and he had given up on her.

When she dropped him off, it was dark. She drove to Forbidden Lake, pulled into a little cutoff road, and stopped. Her lights illuminated a big orange sign that read:

OFF-LIMITS

BROWN WOOD-VIRUS

HIGHLY CONTAGIOUS

CONTACT WILL CAUSE MUTATION OR DEATH

BY ORDER OF CEO NELSON:

She stuck her head out her side window and looked down. Below the sign, three human skulls lay next to a pile of brown wood. One of the skulls was broken. The skull didn't look normal. She wondered why. But she wasn't getting near a pile of virus-wood to find out.

She flicked off the OvalCar lights and stayed in the car waiting for her eyes to adjust to the dark. Then she scammed the shoreline for signs of movement. Next to the shore, a few reeds and tree branches waved; but she couldn't make out if it was the lake breeze or some animal causing the movement. She stepped out of the OvalCar for a better look. Off to the right, a little green light flashed. She stepped toward it and waved. The light went out.

"Come on, you big dummy," echoed across the lake.

She yelled across the dark water, "John McQueen, is that you?"

A hundred meters from the car, the green light flashed again. This time it flashed a few feet from the shoreline. Another voice shouted, "Come around this side."

Danielle fixated her eyes on the green light. As if she were hypnotized, she plunged into the dark and walked toward the green beam. A few meters from the green light, an ugly pale-skinned Dinky with stringy no-color-hair, jumped up laughing. "You big dummy. You're standing in virus vines."

Danielle looked down. She wasn't standing in virus vines. She was standing on blue gravel. The green light went out. She was night blinded. She held out her hands and tried to feel her way back to the OvalCar. Flat heart-shaped leaves tumbled down and covered her face and body.

"Real virus vines!" the little Dinky's voice yelled, and water splashed into her face. "Now you'll be a Dinky."

The laughter of another Dinky wafted in the night, and it spoke. "Go back and jump on that pile of plastic—" he said and suddenly stopped.

Another voice stamped on his words. "Shut up, you fool."

The Dinky's laughter faded into the dark night.

Danielle pulled the vines from her wet face and untangled them from her body. Groping in the dark, her foot sloshed into a shallow stream of virus water.

"Damn!" she said with disgust. "What's the difference? I should have never gotten out of the car. Things are turning out just great. I'm exposed now." She looked down the road. "I have to get back to the base in time to be decontaminated and get the antidote."

She walked back to the orange sign and stopped next to the woodpile. She didn't have time to waste, but that broken skull bothered her.

With the sleeve of her blouse pulled over her hand, she picked up the broken skull and carried it to her OvalCar. She could see something inside the skull, but there wasn't enough light for her to make out what it was. She reached into her OvalCar and turned on the headlights. She stepped to the front of the car and held the skull in the light beam. Inside was a label:

Made in Patagonia.

Under exclusive contract for:
The Friends of the Earth Corporation.

She squeezed the skull. It gave under her touch. It was plastic. All this time someone had been putting plastic skulls around the lake to scare people away. She sighed and said to herself, "Oh well, it works. Maybe the wood's plastic too. But I must get back to the base. I need that antidote."

She tossed the broken plastic skull into the woodpile and jumped into her OvalCar. Then she drove back to the base dispensary, parked her car, and ran toward the decontamination chamber. No one was at the door. She placed her eye in front of the scanner outside the chamber. The computer spoke. "Driver cleared to enter."

She stepped into the decontamination chamber, pulled the lever that activated the ultraviolet laser's excited glow, and looked out the glass door. There was movement down the hall, but she couldn't make out who it was.

The "virus contained" light flashed and the computer voice spoke. "Driver clear to receive the antidote."

The glass door opened automatically. She stepped out. A stern-faced medic with a thick chest grabbed her by the arm. "Driver Fairchild, where do you think you're going?"

"To get the antidote. I've just been exposed to the virus vine. Let me lose."

The medic held her tighter. She looked into his face. It was the drunken medic she had went out with at the Dance Box. The date had started out all right, but after a few drinks he had changed. He had become someone worse than Burke. She had flatly

130

refused to continue the date and had left him standing in the middle of the dance floor. When she went through the Dance Box's doors, his warrior friends had applauded her and laughed at him. And now he was holding her, and his strong grip hurt her arm.

"It's too late for the antidote," he said, and the smell of alcohol wafted into her face.

"You're hurting me," she cried. "Turn me loose and get someone in here to give me the antidote."

The medic released her, leaned back, and held the lapels of his white medic's coat. "No need to bother the crew. I'll give you the antidote."

Time was running out. Even though he was drunk, she figured the freak should be able to give her the antidote. It could already be too late, and she didn't have time to argue with him. "Go ahead," she said, "but hurry." She pulled the flexible sleeve of her uniform up and exposed her arm.

The medic jerked his head toward the antidote room. "Be my guest." He stepped aside.

Danielle stepped into the room and nervously waited for him to draw the antidote from the locked supply cabinet on the wall.

He placed his uncoordinated fingers on the code bar and tried to open the cabinet. It wouldn't open. He tried again, but he was too inebriated to punch the numbers in the right order.

"What's the code," she said, and stepped to the cabinet.

"I can't tell you. If someone finds out, I'll be recycled."

"You'll be recycled if I tell the housing authority that you were intoxicated while on function status."

"The medic staggered backwards. "Hey, you don't play fair."

Danielle didn't want to, but she needed to try a different approach. She reached up and caressed the warrior's face. "Come on, baby, we can both do each other a favor. Give me the code."

The medic wiggled his finger in a come-here-gesture and said, "Come close. I'll whisper it in your ear."

Danielle winced at the thought, but she knew a drunken slob hanging on her was better than turning into a Dinky or dying; and time was running out. She could always wash his stink off her body, but she couldn't wash off the mutant virus.

"Come here, honey," she said, and braced for the worse.

As the medic's hot drunken breath wafted down her neck, he whispered, "One, two, three."

"That's it?" she questioned.

"Try it and see," he said, and smiled. "If that's not it, we'll try again."

Danielle reached up and punched in the code. The cabinet did not open. Again, the medic wiggled his finger in a come-here-gesture. "Come on back, baby. We'll try until we get it right."

Danielle knew he would play his stupid game until he got what he wanted. She reasoned that he must have the numbers but in the wrong order. She reached up again, and punched in three, two, one. The door wouldn't open. She punched in two, three, one. It still wouldn't open. She turned and looked at the staggering medic. No one else was in the dispensary. He was probably covering for the others who were out partying. She didn't want his stinking breath down her neck again. She turned and looked at the code bar. She reared back and slammed her fist into the bar. "Open you piece of junk!"

The cabinet flew open.

The medic stepped to the cabinet. "Okay," he said, "I got it from here."

Danielle held her uniform sleeve up and waited for him to load the syringe fingered glove. The dose was pre-measured and only one antidote to an exposed patient was allowed by law.

The medic placed the tip of the syringe into the antidote supply tube. Slurring his speech, he said, "Put your eye to the pupil identification scanner."

She did. The antidote released from the supply tube and flowed into the syringe. He staggered backward, but caught his balance.

Danielle looked at the time. This jerk had already caused her to wait another fifteen minutes. Maybe it was already too late. She reached for the syringe fingered glove. "Give me that," she said. "I'll give it to myself."

The medic teetered back on his heels and held the syringed-fingered glove on his hand. "No way, baby, this is where I have to draw the line. I must give all the antidote shots on my shift."

"Well, do it," she said, tapped her foot, and waited. He slowly and deliberately held the finger syringe next to her arm. "Okay, baby, here we go."

She didn't want the big blockhead to make a big production out of it. It's was her life he had in his hands. She barked at him, "Just do it!"

"Don't get excited," he said, and fell into her. The syringe went into her arm. The high-pressure air-needle hit her arm at a steep angle. The antidote serum entered her thin outer layer of skin and exited out the other side."

"You dumb ass!" she screamed. "The serum went out the other side."

The medic steadied himself and looked at the syringe. The little orange "Patient inoculated" light was on. "Oh no, you're wrong. It went in. The light's on."

"No it didn't. Can't you see the serum on the floor?"

The medic tramped on the wet stream of serum and dragged his foot across it. "That's just a spot on the floor. It's been there for years."

"Give me another antidote," she screamed."

The relief medic came through the door. The drunken medic straightened up and looked mean. "Only one to a customer. You can leave now."

The relief medic stopped next to the opened door of the unlocked cabinet, slammed it shut, and locked it. He folded his arms across his chest. "What's going on here?"

"Driver Fairchild was exposed to the vine wood-virus. I just inoculated her with the antidote. She says she wants another antidote."

"The relief medic looked at her arms. Redness showed on her skin. "It doesn't matter," he said with an air of superiority. "It's too late now. No antidote can help. If she doesn't die, she'll become a Dinky."

Danielle spoke up. "But I didn't get the

134

antidote. It went—"

The drunken medic put his hand over her mouth. "She's crazy."

The relief medic turned and pointed to the exit. "We don't want to be cleaning up your dead body. Get the hell out of here."

The drunken medic took his hand from her mouth. She yelled, "Just where am I supposed to go?"

"Go back to your quarters," the drunken medic said. "The death squad will clean up your remains."

She shuddered and then screamed, "I'm not going anywhere without that antidote."

The drunken medic put his hand back over her mouth and held it there. "Driver Fairchild, you will leave now. There are other people waiting."

Danielle turned to leave. "Wait," the relief medic said. "There's no welcome mat for you anywhere. You are now officially banned from driving. The warrior at the door will guard your OvalCar until it can be towed to the decontamination garage."

"But it's my OvalCar," Danielle pleaded. "I'm responsible for it."

"Sorry," the relief medic said. "It's the law. No virus-exposed drivers are allowed back in their vehicles."

Danielle turned and walked out the door. She wished she had never gotten out of her OvalCar. She began the long walk back to her quarters. The closer she got the more she thought about McQueen. The last time she had seen him he had been at the water house. Maybe he was there now. She thought about going just to see if he was there.

Maybe before she died, she could see him one last time. Maybe she could walk there. But warriors in OvalCars would be on the roads. They would pick her up and bring her back. It would be useless. With visions of death and mutation, she walked toward her quarters.

CHAPTER 10

Miles from the water house, the trees became smaller and smaller, and then sickly. Then the forest ended. At the path's end, McQueen and Tommy looked across a stretch of land that once was alive with tall trees and teaming with wildlife.

Before them, tree stumps stuck up like black tombstones. Here and there, pale plants struggled to survive in a toxic soil. The air was a dusty-gray and smelled like snakes.

It reminded McQueen that he would be dead by sundown. He had been suppressing the thought of dying. Now, the dead land before him caused him to become sick and confused. "Tommy, what happened here?"

Tommy kicked at the dead dirt. Powdery purple dust puffed into the air. "Before the wood virus epidemics," he said, and irritation flashed in his faced. "The pig people poisoned the land so that only money making cherry trees could grow. Then they cut them down." He flashed a nasty grin. "This is what they left."

"Hardly anything grows here," McQueen said. "Why didn't they replant?"

"They didn't care about tomorrow. Before the pig people were forced to live on the blue grass, they'd take whatever made them money and move on to the next place."

"Maybe they knew about the wood virus and they were cutting the trees down to get rid of it."

"Yeah, right," Tommy said, and started walking across the lonesome land.

The dead black stumps flashed in McQueen's

mind. Soon he would be just as dead. He shuddered. "This place is ugly. It gives me the creeps."

At the edge of the purple-gray soil, the green forest began again. At its edge, a stand of tall green grass blocked the little footpath that ran through the forest. McQueen stopped and watched Tommy. Tommy started tramping down the grass. Then he stood on one foot; and with the edge of his little foot, he whooshed the grass flat; and its ends broke with little tender muffled clunks.

Between the whooshing, McQueen asked, "Is it still there?"

Apparently Tommy didn't hear him. "Don't be afraid of a little green stuff," he said.

"I'm not talking about the grass."

Tommy stopped whooshing the grass. "Well, what are you talking about?"

"Hidden Lake, with all the big bass?"

Tommy stood on the tramped-down grass. "What would you want to go there for?"

"Maybe we could cut some sticks and make some wooden poles. McQueen lifted his hand as if he were holding a fishing pole and jerked it like he was setting the hook. "Maybe we cold catch some fish."

Tommy's face clouded with disappointment. "What would we do with them after we caught them?"

"Just like when we were kids, we could build a little fire and roast them."

Tommy's face reflected agonized grief. "We can't eat fish from that lake."

"You look like someone just told you your best

138

friend died. Why can't we?"

"They're contaminated," Tommy said, and tears formed in his little eyes. "A lot of kids ate those fish after we did. Then, the great Friends of the Earth Corporation dumped a new pollutant into the water."

"I remember that," McQueen said. "The fish tested positive for a new strain of chronic wasting disease, but the corporation claimed there was no evidence that the disease had ever been contracted by a human."

"They lied." Tommy turned his tear-filled eyes from McQueen. "I don't know what it really was, but my friend, Freddy, said a neurological disorder attacked the kid's brains."

Tommy walked off the tramped down grass and onto the footpath that led into the forest. "Before those kids died, they walked around like living skeletons."

McQueen stepped over the bent-over grass and walked behind Tommy. "Maybe we got a touch of it when we ate the fish, but now it doesn't matter. When Burke hit me in the chest, I swallowed that virus-water. He said I'd be dead before sundown."

"So?"

"I've accepted the fact that I'll die, but I would like to die sitting next to the lake."

"Why?"

"If I die with the setting sun, I'll have some sort of control over the process."

Tommy cracked a faint smile. "That sounds like a plan."

Walking behind Tommy, McQueen looked at the back of his shoulders. They shook as if he were crying. McQueen thought if Tommy were going to die, he would cry for him, too.

They walked into a little meadow. Above their heads, a lone bird soared and cried. McQueen stopped walking and looked up. The sky was blank. "Was that an eagle?"

Tommy's shoulders quit shaking. "I doubt it. The corporation said when they built their nests in trees, the wood-virus killed them all."

McQueen continued walking and glanced at the sky. "For one last time, I would like to see how the world should be."

"It might get better," Tommy said. "Now that the pig people stay on the blue grass, pollutants have decreased to almost zero."

At the edge of the meadow, they walked over a broken-down wooden-rail fence and walked under a canopy of tall trees. A kilometer farther into the thick forest they stopped. Hidden Lake appeared before them.

An unusual blue sky blended into the evening horizon and reflected to a purple sheen that shone on the top of the silent water. On the left, a triangle of white swans, with green corporation identification bands around their long slender necks, swam off the tip of a little grass-covered peninsula.

McQueen watched the swan's gliding bodies cut a gentle vee on top of the water and send tiny waves outward like little rolling ropes of chrome. He felt at peace.

Across the lake, lines of full-leaved trees, big, small, fat, and skinny, stood like warriors on leave, basking in the beauty of a paradise. At the horizon, easygoing tree branches stretched upward against a blue and white sky and blended to soft silver.

After they had walked to the edge of the lake, McQueen noticed the water was clearer than when he had last seen it. He breathed in deep. The long lost taste of lakeside air flowed down into his lungs. A little red-ear sunfish swam a few meters offshore.

"Watch!" Tommy said, and pointed to the sunfish. Suddenly, a three-headed, big-mouthed bass, charged in from the deep. The little sunfish fluttered its tiny tail. The bass jerked to the left, opened its middle mouth, scooped in the sunfish, and dashed back out into the deep water.

McQueen stood with his mouth agape. Tommy shook his head as if it were an everyday occurrence and sat down on the grassy bank.

"Now that the pig people are afraid to come here," he said, "except for a couple of mutated fish, the lake has cleaned itself up very well."

McQueen sat next to him. "The people of Blue Town used to be called fair people. How did they get the name pig people?"

"They earned it. We started calling them pig people and the name stuck."

"What do you mean, they earned it?"

"When they came here they always threw garbage, broke down green trees, and then they tried to burn them. When the green wood wouldn't burn they burned that stinking plastic. That black smoke stunk up the whole lake, gave everybody a sore throat." Tommy rubbed his neck. "That smell stayed for days."

"If it smelled so bad why didn't they leave?"

"It didn't bother them. They were drunk. When they caught fish they didn't like, they'd kick them like footballs and leave them on the bank to die."

"I can't believe educated pig people would act like that."

"I didn't either, but after I watched them stagger around, piss anywhere they pleased, and shit behind every tree, I knew they cared about noting but themselves."

"Come on, Tommy, they weren't that bad, were they?"

Tommy smiled a thin smile. "If you were here, you would have stepped in it." His smile vanished. "If you give those pig people clean water, they'll poison it. Give them clean air and they'll pump it full of toxic things you don't even know you're breathing."

"All the pig people aren't like that."

"From what I've seen, most are. Give them the chance and they'll turn the whole world into one gigantic hog pen."

"I guess you should know." McQueen looked across the lake. The bottom of the aluminum sun hit the horizon and created silver sun-flashes that twinkled over the water.

"It won't be long now," Tommy said, put his hands behind his head, and lay back.

McQueen looked at Tommy and wondered why he wasn't concerned. He only had a few more minutes to live and his friend was acting like it was nothing.

The sun dropped halfway below the horizon. It was half of a big ball. McQueen felt tears forming in his eyes. "Well, Tommy, this is it." He took a deep breath. "But I don't feel anything."

"Do you have any last words?"

"I don't think so," he said and paused. "But tell me one thing."

"Tommy lay on his side and leaned on one elbow. "What?"

"CEO Nelson really wanted me to capture Augur. Why is he so important?"

"He's supposed to have special powers. I haven't seen him. But a few months ago, Freddy did. He said Augur was in the tunnels, but he had to get back to Patagonia because a big Dinky revolt was brewing. He only came to the secret cave to see if we had discovered the serum for the antidote-bullets."

McQueen's mind changed from depressed and defeated to one of hope. "Serum!" he shouted, and sat up. "I might be able to take the serum and live. "He reached over and shook Tommy's shoulder. "Do you have the serum?"

"Don't get excited," Tommy said. We don't have it. Augur left to try and stop the Patagonia revolt without it."

McQueen lay back and his mind jumped back into the defeated mode. He let out a disappointed breath. "Patagonia?" he questioned. "That area is off limits. It's really contaminated."

"That's what they want you to believe."

McQueen didn't want to talk anymore. He wondered what it would be like after he died, but he would know soon enough.

The sun sank again. Only the curve of its top was visible.

He watched it sink more. A lone eagle flew across the sky and cried into the late heavens.

143

Tommy held his hand toward the eagle. "There's your old buddy."

As if he were in a trance, McQueen watched the eagle. "I knew I heard him," he whispered. "Maybe my Indian roots are calling me. But what's the difference? I'll be dead in a few seconds."

McQueen's heart pounded in his ears. He sat up, jerked his head around, and searched for something, anything to help fight off death. He saw nothing that would help. He had nothing to fight death. No one did.

He leaned back on his elbows and watched the sun. Its final purple-orange rays flickered through the treetops. "Tommy, it was nice knowing you." Holding a whimper, he paused. "Maybe I'll see you on the other side."

"Yes you will," Tommy said. "I'll see you on the other side of the water tunnel."

"The great water tunnel in the sky?"

Tommy turned his head away and didn't answer. The sun blinked black. The lake turned dark-green and smoothed to a gloss plane. It was night. Tommy lay on the bank and waited. A lone muskrat, with a black scar where a patch of its fur had been burnt off, swam across the lake and scrambled up under the bank. Tommy sat up and looked at McQueen. "Hey, you big dummy, are you dead yet?"

"What's the matter with you, Tommy," I only have a few seconds to live and you're calling me a dummy. Don't you have any respect for the dead?"

"Let me know when you're dead. I'll give you all the respect you want." Tommy turned and put his face an inch away from McQueen's face. "Are

144

you dead yet?"

McQueen sat up and looked at his hands. "There is no virus rash," he said, and looked toward the horizon. "The sun is down. I'm not dead." He looked at his hands again. "I'm not dead. I'm not mutating into a Dinky." He turned toward Tommy. "Did Burke lie about the virus?"

"Maybe?" Tommy said, and there was a hint in his voice that he knew something McQueen didn't know.

McQueen hit himself in the head with the palm of his hand. "How stupid can I be? I'm not dying."

Tommy stood up. "It's about time you figured that out. You ready to go back, or do you want to stay here and die some more?"

"Hey, wait a minute," McQueen said, and raised his voice. "You knew I wasn't going to die, didn't you?"

"That's right. Why do you think I kept calling you a big dummy?"

"Ahh, man," McQueen said, and exhaled a deep breath. "Back there on the path when I thought you were crying, you were laughing. I feel like an idiot. Why didn't you tell me?"

Tommy pointed to his own head. "Your head's not on straight yet. I figured it would help your memory if I let you figure it out."

McQueen didn't answer. He sat on the ground, held his head in his hands, and let what had just happened sink into his crippled mind.

Tommy whistled a low slow. "Cuckoo!"

McQueen looked up with a jerk and smiled. "Maybe I won't die. But I'll still turn into a Dinky." He stood up and looked across the dark

145

lake. It looked peaceful, like a place that had a sacred purpose. It reminded him of his father's secret stones. "Tommy, do you know where my father hid the secret stones?"

"The last time I saw them they were in that tunnel he was digging from the cellar to the water house."

"I remember that," McQueen said. "My father told me the secret stones of life could cure the world's problems. Maybe they could keep me from turning into a Dinky."

Tommy rolled his eyes and looked skyward. "Maybe, but what's so bad about being a Dinky?"

McQueen put his hand on Tommy's shoulder. "Nothing. I only have one thing against you."

"Tommy looked at McQueen's hand on his shoulder. "I know, your hand."

McQueen laughed. "When we were kids, I used to do that to you all the time."

Walking away from the lake, Tommy said, "Let's go. The housing authority is afraid to creep around in the dark. We should have a safe path all the way back to the water house."

McQueen followed. "It'll be nice to see what you did with the secret cave."

* * *

At the water house, McQueen watched Tommy push the wooden lever next to the drinking pipe. They dove into the pool and surfaced inside the secret cave.

Freddy, Tommy's Dinky friend, was on guard. He jumped up from the bunk. "All right! Tommy," he said and a big welcoming smile spread across his face. "You made it back." He reached out his hand to help him out of the pool. "Glad to see you got here in time to pull your shift."

Tommy grabbed Freddy's hand and swung up out of the water. "Why? You got a hot date tonight?"

"I got a date with some outside air and freedom to move around."

"I know what you mean," Tommy said. "Before they put up that off-limits sign, warriors were all over the place. One time, I had to stay down here for six months."

"What happened?"

"My skin turned pure white. When I finally did get out, the light from the sun hurt my eyes."

McQueen pulled himself up out of the pool. His head scraped the top of the cave. He slouched over and water dripped off his body. "You guys got anything to dry off with?"

Freddy reached under the bunk and pulled out a hand cranked heater. It had a wheel on the back with two long ropes hanging down from the wheel. He hung the heater on a metal hook that had been pounded into the stone wall of the cave. Then he handed the ends of the ropes to McQueen. "If you pull these ropes, it will heat up and blow almost warm air on you."

McQueen looked at the dryer. On the side, in his father's painted letters it read: Pretty Good People Dryer.

That was something his father would have written. He always did things that made a person's mind work. He used to say, "Dead things draw flies. You got to keep your mind working. It keeps the flies off."

Freddy stepped to the pool. "I'm going outside before the sun comes up." Before anyone could say good-by, he plunged into the water.

McQueen and Tommy took off their wet clothes.

McQueen picked up the ends of the ropes. "You stand under the dryer and I'll pull."

Tommy stood under the dryer. Pulling the ropes, McQueen said, "You guys sure improved this place. It must have been a lot of work. Dinkies are watched every minute of their working day. How did you guys find time to do this?"

Tommy shook the water from his wet head. "You know about all those missing Dinkies?"

"I sure do. Nelson keeps telling the pig people that the Dinky population is shrinking because the wood and water-virus is killing them."

"Do you believe that?"

"I don't know what to believe anymore, but Nelson's always pushing the warriors to find out where the Dinkies are going."

"They're going right here," Tommy said, and stepped out from under the dryer. "This thing isn't working too hot."

McQueen stepped under the dryer and handed Tommy the ends of the ropes. "Here, let me try it."

Tommy pulled the ropes and with the warm air from the blow-drier blowing on his body, McQueen looked around the secret cave. "What do you mean they're going here? There's not enough room in here to house all those Dinkies."

Tommy quit pulling the ropes and pointed to a high stone leaning against the wall. "That's true, but when you look behind that stone you'll be

148

surprised."

"Did you finally find those old hand-and-knee coal mines my father was digging for?"

"I think we did."

"I got to see this," McQueen said, leaned toward the stone, and looked toward Tommy.

Tommy didn't move. "Not now."

McQueen leaned back. "Why not?"

"When Freddy gets back, we'll slide that stone to the right. You'll see there's room for a lot of people."

"Do they have a signal lever, too?"

"We've got everything. We have to. If this place gets compromised, we'll have no place to live."

Tommy and McQueen sat on the bunk and wrung the water from their clothes.

McQueen stood up beside the bunk. His head hit the ceiling, again. He rubbed the top of his head. "After I become a little Dinky I won't have to put up with this." He smiled. "My clothes are still wet. You want to pull the ropes again?"

"If you can wait, we won't have to. There's an electric heater inside."

"What are we sitting here for? Let's get in there and use it?"

"Can't, we'll have to wait until my shifts over. We don't want anyone wandering off the guard post. Someone might signal or a warrior might come up."

"I haven't seen power lines for years. Where do you get electric?"

"There are streams of water that run through the mineshafts. We have generators that run off water wheels."

McQueen shook his head with amazement. "That's ingenious. Why don't you string the electric out here?"

"If someone finds this place, they'll trace the wires into the mineshaft."

"Has anyone ever found the water tunnel?"

"No, your father did a good job designing it, but this entrance has to be watched. Every Dinky takes their turn."

Stepping into his damp uniform, McQueen said, "That's a pretty big job."

"Not when a lot of Dinkies help. The more help we get, the fewer things each one of us has to do."

McQueen smoothed the front of his uniform. "Even if we peek inside, we'll still be on guard." He put his hand on Tommy's shoulder. "Can't you slide the stone now?"

Tommy shrugged away from McQueen's hand. "Not now. You sound like a little kid."

"I feel like a little kid. My father said those old mines were just high enough for a person to crawl around on his hands and knees.

Tommy looked at him as if he had limited comprehension. "Don't you think that's why they called them hand-and-knee mines?"

McQueen was embarrassed about his temporary ignorance. "I know that, but I'm trying to think. I remember that I always wanted to see them. Let me take a peek."

"I can't. The stone never gets slid until there are two guards present."

McQueen stood under the dryer and slowly

150

pulled the ropes. "Things sure did change since the last time we were here."

"More than you know."

McQueen shook the wetness from his long hair. "They didn't tell us much in youth camp and even less in warrior school."

"They didn't tell you because they didn't want you to know?"

McQueen stopped pulling the ropes. "I can see that now, but I couldn't then. Some things still aren't clear, but they keep coming back." He started pulling the ropes again.

"It's a good thing," Tommy said. "You don't know how close you came to being drowned in the tunnel."

"I know," McQueen said, took a deep breath, and stopped pulling the ropes. "I'm out of shape and Burke kicked me in the chest just before I went in."

"But that's not why you would have drowned."

McQueen's eyes widened. "Oh yeah, what's the reason?"

"If you wouldn't have remembered about the poison ivy, I would have known that you had been permanently brainwashed."

McQueen leaned over and hung onto the ropes for support. "So what? I'm almost recovered."

"I found that out just in time."

Smiling, McQueen hung on the ropes and swayed his body to and fro like a little kid on a tire swing. "I didn't know we had a time limit."

"If I had pulled the wooden lever at the drinking pipe, it would have signaled Freddy. After you got inside the tunnel, he would have slid the gates shut."

McQueen quit smiling. Suspicion flooded his brain. "Were you going to pull that lever before my memory came back?"

"It was my obligation to pull it. But I don't know if I could have done it."

McQueen shook his head and flashed Tommy a look of understanding. "You couldn't pull that lever and I couldn't shoot you."

Tommy nodded and smiled. "I think the real reason Freddy and I didn't trap you in the water tunnel, is because we would have had to drag your dead ass out and bury you."

McQueen smiled again. "I'm glad I saved you that chore."

"Thanks, I really appreciate it." Tommy smiled back at McQueen. "I'm glad you're getting your old self back. It's almost like old times."

McQueen dropped the ends of the rope and sat on the end of the bunk. "Tommy, one thing bothers me about my father. Maybe you know something."

"You want to know something, just ask."

McQueen lowered his head and stared at his boots. "My father was never sick. He never had any rash. We went into the same forest, swam in the same water, and lived in the same wooden house." He paused and looked at his hands. He had held the poison ivy vine at the door to the water house. There wasn't even a hint of poison ivy or wood virus on his hands. "How did my father die from wood-virus so quick, and I never have had a trace of it?"

"That's simple, you big dummy."

McQueen threw his hands into the air. "There

you go again, calling me a dummy. Why do you keep doing that?"

Tommy smiled a compassionate smile. "Because I thought you would have figured it out by yourself."

"Figured out what?"

"Think about it. Your father died only after the housing authority gave him the antidote."

"They said he didn't get it in time."

Tommy tilted his little head in a quizzical slant. "Then why haven't you had any signs of any type of virus?"

McQueen felt as if he were being backed into a corner where he wasn't sure of anything. "Maybe the wood and water viruses have cleared up." He gripped the edge of the bunk. "Maybe the whole world is virus free. I don't know. Maybe I just have good genes."

Nodding his head, Tommy said, "You do have good genes." He waved his hands in the air. "That's one reason why the corporation only allows only certain people to reproduce."

"One reason? Is there more than one?"

Tommy shook his head and whistled low. "Yes, when they sent you to youth camp and brainwashed you, they used you for a trained source of genetic breeding experiments."

"That's hard to believe. Scientists can clone the genes?"

Tommy sat on the bunk next to McQueen. "Incompetent scientists were appointed to the jobs of authority." He exhaled a long breath and put his hands on his knees. "You have firsthand experience about how unqualified people are positioned in the corporation."

McQueen shook his head in agreement. "Burke is proof of that. I helped him as much as I could, but I knew he would never make it out of warrior school."

"So, how did he get through?"

"Orders came down from the top and he graduated."

Tommy lifted his hands from his knees. "That's typical. He probably gives half his monthly credits to Nelson."

McQueen scooted himself sideways and faced Tommy. "I must have been brainwashed. All those years, I thought Nelson was an honest man."

"Over the years, it got even worse." Tommy moved his hand side to side in a negative gesture. "Politics, not ability, determines who is picked for jobs."

McQueen felt his long suppressed mind expanded with past memories. "I remember when my father told me about that."

"Maybe you're getting better," Tommy said and hope crept into his voice. "What did he say?"

"He said that the few good people left in the corporation were like Diogenes. You know Diogenes, don't you?"

"He was that old guy with a lantern, searching in the daylight for an honest man."

"That's the one. My father said that if they don't find an honest man soon, some day it will catch up with them."

"Some day is here," Tommy said. "The corporation has found honest people, but they keep them in the dark. The ignorant people don't have enough honesty to stand in Diogenes' shadow, and they're the ones who are in power."

"It sure seems that way."

Jerking his finger at McQueen, Tommy said, "Now, the corporation, instead of putting people in power who know something, is trying to repair their genetic defects by stealing off generations of working and thinking people like you."

McQueen felt Tommy was unconsciously building him up. "Don't make me out more than I am. If they wanted strong genes they should have gotten them off my father."

"They wanted to do just that, but your father was not cooperative. You have his resistance in your genes, and you have the quality they are looking for. They probably drew blood from you at least once a week."

McQueen looked where the needles had been pushed into the veins of his arm. "They did. They said it was to check for the wood virus."

"They were taking your blood and trying to make some kind of a smart serum."

"With the advances in technology and science that should have been a pretty easy task."

"It might have been at one time," Tommy said. "But the pig people's selfishness and ignorance have crippled science. The information they use isn't even based on things that have already happened."

McQueen looked at a broken TV setting in the corner. "What happened to the world's communication systems? We can't even get a decent picture on TV anymore?"

Tommy moved his little hand and talked. "The

electrical fields and the communications signals are constantly interrupted."

"That didn't used to happen. Why does it happen now?"

"I'm not sure, but when they exploded all those underground nuclear tests, the earth's molten iron core began to cool. If that wasn't cooling it enough, the pig people came along with a process called fracking, where they pumped chemical-laced water down deep wells to extract natural gas and oil."

McQueen leaned back on one elbow. "Why don't I feel the earth cooling down?"

"The earth's molten iron core creates the magnetic fields. When it cools, the magnetic fields move or are eliminated."

Even though Tommy was his boyhood friend, McQueen figured that this was a lot of knowledge for a little mutant Dinky to understand. "You sound pretty well informed. Where did you learn all this?"

Tommy shot McQueen a slit-eyed stare of caution. "You sound like you don't believe what I've been telling you."

"I have a hard time understanding it myself."

"If you wouldn't have stayed in that youth camp, you wouldn't have that problem."

McQueen felt his mind expand again and felt the need to know more. "Maybe you can teach me."

"Freddy's the one who knows all that stuff. I'm not that smart."

"You know more than I do."

"I only know what Augur told Freddy. He said that if someone doesn't do something, and soon, it would be the end of the earth as we know it."

156

McQueen shook his head in disbelief. "I don't think it will ever get that bad."

"Don't kid yourself," Tommy said, with an edge of warning in his voice. "The earth's core has already cooled and changed the magnetic fields. There are already solar winds. The ozone layer is messed up. If it continues to deteriorate, it won't block radiation that comes from space, then all life will end."

"But the Friends of The Earth Corporation have computers to take care of that."

"They may have at one time, but the interrupted magnetic fields wiped out most of the computer's stored knowledge."

"Nelson told us warriors that although temporary global warming was wiping out a lot of the earth's protective atmosphere, the harmless radiation from sun flares would only temporarily interrupt the TV and computer signals."

Tommy shook his head and smiled a half smile. "When it comes to nuclear testing, they'll tell the people anything."

"Then it isn't temporary?"

Tommy looked dejected and tired. "Temporary eventually becomes permanent. They're still planning to set off bigger and stronger nuclear bombs."

"The corporation will eventually learn they are destroying the earth and fix the problem."

A dark cloud crossed Tommy's brow. "Over half the earth is radioactive, and because the melted poles stopped the warm currents, about a fourth of it is too cold to sustain human life. Didn't you learn anything in that youth camp?"

McQueen stared into the pool of water. He was amazed how much the little Dinkies, who were supposed to be ignorant, had done. "I have learned things, but it looks like I haven't learned anything about the workings of the real world."

"You're learning now," Tommy said, and his voice tinged with relief. "The corporation no longer appoints people on what they know or how smart they are. They are appointed because of who they are or who they know. The earth has no competent minds to fix anything or create anything new."

"But the world should be able to get by on what they already have."

"It might get by for now, but when something breaks, the appointed pig people don't have the brains to fix it."

McQueen wanted to keep his faith mankind and keep an optimistic outlook. "In time the pig people should learn by the example the Dinkies set. Then, they will be able to gain back that lost knowledge."

Tommy shook his head so hard his ears wiggled under his floppy hat. "Not as long as the pig people control this world. The influx of ignorant people into those unearned positions of honor has taken over every field of research in the land."

Plonk! The signal lever next to the cot dropped down.

Tommy jerked to his feet. "Someone's coming through the tunnel."

They stepped to the pool and watched. Freddy's little head bobbed up through the surface of the water.

McQueen reached down and pulled him out.

Freddy walked to the stone door and slid it aside. "Okay, Tommy, I stand guard. You and your buddy can go in."

McQueen bent over and looked into the opening. As far as he could see, the hand-and-knee mineshaft extended into a prospective point that vanished into a dot of dark. He looked at Tommy and Freddy. "You guys were busy while I was gone."

"A little bit," Freddy said, walked to the dryer, and pulled the ropes.

Tommy took McQueen by the arm. "Come on. I'll give you a tour."

McQueen bent over and entered the tunnel-mine-shaft system. The tunnels were lower than the cave room. He squatted down and duck-walked to a big wooden barrel at the head of a big meeting room.

Boom! Boom! Boom! Tommy pounded on the barrel. Dinkies wandered out of the mineshafts and stood in the room.

McQueen looked at the side of the wall to his right. On square metal pegs, pounded into the layers of the flat-stoned wall, old rusting slave irons hung like bad memories of the past. In the center of the room, a four-meter-wide solid stump of gray coal supported the stone ceiling.

A Dinky's voice from behind the stump rang out. "I know that's you, Tommy. What do you want this time?"

"Sorry to wake you," Tommy said, and a crowd of complaining Dinkies gathered around the barrel. Tommy pounded on the barrel once. A hush fell over the crowd. He began, "I would like to

159

introduce, Sergeant John McQueen."

McQueen dropped to his knees, walked behind the barrel, and stood next to Tommy. "I am sorry I have invaded your world. I have been exposed to the virus, and in time, I will become one of you."

"Yeah, right!" a Dinky said from within the crowd.

Tommy lowered his head and held up his hand. "Let's not get off on the wrong foot. McQueen will be staying in the tunnel system for a while. Let's try to make him feel at home."

There was no response from the crowd.

McQueen leaned over and whispered in Tommy's ear. "Maybe I should go back outside."

"Give them time," Tommy whispered back. "They're like poison ivy. They'll grow on you."

McQueen smiled a faint smile and whispered, "When I start to become a Dinky, I'll grow down to their size."

Someone in the crowd yelled out, "Speak up. We can't hear you."

Tommy turned to the crowd. "I was just telling McQueen that we still need the antidote. If we're going to get it, we'll have to go outside and gather some information about Augur's hideout." He turned toward McQueen.

McQueen remembered when Burke was about to shoot him at the lake and how Danielle had screamed. She had saved his life. He wanted to talk to her again. "No problem," he said. "While you get the information, I'll sneak around and see Danielle."

Tommy's forehead wrinkled. "No way! If Augur's bodyguards see you, they'll never let me

160

near him."

McQueen slowly nodded. "I guess I'll have to stay here." He looked toward the crowd and smiled. "I'm a big boy now, but in a few weeks, I'll be a little Dinky. I'll fit right in with you guys."

The crowd began to mumble and move uneasy. A stocky thick-armed Dinky made a sour face and pointed to McQueen. "How long is he going to stay down here?"

"We don't know," Tommy said.

The crowd began asking questions all at once. Tommy pounded on the barrel. The crowd hushed. "While I'm gone," Tommy said, and pointed to McQueen, "he will answer any questions you have." He turned, gave McQueen a thumbs-up signal, and walked toward the exit.

McQueen yelled after him. "Tommy, are you going to leave me here?"

Tommy stopped at the stone door and turned. "You'll be okay. Like you said, 'You're a big boy now.'" He passed through the stone door and left McQueen alone with the Dinkies.

The Dinkies gathered around McQueen, and a barrage of questions avalanched down on him.

"What have you ever done for mankind?"

"Do you think you're going to stay here and freeload?"

"We all earn our keep down here. Do you know how to use a shovel?"

The Dinkies looked as if they were going to mob him. McQueen threw up his hands in a halting gesture. "Wait a minute. You don't have to stay down here."

The Dinkies stop talking. All heads turned

toward him. The thick-armed Dinky asked, "What are you talking about?"

"My father's hidden stones of life have a power that will change all your lives."

"How do you know that?"

McQueen knee-walked away from the barrel and got closer to the gathered Dinkies. "If the stones were found, we wouldn't be in the mess we're in right now. In fact, the world would not be in the mess it's in right now."

The stocky thick-armed Dinky waved his shovel in the air. "You're the only one in a mess."

A Dinky's voice rang from the back of the crowd. "You tell him, Sludge."

The Dinkies' faces turned mean. Still on his knees, McQueen stepped back from the advancing group and kneeled behind the barrel. He held up his hand. "I'm telling you the truth." He pointed down the mineshaft and to a little tunnel that branched off to the right. "The stones may be buried in that tunnel."

A skinny Dinky, with a pointy pick in his little hands, shook his head from side to side. "We dug up every place we can. We ain't never found no stones you talk about."

Sludge waved his shovel in the air and jerked it toward McQueen. "What are you tryin' to do, freeload off our work?"

As if he were poking him, a Dinky with a ripped sleeve in the elbow of his long-sleeved shirt shook his finger at McQueen. "Freeloading works on the surface, but it ain't gonna work down here."

An old Dinky pounded his staff on the wooden platform he was standing on. Silence invaded the cave. All Dinkies looked in his direction. He twirled his staff in the palms of his hands three times, and then he spoke. "I know of the stones of life. They were outlawed years ago. They were only something the corporation made up to control us mutants."

Sludge pointed the sharp tip of his shovel at McQueen. "That's right! What are you tryin' to do, feed us a crock of corporation crap?"

The Dinky with a raised fist, shouted at McQueen. "Tell it like it is, McQueen. You're a fucking sergeant in corporation's army of assholes."

As McQueen tried to reason with Sludge, the crowd of Dinkies grew. They gestured, argued, and worked themselves in to the irreversible single-minded mentality of a mob. Shouts and threats rang out. Suddenly, the Dinkies' sharp shovels and pointed picks jerked in McQueen's direction. Then like a hoard of little ants attacking a grasshopper, the angry army of Dinkies came at him.

He wasn't sure of what he should do. He could easily pick up the barrel and bat the little Dinkies aside. But, they were Tommy's friends. He didn't want to hurt them. He looked at their sharp shovels and pointed picks. They were raised and threatening. But if he didn't fight they would swarm on him like mad bees. They would kill him. He looked down the long tunnel on the left. More Dinkies rushed into the room.

He crouched behind the barrel and hesitated. Sludge waved his shovel and yelled, "Surround him."

McQueen stepped sideways. In a crouched over position, he half ran, half duck-walked down the low, dim-lit mineshaft on the right.

In the crouched over position, he tried to run hard and fast, but his head kept bumping and scraping the stone roof of the low mineshaft. He stopped where the mineshaft split into two tunnels. Then he turned and rushed down the dark tunnel on the right. It narrowed and got lower. He dropped to all fours. On his hands and knees, he crawled as fast as he could. Maneuvering his body through a maze of turns, little mounds of mined dirt popped up every few meters. Gasping for breath, he stopped and looked back. He didn't see the Dinkies following him. But he heard shouts.

"Catch him!"

"Tie him up."

"Drown him in the tunnel."

In the dirt, McQueen lay on his side and sucked for air. Vibrations, from running Dinkies' feet pattering on the tunnel floor, ran up his arms. He heard one say, "After he drowns, he'll float up to the other side. The housing authority will carry his dumb ass away."

McQueen hoped there was another way out. He looked back to tunnel where he had just come from. He figured the Dinkies had to have another entrance to wheel dirt out. But if they put dirt on the surface, the housing authority would find it. The mines had already been mined out for the coal and the entrances had been filled in. The Dinkies must transfer dirt from new tunnels to old tunnels. That dirt never sees the light of day. If they had another way in or out, they wouldn't have to get wet all the time. His reasoning told him there was no other way out. He turned into a dark tunnel and crawled deeper.

Trying to make his eyes adjust to the dark, he saw a speck of light. The sides of the tunnel brightened. Yellow dirt of a newly started tunnel loomed up. He stopped and looked back. Little Dinkies with little headlights strapped to their foreheads, turned down another tunnel and vanished.

McQueen twisted and turned down a long yellow-dirt tunnel. In the semi-dark a light beam flicked in the air in front of him. He stopped. Like a four-legged animal, he leaned the side of his tired body flat against the soft dirt wall. Listening for the searching Dinkies, he reached up and gripped the sides of the wall. He breathed easier and listened. Muffled sounds of Dinkies scrambling around in the dirt filled his ears. Bits of bright beams of light from the Dinkies' headlights sprinkled into the dark but did not intensify. He was safe for the moment. He could rest.

He thought of Danielle. Like a phantasmagoria, she appeared in his mind: An ethereal creature with wide, strong dark-brown eyes and a treasure of flowing black hair. He did not know how she would look the next time he saw her. He wondered if he would ever see her again. Any way she looked would be okay with him. Maybe he had only imagined her. After he had not shot Tommy, it had been a stressful time. Maybe she was a spirit, some kind of a goddess; such beauty was not of this virus-filled earth.

A long beam of white light flashed from out of the black tunnel. He turned and jerked back into the wall. His elbow slammed into the soft dirt side of the cave. His plethora of Danielle disappeared in an instant.

He moved away from the wall. His elbow was buried in the dirt. He pulled it out and turned toward the wall. A small hole appeared. He looked into the hole. It was dark, but fresh air flowed into his face.

With his bare hands, he dug, scraped, and scooped dirt. The small opening grew. For more leverage, he braced his shoulder on the wall; it fell through. His head followed.

His mind shouted with hope. "Maybe it's another tunnel."

The patter of the Dinkies' feet vibrated under his knees. He felt into the dark of the new tunnel. Empty space welcomed his hands.

His mind screamed in relief. "There's a way out."

The vibrations of the Dinkies' pounding feet increased. He dug his toes into the tunnel floor and pushed toward the opening. Thick yellow dirt enveloped his shoulders and stopped his forward motion. He repositioned his feet and pushed harder. Suddenly, his body slammed through. But the tunnel behind him caved in. Dirt trapped his feet, but his head and shoulders were free. Old boards creaked. Spiders and bats fluttered above his dirty sweating head. He reached out in front of him, clawed his fingers into the dirt, and pulled. Just as his feet pulled free, the opening to the tunnel behind him, crumbled and fell more. It blocked the Dinkies from coming through the new opening. He rolled his body away and stood up.

This tunnel was taller that the mutant tunnels.

He hoped it was the old escape tunnel his father had tried to dig. That tunnel was under the cellar steps, but he had never finished it. Before the housing authority came and gave him the antidote, he had said he only had a few feet to go.

McQueen looked down the long tunnel. A small shaft of light threaded its way into the dark. He walked toward it. Near the light, the soft gray slate on the sides of the tunnel was sandwiched in yellow dirt. It looked like the same kind of dirt his father had on the knees of his pants when he died.

McQueen walked to the light and recognized what was in front of him. He stopped, wiped the sweat and dirt from his face; and on a dirt-covered familiar cot, he lay down. He was home again. He felt at peace.

He only wanted to rest for a few minutes, but went to sleep.

CHAPTER 11

Danielle didn't go back to her quarters. Even though she knew it would be useless to try and walk to the water house, it just didn't matter. She was going to die anyway. Even if the walk were impossible, she would rather die walking toward something than waiting in her quarters feeling sorry for herself. If she made it to the water house and didn't die, she would mutate into a Dinky; and if McQueen was still alive, there was a bright spot. They would be Dinkies together.

With the fading lights of Blue Town seeping on her back, she walked down the blue asphalt road. After a while, the light paled and the road turned to a sad gray. When she had sped down the road in her OvalCar she had never taken the time to look at the surroundings.

Now walking, she studied each side of the road. Shadows, she had never noticed before, spread mysterious veils of fear. Where the forest began, movement rustled in the night; and like a ghost, strange disturbances flitted across the dark treetops. She was a city girl walking in a strange new place.

The rustling leaves and the wind swishing blue spruce branches sounded like nothing she had ever heard before. Even though the darkness makes the road look gray, she knew it was blue; and just knowing it was blue gave her a connection to the sameness of the blue grass and the safe blue world she had known all her life. Although many things she didn't understand or recognize were happening all around her, it was as if she were walking on a road of calm. The road made her feel safe.

On down the road, the smell of green dew-covered grass was in the air. She had always feared this; but now even though she was dying, she wondered why she had not done this before. The night air made her feel fresh. It charged her with energy. She realized what her father was talking about when he had said that the threat is always worse than the actual deed. Now, without a constant threat of being exposed to a virus, she could die a happy death.

Wrraammmm! Behind her, the sound of an OvalCar threatened. She jumped off to the side of the road and plunged down into a ditch full of water. "Water!" she gasped. "Water virus!" She lifted her wet hands to her face and felt the water. And then she laughed. She had already been exposed. The damage was done. Now, the virus was nothing to fear.

Before being exposed, she had felt a sad sense of envy. While she had to stay on everything blue, Dinkies could go wherever they wanted. They could do whatever they wanted. Except for the warriors that hunted them, the escaped Dinkies were free.

The OvalCar zoomed past. She crawled out of the ditch and walked toward the road. Then she heard a sound she had never heard before: her wet feet squishing with each step. The wet was new. The feeling was new. Everything in this virus world was different. She felt she had been missing something all her sheltered life. She no longer envied the Dinkies for being free. A sense of freedom enveloped her. She continued walking down the road.

Another OvalCar loomed behind her. Again, she jumped off to the side of the road. This time she landed in dew-covered virus-grass, weeds, brush, and all kinds of wet foliage. The OvalCar slowed, its spotlight shining great scythes of light, searching. She didn't want to be captured and taken back to her quarters to die. She imagined that she was surrounded with all kinds of snakes, crawling things, and buzzing things that could bite; but she didn't move.

The beam of light nipped the top of her wet head, but the OvalCar continued searching on down the road.

She stood up, took a few steps, and tripped. She fell into the softness of a bed of grass. In the dark, she couldn't tell if the grass was blue or green. She didn't really care. It was relaxing. All of a sudden, she needed to rest. She closed her eyes.

* * *

When Danielle opened her eyes the sun had come up. She didn't know what time it was. She looked up to see the position of the sun. It was hidden behind a great gray sky.

She walked around the bend in the road that led to the water house and looked up at McQueen's father's burnt down farmhouse. As she scanned the ruins, her eyes stopped. She blinked to make sure she wasn't seeing a mirage. As the figure came into focus, she recognized the warrior standing on top of a pile of wood ashes. His chin was lifted high, and his jet-black eyes were glittering. Suddenly, she could scarcely hear what was going on around her.

Never had she seen such a handsome man as this Sergeant McQueen. Although his spruce-tree-

170

blue warrior uniform was spotted with patches of yellow-dirt, he showed no signs of mutating into a Dinky; and she was glad he was still alive. A clean fresh image radiated from his body. She remembered his smell. He was not a bit like most warriors. He didn't reek of booze and steroidal workout sweat. She didn't know why, but just the sight of him relaxed her and made her feel safe.

A gentle breeze blew in from the north. Beneath his wind-blown pants legs, his slender leg muscles rippled. His gold sergeant stripes pointed upward like they belonged on his arm. His long hair blew around, and he placed his hand on a glistening purple feather that was in his hair. She had never seen that before. He was uniquely attractive and had a look of controlled power.

Without warning, Danielle felt weak-kneed. A strange flip-flopping sensation eased into the pit of her stomach. She had had crushes on men before. But this time it was different. These feelings were new. For the first time in her life she was hopelessly attracted to a man. And this was not just any man. He was an outlawed warrior, and she was an outlawed driver.

But she was wet and dirty with a rash all over her hands, hardly a presentable image to project to a warrior. She ran her hand through her hair and brushed the dirt from her uniform. She didn't know if her face was dirty, so she ran the sleeve of her uniform over it.

McQueen turned and gazed at her over his shoulder. She felt her face do something she had no control over. It blushed.

A happy and surprised look beamed in

McQueen's face. He called out to her, "Danielle!"

She wished she had a mirror. She didn't know how bad or how good she looked. She hoped she didn't look bad enough to scare him away. Trying not to think about her appearance, she put on her best seductive smile and waved to him. He jumped off the ash pile and took long strides toward her. She tried to control it, but her heart raced. She thought it could be from the virus attacking her heart. After all, the rash was spreading all over her body.

McQueen stood before her and nodded. "You went and done it."

Danielle lowered her gaze. "Yes, I know, I have been exposed to the virus. I can never go back now."

"I had a little bit of a run-in myself." He paused and looked at her hands. "It looks like we're on the same team."

Danielle wanted to run up to him and jump into his strong arms. But she didn't know him well enough. She lowered her head like a bashful schoolgirl and played in the dirt with the toe of her foot. "I don't know if I'll be able to live like a Dinky. They seem so stupid."

"That's what they would like you to believe."

She looked at her swollen hands. "How long do I have before I change?"

"I think we can have you back in shape in a few days."

She jerked her head upward. "Do you have a cure?"

"As a matter of fact we do."

All of a sudden, Danielle wasn't sure she liked

172

this warrior. "Don't play games with me. This is a life changing disease. If a cure had been found, Chief Earth Officer Nelson would know about it. The whole world would be cured."

"The mutants have a white powder," McQueen said, and rotated his hand as if he were stirring something. "They mix it with water. It'll take care of that rash you have."

"But won't the water make it worse?"

"Didn't you ever hear of poison ivy?"

"I know little about the green world. Until yesterday, I had never been out of the blue grass boundaries."

A happy look appeared on McQueen's face. "I have lived in the green world."

Danielle wondered why he was smiling. Maybe the virus invaded his brain. She stood back. "Why aren't you dead or mutated?"

"I was just a kid then. I'm glad I picked up that rash. It saved my life."

"What are you talking about?"

"I'll tell you on the way. Come with me to the water house."

"We can't. The Dinkies will be there."

"We should be okay. They're looking for me in the tunnel system."

"What tunnel system?"

He turned and started walking. With his back turned to her, he waved his arm and said, "On the way, on the way."

Following behind McQueen, Danielle saw the vistas of green foliage and forest glades. In the distance, soft bits of silver light shot through the wind-tussled leaves. She had never been this close

173

to the green forest in the daylight. This sight was new to her and its exact detail was veiled in a purple haze. Somehow, she knew behind that purple haze was the glamour of the unknown and a lure of romance.

If this were part of being a Dinky, it would be an adventure. She would never be bored. There would always be something for her little deformed head to think about. And she would always have something to do with her little hands. It would be difficult. She would have to learn a new way to live, and she wasn't about to give up. It would be a new world to conquer.

In the thick foliage behind the water house, McQueen held out his arm and whispered, "Let's wait here and watch."

He crouched down. Danielle crouched down beside him. She couldn't pretend not to like him.

She looked at him and felt a little startled, but something about him warmed her. Maybe she had been cold all her life. She leaned toward him. For a man about to become a Dinky, he was a blazing man, like a friendly fire spouting forth strength and health. She felt him lean toward her. It frightened her at first. It was an effort to resist. There was an impulse to shrink away from him. She was repelled by the thought of how the other warriors had treated her. But McQueen was different. His hands didn't have those typical warrior blue-grass lacerations. He didn't have those bulging warrior muscles that she despised, and he wasn't obnoxious and self-centered.

She thought about what a Dinky had told Burke. "You have muscles in your head that you'll

174

never use." And she laughed inwardly.

McQueen was different, and it made her leery but she liked it. The draw of him was overwhelming. She wondered how any man could have this kind of power; and at that moment she decided that with McQueen at her side, being a Dinky wasn't going to be so bad after all.

McQueen stood up, reached down and placed a gentle hand on her shoulder. "Let's go in the water house. I think it's safe."

Inside the water house, McQueen reached up into the side of the pool wall and pulled out the little square stone that hid the white powder. He dumped a small amount on the edge of the water house pool wall. "Dip your hand into the water and make a paste."

Danielle automatically jerked back. "That's virus-water."

McQueen smiled a big teasing smile. "What's the difference? You're going to turn into a Dinky anyway. The water won't make it worse."

Danielle stepped up to the pool wall. Although she had slept in green grass all night and had been covered with water, she was still leery. Timidly, she dipped the very end of her slender finger into the water. "Now what?"

McQueen scooped a hand full of water off the surface of the pool. "It's not enough." He drizzled the water onto the powder. "Mix it up and put in on your poison ivy."

He stepped to the door and watched for trouble. Danielle felt like a kid playing with food she did not want to eat, but she mixed the powder into a white paste and coated her rash. Just as she spread the last of it onto the back of her hand, McQueen rushed toward her. "Someone's coming."

He grabbed her by the arm and gently pulled her out the door. "We'll have to find Tommy before we can come back here."

CHAPTER 12

When Tommy surfaced in the secret cave pool, Freddy told him how Sludge and his gang had chased McQueen down the mineshafts and into the tunnels.

Tommy ran to the meeting room and pounded on the wooden barrel. The beat patterns signaled to all in the mine-tunnel system that this was an emergency meeting.

The Dinkies flocked to the room and Tommy began. "My friends, what have you done?"

Sludge waved his hand in the air. "We did you a favor. We chased the enemy into hiding. He'll never find his way out of the tunnel system. He's gonna starve to death."

Tommy shook his head from side to side. "I leave my friend and your friend here for a few hours and you have forced him into hiding."

"He ain't no friend," Sludge said. "He's a warrior for the corporation. One more capture and he woulda caught five hundred of us."

"That's true," Tommy said, "but he has never killed a single Dinky, not one."

Sludge tilted his head and stuck his finger in his ear. He shook his head as if he were shaking water from his ear. "That don't matter." He lowered his finger and straightened his head. "He's a warrior under the control of that pig, Nelson."

"Whoa! Back up," Tommy said. "Sergeant John McQueen gave up a lot when he did not shoot me with the antidote bullets. That shows us that he wouldn't do a single thing to harm us."

"How do you know that?"

"You all know that his father started our tunnel system. In fact, the very land you stand on was owned by Sergeant John McQueen's father."

A murmur waved through the crowd.

"That's right," Tommy said. "You have actually chased McQueen off his own land."

Sludge looked hard at Tommy's face. "What are you, part of the corporation?" He jerked his hand toward the ceiling of the room. "The thievin' pigs already stole everything from us on top of the earth. Are you tryin' to give them what we dug out below it?"

Tommy paused and took a deep breath. He was familiar with this Dinky. Sludge was always mouthing off just to mouth off. If a person said something was blue, just out of habit Sludge would say it was green. Tommy knew the best way to get his goat was to talk over his head. People like Sludge never liked to admit it when they didn't know something. They always tried to weasel their way around it. Tommy figured he might be able to dazzle Sludge with some of the knowledge Freddy had taught him.

He looked directly into Sludge's eyes. "Of course you know that it has taken two billion years for primitive cells of the earth to incorporate into a nucleus."

Sludge tilted his head and looked puzzled. "We know that."

"Then, you can help me explain to the others about how these primitive cells were the first step toward complexity."

Sludge's voice wavered, but he nodded his head as if he understood. "Yes, I could."

178

"You could also advise the others that it has taken only two hundred million years for us to evolve into multicellular animals."

Sludge turned. Behind him, the other Dinkies stared at him, waiting for him to speak. He turned back toward Tommy. The ends of his little ears reddened. "So what's all those big words got to do with the corporation?"

Tommy pointed to Sludge's forehead. "A Dinky of your intelligence will know that it is futile to argue that it took four million years to go from small-brained apes that had crude bone tools to mutate into the modern Dinkies we are today."

Sludge's ears whitened and his face became stern. "We don't care about that book-learnin' crap. McQueen's a warrior. He's our enemy."

The crowd of Dinkies grumbled and agreed.

Tommy pounded on the barrelhead. "If it weren't for McQueen and his father, we wouldn't be here today."

Sludge looked up at Tommy. "What?"

"You heard me. When we were kids, McQueen and I stood guard and helped his father dig the water tunnel and the cave."

Sludge stepped forward. "That don't mean nothin'. What are you tryin' to pull off?"

Clomp! Clomp! The old Dinky, standing on a wooden platform, pounded on the platform with his staff. "Let him speak." All eyes turned toward Tommy.

Tommy hesitated. He knew if he continued talking about digging, Sludge would say that any Dinky could have dug the tunnel. He would have to change his line of thought. He paused to think.

But Sludge would have none of it. He wanted an immediate answer. "What are you trying to pull off?"

"I'm not trying to pull anything off, Sludge. But as you know, the corporation has created a large population of dumb scientists that work together. And if that isn't bad enough, they actually share their ignorance."

The old Dinky nodded in approval. Tommy continued. "And they don't even have as much intelligence as a colony of ants. They cannot work together and accomplish any goal."

Sludge turned to the crowd and smiled. "They're doin' a pretty good job of accomplishing their goal when they catch us."

A Dinky in the crowd laughed.

Tommy knew that best way to combat ignorance was to mock it. "That's not what I'm talking about. You can all remember the corporation's last great scientific project."

"Which one?" Sludge asked.

"The one they started when one of them accidentally discovered that farts were methane gas, and burned with a blue gemlike flame."

A ripple of laughter waved over the crowd.

"If it weren't for McQueen's father, our Dinky friends would still be on the outside. Every day, they would still be collecting jars full of invisible farts."

The old wise Dinky smiled and said, "The energy branch of the corporation claimed that it was a great untapped natural resource."

Tommy smiled back. "Too bad it took them two years to find out it took more energy to collect it than it produced."

A great wave of laughter welled up in the crowd.

Tommy continued. "The pig people and the other warriors can't help us, but McQueen can. We must try to work with him."

Sludge raised his fist and opened his mouth to speak. Tommy looked him in the face and talked directly at him. "Sludge, wouldn't you agree that the pig people are obsequious to the corporation?"

Sludge wrinkled his little brow in befuddlement. Another Dinky spoke up and bailed him out of his ignorance of the meaning of the word. "That's right, the pig people are obsequious. They are just like children trying to please a parent."

Sludge lowered his fist. "That's right they're just a bunch of ignorant ass kissers."

The old Dinky spoke. "To survive, they do what they have to do. They know no other way."

"That's true," Tommy said. "Thanks to McQueen's father, we have moved ahead in life. The pig people haven't. And that is their greatest weakness."

"The way you're talking," the old Dinky said, "you sound like you have a weakness for warriors."

Tommy paused. He knew he was losing the argument. He took a deep breath, rolled up his little sleeves, and stood tall and straight. If he were going to save McQueen, he would have to create in their minds, life before the mine-tunnel system.

When he didn't speak right away, Sludge yelled to the crowd, "He don't know what he's yappin' about. We're just wastin' time. We got tunnels to dig. Let's git back to work."

The crowd started to break up and head for the various tunnels.

Boom! Boom! Boom! Tommy pounded on the barrelhead. "Years ago," he said, and stopped.

The crowd stopped walking away and turned their faces toward him. "Years ago," he continued. "I was a member of the Chief Earth Officer's barracks crew. I had smuggled food to starving runaway Dinkies, McQueen's father had helped. Back in those days he hid many Dinkies in the attic of his house. I got caught with a weeks' worth of food and was thrown into jail. But I escaped and made it back to the secret cave. I would have had to hide in that little cave for the rest of my life or come out and be shot with the antidote bullet, but McQueen's father swore he had given me the food when I was with him at the farm. He saved my life. He saved the future of our tunnel system.

"That's bull," Sludge said. "The guards woulda recognized you."

"Not back then. Those guards always said, 'All Dinkies look alike. We can't tell them apart.'"

A Dinky spoke from deep in the crowd. "I still hear that."

Tommy continued. "Maybe because McQueen's father saved my life is the reason he was killed, but he couldn't help it. It was his cause to help us and reveal the truth."

Tommy looked over the sea of Dinkies. Wide eyes and silence prevailed. Tommy knew they were seeing what he had seen. But would it be enough to get McQueen back into the secret cave.

A young red-haired Dinky stood up. "We don't

182

care what you say. He's still a brainwashed warrior. None of them are worth saving."

Tommy needed to bring something up to convince the doubting crowd. He needed to say something that would jar their senses.

He held up his hand and pointed to a group of young Dinkies. They had their legs crossed and were leaning against the cave wall. "You younger Dinkies don't remember the warriors of old," he said. "You don't remember their evil slithering eyes. You don't remember them inflicting pain."

"That was then," Sludge snapped. "This is now. Those things don't happen anymore."

"Those things don't happen because the corporation did away with the death camps and replaced them with antidote bullets."

Sludge grunted disapprovingly. "That was still then."

"If you want to talk about back then," Tommy said. "You'll remember back then Dinkies could inherit their forefathers business." Tommy pointed his finger at the crowd. "How many of you can do that today? Don't be bashful. Raise your hands?"

Not one Dinky raised his hand. Tommy continued. "The pig people have stolen your very heritage and claimed it for themselves."

"But it's different today," Sludge said. "We're getting some things back."

Tommy reached out, turned his palm up, and gestured toward Sludge. "Sure it's different today. It's different and worse. Our friends on top are still slaves." He made a face and pointed to the old slave irons hanging on the cave wall. "We are not put in irons anymore. Now, when we rebel, we are eliminated."

A young Dinky uncrossed his legs and stepped away from the wall. "So what can this Warrior McQueen do for us?"

Tommy felt a sense of achievement. They were beginning to understand. "McQueen has been on the inside," he said. "With me, he has been on the outside. He knows both sides."

Sludge waved his hand in the air. "That don't mean nothin'."

"But it does," Tommy said. "With his help, it will be possible for us to defend ourselves. With his help, we will win back our rightful place in the outside world."

As if he were yawning, Sludge stretched out his arms and looked around the room. "We're doin' all right down here."

Tommy looked up at the dark cave ceiling. "There is no sun down here?" He looked at the crowd. "What do you want to do, live like moles all your lives?" Waving his hand toward the young Dinkies leaning against the wall, he raised his voice. "Do you want your offspring to live like rats?"

A roaring, "Noooo!" moaned from the crowd.

"Warrior McQueen comes from good stock. He could be the only person qualified to help us. He's already a hero in the pig people's eyes. With our help, maybe they'll escalate his fame into the corporation and bring it down."

The little Dinkies paused, open-mouthed, on the verge of awe and cheering. Tommy couldn't believe what he had just done, but he knew he was swaying them. He didn't feel like his usual jovial self. This was the first time in his life that he had actually used something other than his crazy antics to change people. His confidence grew.

What more could he say? He had to say something that sounded great. If he could remember some of the things Freddy had told him, he might be able to pull something out of his rear end.

Pointing to the old slave irons, he said, "We do not need reminders like these. We do not need slave irons to tell us what has become of our lives. Some might say, 'It's merely work.'" He paused and searched his mind for the right words. From an unfamiliar hallowed place, thoughts of an eloquent and skilled public speaker appeared in his head. He jerked his head in surprise, and his voice became stronger, orator like. "We do not have to be unaware of what we do. We can have the freedom of romance, beauty, and high vigor. With McQueen's help, all our repressed dreams can come true."

A slight applause rippled across the crowd. Tommy felt its strength. He raised his hand and spoke louder. "We can make living something more than a utilitarian function for the pig people." He paused. He wasn't sure of the meaning of the word, utilitarian, but it sounded good. He continued. "We are slaves wishing our lives away. We have no love of life. We are starved for it. Let McQueen come live with us. Let him help us. Let him finish what his father started."

Sludge mumbled and Tommy barely heard what he said. Tommy repeated it and yelled it into the crowd. "Sludge just said, 'We're not smart enough.'"

A big, "Booo!" echoed from the crowd and traveled down the dark tunnels.

"By God!" Tommy cried. "We're just as good as they are, in fact, we're better. They might know things that we don't know, but we'll learn them." He paused and stared at the irons. "Knowledge is a wonderful thing. And we'll use those things against the unceasing evil they have brought to rest upon this earth."

"So what," Sludge said. "We'll let McQueen live. But we ain't gonna let him live down here."

Disagreement rumbled throughout the crowd.

"I'm sorry you feel that way, Sludge," Tommy said. "Because of us, McQueen has no home except with us. You should feel ashamed that you forced him form the very home his father started."

The Dinky, with a muscle shirt pocked with holes, stood next to the old wise Dinky and drew a breath of air into his little lungs. "Tommy!" he said in a voice of awe and wonder.

Tommy heard him, but he was looking into the crowd

"Tommy," the Dinky repeated.

Tommy looked down at him. "Yes?"

The little Dinky scratched his haystack hair and put his hand into his pocket. "I think you're right."

The old wise Dinky pounded his staff on his wooden platform and twirled it three times. The crowd of Dinkies stood in silence and waited for him to speak. "I believe no harm can come from Sergeant John McQueen. He will be permitted to live amongst us."

A few cheers went up and a few disgruntled Dinkies shook their heads in disapproval.

186

A horde of Dinkies mulled around for a while, stretched, and talked to other Dinkies close to them. Dinkies on tunnel digging function status collected their shovels and picks and wandered off into the various branches of tunnels. After a certain percentage of the audience had gone, the remaining Dinkies stopped milling around and left quickly. It was a focus change. Tommy didn't know where McQueen was, but it would be okay for him to come out of hiding. Tommy was glad.

CHAPTER 13

McQueen and Danielle walked through the outer leg of the forbidden forest and stopped. Forbidden Lake was before them.

At the shoreline, next to a fallen log, long straw-like weeds slanted toward a lavender pane of silky water that spread out in all directions. At the opposite shore, reflections of trees, some golden, some tangerine, and some green, stretched across the water, turning the simple lake into a magnificent sight.

McQueen expected to see Tommy dancing along the bank of the lake, waving, and calling him a big dummy, but he was not.

He turned to Danielle. "He's not here."

With her soft dark eyes, she looked toward McQueen. "What do we need him for?"

"He knows about the secret levers. If we try to get into the secret cave without knowing where the levers are, we'll be trapped in the water tunnel."

McQueen guided her to the fallen log where he had left his boots. They sat down and let their feet hang over the log's edge.

Danielle moved her finger across McQueen's arm. "Tommy's always been a jokester. Are you sure he won't drown you just for the fun of it?"

McQueen leaned toward her and searched her face. "You know he wouldn't do that."

A teasing look shone in her bright eyes. She put her arm around his waist and held him close. "I know. I was just fooling."

McQueen looked at his hands. There was no virus rash forming. He looked at Danielle's rash-covered hands. He was pretty sure it was poison ivy, but he hadn't had it for years. But even if it wasn't poison ivy, she was pretty joyful for being a few days away from turning into a Dinky.

Green leaves above their heads rustled in the breeze and sounded like falling rain. Gently, McQueen placed his arm around Danielle's shoulders and looked at the left side of the lake. Wildflowers in a field nodded and drooped their faces earthward as if the wind were gently rocking them to sleep. Next to that, like skinny pickets in a fence, lines of long green cattails stood at the edge of the water. A big fish jumped and splashed the water next to the shore. The image of the three-headed bass, McQueen had seen at Hidden Lake, flashed in his mind. A few minnows scattered across the smooth surface of the water in all directions. He turned toward Danielle. "Now we're the prey and The Friends of The Earth Corporation are the predators."

He stood up. Danielle looked up at him. Her dark eyes softened and melted into him. He reached down for her hands. She twined her fingers in his. That bass jumped again and scattered his thoughts of love in all directions. Looking for lurking warriors, he quickly turned his head to the right and then to the left. He didn't see anything, but he had a feeling of being watched. He urged her to her feet, and held her in a gentle embrace. "We can't stay here." He released her and stepped off the log. "Sooner or later, Tommy will go back to the water house."

Danielle stepped away from the log. "We'll just have to go back and wait for him."

189

McQueen turned and stepped into the green bushes.

A voice whispered from behind a big tree. "Hey, you big dummy."

McQueen turned toward the sound.

"Don't turn around," Tommy whispered. "You're walking into a trap."

McQueen turned from Tommy's voice.

Danielle tensed and looked straight ahead. "What?"

"Burke and the housing authority have set a trap for you. He's waiting just around the bend in the path."

McQueen crouched, looked down, and pretended to be examining a plant. "What should we do?"

"Keep walking. When you get to the bend, step off into the bushes, but don't run. Act like you're looking for something. When you get to a big tree, just stand there. My buddies will do the rest."

McQueen stood up and looked at Danielle. "You ready?"

"Any time you are."

And they walked down the path.

Just before the bend, McQueen feigned excitement and pointed into the trees. "I think it's over there."

They made a sharp right turn and walked into the brush. The big tree appeared right in front of them. Danielle tugged at McQueen's sleeve. "Let's keep going."

McQueen held her by the shoulder and gently pulled her behind the tree. "Just stand here and watch."

They peeked through the Y of a low branch. On the left side of the path, a small bush shook.

Standing on the path and sounding like a muffled donkey's he-haw, Burke yelled through his facemask, "Get them!"

"They're over here," a plastic-suited housing authority hunter yelled, and crashed into the bushes on the left side of the path.

Off to the right, a stand of tall grass swished.

Another hunter pointed to the grass. "They're over there."

"Somebody's right here," another plastic-suited hunter said and searched an area ten meters from the path.

Burke stood in the middle of the path like a confused traffic cop in a white plastic suit. He-hawing commands, he turned his face-masked head and directed hunters where to charge. Each time it was a different place and nowhere near the tree.

Tommy stepped out of the brush and walked up to McQueen and Danielle. "Okay, we can go now."

Danielle stiffened and stepped closer to the tree." Are you sure?"

"Burke doesn't know which way to turn or who to chase. He'll just stand there like the dumb jackass he is."

McQueen laughed. "Looks like he'll be busy for the rest of the day."

Tommy put his little hands next to his ears and flopped them like a donkey's ears. He-hawing like a donkey, he led the way. McQueen and Danielle followed at a leisurely pace all the way to the water house.

Inside the water house, next to the pool,

Tommy pulled the wooden alarm lever. "You know I have talked the Dinkies into accepting you."

"That's apparent," McQueen said. "If you hadn't, they wouldn't have tricked Burke and his cronies."

Tommy took his hand off the wooden alarm lever. "It's off. Let's go in."

Danielle backed away from the pool. "I can't swim."

McQueen took her hand. "You won't have to. Hold onto my feet and I'll pull you through. All you'll have to do is hold your breath."

"Danielle went rigid and pulled her hand back. "That's virus water."

"So what?" Tommy said. "Would you rather go back outside?"

Danielle lowered her head. "I'm sorry. It's just that I was brought up to fear water."

"Don't worry," Tommy said. "I'll be right behind you."

"But I can't hold my breath that long."

McQueen put his hands on her shoulders and looked into her face. "Sure you can. Just don't think about breathing. Before you know it, we'll be on the other side."

She didn't speak. She nodded her pretty head in agreement.

McQueen jumped into the pool. Danielle stuck her foot into the water and pulled it out. "That's cold."

"I'm not going to stay in this water house all day," Tommy said playfully. "Get in there before I push you in."

Danielle stepped over the wall and eased into

192

the pool. McQueen grabbed her by the shoulders and looked into her face. "Deep breaths now."

Together, they breathed in deep breaths of air. "Now," McQueen said, and guided her under the water. She let him pull her under a few feet and jerked free. She panicked and struggled to the surface. McQueen turned and swam back up. He looked across the water. Danielle was splashing and spitting water. He grabbed the collar of her uniform and pulled her to the wall. She quit thrashing and coughed a few times.

"I can't make it," she whined. "Go on without me."

Tommy stepped into the pool and held onto the side of the wall. "Okay, stay here." He dove in.

McQueen knew Tommy had gone after the facemask, but some day when he wasn't around she might need to escape through the tunnel. She needed to learn how to swim through without it. He looked at her scared face. "Don't get excited. It's only water. We can make it. Just hang on this time."

"There isn't going to be a next time," she said. "This virus water gives me the creeps. I just can't do it."

McQueen put his arm around her shoulders and sat on the underwater ledge with her. "Okay then, we'll just stay here the rest of our Dinky lives."

Danielle smiled a little smile, but then turned serious. "If the warriors come, and you know they will, you can dive in. I'll just go with them."

"I could never leave you," McQueen said and paused. He knew it was too soon to tell her, but he wanted to tell her anyway. "I think I—"

193

Suddenly, in the pool's center, Tommy's little round head broke the surface of the deep water. "Hey, you big dummy, you might need this."

He held up the facemask with an air-hose attached to it.

Swimming over to McQueen and Danielle, he spoke with the facemask in his hand. "We usually use this for older folks. But since it's your first time, we'll make an exception."

Danielle looked at the mask in Tommy's outstretched hand. "What is it?"

"It's a facemask. My buddy on the other side is pumping air into this thing. When you put it on your face, you don't have to hold your breath. You can breathe."

McQueen figured she could learn to swim through the tunnel without the facemask some other time. He took the facemask and held it over her head. "Here try it on."

Reluctantly, she pulled her wet black hair back and let McQueen place the mask over her face.

"Perfect fit," Tommy said. "Now let's get out of here before someone comes in."

"Good idea," McQueen said. "I don't want to run around in the forest and wait for another bunch of warriors to go away."

Danielle's muffled voice came from inside the facemask. "I can breathe."

"Excellent," McQueen said, and they descended into the deep pool. They made it through the water tunnel with ease and surfaced on the other side.

Freddy was in the corner, pumping the air compressor. Danielle pulled off the facemask.

Freddy stopped pumping and wiped his forehead. "It's about time. I thought my arms were going to fall off."

McQueen pushed himself out of the pool and stood up. Clunk! He hit his head on the low ceiling. "Ahh, man." He rubbed his head. "I should have listened to my father and made this ceiling higher."

"We didn't have to," Tommy said, treading water. "We were just little kids then." He took the facemask from Danielle and handed it to Freddy.

Freddy placed it next to the compressor and pushed the compressor into a hole in the wall. "We have to keep this thing hidden," he said, and covered the hole with a flat rock. "If those pig people ever find out there is no virus, they'll come in here and use the mask to bring all their pig friends."

Tommy's words, "If those pig people ever find out there is no virus," stuck in McQueen's brain, and all other thoughts stopped. He looked toward Danielle. It was a delayed reaction. Hanging onto the side of the pool, she gasped, and her wet eyes bulged wide. They both looked at Tommy. McQueen pointed at Freddy. "What's he talking about?"

With her eyes looking like guns about to be fired, Danielle snapped, "Yes, we would like to know."

Tommy stuttered a little and said, "We were going to tell you, but we had to make absolutely sure you weren't brainwashed." Tommy shrugged. "And besides, I needed to pay you back for that time you tricked me into believing that standing in fresh horse manure would make me grow taller."

McQueen smiled at the thought of how he had tricked him. For a week, Tommy had went out to the barn every evening and stood in the horse manure for fifteen minutes.

"I guess you owed me one," McQueen said. "But this is different."

"Yes it is," Tommy said, and pulled himself up out of the pool. "But it was still nice to get you back." He offered his hand to Danielle. She glared at him for a long moment. Then, she grabbed his hand, and he helped her out of the pool.

While Danielle wiped the water from her body with her hands, Tommy walked toward the little cot and talked. "Actually there is more to the virus than you think. But if I would have told you, you wouldn't have been able to control yourself."

"What are you talking about?" McQueen said.

"We need all the help we can get," Tommy said. "We don't need a dead hero."

McQueen blinked his wet eyes with surprise. "You know me better than that, Tommy. I would never get excited and do something stupid enough to get killed."

"Oh yeah," Tommy said. "You're here aren't you?"

McQueen nodded his head in agreement. "You got me on that one."

Tommy lifted the thin mattress on the cot, sat his wet rear end on the exposed springs, and motioned to McQueen with his arm. "Come and sit down. I think I can tell you now."

Danielle walked over and dropped to her knees. Knelling next to the cot, she placed one hand on her hip, leaned her shoulder against the cave's hard stone wall, and turned her head toward Tommy.

Tommy began. "Do you remember when your father died?"

McQueen bent over, walked over, and sat on the exposed springs on the edge of the little cot. "Plain as day. I saw the virus rash on his arms. He said it was poison ivy."

Tommy looked at him as if he were lying. "Was it?"

"Don't look at me like that. I don't know."

He gave McQueen a slight shrug as if to say okay, but persisted. "Are you sure?"

"The housing authority gave him the virus antidote." McQueen took a deep calming breath. "But they said he was too far-gone. He died a few minutes later."

There was strain in Tommy's voice. "I thought you would have figured it out by now."

"Come on, Tommy, quit screwing around. I know he had the virus, and the housing authority gave him the antidote. But it was too late. What else is there to figure out?"

Shaking his head, Tommy took a deep bracing breath and exhaled. "No one has ever died from any virus."

In disbelief, McQueen's jaw dropped. "What?"

Tommy flashed a weak smile. "The antidote doesn't cure anything but life itself."

McQueen stood up too fast. He bumped his head on the ceiling. "Aarrgh!" He reached up and rubbed his head. "You're driving me crazy."

"Talk about driving someone crazy," Danielle said. "It's not right to let us think we were going to

197

die."

McQueen jerked his head back. His head banged on the low ceiling again. The pain seethed into his heart and masked the pain on the outside of his head. "They murdered my father!"

"Calm down," Tommy said. "Now, you can see why I never told you before."

McQueen grabbed the top of his head, hunched over, and paced back and forth across the dirt cave floor. "I don't understand. I know my father was helping the Dinkies, but why would anyone just out and out kill him?"

Tommy's bright eyes seemed to lose their light. "He had found out the virus was fake. And he had the stones of life. The Friends of the Earth Corporation had to get rid of him to keep control of the pig people."

"What do you mean control? The warriors control everything."

"Is that right?" Tommy said, leaned back, and tilted his head to one side. "You're a warrior. How much are you controlling now?"

McQueen quit pacing. "How long does this brainwashing thing last? When I found out that you were not a dumb Dinky and wouldn't shoot you, they were going to give me the antidote."

"Sure they were," Tommy said. "That's how they control people who get too smart or find out too much."

McQueen's face beamed with realization. "One shot and all their troubles would be gone. And all they have to do is say it was the virus."

"The housing authority killed your father and there is no telling how many more people The

Friends of the Earth Corporation have murdered."

"It makes sense to me," McQueen said. "Nelson is a devious man."

"Even his title is deceiving," Tommy said. "CEO doesn't stand for Chief Earth Officer. It stands for Chief Executing Officer."

Danielle took her hand from her hip and rubbed the poison ivy on the back of her hand. "You mean if that drunken medic had not botched injecting me with the antidote, I would be dead?"

Tommy pointed at her as if she had just won a carnival prize. "That's right."

"It doesn't understand it," Danielle said. "If there's no antidote, do I have the virus or do I not?"

"Tommy and Freddy smiled big ear to ear smiles and talked in unison. "There is no virus."

"You mean I won't turn into a Dinky?"

"I don't know a single person that has," Tommy said.

Danielle looked at the rash on her hands. "What about this rash on my hands and face?"

Tommy gestured to her arms. "That's a variation of poison-ivy, something the Friends of the Earth Corporation keep around. They give it to people who they want to scare or get rid of."

"That's right," McQueen said. "Poison ivy has been around forever."

Danielle persisted. "But what about the water-virus? And why does everyone have to drink bottled water that has an expiration date of one week?"

Freddy spoke up. "That's an even better farce. I worked at the bottling factory. The workers bring in the expired bottles of water, change the date and

199

ship them right back out."

"But we have factories making things for the blue world people," Danielle said. "If there's no virus they would be out of a job."

Tommy looked to Freddy. "Freddy can answer that."

Freddy cleared his throat. "When there is no work, those factories mimic war. That way, the pig people feel like they have a purpose in life."

"That's pretty farfetched," Danielle said. "How can they do that?"

Freddy pushed his glasses up off the bridge of his nose. "In war three things happen." He held his hands together. "First they make something, then" — he jerked his hands apart as if they had just exploded — "they blow it up." He moved his hands as if he were making something. "And then they rebuild it again." He dropped one hand to his side and held his other hand in the air pointing with his finger. "The factories make things on first turn." He jerked his finger. "The next turn comes out and smashes it." He jerked his finger again. "And the third turn recycles the smashed stuff and gets it ready to be made again on the first turn."

Danielle looked confused.

Freddy turned his head sideways and smiled a cocky full-toothed smile. "See, it's just like war. People destroy things then rebuild them, only this way not many people get killed."

Tommy stood up, raised his hands in the air, and walked in a little circle. "That's only a small part of what the so-called Friends of The Earth Corporation can do. Without the fake wood and water viruses there would be no control. Fear of the

200

virus is control. It's even a better fear than losing money credits."

"Danielle stared at the rash on her hands and sobbed. "What about the green grass?"

"It's just as safe the blue grass."

Danielle's face took on a look of disbelief. "I think you're just saying that because you have already turned into a Dinky."

McQueen looked at Tommy with suspicion. "If there is no virus, why are there so many Dinkies?"

Tommy let out a long breath of air and looked at Freddy. Freddy took off his glasses and polished them with his shirttail. "That's a good question. Tell them Tommy."

"I'm not too good at it, but I'll try to explain it."

Freddy put his glassed on; and encouraging Tommy to continue, he rolled his hand in a circle.

Tommy shook his head as if to say, okay, and started. "Do you remember when the world used nuclear power to produce electricity?"

"Yes," Danielle said. "That was when the world had a decent government and it claimed radiation was safe."

That's what the government wanted the people to believe," Tommy said. "Actually, just as long as the corporations made money, they said and did anything they wanted."

"The government was honest back then," Danielle said.

"Only until it came to making money," Freddy broke in. "The leaders were paid off, claimed that low levels of radiation were harmless."

"It must have been harmless," McQueen said.

"They used it in everything from smoke alarms to glow in the dark watches, even used them to power the satellites that used to circle the earth."

"That's the catch," Freddy said. "Low-level radiation can't go through a person's skin or pass through a piece of paper."

Danielle stepped away from the wall. "So there was nothing to worry about."

"That is exactly what people thought. But once that low-level radiation is breathed in or swallowed, it mutates cells inside the body and those cells don't die."

"There are millions of cells in the body," Danielle said. "A few bad ones shouldn't hurt anything."

Freddy threw both hands up and looked to the ceiling. "Our ancestor's chromosomes in those few cells were mutated."

As if it were the end of a play, Tommy opened his arms, turned his palms up, and bowed. "And that's how we were created."

"If that's true," McQueen said. "Then the whole world should be Dinkies."

"Not everybody had the same level of exposure," Freddy said. "Some people got more some got less."

"Because I'm not a Dinky," McQueen said, "that means that my Indian ancestors were only exposed to small amounts of radiation."

Freddy shook his head. "Not really. In fact, it's just the opposite. High exposure kills the cells and that is the end of it. With low levels of exposure, only a few cells are maimed or maligned. Those few cells reproduce in the maimed form and

202

then reproduce again and again. This is why it took years for government's suppression of the low-level radiation's genetic effects to see the light of day."

"I don't understand everything about it," Tommy said. "Freddy's the expert. All I know is that it just sort of just snuck up on us."

All heads turned toward Freddy.

Freddy's face took on a slight glow of embarrassment. "I'm no expert. But I do know that the effects from exposure to ionizing radiation, pollution, and poisons put on the food for the good of mankind, did not appear for years, even though it was linked to many forms of genetic effects that were carried for many generations."

Tommy bent his wrist, held his hand to his side, and limped. Deforming his mouth as if he were retarded, he said, "Severe mental retardation is notable even at low levels of exposure."

Freddy smiled at Tommy's antics. "Maybe Burke came from this long line of mentally defective people."

Danielle leaned back against the wall. "You're right about that. Something has definitely altered that man's brain."

Tommy unbent his wrist, stood normal, and a mischievous grin spread over his face. "I heard the corporation was going to examine Burke's brain. But they couldn't find it."

Danielle smiled a slight smile, but it faded.

"Talk about no brain," Freddy said. "At one time, the old government proclaimed that there is no known safe dose of ionizing radiation, no threshold level."

Tommy sifted uneasily on the cot. "And they

203

were going to do something about it."

Freddy jerked his thumb across the palm of his hand as if he were counting money. "But the corporations bought them out. They lost their brains in piles of money."

"That was years ago," McQueen said and lowered his voice as if he weren't sure. "The radiation would have decayed by now."

Freddy lowered his voice an octave. His words came out with feeling of great truth and confidence. "That is not true. "Uranium-235 has a half-life of seven point one billion years. Uranium-238, that was used in nuclear power plants, has a half-life of four and a half billion years."

"Now you got him going with the numbers," Tommy said. "If you keep it up, he'll give you a headache."

"Headache or not, that's a long time," Danielle said, "I don't think any government could delude the public about the dangers of low-level radiation for that many years."

"They did and they could," Freddy said and lowered his eyes. "People didn't realize that if radiation didn't kill you at the time of exposure, it didn't mean it wouldn't get you later on."

Danielle started to scratch the rash on the back of her hand, but stopped. "You guys sound like a bunch of textbooks."

Tommy leaned over and looked at the dirt floor. "That was part of the problem. People didn't care about the effects of radiation until it took a hold of them. They didn't even want to read about it. When they finally did, it was too late." He looked up. "Three-quarters of the earth is uninhabitable because of radiation, and the Friends of the Earth Corporation are still exploding nuclear bombs in the air and under the ground."

Freddy nodded with approval. "You got that right. When it comes to making money, people in power don't play fair. Chief Earth Officers like Nelson always said, 'If you can't tell them the truth then fool them.'"

"I thought he was joking," McQueen said and wrinkled his brow in thought. "But I recall Burke saying, 'They are ours for the taking. We'll fool them out of every cent they have ever saved, earned or will earn or inherit in the future.'"

Freddy pointed to his own head. "They are sly ones. Radiation got a big foothold in the genetic chain when irradiation was sold to the gullible public as being one more step in food processing that would prevent someone from dying or getting sick from food poisoning."

Freddy made a face and shuddered as if he had a bad taste in his mouth. "Actually," he said, "it was just another way to fool the people into buying rotten meat."

McQueen stepped to Danielle and held her close. "We were never exposed to radiation. We are not going to turn into mutants."

Danielle slumped and lowered her head as if she were giving thanks. Almost crying, she said, "That's wonderful."

"It would be," Tommy said and threw his hands into the air, "if the world knew."

McQueen turned from Danielle. "Well let's just go out and tell the world."

CHAPTER 14

McQueen and Danielle squatted and began to duck-walk into the mine shaft. But walking in this unnatural position was difficult. They dropped to their knees and knee-walked behind Tommy. He led them into the entrance of the mine-tunnel complex where the old wise Dinky stood.

"Welcome to our world," the old Dinky said and extended his little hand.

McQueen looked deep into his eyes. "I think I know you."

"I don't think you could. I came from a place far from here."

McQueen half closed one eye and studied the old Dinky. "Years ago, I saw you on the blue grass." He looked at the old Dinky's staff. "I remember your staff. I watched you slip it in front of Burke's feet when he was chasing another Dinky onto the green grass." McQueen let out a little laugh. "He tripped and went flying head over heels."

The old Dinky's eyes opened wide. "Was that you?"

"Yes, the other warriors got a big laugh out of it. But I almost got recycled because I didn't turn you in."

"Yes," the old Dinky said, and forced a cautious smile. "That Burke is strange person."

McQueen nodded his head in agreement. "When I finally realized just how rotten he was, it was too late to do anything about it."

The old Dinky looked at Tommy. "Have you informed them that they are not going to become

Dinkies?"

"Yes," Tommy said in an almost obsequious manner. "We told them."

"The old Dinky tipped the end of his staff at Danielle. "Glad to make your acquaintance ma'am."

Danielle extended her hand in friendship. "I'm glad to be here with you."

The old Dinky shook her hand. "Do you have a choice?"

"Not really."

"We're both wanted by the corporation," McQueen said.

"We know," the old Dinky said. "Rewards have been posted."

Danielle gasped. "I didn't think the corporation would do that."

The old Dinky sighed. "There will be many things you won't think they will do. They're a mean bunch."

McQueen extended his hand to the old Dinky. "We're here to help."

Shaking McQueen's hand, the old Dinky repeated his question. "Do you have a choice?"

"I could go back and possibly get recycled."

The old Dinky's proud face looked hurt and vulnerable. "So, when you capture your five-hundredth Dinky, you will go back to CEO Nelson?"

"No," McQueen said immediately. "It's no longer like that."

"Like what?" the old Dinky snapped back.

"I was propagandized at the youth camp." As if he were signaling that there was something wrong with his head, McQueen lifted his hand and shook it next to his ear. "There was something blocking my thoughts. If I could have beaten the block sooner, I would have come back here years ago."

A flicker of doubt crossed the old Dinky's eyes. "How do we know you won't go back and betray us anyway?"

Losing his obsequious tone, Tommy spoke up. "McQueen's my friend. He'll never do that."

McQueen placed his hand on Tommy's shoulder. "Thanks, Tommy," he said, and looked at the old Dinky. "I can't explain it. It's just something ingrained into my soul. I don't know what it is. But I do know that I must follow in the footsteps of my father."

The old Dinky looked puzzled. "Why would a trained warrior do that?"

McQueen paused and answered. "My mind gets clearer every day. Some internal or external force has put me here for a reason. I know the ways of the world are not how they should be."

"Why would you be any different from the other stone-faced warriors?"

"Stone?" McQueen said and paused. "Stones . . . Stones of Life. That's it. Maybe it's because I have touched the stones of life."

The old Dinky jolted back as if he had been shocked. "You have touched the stones of life?"

"Yes, but I was very small. I remember my father lifting me up to touch them. I may have not been able to walk at the time, but I remember them clearly."

"Augur has talked of the stones of life. He claims they hold the key to the troubles of the world."

"I don't think they have that much knowledge. They weren't that big."

"We need all the help we can get. Maybe you could remember where your father hid them."

A lose stone fell from the ceiling and thudded on the floor. McQueen flinched as if someone had suddenly struck him. He looked at the rock and relaxed. "I have no idea where they might be." He took a deep breath, and exhaled. "I think the only help we can expect is from ourselves."

The old Dinky's face took on a look of disappointment. "Without the stones of life, what do you plan to do?"

"I'm still considered a hero. The pig people have been told that the wood virus caused me to commit suicide. When they find out I am still alive, they might revolt."

"I don't think you know the value the corporation places on life."

"I know it's pretty low, but I still think if the corporation has me killed they will have to make it look like it wasn't their fault."

"They already have a head start on that," the old Dinky said. "The pig people believe you have the virus."

McQueen began to answer, but Sludge and his band of rebels walked out of a long dark mineshaft. "McQueen," Sludge yelled, and a crooked grin formed on his night-crawler lips. "You got out. We figured you'd be dead by now."

The Dinkies behind him laughed and babbled excitedly.

This bothered McQueen, but trying to keep the

peace, he extended his hand in friendship. Sludge grasped it and squeezed. The strength in Sludge's hand told McQueen this Dinky was a tough little bugger. He turned to the gathered Dinkies. "I'm sorry to disappoint you, but I'm still alive"

Sludge lifted his little shovel and offered it to McQueen. "You gonna to help us dig?"

McQueen didn't take the shovel. "When the truth is known, no one will have to dig tunnels ever again."

"What you gonna to do?" Sludge asked. "Git digging machines down here?"

"Nothing like that. Tommy and I have a plan."

Sludge glared at McQueen. Suspicion filled his face. "No pig person ever had enough brains to make any plan work."

Tommy held up his hand. "The fake virus has to be exposed. We're going to alert the pig people over live TV."

Sludge tilted his head back in an arrogant manner and looked down at Tommy. "So what's the big deal?"

Pointing toward the ceiling of the mine, Tommy said, "When they find out there is no virus, they won't be afraid of turning into Dinkies."

"So what?" Sludge said. "If we go up top, we'll still be slaves."

"No we won't. The pig people won't be afraid to go into the fields and do their own work. We'll be able to live like real human beings."

Sludge's brow furrowed. "Your plan ain't gonna work. TV only gits broadcasted if the moon is in the right place."

"So when should we do it?" Tommy asked.

A look of importance beamed from Sludge's face. The workers behind him listened with interest. "You gotta wait for high tide."

Tommy nudged McQueen in the ribs and asked, "Why is that, Sludge?"

Sludge clasp his hands behind himself, turned toward his Dinky friends, and bent his head low as if in thought. A Dinky with a straw hat stepped forward and whispered in his ear. Sludge turned back toward Tommy and stood like a kid in front of the class who knew all the answers. "When the moon's gravity pulls on the space junk, it pulls on the other stuff that blocks the TV signals. Sometimes it makes the TVs come in clear."

McQueen knew no one knew the real reason TV signals were unreliable, but he decided to feed Sludge's ego. "There will be a high tide tonight."

Danielle stepped next to McQueen. "I don't remember a time when TV came in clear."

"No one has found the real reason why TV isn't reliable anymore," Tommy said.

Sludge turned his palm up and talked to his buddies. "Duh! Maybe it's because the pig people are too dumb to run it?"

The old Dinky spoke. "The elimination of clear dependable TV was a great blow to The Friends of the Earth Corporation. All the powers lost control of subliminal messages that were broadcast clandestinely over the TV waves. Now they can't control the pig people as easily as they had done in the past."

Tommy lifted his finger to interrupt. "What does Augur say about it?"

"Augur has told us that after the TV was lost,

the wood-virus came. The corporation created an epidemic, and it gave them an excuse to put people out of their wooden houses. But it was not enough to really control them."

"I remember that time," Tommy said. "People were still living in tents and wooden houses on green fields and growing their own food. Many outcast pig people and Dinkies lived independently and didn't buy corporation grown food or drink corporation filtered water."

"There was a big run on water back then," McQueen said. "The CEO declared a water shortage and raised the price."

"But it was not enough money," Tommy said. "The people living outside the controls created a big money loss for the Friends of the Earth Corporation."

The old Dinky nodded. Wasn't it coincidental that when the green water-virus epidemic occurred, the Friends of The Earth Corporation just happened to have virus-free blue grass, and blue plants, and blue trees for sale?"

"And," Tommy added, "under warrior protection, the pig people ran for the safety of the blue grass and the shelter of the non-wooden houses."

Out of a passage that led into darkness, a Dinky with his arm in a sling and a sickly pale face walked up to Sludge. I'm tired of living down here with no sun. When are we going to take back our land up top?"

Tommy's brow furrowed. "Just be patient. We'll be back on top sooner than you think."

"Sludge held up his hand like a man signaling

212

in some sort of sports game. "Time out. We heard all this before. What's your plan?"

"Simple," Tommy said. "When the TV station is broadcasting live, McQueen and I will go to the TV station and tell the world there is no virus."

"What makes you think the people will believe you?"

Danielle broke in. "The TV has already broadcasted that McQueen had been killed by the wood-virus."

McQueen nodded once. "That's right. When I show up on TV, I'll tell them the truth. They'll know they have been living a lie."

Sludge smiled a wry smile and shook head slowly. "They're gonna twist it around. It don't matter what you do. They're gonna make you look like a liar."

Tommy looked at Sludge. "And what do you suggest we do?"

"We had planned to keep diggin' our tunnels."

"Then what?"

"Then we woulda brought more Dinkies down here. Then the pig people wouldn't have no one to plant or harvest their food."

"If it ever got that bad," Tommy said, "they'd probably tell a few warriors or housing authority people the virus is fake and give them the jobs of planting and harvesting."

"Let them," Sludge said. "All those idiots know how to grow is red cabbage and purple beans." He turned to his buddies. "Let doze pigs eat all the red cabbage and purple beans they want. Let 'em fart themselves right off the face of the earth."

Sludge's buddies laughed in unison.

Sludge gestured to a sickly pale Dinky. "If we don't get enough sunshine, we'll all be white as ghosts. We got enough Dinky strength to go up top and overpower them right now."

"We won't overpower them," McQueen said. "They have all the weapons. We have none."

Sludge's eyes widened with excitement. "What do you mean we don't got no weapons? Just as soon as we steal a hose from the bottled-water plant we'll have our water pumper going. The stupid warriors that don't run from the fake water-virus will be blasted right off their feet."

The Dinky in the straw hat pointed to a two-by-four leaning against the dirt wall. "And those warriors run away from wood virus."

McQueen place his hand on the wooden two-by-four and looked toward the Dinkies. "Water and wood will only scare warriors for a short time. Then, they will start shooting poison antidote bullets."

Sludge growled and took on a look of defiance. "So what? If we gotta sacrifice a few lives, we will. Our lives are worthless down here anyway. I say we revolt, and the sooner the better."

"The Dinky with the straw hat grabbed the two-by-four and raised it above his head. "That's right. Even a rat fights his way out of his hole sometime."

Sludge's buddies nodded, raised their fists and chanted, "That's right! That's right! That's right!"

The old Dinky raised his staff and twirled it three times. The Dinkies stopped chanting. All heads turned toward the old Dinky.

"All life is precious," he said. "We cannot

waste it foolishly."

McQueen's heart ratcheted up a beat. He would never get on TV if Sludge started a revolt. The warriors would be out in force. McQueen held up his hand. "Before you do anything, can't you a least let Tommy and me try."

Sludge shook his head slowly. "Dah only thing doze corporation pigs know is violence." He smiled an exaggerated ear-to-ear cocky smile. "And we're just the ones that can give it to 'em."

"What about Augur?" Tommy said. "He doesn't believe in violence."

Shaking his head, Sludge held his hands up in a halting gesture and waved them in a negative motion. "There ain't no real Augur. "Everybody knows he's just a myth."

The old dinky cleared his throat and stared at Sludge. "the least we could do is let's let McQueen and Tommy try to do what they want to do."

Sludge shrugged and waved his hand down. "Ah, what the heck? I could use a few laughs. I'll give them some time to make fools of themselves."

McQueen looked at Tommy. "You ready to be on TV?"

"Anytime you are," Tommy said, and turned to walk away.

"Whatever you guys do," Sludge said, "it ain't gonna work. I'm only gonna wait three days. If you ain't changed anything, we're goin' into Blue Town and take it by force."

"Then it's settled," the old Dinky said. "McQueen and Tommy will go to the TV station."

Sludge turned toward his fellow workers. "Let's git back to work. While McQueen's wasting

Tommy's time, we'll be gittin' ready for the revolt."

Sludge waded into his pack of buddies. They patted him on the back and followed him into the dark tunnel on the right.

In preparation to go up top, Danielle rose to a squatting position and brushed the dirt off the knees of her uniform. "Let's get out of here."

McQueen looked to Danielle. "You can't go with us."

"Why not?"

"You still have the rash. The TV people believe that your poison ivy is the contagious wood virus. They won't let you get near them."

"What will I do here?"

"You can keep help keep the Dinkies from revolting. When we get into the TV station, if they're revolting, it'll draw the TV viewer's attention away from us."

"That's right, Tommy said. "If Sludge goes into the street, all the people will come out to watch. We'll be on TV with no one watching."

"But," Danielle protested. "I don't want to stay here alone."

"The old Dinky put a gentle hand on hers. "I'll protect you."

Danielle gave McQueen a puzzled look.

McQueen smiled. "The Dinkies respect this man."

Danielle shook her head in disagreement. "But I want to go with you."

Tommy patted her on the back. "Stick with the old-timer. You'll be okay."

McQueen and Tommy left for the TV Station.

216

CHAPTER 15

McQueen and Tommy plowed their hands across the clear water, gave Danielle a playful splash, and disappeared down into the pool of the secret cave. She sighed and turned toward the old Dinky. "Follow me," he said.

She bent over, slouched just enough to clear the mineshaft's ceiling, and followed him. He took her to a tiny round cave room. Inside, an electric heater sat next to a single wood-slatted-cot.

The old Dinky patted the end of the cot. "It may be a little short. But we weren't expecting guests as tall as you."

"Thank you," Danielle said, and sat on the little cot. "This will be just fine. I'm sure McQueen and Tommy will be back soon."

"You look a little damp." The old Dinky reached down. "I'll turn the heater on for you." He twisted the switch on the electric heater. Warm air wafted out onto her cold wet legs. "Turn it off when you're dry."

She curled up on the bunk. The old Dinky left and she closed her eyes. She had always done things for the corporation. Sometimes they were dangerous, but she was never told to stay behind for any reason. She always worked through the assignment, no matter how bad it was. She was not just a helpless creature of another sex. She was a warrior driver.

She rolled over and stretched out. With her feet hanging over the hard edge of the short bunk, she dozed off.

When she woke up, she was sweating. Needles

and pins sensations flowed like electricity over her legs. She looked down. The hard edge of the bunk had cut off the circulation to her legs. They had fallen asleep. She reached down, turned the heater off, curled her knees up to her chest, and looked out the little cave room door. Little Dinkies, pushing tiny wheelbarrows full of tools, scurried past as if they were on their way to some important job.

She smiled and figured that if she didn't get out of the mine she would be like Snow White and a hundred dwarfs. She wouldn't eat a poison apple and fall asleep, but it would be nice when McQueen got back. He could be the handsome prince that wakes her with a kiss. She didn't want to sit and do nothing. She searched her mind for a way to help McQueen. She knew the antidote was poison. Suddenly she realized that Sludge was right. McQueen's plan wasn't going to work. If he went on live TV and announced that the virus was fake, Burke would go on live TV, too. He would line up a few people and say they had the virus. Claiming he could save them, he would inject them with the poison antidote. After they died from the poison antidote, he would claim the virus still kills. The pig people would not believe McQueen. They would not believe the virus was not real. No matter what McQueen did, Sludge was going to revolt. And that gave her an idea.

She had gone out with Judd a few times. He was Nelson's bodyguard, but he was also McQueen's friend. If she could go out with him again, she could get him to help McQueen. But she decided that idea won't work. She would be recognized. Burke would catch her for sure.

A little red-headed Dinky stopped at the entrance to her room, made a comical face and ran away.

Danielle smiled. The Dinky had given her another idea. She would go to the warrior fantasy bar. Judd sat at his usual table just about every night. She would dress up in a warrior's fantasy costume. She would even dig out her fake nose. No one would recognize her. She would convince Judd to switch vaccines in the antidote bullets. He was probably in the ammunition room every day. He could replace the antidote-death serum with sleeping serum. When the warriors shot McQueen, he wouldn't die. When the warriors shot the Dinkies the warriors would believe they were dead, but they'll be sleeping. Fake bullets would be McQueen's and the Dinkies' only chance. McQueen wouldn't know it, but he and Danielle would be working together. They would expose the wood-virus for the farce that it was. But she couldn't hold her breath long enough to get out of the tunnel. Maybe she could get Freddy to run the air pump to the facemask.

She felt a tingling on the back of her leg and reached down to scratch it. "Damn, that poison ivy is in a new place now." She reached over, picked up her mixture of white powder and water, and spread it over the rash. She wanted to see Judd right now, but she would have to wait until the itchy poison ivy went away.

CHAPTER 16

Under the lighted window at the TV station building, Tommy dropped to all fours. McQueen placed his feet on Tommy's back, stepped up and looked through the window. The eastern hall of the building was partly obscured by a warrior standing guard in front of the transmitting equipment. There seemed to be no one else in the immediate vicinity. McQueen pushed on the bottom of the window. It wouldn't budge. He would have to find another way into the station.

He stepped down off Tommy's back. Tommy got up. With his dusty hands, he quietly tried to whisk the dust from his knees. Then they turned their backs to the station, eased into the concealing darkness behind the blue hedges, and squatted down. "That was quick," Tommy said. "Can we get in?"

"Not here," McQueen said. "The window's jammed solid, and there's a guard."

"We might not have to get in."

McQueen jerked his head toward Tommy. "What?"

"When you were on my back, I watched a reporter walk in and out of the building. He looked like he was waiting to meet somebody."

"How many cam-fingers does he have?"

"I couldn't see for sure, but it looked like only one."

"He has only has one chance left to report something that Nelson wants him to report. Did anyone else come out?"

"Just him. He came out twice."

Tommy pointed through the blue hedges and to the main entrance. "There he is again."

McQueen wanted to go into the TV station and make his case in front of the big TV cameras, but it would be easier and safer to do it with the reporter. "I guess it doesn't matter who gets the story," he said. "If it's live, it'll go out anyway."

"Are we going to talk to him?"

An uneasy feeling invaded McQueen's body. "That's what we came here for," he said, and shook off the feeling. "Stay here and watch. I go first. If it's safe, come on over."

McQueen walked up the cement steps and into the light. Like a man who owned the station, he sauntered over to the reporter and stopped. This reporter was a big man with an aggressive air. He stood with his legs apart. His right arm was around his stomach and the other arm was bent at the elbow. He rested his chin on his full-fingered left fist as if he were in deep thought. Dropping his hand, he turned and looked straight at McQueen. Like he had just seen a ghost, he blurted out, "Warrior McQueen, is that you?"

"Get your cam-finger out," McQueen said. "I want to give you a real story."

The reporter lifted his right hand, put his single cam-finger in front of McQueen's face, and then dropped it back to his side. "Wait!" he said. "Your best friend, Sergeant Burke, has just finished his interview about your death. He'll be glad to know you're still alive."

"I'm sure he will. But I have a bigger story."

"Good, you can tell your best friend and fellow warrior that you're alive. And you can do it right

221

on live TV."

McQueen figured Burke wouldn't stupid enough to do anything to him on live TV. "Okay," he said. "I'll wait here."

The reporter turned. Rushing toward the door, he said, "I'll be right back."

He opened the station door and held it open with his cam-fingered hand. Down the hallway, like some kind of spasmodic nightmare, Burke appeared. His happy smiling cheese-face distorted and flashed with fear and hate. Immediately he broke into a full run. Rushing toward McQueen, he pulled his sidearm out of its holster and shot through the opened door. The bullet whizzed past McQueen's head. McQueen ducked behind the pillar on the front of the station entrance. Burke ran up to the reporter and stopped. The reporter stood with his cam-finger sticking over the edge of the opened door.

Burke reached into his vest pocket, and screamed, "You made me miss."

"But he's your best friend," the confused reporter stammered out.

Before the reporter had a chance to react, Burke pulled out is razor-sharp pruning shears. And with one swift motion, he snipped off the reporter's last cam-finger. It fell to the concrete below. Screaming in pain, the now-out-of-work reporter grabbed his bleeding fingerless hand with his other hand and dropped to his knees. Burke stood over him with his foot raised. "This will teach you the finger lesson." He tromped down on the cutoff finger. With the thick heel of his warrior boot, he ground it on the white cement until it was a red smear.

McQueen turned and ran toward the blue hedges. He leaped over them, ran into the concealing darkness, and stopped next to Tommy who was crouching in the night-blue bushes. Tommy stood up. "What happened?"

"Nothing we wanted to happen. Burke was there."

"But you're supposed to be a hero. Why didn't you get on TV?"

"Maybe I'm old news."

"I didn't think it was going to be this hard."

"Now what?" McQueen asked.

"We'll have to find Augur."

CHAPTER 17

Danielle got Freddy to pump air into the facemask. Although she couldn't swim, she pulled herself along the stones of the water tunnel. On the other side of the tunnel, she placed her feet on a stone ledge and pushed herself to the top of the pool in the water house.

Avoiding occasional OvalCars by jumping into tall green grass and hiding behind green trees, she walked back to Blue Town. At the fence that ran around the green grass border of the OvalCar motor pool, she stopped.

In the past she had watched Dinkies slip out a trap door somewhere in the green grass. She knew they had dug a secret tunnel into the motor pool, and that they used it as a shortcut when they had come in from working long days in the fields. She had never reported it, but in the semi-darkness she wasn't sure where it was.

Where the grass had been tramped down, she tapped the ground with her foot. When she heard a hollow sound, she bent over and lifted a green grass-covered trap door. There were no Dinkies inside. She stepped down and duck-walked through the dark tunnel. On the other side, disguised as a plastic manhole cover, was another door. When she opened it, she was at the edge of the motor pool parking lot.

Watching for guards, she made her way to her OvalCar. No one was guarding it. Just as she had done for years, she disabled the alarm system with her metallic fingernail and lifted the dome of the OvalCar. Watching for guards, she reached in, grabbed her personal-belongings case, and took it out. When she eased down the dome of the car, a warrior guard's shadow loomed around the corner of the white cement-block garage. She ran behind the OvalCar, lifted the manhole cover, and walked back through the tunnel.

After she went out the grass-covered trap door, she slunk off into the green grass, stooped down, and opened her case. It was too dark to see what was in it. She stood up to let light from the parking lot shine into the case. It still wasn't bright enough. She walked closer to the fence, stopped, and looked next to the white building. Walking with a slow searching pace, a warrior guard flashed his flashlight into the OvalCar. She ran back to the trap door, lifted it, and stepped into the tunnel. Then, she closed the door, leaving a small slit to watch through. When the warrior began to flash the light in her direction, she slowly shut the trap door. Faint light beams danced on blades of tall green grass around the edges of the door, but she was sure he hadn't seen her.

When the guard left, she went back through the tunnel, out into the parking lot, and stood under a light pole. Now she could see into her case. And it was still there: the ugly latex nose that she used to put on when she didn't want warriors trying to take her out. But she still needed a costume, maybe a medic's uniform. If that drunken medic that had botched her antidote injection was on function status, maybe she could sneak past him and get a uniform. She worked her way through the velvety safe shadows of the tall grass and made it to the clinic without being seen.

The clinic's front door was held open with a stone. She looked in. There was no movement. Because the door was open, she figured the drunken medic was probably trying to get some fresh night air for a hangover; and he was probably sleeping.

Stepping softly, she stepped through the door and eased on down the hallway. Garbled grumbling came from the open door of the medic's office. She peeked around the corner and looked in. The medic's eyes were closed. He looked like he was drunk, but she couldn't tell if he was awake. His face was round and red. There was a weak smile on his face, and he had an ugly mustache that grew into his nostrils. Drunk or sober, he was no handsome prince.

She scurried past the opened door and slipped into the uniform closet. A voice like a grunting pig echoed from the office. "What was that?" it asked.

Danielle closed the closet door and listened. Slowly, soft-soled shoes scraped on the concrete floor, shuss . . . shuss . . . shuss. The medic or someone walked past the closed door of the closet.

Danielle stared at the closed door, trying to will it to stay closed. Maybe it's was the medic. Maybe he knew she was there. Maybe he was just playing with her. She prayed he wasn't. She could never outrun him.

The shuss stopped. Danielle waited. There was silence. She opened the door, just a crack, and looked through the tiny slit. The drunken medic sat in a chair with his hands hanging down close to the floor. His mushy mouth was open and his eyes were closed. He was passed out.

She jammed the uniform and shoes into her

226

case and stepped out of the closet. Without warning, the drunken medic sprang to his feet. She ran into the shot room, slammed the door shut and locked it. Through the door she heard the jingle of keys. The knob on the door turned. The drunken medic was unlocking the door. She was supposed to be dead. There was no telling what he would do. She jammed a chair under the knob. He unlocked the door and pushed. The chair stopped it from opening.

His voice rumbled like threatening thunder. "Open that door!"

Danielle kicked the chair. It jammed tighter against the knob.

He slammed his shoulder against the door. It opened a few centimeters. For a moment their eyes met.

He flashed a slobbering smile. Then with a low menacing voice, he said, "You're all mine." He reared back for another slam.

Pushing on the door and swinging her hip, Danielle slammed the door shut again. Again, she jammed the chair under the knob.

He slammed his big shoulder into the door. The chair's legs skidded across the floor. The door opened a full meter. Laughing an exaggerated laugh, he leaned toward the opening. But in his drunken state, he wasn't fast enough. Before he could regain his balance, she slammed the door shut and kicked the chair until it was jammed tight under the knob. He crashed again and again, and then he quit laughing.

She knew the door couldn't hold out against his brutal crashes. So . . . she timed them. When he least expected it, she grabbed the chair, pulled it away from the door, and stepped to one side. The medic crashed into the door. The door blasted open. His uncoordinated slob body caused him to stumble forward until he landed on his face. Like a Humpty Dumpty man, he struggled, rolled over, and sat up with his knees straight and his legs apart. She picked up her suitcase. Bonk! She hit him over the head with it. He reached up, grabbed his head and moaned. She jumped over his outstretched legs and escaped out the door.

In the safety of the green grass, she put on her ugly rubber nose and changed into the medic uniform. Then she made her way to the fantasy bar and stepped inside.

The long, narrow bar had a blue ceramic floor, a low ceiling, and all around the tops of the walls, blue lights interlaced with a few sparkling yellow and red lights. She figured the person that redecorated the place was color blind or related to a plastic Christmas tree.

At the end of the bar, just inside the door, drunken warriors were lined up like hogs at a trough, leaning over, and slobbering on prospective dates.

At the back wall, McQueen's bodyguard friend, Judd, sat at his usual table. He was talking to a well-built bottled-water-worker woman. She chittered at him and swung her long blond hair around like some kind of mutant bird signaling for a mate.

Danielle walked up to his table. "Is there a man here, who can buy a lady a drink?"

Jud immediately stood up and looked at her

fake nose. A puzzled look came over his face. "Is that you, Danielle?"

"I'm sorry," she said. "Are you with someone?"

"It's just business," Judd said. "Please sit down. Candy was just leaving. Weren't you?" He glared at Candy.

Candy shot antidote-bullets with her eyes in Danielle's direction. Danielle couldn't risk making a scene with this girl. She looked away as if she were disinterested in Judd. Candy stood up, grabbed her purse with a deliberate smack of her head, and left.

Danielle sat down. Judd order her the best drink in the house and looked at her nose. What happened to your nose?

"Nothing, you know I'm wanted?"

"The posters are everywhere, yours and McQueen's. Is he still alive?"

Danielle lowered her voice to a whisper. "He's alive. That's why I'm here."

Judd looked concerned. "What's the matter?"

"He needs your help."

"Anything for my old friend."

"We found out that" — Bam! Candy slammed the restroom door — "there is no virus."

Judd raised his voice. "What?"

People at the next table quit talking and looked in their direction. "Take it easy," Danielle whispered. "I don't want to get caught in here."

Judd lowered his voice and leaned toward Danielle. The people started talking again. "I think your brain has been infected with the virus. I can see the rash under your gloves."

"It's not virus. It's poison ivy."

"Same thing," Judd said as if he weren't afraid of the virus, but he backed away. "What can I do to help McQueen?"

"You're Nelson's bodyguard. You have access to all the antidote bullets. Could you get into the ammunition room and take out the antidote serum in the bullets and replace it with a sleeping drug?"

"I could replace the antidote serum with an anesthetic that will put the injected person asleep for a few minutes." He looked into her eyes. "What's in it for me?"

"You'll be part of the new virus-free world."

Judd smiled as if he were humoring her. "What do *you* have to offer?"

"Nothing now, but when I get rid of this poison ivy we can go out again."

"Like old times?"

"No, better. There will be no virus."

Judd took a long drink and put the glass down on the table. "I have to be out of my mind, or I have the virus myself."

"Then you'll do it?"

He reached under the table and placed his hand on her thigh. "Anything for you, baby."

She didn't like his hand on her thigh, but she didn't object. To save McQueen, she would do anything she could. Judd probably thought she would go with him tonight. She didn't want to, but if it got the job done, she would have to lead him on.

Jud placed his hands on the table and stood up. "I see a medic over there right now. "Wait here. If he can get me the anesthetic, we can get out of here."

Danielle sipped her drink, leaned back, and watched. The entrance door opened. Burke and three warriors walked in. She needed to get out of there.

While Burke pushed lower ranking warriors away from the bar, his obnoxious voice thundered across the room. "Make room for some real warriors."

Candy walked out of the restroom and high-heeled her way toward the warriors. With each sensual sway of her hips, her long blond hair swung across her clinging dress that magnified the firm curves her body. The warriors' heads turned in her direction. As she walked closer they inflated their massive chests and sucked in their beer guts.

Danielle didn't wait for their perverted mouths to drool. She turned her back, got up, and walked into the restroom.

Inside, all the lights were out except one tiny bulb. She checked the window. It was cemented in solid. She tapped on the glass. Dull clicks rapped. It was too thick to break and escape if she had to.

The door opened. A stripe of yellow bar-light illuminated a uniformed driver. She walked in. The door closed and the restroom returned to its darkened state, but Danielle recognized her friend. "Sally!"

Sally gave Danielle a quick hug. "I saw you and your funny nose. Judd's outside talking to Burke. How are you going to get out of here?"

Danielle looked at the door, looked at the solid window, shrugged, and looked at Sally. "What can I do?"

"I don't know," Sally said with a tinge of hesitancy in her voice. "It's a shame that you will become a Dinky."

"If that was going to happen, I would walk right out and spit in Burke's face. But he'll take me back to the base and torture me until I tell him where McQueen is."

Sally covered her face with her hands and gave a startled gasp. "McQueen's alive?"

"So far."

Sally dropped her hands and exhaled a deep breath. "I just knew he was."

"He's a tough man to kill."

"Danielle," Sally said. "It looks like you haven't been infected, but I owe you. I can't let Burke get his crummy hands on you."

"I don't want him to either. But what can I do?"

"Let's change uniforms. If Judd is telling Burke about you, they'll be looking for a medic's uniform."

Danielle didn't think Jud would tell Burke anything, but even if he didn't, she couldn't let Burke see her. She was glad it was dark. If Sally saw the poison ivy she would run for her life, but Sally didn't hesitate or show any fear. She unzipped the front of her drivers' uniform. "After we change," she said, "what will you do? You can't stay in her forever, and the window is solid glass."

Danielle slipped off her medics' uniform and handed it to Sally. Putting it on, Sally said, "I'll go and sit at Judd's table with my back to Burke."

Danielle jumped into the drivers' uniform and zipped it up. "It might work," she said. "We're

232

about the same size."

Sally buttoned the medics' uniform, reached up and pinched Danielle's cheeks. "Okay, sweetie, after I sit down, come out the door like you have to pick someone up, and then, get out of here."

Danielle held the restroom door open a crack and waited until Sally sat down. Burke was with Candy, flexing his arms and pointing to his sergeant stripes. Danielle opened the restroom door, lowered her head, and walked toward the exit. When she put her hand on the doorknob, Burke shouted at her. "Driver!"

Danielle stopped. Her heart beat so hard and fast that she could feel it in her neck. She took a deep breath, exhaled, and lowered her voice. "Yes, Sergeant Burke."

"We'll be out in a few hours," he yelled, and roared a big mule's heehaw. "Wait for us."

"Yes, Sergeant Burke," she said, opened the door, and walked out.

A warrior slipped out the door and called after her. "Hey, honey, how about we get together in your OvalCar?"

Danielle kept walking. "Go back in, warrior. I'm Burke's girl."

With great disappointment the warrior said, "Oh," and slipped back into the bar.

Danielle ran off the blue grass and onto the green grass. Under the green leaves of a tall tree, she slowed to a walk. She had just done her part. She had helped McQueen. Now, even if the Dinkies revolted they would only go to sleep for a while. They wouldn't be killed. Everything was going to be all right. She happily made her way back to the water house.

CHAPTER 18

After McQueen had avoided death at the TV station, the warriors were put on full alert.

McQueen and Tommy weaved their way through green bushes and tall trees, crossed a few fields of green grass, and made their way back to the water house where they dove into the pool, swam through the tunnel, and surfaced in the hidden cave.

Freddy jumped from the cot. "I didn't see you guys on TV. Are you going to Patagonia?"

All Blue Town warriors knew Patagonia was a place to stay away from. As McQueen treaded water and stared at Freddy, his face took on a puzzled look. "Are you crazy? Nobody goes to Patagonia?"

"Don't look so puzzled," Freddy said, giving McQueen a sly smile.

McQueen grabbed the side of the pool to pull himself out, but hesitated. "But that land's contaminated."

Tommy crawled over the edge of the pool and stepped out. "Patagonia's The Land of Augur."

"And Patagonia is on the off limits list," McQueen said, pulled himself up, and sat on the wall of the pool. "I don't know any warriors who have gone there."

Tommy let a big alligator smile spread across his face. "No warriors from around here have gone there. Augur has been a good influence in Patagonia. Nelson is afraid he will convince the warriors and the pig people that there is no virus."

McQueen jumped up out of the pool. "Well

let's get some gear and go there."

"Sorry, old buddy," Tommy said. "If the Patagonia Dinkies see a warrior, which you are, we'll never get near Augur or anyone close to him."

Freddy spoke up. "That's right, those Patagonia Dinkies are strange. They don't trust anyone associated with the corporation."

Tommy looked at McQueen and spoke with authority. "Freddy knows what Augur looks like. I don't. In the morning, when the dew is all over the grass, Freddy and I will go to Patagonia."

"What are you going to do when you get there?" McQueen asked, but seemed a little taken aback at how Tommy had spoken so forcefully.

Tommy figured McQueen apparently didn't realize that while he had been at warrior school he had become a pretty good leader himself. It seemed that McQueen still had his doubts about his intelligence. Before Tommy could confront him about it, Freddy stepped between them. "Heck," he said and smiled. "We don't even know if Augur is still alive."

Tommy gave a heavy sigh. He wasn't sure Augur was alive, but he knew he would have to go to Patagonia and make sure. "Augur may have found the antitoxin for the poison antidote-bullets." He looked to McQueen. "While we're gone, try to keep Sludge from starting a revolt."

"Don't take any crap off him," Freddy said. "We don't need any more dead Dinkies."

McQueen clasp his hands behind his back in a position of parade rest. With a stone face, he held the stance for a moment, and then said with authority, "Yes, sir!"

236

Tommy's gasp. He figured McQueen had reverted back to his brainwashed days.

McQueen's stone face cracked with a slight smile. He relaxed his parade rest stance, then he burst into a laugh.

Tommy smiled. "You got me that time."

McQueen patted him on the back. "You're the best friend I ever had. Be careful out there."

CHAPTER 19

Tommy and Freddy crept out of the water house and looked into the new morning. The silver sun shone out of the sky and turned the dew-covered grass sparkling silver. Although the air was calm, like a tiny tornado, a strange little whirlwind whirled down the dusty road. It danced toward the water house, spun right outside the door, and caused the poison ivy vine to slap three times against the side of the water house wall. Then, as if someone had turned a switch, it whirled into nothing and was gone. Then, a dark cloud covered the silver sun.

Tommy felt as if a cold hand had just grabbed the center of his back. He shuddered and looked to Freddy. "I've never seen that happen before."

Freddy playfully pushed on Tommy's shoulder. "Are you afraid of a little puff of wind? Get going."

"I'm not afraid," Tommy said, and stepped forward. "But it just seems out of place, like some kind of a sign."

"Don't start that superstitious crap on me." Freddy waved his hands in the air. "The way the pig people got the atmosphere ruined, stuff like that happens all the time." He paused and looked back at the poison ivy vine. It hung down motionless. "Maybe it's a good omen."

Tommy started walking. "The only good omen we're going to get, is to get outa' here before the grass dries and those housing authority morons come."

Walking behind Freddy, Tommy's eyes searched for movement in the tall weeds and trees. "They want McQueen pretty bad," he said.

238

"They'll shoot anything that moves."

Freddy increased his pace and walked toward the forbidden forest. Seeing nothing suspicious, Tommy followed. With a playful intent, he stepped on the back of Freddy's shoe. It came loose. Freddy stepped out of it. Bending down to pick it up, he said, "All right, Tommy, cut the crap."

Tommy put his thumbs in his ears and waved his fingers at Freddy.

Freddy jammed his foot back into his shoe and ran ahead of him. At the path that led into the forest, he stopped, took off his glasses, and waved back at Tommy. "Come on, you big dummy?"

Tommy ran toward Freddy. "Hey, wait on me."

Ten meters from Freddy, Tommy looked beyond the orange off-limits sign. "Get out of there!" he cried. "There's a hunter behind that sign."

Freddy held his glasses in his hand and turned toward Tommy. "What?"

The plastic-suited hunter took aim and shot. Freddy dropped his glasses and grabbed his back.

Something sprayed into the side of Tommy's face and stung like a swarm of bees. He reached up, wiped his face with the palm of his hand and looked at it. It was covered with blood. Like little slivers of ivory, yellow-white bone fragments stood out in a coating of red and stuck into the palm of his hand.

The hunter stepped out from behind the sign and shot Freddy again, and again. Another plastic-suited hunter came in off the path and pointed his sidearm at Tommy. Tommy turned and ran toward the burnt down farmhouse. The hunters ran after him. He raced into the tall green grass, dropped to the ground, and looked back. One of the hunters shot in his direction, but stopped at the edge of the grass.

Tommy knew they would be watching the water house. If he went back that way he would be shot. He decided to make his way into the cellar of McQueen's father's burnt down farmhouse and cover himself with ashes. If he could get that far, he could hide until they went away. But everything was a big if.

Concealed in the tall green grass, he crawled to the farmhouse. Then he dropped down into the cellar, and slipped under the shadow of the old steps. A dim orange-tinted light of the morning sun snuck through the shadow of the steps and shown on the burnt rubble and charred wood beams. Its soft light illuminated an old dirty cot. Tommy crawled over to it and sat down. In his mind, he saw Freddy being shot. It was like an eternal movie ran on a single loop. The same scene of Freddy being shot flashed again and again. The same red blood and the same yellow-white bone fragments sprayed into his face. He looked at his hand. The bone fragments had been scraped off when he had crawled across the ground, but he could still see them. He wiped his hand on the cot and looked at it again. The bone fragments in the horror movie of his mind faded, and his hands turned the color of gray wood ashes.

Freddy just got killed. Tommy wondered if his life worth it. Maybe Sludge was right. Maybe the Dinkies should revolt. They could storm the main barracks. In the chaos, Tommy would do something he would really like to do. He would rip Nelson's head right off his rotten steroid shoulders. They could attack with wooden sticks. Those dumb warriors were afraid of wood. That was it. He might as well just give up the whole idea of fighting those rotten warriors and pig people with nothing but tricks and words. It wasn't working anyway.

He looked at his gray hands. The vision of Freddy's bone fragments appeared again. He slammed those hands on his thighs. Thoughts squirmed in his brain. "It's just not worth it," he screamed inside himself. "I'll just quit."

He held his head in his hands and looked at his little feet. Fresh yellow dirt was under them.

That dirt looked pretty fresh. Maybe some kind of an animal had dug a den somewhere close. Or maybe it was dirt form the old tunnel entrance McQueen's father had started to dig.

He hit himself on the side of his head with his palm. He wondered what was wrong with his mind. McQueen had told him that he had found his father's tunnel when he escaped from Sludge and his cronies. He said it was in the yellow dirt. This might be it.

Tommy stood up and picked up an old burnt board. With its pointed end, he dug into the soft earth.

From up above, a hunter's face-masked muffled voice filtered down into the cellar. "Maybe that dumb Dinky fell down there."

Tommy stopped digging and stood silent.

"I'm not going down," another hunter said.

"I don't blame you," the first hunter said. "That place is filled with wood virus. It killed

McQueen's old man. There's probably a super strain of stagnant water virus down there, too."

"We'll wait here a while," the second hunter said. "If that Dinky's down there, he'll be dumb enough to try and sneak out."

Tommy crawled into the little hole he had dug with the board and leaned against the yellow dirt wall. He relaxed and figured that if he had to, he would wait for the hunters to go away. And It didn't matter if it took all day and all night.

"The stern voice of another hunter bellowed into the air. "Get down there and shoot that Dinky."

The booted feet of a hunter thudded on the cellar floor. Tommy jerked with fright. The dirt he was leaning on gave under his tiny weight. He pushed his hand through the dirt. A hole appeared. It could be the tunnel.

Another hunter's feet thumped on the floor. Tommy dug the dirt away as fast as a wild animal after an escaping meal. When he had an opening the size of a small dog, he plowed his body through and landed inside the safety of the tunnel system.

He had found it just in time, but he couldn't tell Sludge. He didn't know what he would do after he found out Freddy had been killed. If Sludge blamed McQueen for his death, he might get the other Dinkies riled up. Then McQueen would need a way to escape. For the time being, the new entrance would have to be an emergency exit.

He stood on the other side of the wall. With both hands, he scooped up dirt, and pitched it over the entrance. With each scoop of dirt, his need for revenge blazed brighter. That's what we'll do, he told himself. We'll revolt. But we can't go into

Blue Town without a plan of action. Any revolt must be organized. For starters, I'll pound on the barrel and announce that I have changed my mind.

CHAPTER 20

With a lantern in his hand, McQueen duck-walked down the dim mineshaft and into the tunnel complex. He was searching for the escape tunnel that led to his father's cellar. When he saw Tommy pitching dirt over it, in a playful mood, he dropped to his knees, and knee-walked until he was behind him. "Need any help?"

Tommy didn't jump or jerk with surprise. He kept scooping and pitching dirt. "There are at least two hunters up there." He grunted between pitches. "If we don't get this filled in, they'll be down here."

McQueen set the lantern down and joined Tommy. "The dirt pitching twins," he said, and looked at Tommy for approval.

Tommy didn't smile or acknowledge McQueen. He just kept scooping up dirt and pitching it over the entrance.

McQueen smiled big and threw more dirt. "Okay, little brother, don't talk. Let's make this dirt fly."

Tommy held his hands together and scooped up a big handful of dirt. "I didn't know it was a contest." He slung the dirt into the almost concealed opening.

Out of nowhere, a loud agitating voice beamed. "Just what do you think you're doing?"

McQueen looked up. Just above the lantern in his hand, Sludge's face glowed in the orange light like some sort of grotesque pumpkin. He put the lantern on the floor, leaned on his shovel, and motioned with his hand. "Can't you guys do anything right?"

244

"Don't help or anything," McQueen said sarcastically. "Just stand there. The hunters will be in here in a few seconds. Then you can start your revolt early."

Sludge lifted his shovel and offered it to McQueen. "Does the big brave warrior know how to use one of these?"

McQueen snatched the shovel from Sludge's hand. "Sorry I don't have time to argue with you now, Sludge. I can hear the hunters on the other side."

While Sludge stood and watched, McQueen jammed the shovel deep into the mine floor, scooped up huge shovelfuls of dirt, and frantically threw them at the shrinking opening. When no light came through, Tommy kicked the dirt tight with his feet. McQueen threw a few more shovelfuls for good measure. Out of breath, he stopped and wiped his forehead. Then he offered the shovel back to Sludge. "Thanks for the help, pal."

"Anytime," Sludge said, took the shovel, and leaned on it.

McQueen rested his back against the tunnel wall and slid down to a sitting position. "What happened, Tommy? Did you find Augur already?"

Tommy shook his head. "We didn't even get into the forbidden forest. The hunters shot Freddy."

McQueen reached up and put his hand on Tommy's shoulder. "Is he going to be all right?"

Tommy leaned his back against the wall. "He's all right now." He slid down the wall and sat cross-legged on the dirt floor. "He's as all right as he'll ever be. In fact, we should all be as all right as he is. Now he doesn't have to put up with all this crap." He crossed his arms across his chest as if he were lying in a casket. "He's dead."

"Are you sure?" McQueen asked. "We can go up top and check him out."

"They wanted him dead. They used high-powered bullets. Shot him at close range." Tommy's voice became strained as if rigor mortis was setting in. "The syringe-bullets blew his face right out the back of his head."

Sludge held onto his shovel with one hand and jerked his finger at Tommy. "See, I told you. Your dumb stupid ways won't work."

McQueen broke in with strained politeness. "We never got the chance to try."

"Why try," Sludge said and clutched Tommy's arm. "We'll just go up and take back what's ours."

Tommy gently waved off Sludge's hand. He looked down and scooped up a handful of dirt off the floor. Staring at it, he let it fall through his fingers. With tears in his eyes, he looked up at Sludge. "I didn't believe you before," he said. "But this time, I think you're right." He wiped the tears from his face with the sleeve of his shirt. "We have enough Dinkies who can fight. Those warriors and hunters are afraid of wood. We'll overwhelm them with wooden two-by-fours."

McQueen's mouth dropped open in surprise. "Come on, Tommy. I know Freddy was your friend, but you have to keep a sane mind."

"How can I keep a sane mind when we have to live like stinking rats in a stinking hole?"

Sludge threw his clinched fist into the air. "That's right. Let's get our forces together and wipe the bastards off the top of the earth."

McQueen felt like a wounded dog that had just been shot by someone he trusted. "Don't do this to me, Tommy," he pleaded. "You don't stand a chance."

"Tommy lowered his head, scooped up another handful of dirt and held it. "It just keeps getting worse. Pretty soon we won't be able to come and go at all. I can't live in these tunnels forever. I got to be outside, up top in the good air."

The old Dinky stepped into the light and thumped his staff on the tunnel floor. "You can't fight fire with fire. If you do, you'll burn the whole house down."

Tommy slung the handful of dirt onto the floor and looked up. "And what's wrong with that?"

"Tommy, Tommy, Tommy," the old Dinky said as if he were shaking his finger at him. "Don't make one of your quick decisions. You know as well as I that things gained by force have to be retained by force."

"So what," Sludge said. "We'll finally be free."

The old Dinky's brow furrowed in thought. "The odds are against us. But just suppose," he said, and paused. "Just suppose, by some quirk of fate, we overtake the warriors and the hunters."

"Quirk nothing," Sludge objected. "We'll do it."

The old Dinky gave a slight shrug as if to say it could happen. "You just may," he said. "However, you and I both know Nelson will send more and more warriors. They will overtake us, and then we will go underground again and start the process all over. It will take at least another twenty years to be able to rise up and overtake them. We will be forced to repeat the process again and again. It will never end."

Sludge stabbed the end of his shovel into the dirt. "So what? At least we'll have a time of peace until they come."

"You may have a few days, but at what cost. Those of us that they don't kill will be put back into bondage. Do you want to be a slave again?"

Sludge jerked on the handle of his shovel as if it were a spear. "There will be no slaves when there are no warriors."

The old Dinky glanced at the shovel, but acted like he didn't see it. "What difference will a few days make," he gestured to McQueen and Tommy. "Let them go to Patagonia and find Augur."

Sludge's took on a look of defiance. "We're not waitin' on nothin'.". He pulled his shovel from the dirt and violently jammed it back in. "The bastards are killin' us right outside our own water house."

Danielle duck-walked into the light. Her hair was tied into a ponytail that gave her a sassy, happy look that definitely did not fit the situation. She smiled and laughed with delight. "I think you may want to wait a little longer."

"Where have you been?" McQueen asked.

"I snuck out and talked with Judd, your bodyguard buddy."

McQueen let out a low moan. "What? Are you nuts? You're a wanted women."

Danielle maintained her smile. "I didn't know you cared," she joked. "Judd said he could disable the antidote bullets that the warriors shoot. He said

248

he can replace the poison serum with an anesthetic that will put the injected person asleep for a few minutes."

Sludge's eyebrows shot up, and his eyes opened wide. "Did he do it?"

"He can do it," Danielle said, and offered a faint smile. "But he said he will need time."

Sludge breathed a sigh of relief and leaned back onto his shovel handle. "Now that's something I might wait for."

"This is good," the old Dinky said. "But the warriors will find out and change the bullets back. It's only a short term solution."

"I think a simple bullet change is worth waiting for," McQueen said. "Just think how a revolt would be with antidote bullets that don't kill."

"That would be great," Sludge said. "But what if your great friend doesn't change the bullets?"

"If you wait for us to come back with the antitoxin it won't matter what kind of bullets they use."

That's right," Tommy said. "Augur is said to have found the antitoxin. It makes those poison antidote bullets useless."

"Okay," McQueen said shaking his head in defeat. "If we must revolt, let's get the antitoxin first."

Sludge looked up with realization and hope in his eyes. "That sounds good to me. If Augur's got this antitoxin, there's no way we can lose."

The old Dinky turned toward Sludge. "Then you will wait?"

As if he were trying to keep the words from coming out of his mouth, Sludge talked through

249

clinched teeth. "I'll give you a few days. If you haven't returned by then, I'll know you have been killed or captured." He lifted his shovel and poked the air in front of him. "Then we're goin' in."

McQueen looked down toward Danielle's foot. A twisted vine of poison ivy was wrapped around her ankle. "You'll never get rid of that poison ivy if you keep towing it around all day."

Danielle jerked her head toward her feet. Her black pony-tailed hair whipped over her shoulder. "What?"

Tommy pointed to her ankle. "You got it on your foot."

Danielle lifted her foot and looked at the poison ivy. "I was so tired last night I didn't notice."

Sludge placed the end of his shovel on the end of the vine and pulled. It unraveled from her ankle. She bent over and held out her two fingers to pinch the vine and pick it up. "Thank you, Sludge," she said. "When we go up top, I'll take it outside."

Sludge placed his shovel on the vine and pulled it away from her fingers. "I'll take care of it."

McQueen studied Danielle's face and hands. The poison ivy rash stood out red and blistering. He sighed. "You can't come with us.

Danielle's face turned ugly. "Why not?"

"When the Dinkies of Patagonia see your rash they'll run away from us."

"Why should they?" she asked with a hint of contempt. "They know it's only poison ivy, and Augur should have better accommodations than this."

Shaking his head, McQueen gave her a compassionate smile. "We're not staying in a hotel.

250

We'll be lucky if we get out of the weather the entire trip."

"I could still go and help in some way."

"You probably could. But we're going to have to talk to both sides."

"That's a fair assumption," the old Dinky said. "McQueen can talk the pig people into changing, but Tommy cannot talk the Dinkies into changing."

"Why not," Tommy growled. "I can talk just as good as anyone else."

"I'm sorry Tommy. But over the years, your sham as a dumb Dinky has brought you unwanted popularity. Your antics and jokes have made people think of you as a jester or a fool."

Sludge let out a little laugh. "Those warriors didn't think it was so funny when we wrapped that green plastic around their heads."

The old Dinky lifted his hand and pointed upward. "All the more reason we will need known heroes on both sides. McQueen and Augur can unite the people of the world." He pointed to Tommy. "But you and your friend will have to find Augur, and bring him back. He will know how to handle the people after the revolt."

Tommy nodded with approval. "Yes he will, but what if he is not in Patagonia?"

"They say he lives in harmony with the pig people of Patagonia. They will know where to find him."

Danielle jerked her ponytail off her shoulder. "But what am I supposed to do here?"

"You can keep the Dinkies from revolting," McQueen said, and looked at the old Dinky. "You can help her with that, can't you?"

"I'll take her under my wing. There should be no problem."

"No problem at all," Sludge said with an arrogant air. "When you're not back in three days, we're revolting without you."

"We can do this in two days, Tommy said, but if we run into trouble we may need more time."

"Maybe you're right," Sludge said and grinned. "You'll need a few extra days for your funerals."

McQueen momentarily sagged against the wall. "Gee, Sludge, thanks for the vote of confidence."

The old Dinky glared at Sludge.

Sludge turned his head away from the old Dinky's stare and looked to McQueen. "All right, I'll give your week. But no more."

CHAPTER 21

Danielle saw McQueen and Tommy off in the hidden cave. Then she mixed up another batch of paste for her poison ivy and carried it back to her little cave room.

Spreading the white paste over the rash on her face, she began to have doubts about what it was. The paste made the rash feel better, and she hoped it was poison ivy and not the virus-rash. But if it was poison ivy and the Dinkies revolted, they could be killed. Then she would never know what the white powder was.

She sat on the cot, took off Sally's OvalCar drivers' uniform pants, stretched her long slender legs, and smoothed the paste over her thighs and ankles.

A thudding knock pounded on the outside entrance to her room. A baldheaded Dinky, with his floppy hat in his hands, appeared in the doorway. "Excuse me, ma'am, can I talk to you for a moment?"

Danielle covered her thighs with the blanket on the cot. "Yes, please come in."

Looking at her legs, the little Dinky walked up to Danielle and extended his hand. "Hello, my name's Parry. I think you would like to talk to me."

"Do you have news of McQueen and Tommy?"

"I have something better," he said, and stepped close. "But you can't tell anyone."

This Dinky gave her an uneasy feeling. She wondered what this little creep was trying to do.

He stood with his knee touching the side of the cot and played with his hat in his hand. "I don't want you to think I am being too forward, but I think you are a very attractive lady."

Danielle pulled the blanket down over her legs and leaned back away from him. "I've been told that before."

"Would you like me to sing you a song?"

Danielle wondered what was this guy? But figured, what the heck, she wasn't doing anything else. She flirted with him with her eyes and said, "It might be nice."

Parry held out his hat. "I can dance for you, too."

Danielle didn't answer. She just stared at him and waited for him to move.

"Somewhere over the rainbow," he sang, and stopped. Danielle grimaced. His one line of singing was so bad it caused her cheeks to pucker.

"Don't sing," she said. "Just dance."

Parry did a few taps with his little untrained feet, but suddenly stopped. He stepped close. "I may not look it," he said and stared at her breasts. "But I have satisfied many women in my time. In fact, a lot of them say that I have satisfied them better than their young boyfriends."

Danielle wanted to tell the little half-wit to hit the trail. But she couldn't get the little pervert mad. If Sludge and the crew decided to revolt early, she would need all the help she could get. She smiled a half smile. "I don't know you well enough to talk about things like that."

The old Dinky walked into the room and shouted, firm and loud, "Parry!"

Parry stiffened. "Yes?"

"You have not completed your share of work

254

for the day. Get back to your tunnel."

Tipping his hat to Danielle, Parry backed out of the little room and stopped in the doorway. "Maybe we can talk later," he said, and stood there.

The old Dinky pointed to him and shouted, "Buzz off!"

Parry frowned. "I just wanted to ask her if she wanted to have a cup of coffee with me."

The old Dinky glared at him. Parry turned and scurried down the tunnel.

"Did he bother you?" the old Dinky asked.

"Not much," Danielle said. "I've dealt with guys like him before."

"I'm sorry if he bothered you." The old Dinky forced a grin. "Old perverts never die. They just show up in our tunnel system."

Danielle smiled. "Any word from McQueen or Tommy?"

"We don't even know if they made it as far as Forbidden Forest. But I'm sure they're doing just fine."

She looked at the rash on the back of her hands. "Are you sure this rash is only poison ivy?"

"Yes, it is. If you had not went out and tromped around in it again, it might have been gone by now."

Danielle glared at her rash. Its red puffy lumps gave her the creeps, and it gave her a feeling of total restriction. She looked to the old Dinky; and with hope in her voice, she asked, "How much longer will I have this rash?"

The old Dinky shook his head like a doctor giving a patient bad news. "It depends upon your immune system." He sighed. "If it is weak and you don't get enough rest, it could talk a long time."

The ugly puff of poison ivy on her right ankle had swollen and now it was itching. She reached over and scratched it. She wondered why a simple rash that the Dinkies said could be cured could look and feel so bad. It was difficult for her to believe there was no virus.

"Don't scratch it," the old Dinky said. "It'll make it worse."

She quit scratching her ankle and looked to him. "Are you sure McQueen isn't just telling me this is poison ivy just to keep me at ease?"

The old Dinky smiled an assuring smile. "We haven't deceived you. There is no virus."

Danielle reached to the rash on the back of her hand and snuck a quick scratch. "I guess I'll just have to watch out for Parry while I wait for this to heal."

The old Dinky walked toward the door and stopped. Turning toward her, he said, "Parry-Pervert gets carried away sometimes. We almost banished him to the world up top. However, he might not keep his mouth shut about the location of our tunnels, so we keep him around."

"I should be okay," Danielle said.

"This should help," the old Dinky said, reached up and pulled a curtain across the entrance to the room. "Please let me know if Parry bothers you again."

"Thank you," Danielle said, and the old Dinky left.

She pulled the cover back off her legs and smoothed the white past on the rash. She still wondered what the strange white power was, but whatever it was, it was keeping the rash from itching. If the Dinkies were right about the poison ivy, and it looked like they were. They might be right about everything else. Her life and McQueen's life, and all the lives of all the pig people of the world, could be affected by an early revolt. War could break out. If the Dinkies were killed, their knowledge of the cure for what they call poison ivy would be lost forever. Until McQueen and Tommy got back with the antitoxin, she would have to do whatever she could to keep Sludge and his crew from revolting.

She placed the paste on the little table next to her little cot. Before she could do anything, she had to get rid of her rash.

CHAPTER 22

Inside the water house, McQueen and Tommy popped their heads up out of the pool. Warrior's voices filtered across the top of the water.

Getting ready to dive back down, Tommy breathed deep and pointed downward. "We going back?"

McQueen looked at a loose stone at the edge of the water house pool. "We don't have time, but if they're still there, we won't have a problem."

"Come on," Tommy said and glanced at the water house door. "If what's there?"

McQueen reached over and pulled the loose stone aside. "I bet you thought I forgot about these."

Tommy smiled a mischievous grin and patted McQueen on the back. "I always wondered where you hid those things."

McQueen reached in and pulled a blue one out. "I hope they still work." He placed the plastic squirt gun under the pool's surface. The gun bubbled and filled with water. He pulled it out of the water and pulled the trigger. Nothing happened.

"There's two more and they're green," Tommy said. Try them."

McQueen reached in, grabbed both guns and handed one to Tommy. "Here, see if this one works."

Tommy and McQueen filled the green squirt guns, pulled them up simultaneously, and pulled the triggers. Like little kids, they sprayed water into each other's faces.

With water dripping down his round face,

Tommy smiled and said, "Just like old times."

McQueen put his squirt gun under the water. "Let's fill 'em up again."

The booming voice of a warrior echoed hollow in the water house. "Dinky, stop what you are doing?"

Tommy looked up from filling his squirt gun, and moaned, "Ahh, man."

McQueen grabbed Tommy's behind, pushed him up out of the pool, and dragged himself up to his feet.

The warrior stood in the doorway and looked at the green squirt guns in Tommy's and McQueen's hands. "Those are illegal green-virus sprayers." He pulled out his sidearm. "Drop them or I'll shot."

McQueen ran up to the warrior, held the barrel of the squirt gun in his face, and ordered him to: "Get out of the way!"

"Wanna a drink?" Tommy asked, and pumped the trigger on the squirt gun. Water streamed onto the front of the warrior's uniform. The warrior reached up and tried to shield his chest with his sidearm.

McQueen knocked the sidearm from the warrior's hand. Tommy pointed the squirt gun at the warrior's face. The warrior jerked his hands up and blocked the stream.

Tommy lowered the squirt gun; and squirting the warrior's groin, he asked, "What are you doing, peeing your pants?"

The warrior dropped his hands and covered below. McQueen squirted him in the face. With one hand on his face and the other on his crotch, the warrior ran out the door and went screaming down the road. "Virus-water! Get me to the decontamination chamber."

McQueen and Tommy dashed out the door. Another warrior, with his hand on his sidearm, blocked their path. McQueen shot water right into his face. The warrior took his hand from his sidearm, reached up, and rubbed his face. "Virus-water!" he cried. "My eyes! My eyes!"

Tommy shot water on the back of the warrior's hands. He dropped his hands and McQueen shot him in the face. The warrior turned. Tommy squirted water on the back of his head. The warrior ran after the other warrior. McQueen scrambled toward the forbidden forest. Tommy lagged behind, shooting streams of water back over his shoulder at anyone who cared to follow.

When they were deep into the forest, Tommy laughed and giggled every few feet.

They kept walking.

* * *

After a day, they had passed through Dinkies' agriculture fields, stopping only long enough to harvest a few things to eat. Then, avoiding housing authority hunters, they ran across open fields, walked in and out of forests, crossed old roads, and swam across a lake.

It was early morning when they stopped at the Patagonia Border. Partially obscured in the fog, an old wooden fence ran along the mountainous land. Many sawn-off round tree branches pounded into the ground created long lines of posts. Three rows of smaller round rods of wood telescoped across and rested on the posts. Missing segments in the fence had been replaced with single strands of

260

rusting barbwire. A Dinky with a giant food-harvesting basket on one shoulder and the long bent handle of a scythe balanced over his other shoulder, walked along its length.

Tommy jerked on McQueen's shirtsleeve. "When he gets close, I'll ask him if he knows where Augur is."

"You can't," McQueen said, and pointed at the fence line in the distance. "A border guard is coming up right behind him."

They eased back into the brush and crouched down. As if he were on his way to a party, the Dinky with the basket and the scythe happily walked past. A few seconds later, a border guard, with an ugly scar on his face, stomped up to the brush right in front of them and stopped. He bent over and talked to himself. "Damn, for a new boot that thing's tight." He untied his tight-fitting boot and retied it. "Dumb Dinkies can't even make a decent boot." He grunted as if he were mad at the world, and continued following the Dinky.

When the guard had disappeared into the distance, McQueen stood up and watched the fog beyond the fence. It hovered thick and white. It began to lift and revealed the land beyond the border. An expanse of green mountains had been terraced for the growing of food. Its rippled rows of plants resembled waves on a hilly ocean.

"There is no place we can cross here," McQueen said. "When the fog lifts, the guards will be able to see anyone for miles."

Tommy pointed to the right. "They might, but look over there."

McQueen looked to the right. Through the fog,

he could see a lone scrubby green and brown pine tree. It seemed to be struggling for life on top of a steep mountain of jagged stones. Below it, smaller surviving trees dotted the little valley; and like a hundred traffic cops, their scrawny branches pointed toward a lone pathway that ran through a dark-green growth of a forest. "We can't go that way," he said. "It looks like Ambush Alley."

Tommy nodded in agreement. "It does look like it could be a trap. But we've already wasted three days, and that's the fastest way across."

McQueen scanned the small passageway before him. "I don't think we have a choice."

Tommy's eyes moved from left to right scanning the area until they stopped and focused on the passageway. "We don't, but Freddy and I have gotten through there before. It's the way to the guarded chain-link fence at the border."

McQueen stepped to the wooden fence. "You mean this isn't the border fence?"

"It's just the start of the guarded border area."

McQueen put his foot on the bottom rail and lifted the barbwire. "The fog's lifting. Let's get going."

Tommy hopped through the opened fence. McQueen dropped the wire, stepped over it, and followed Tommy down the long stony path.

At the first big tree, McQueen looked back. "I think we made it," he said, and then watched a border guard step to the top of the mountain and stop under the scrubby pine tree.

"Keep walking," Tommy whispered. "He might not see us."

"I hope not," McQueen whispered back and

262

stopped. He looked ahead. Up close and beyond the trees, sharp rocks lined the narrow passage and only a few areas didn't go straight up. He shook his head. "This place is worse than I thought."

"It's not that bad," Tommy said as if he'd been insulted. "We have two choices."

"Yeah, we can go in or we can go out."

Tommy reached back and pulled McQueen by the hand. "Come on, have a little faith. We'll make it."

McQueen took one step. Rolling rocks rumbled above his head. A trickle of stones plinked down the mountainside, and a light dust rained down on his and Tommy's head.

"Avalanche!" McQueen cried, and sprang into a sprint. Tommy rushed after him, and they dashed into the thick cover of the lush forest. Behind them, boulders avalanched down onto where they had just been.

The voice of the border guard with the tight boots boomed from the trees on the left. "Border Patrol. Dinky! Halt where you are."

"Ahh, man," Tommy moaned and stopped.

McQueen crouched down behind a big tree. "Get out your squirt gun," he whispered. "I'll stay here. You can scare him right out of his tight fitting boots."

Tommy stopped in front of a wooden stick lying at his feet. "If that doesn't work, I'll throw this wooden stick at him."

The border guard emerged from the forest. Tommy held up one hand and placed the other hand with the squirt gun behind his head.

The border guard walked toward him. "Dinky,

stay right there," he ordered. "Don't move."

When the guard was three meters away, Tommy pulled the squirt gun from behind his head and opened fire. The guard stopped and shielded his face with his bare hands but didn't panic.

Virus water!" Tommy shouted.

The guard dropped his hands, crossed his arms across his chest, and smiled. "Not in Patagonia."

Tommy swooped his hand down and scooped up the wooden stick. Shaking it at the guard, he warned, "Wood virus! Stay away."

"Right," the guard said. "What do you think I am, stupid?"

McQueen noticed that the guard didn't have a protective suit. He must have known there was no virus. But he didn't know McQueen was standing a few feet away. If McQueen could get the guard to chase him, the guard wouldn't be fast enough to catch him and Tommy, too. If no other border guards were close, Tommy or he would make it across the border. It would be like the old days, when Tommy and he raced on foot. Tommy beat him sometimes, and he didn't let him do it on purpose. Some days Tommy could run really fast. McQueen hoped this is one of those days.

McQueen stood up and waved to the border guard. "Hey! Hey! You, big dummy. I'm over here."

While the guard turned toward McQueen, Tommy flipped his athletic body into midair, landed on his feet and took off running. McQueen lifted his arm and motioned to the guard as if he were leading a battle charge. "Follow me, you big dummy."

CHAPTER 23

Tommy dropped the stick, ran away from the border guard, and stopped next to a tree. A poison ivy vine was wrapped around the trunk. He reached down and snatched a piece of the vine up in his hand. Then he ran into a clearing, yipping, hollering, dancing, and kicking up sand with his little feet. When he looked back, McQueen was gone.

Tommy figured he had gotten over the border, and he would, too. No one had ever caught him. He wasn't going to let them do it now.

He jumped up and down and made faces at the guard. "Run, run, as fast as you can," he taunted. "You can't catch me. I'm the mutant man."

The border guard grunted like a big mad hog and chased him. Tommy stopped and turned. Whirling the poison ivy vine over his head, he threatened, "Wood-virus right here. How much do you want?"

The guard laughed. "We don't get poison ivy." He lunged for Tommy.

Tommy dropped the vine. "How about pee-water," he said, pulled out the squirt gun, and squirted a long stream of water into the guard's face.

The guard reached for his face, stumbled, and jerked back. Looking back over his shoulder, Tommy ran free. The guard wiped his face and smelled his hands. "You little asshole. It's just water." He sprinted after Tommy.

Tommy slipped behind a big tree and stopped. The guard turned in the opposite direction and walked toward where McQueen was standing. Tommy jumped out from behind the tree and yelled, "Over here, pee-face!"

The guard spun around and ran toward him. Tommy took off running. He ran down an embankment and though a small crick. On the other side, he slopped through a thick ooze of yellow mud and crawled up a little steep hill. At the top, his muddy feet slipped. He slid back down and flopped into the water and the yellow mud. The guard stood back and pointed to the steep hill. "Try it again, little dummy," he said and laughed.

Tommy started up the hill, again. Halfway to the top, he looked up. Another guard was standing at the top of the hill. With his legs spread and his arms crossed, the guard strangely acted as if he had all the time in the world to wait for Tommy to come to him.

Tommy realized he was trapped. "Ahh, man," he said out loud. "At least I gave McQueen enough time to get away."

He held up his hands in surrender. Off to his right, something moved.

CHAPTER 24

McQueen crouched in a clump of bushes next to the chain-link fence, staring through the diamond openings in the silver wire. The border was right in front of him. All he had to do was climb over the fence and be on his way.

He dropped one knee on the ground, turned, and looked across the road. At its edge yellow-mud coated a steep hill. Tommy was sitting in the middle of the mud. A border guard stood on top of the hill. Behind Tommy, at the bottom, another guard placed on hand on his hip and tapped his foot.

McQueen wanted to distract one of the guards so Tommy could get away, but behind any rock, tree, or brush pile, a guard could be watching and just waiting for him to try and help Tommy. If McQueen helped Tommy there was a better than average chance that he would be captured, too. It would make more sense to leave Tommy there. That way, even though Tommy was caught, one of them could still be free to find Augur. After all, Augur was a powerful Dinky. It didn't really matter what where they took Tommy, with Augur's help, he would be able to find Tommy no matter where they took him. He decided to climb the chain-link fence and cross the border.

He placed one hand on the fence and stopped. Why was he letting Tommy get captured? Augur probably could find him later, but why was he going to depend on someone he might not even find? McQueen felt like a helpless person waiting for a handout. He wasn't crippled. He didn't need help from anyone. He could help Tommy right now.

From his crouched position, in the clump of bushes, McQueen picked up a rock and threw it into a pile of dry sticks. The Border guards looked toward the pile, but they stood in place. The guard at the bottom of the hill walked toward Tommy. Tommy sat in the mud and squirted his squirt gun at him until it was empty.

Smiling a strange smile, the guard kept advancing. He looked like some kind of a freak. McQueen didn't know what any of these guards were like. There was no telling what they might do to Tommy. McQueen had to do something, and quick.

He looked at the border fence and at Tommy. Suddenly, he jumped up and stood in the middle of the road. "Hey, pee-face!" he shouted and waved his arm in a come here gesture. "Come and get me. I'm over here."

The guard at the top of the hill turned and ran toward McQueen. Tommy scrambled up the hill on his hands and feet. The guard at the bottom ran after him, but slipped back down into the yellow mud. Tommy climbed over the top of the yellow mud hill and ran for the border fence.

McQueen reached up, stuck his fingers through the diamond wires of the fence, and gripped. He placed the toe of his boot against the middle of the fence and pulled himself up. Reaching higher, re-gripped the fence, and pulled. The border guard grabbed him by the leg and held on. McQueen tried to pull his leg free. It wouldn't budge. He couldn't climb higher. He looked down over his shoulder. The border guard grabbed his other leg and held tight. McQueen tried to shake it loose. The guard held fast. He looked toward Tommy. He couldn't see what it was, but Tommy threw something. It sailed across the road and clunked in the center of the guard's back. The guard released McQueen's legs and grabbed his own back. McQueen climbed over the fence and plunked down on the other side. The yellow mud-covered guard, who had been at the bottom of the hill, ran across the road after Tommy; but before he could get to him, Tommy scrambled over the fence, jumped down, landed on the other side, and fell down. When he stood up, he turned toward the mud-faced guard, put his thumbs in his ears; and looking through the diamond wire fence, he waved his fingers at him.

McQueen yelled at Tommy, "Quit fooling around. Get out of there."

Tommy ran.

When he was next to McQueen, together they sprinted onto a path and into the forest.

Fifty meters down the path, another chain-link fence blocked their way. Tommy didn't hesitate. He climbed up the side of the metal fence and jumped down on the other side. He looked back through the fence at McQueen. "Come on, you big dummy."

McQueen placed his hand on the fence. A bullet zinged past his head. He ducked down and shouted, "Run, Tommy. I'll catch up with you later."

McQueen ran to the right. A group of guards stood in his path. He turned left. Another guard appeared. He turned away from the fence and ran back to where he had come from. Just before the first fence, at the edge of a small pond, he dove into a thick tangle of wet brush and weeds and sticks.

There was nowhere else to go. Under the cover of the weeds and sticks, with his eyes wide open and searching, he lay perfectly still.

Something moved in front of his face. He watched a little three-headed frog crawl up onto a little stick and stop. The head on the frog's left, hung down and off to the side. Its mouth was open and appeared weak. Sickening clear mucus streamed from it. The head on the right was solid and didn't move. Like lifeless wet stones, its eyes stared straight ahead and blinked as if they were on a timer. Its mouth was small and shut tight. It resembled some kind of a half-witted person. The frog wagged its center head around once and stared at McQueen. He reached out to bat it away. Something jabbed him in the back. Then, the crunch of a border guard's footsteps grew loud. McQueen drew his hand back, curled into a fetal position, covered his head with his hands, and waited for death from a poison antidote-bullet.

He had some comfort in the thought that his death wouldn't in vain. Tommy had gotten through, but he wished Danielle was by his side. He could have at least said good-bye.

CHAPTER 25

Danielle woke to the sound of a shovel banging on the dirt outside her cave room. It just had to be McQueen. He was back. She jumped up off the cot and banged her head into the low ceiling. She ignored the pain and ran a quick comb through her hair. Walking on her knees, she straightened her driver's uniform. Stopping at the door, she placed her hand on the curtain but didn't pull it aside. She wanted to jump into McQueen's arms and hug him forever; and she wanted to make the moment last; but she just couldn't wait. With love and happiness in her heart, she pushed the curtain back. McQueen wasn't there. Her heart fell into her stomach.

To make matters worse, the man at the door was Sludge. He was his usual dirty self, but this time he had his head down, stomping down the dirt floor in front of her cave room.

She took a defensive stance. "What are you doing?"

Sludge stopped stomping and looked up. "Just tidying up." He smiled a big exaggerated smile. "You don't mind, do you?"

Danielle wanted to tell him to go away, but decided to see what he was up to. "No, Sludge, I don't mind. I like neat things."

As if he were her boyfriend, Sludge stepped close to her. "The old Dinky got sick," he said, showing sad puppy dog eyes. "He ain't gonna be comin' around for a while."

Although she felt a little pity for Sludge, his rank smell overwhelmed her. She held her breath and backed away. He stepped next to her and

271

rubbed his dirty thigh against her knee. "You're not bad lookin' for a pig person." He looked at her rash. "You know that ain't poison ivy?"

She jerked her knee from his thigh. "What are you saying?"

"It's really the water-virus," he said, and pointed to her thigh. "You just got a natural resistance to it."

She picked up the paste that was on the little stand next to the cot. "But Tommy gave me this secret power to cure it."

Sludge scoffed at the paste. "That's junk. It don't do nothin'. It ain't gonna cure no virus. Your own body's curing it."

Danielle had doubts, but this old stinking sludge-bucket might know something she didn't. For a middle aged Dinky he looked old. If he didn't know something, he wouldn't have lived this long. She looked at her rash and then looked at him. "How do you know the powder doesn't cure?"

"Everybody knows the powder works like a phony sugar pill. I don't know why Tommy never told you the truth."

"Are you saying the powder is a placebo?"

Sludge's forehead wrinkled with confusion, but he shook it off. "It ain't something that's gonna make you see bows better," he said, and looked to Danielle for approval.

Danielle held in a laugh. The dummy didn't know what a placebo was. But she couldn't get him angry. If she did, he wouldn't tell her anything. "I'm glad you explained that," she said, and nodded her head in approval.

Sludge puffed up his chest. "Face it, honey,"

he said with self-importance. "They lied to you."

"Tommy and McQueen go back a long way. They have no reason to lie to me."

"Don't you know?"

"Know what?"

"With your immune wood-virus genes and my mutant Dinky genes, if we got together, we could make a super race of people. Everyone would be safe from all the viruses of the world."

Danielle knew Sludge wasn't making sense, but the whole virus thing didn't make sense either. She wished McQueen was standing by her side. Sludge was a stinking clod with more bull than a warrior on a weekend pass. He was probably trying to seduce her. But if she wanted to keep Sludge from getting angry and starting the revolt early, she had to be nice to everyone. "I don't think there is much chance of us reproducing," she said, and smiled. "When the time comes, my reproductive abilities will go to Johnny McQueen."

Sludge's face turned mean. "If that's the way you feel about saving the world." He raised his voice. "Then you can stay here and wait for him until you're an old maid."

Trying to keep her true feelings under control, she looked at Sludge with fawn eyes. "Why, Sludge," she said, and placed her hand on his shoulder. "I do believe you're jealous."

"You ain't nothin' but a virus resistant gene carrier."

She wanted to tell him to just go away, but in a sweet loving voice she asked, "Is a virus resistant gene carrier a bad thing?"

Sludge reached up and knocked her hand from

his shoulder. "Don't start gettin' smart with me." He growled. "Now that Tommy's gone, I'm gonna have ta take over da tunnel complex"

Danielle's voice took on a serious tone. "Are you going to wait for Tommy to come back before you start the revolt?"

"That depends on what happens."

"What are you trying to say?"

"I'll talk it over with the others. But I'm gonna tell you one thing. If I take charge, you're gonna be diggin' just like the rest of us. There ain't no free ride down here. We all have-tah work."

"I'm not afraid to work," Danielle said.

Sludge looked at her swollen hands. "Your rash is gonna be gone by tomorrow. If I'm in charge, you better git ready to git your clean uniform all dirty."

Danielle's voice lost its sweetness. "I can work without getting dirty."

Sludge reached down, unplugged the heater next to the cot, and tucked it under his arm. "Good, then you won't need to wash up, and you won't need this to dry off."

Danielle liked the heater. Without it, her cave room reeked of dampness. She didn't want him to take it. So, she tried to change his mind. "But how will I keep warm?" she asked with a sweet begging tone.

Sludge tightened his arm around the heater. "That's your problem." He turned his back to her and walked toward the curtain door. Holding the curtain open, he turned back. "Just be ready to git to work, first thing in the morning." He let the curtain fall behind him.

274

Danielle needed that heater to keep that moldy feeling off her body. She looked toward the floor in front of the curtain. The end of the heater cord was sticking out from under the curtain. She bent over and pulled the curtain open. When she stepped out, Sludge was outside. The heater she wanted was still under his arm.

In the most pleasing voice she could muster, she asked, "Sludge, would you please let me have the heater?"

He turned toward her. "Have you changed your mind about reproducing?"

She shook her head and didn't say anything. She put her back against the dirt side of the tunnel and slid down to a sitting position. A group of Dinkies walked down the tunnel and stopped in front of her. Sludge turned his back to her and motioned to the Dinkies with a wave of his hand. "Let's go," he said, and walked away. With the heater's cord trailing in the dirt behind them, the group followed Sludge and the heater down the dim tunnel complex.

Out of the darkness, Danielle heard Sludge say, "What's she doing here anyway?"

She wanted to call him a little creep. On the worst day or her life she could work anyone of their little butts under the table. She was no stranger to work.

She started to rise and banged her head on the ceiling. Dirt fell onto her shoulders and covered her head. Shaking it off, she knee-walked back into her cave room. She tried to comb the ceiling dirt out of her hair. It was useless. She had to wash it out. A long duck-walk or crawl to the water pool entrance

275

was next.

All she wanted to do was go to the pool, jump in, and rinse the dirt from her body. But Parry-Pervert would be on guard function status. She would have to keep her uniform on, but she knew she could pull the ropes and try to dry out with the drying fan.

If she weren't waiting on McQueen, she doubted if she could stay in the tiny room a minute longer. She wished she were back at her barracks room. She would be away from all the dirt and the filthy unorganized, so-called, tunnel complex. With the old Dinky down sick, she would have no one to protect her from the pervert, but maybe she could lower herself to his level. He could prove to be most entertaining. She had manipulated crude no-mannered warriors for years.

She walked down the mineshaft and slid the stone door open to the hidden cave. Parry-Pervert jumped off the little cot and walked up to her. "Are you going out?"

"No, Parry, I just thought I would take a dip in the pool to wash off a bit."

"Oh, you get them too?"

"Get what?"

"The itchies, I get them when I stay in one place too long."

Danielle looked at Parry. He looked like he hadn't bathed in years. She figured it was probably bugs or something crawling around under his filthy clothes making him itch. She stepped away from him. He followed her to the edge of the pool, and his putrid smell saturated her nostrils.

Like a dog panting with its tongue hanging out,

Parry asked, "Are you going to take your uniform off?" He paused and his face turned a light shade of red; but he hurried up, and said, "I'll turn my back."

Danielle looked down at Parry staring at her. If his eyes were as filthy as his body, his stare would burn a hole right through her body.

"I won't have time to take my uniform off," she said. "Tommy and McQueen should be back any time now. I want to go to the Chief Earth Officer with them."

"Didn't you hear?" Parry said with an increasing edge of warmness in his voice.

"Hear what?"

"I was out last night," he said, shaking his head in disapproval. "TV was on for a brief time. Nelson came on and said that Sergeant McQueen and his Dinky friend were surrounded. And that it would only be a matter of time before they were taken into custody."

Danielle didn't want to believe what she was hearing. "Are you sure?"

"As sure as I can be," he said, staring at her breasts." The old Dinky would have told you, but he's sick. I'm sure he passed the information on to Sludge. He'll tell you as soon as he sees you."

Danielle wanted to say, Nice try, you little creep. Sludge didn't tell me anything. Something is wrong here. But she needed to find out what it was. She decided to work on the little pervert.

She reached around her waist and pulled up her uniform shirt. Parry's mouth opened, and he stood like he was hypnotized.

"Can you stand guard while I take off my blouse?"

277

As if he didn't want to miss seeing a single thing, his eyes widened. His mouth dropped open, more. He didn't speak.

Danielle winked at him. "I just have to rinse off those itchies?"

"Yes, sweetie," Parry said. "Would you like me to sing for you?"

She cringed at the thought. "No, but thank you," she said, dropped down into the water, and took off her top. As if he weren't looking, Parry turned sideways. But she knew he still had a clear view of her.

She held her hands up out of the water. "Parry does my rash look like it's getting better?"

Parry ran to the cot, scooped up the lantern, and placed it on the stone wall of the pool. He turned up the orange flame. The room brightened and the water turned to a tangerine glow. Standing at the edge of the pool, he looked beyond her hands. In the new light, his eyes fixated on her neck and shoulders. "Yes, I think the rash is getting smaller."

She wanted the rash to be poison ivy and needed to know it wasn't the virus. "Then the cure is working?"

"Oh my, yes, it works every time," Parry-Pervert said. "But you know, if we all get killed in the revolt, the cure for the poison ivy will be lost."

Danielle wiped her hand with a washcloth and examined it. She held her hand up toward Parry. "It is just poison ivy, isn't it?"

Parry stretched his neck over the pool and looked closer. "I'm not sure. Sometimes they tell people things just to keep them at ease. They don't want them to get excited about turning into a

278

Dinky."

Danielle was brought up in Blue Town, she didn't know about those things. She began to have doubts. What if she didn't have poison ivy? Maybe these Dinkies were using McQueen. Maybe they were using her. If they didn't have a cure, McQueen and she would continue to mutate. They would shrink down to nothing. Maybe she did have the virus rash and the Dinkies had the cure. She paused and remembered that Parry had just said, "...if we all get killed in the revolt." Maybe it was a slip. Maybe Sludge and the crew were not going to wait. This little pervert was probably afraid to tell her the truth. Maybe she could work him some more.

She held the washcloth out toward Parry. "Parry could you take this and rub my back. I still feel those itchies you were telling me about."

With a delicate left hand, Parry took the washcloth. "Sure, anything for a beautiful lady like you."

Danielle turned her back to him. He stroked her back with the little washcloth.

"You're different from the others," she said. "Why do they treat you so badly?"

"They know that I am going to find the stones of life."

"How thoughtful of you. It will surely help the world."

"Sure it will, but it will help the person that finds them even more. When I find them, I'm going to sell them to the highest bidder."

Apparently Parry didn't realize that Dinkies were not issued money credits. They were slaves.

If they were issued money credits the corporation would lose some of the power it held over them. Sometimes a dream was the only thing a person lived for. She didn't want to spoil his dream. She smiled at him. "What will you do with all those money credits?"

"Me and some lucky girl will have total freedom to be ourselves. We'll never have to worry about where we'll sleep next. I'll make you the queen of my cave room. I'll never be stuck here on stupid guard function status again."

Wanting to get him to trust, her she lied, "I have seen the way the other Dinkies look down at you. I think it's just awful."

"I can fix all that," Parry said with happiness in his voice. "With those big credits, we'll be somebody. I'll sing on stage. When I'm a star, and I have you on my arm, the other Dinkies will be envious of us. I'll show them all."

"That would be nice," Danielle said. "But if everyone gets killed in the revolt, the credits won't do anyone of us any good."

Parry stopped stroking her back. "That's right. I'm not supposed to tell anyone." He looked around the cave room. "The old Dinky isn't sick. Sludge hid him in the tunnel complex. Right now he's gathering forces for the revolt."

Danielle jumped up out of the pool. Parry's eyes gaped wide open. She shook the water from her nude upper-body and put on her uniform top. "Parry, can you take me to the old Dinky?"

"I don't know where they took him," he said, stuttering. "Sludge will kill me if he finds out what I told you."

"We've got to do something to stop this revolt. I know McQueen and Tommy will get the antitoxin. They'll bring Augur back with them, but we need time."

"It's too late," Sludge said from the stone door.

Sludge's body odor wafted toward Daniel. She waved her hand in front of her face. "It's not too late," she said. "They'll make it back."

"They ain't gonna make it," Sludge said. "The TV just said they caught 'em. And they're bringin' 'em back. Nelson's gonna give them the antidote. Gonna do it on live TV."

The awful news and the extra-unwanted attraction of Sludge's stinking body invaded her sanity. Damn it. She had never liked walking around the stinking tunnels, bent over, living like a dirty Dinky. The little bastards were getting ready to revolt and she couldn't stop them. They would probably turn on her. If she were in her OvalCar, she could drive away from all the bullshit. But she didn't have her OvalCar. She didn't have anything in the stinking place. Somehow she had to save McQueen. She looked at the orange lantern light reflecting on the pool of water. She could dive in right now. All she had to do was hold her breath. But if she dove in and Sludge pulled the water tunnel switch, she would be trapped in the tunnel. She would drown. She would rather die than stay in the mine without McQueen. She took a deep breath. The stinking smell of Sludge and Parry had gotten worse. It entered her lungs like a disease. She wondered how anyone could smell that bad and still be alive. She turned her head away from them, breathed in deep, and dove into the water.

CHAPTER 26

Like a little kid playing hide-and seek, a voice sang out: "One-two-three on Johnny!"

McQueen slid his hands from his head, turned, and looked up. Outside the cover of thick growth of sticks and shrubs, Tommy's face appeared. A big ear-to-ear grin spread across his face. "Come on, Johnny, I found you. Get up."

McQueen wondered if a return to his childhood when Tommy and he used to play hide and seek was what it was like to be dead. He uncurled from the fetal position he was in and looked at his own feet. They weren't the dirty bare feet of a little boy. They were his warrior boot-covered feet of the present time. He was still alive.

He shook his head, cleared the thoughts of death, and looked up. Tommy was still there, looking through the sticks and shrubs. "Come on out," he said. "These guys are on our side."

McQueen crawled out of the shaggy mass of thick brush and sat on the ground. He felt something in his back. He reached back to pull out what he thought was an antidote bullet. To his surprise and relief, all he pulled out was a thorn. He let out a breath of air and looked up at Tommy. Two border guards in black uniforms stood next to him. A guard with weird eyes, one looking up and the other looking down, stuck out his hand. "My name's Frank," he said as if he were a long lost friend. "Glad to meet you."

Looking at the guard's crooked eyes caused McQueen's eyes to cross. He shook his head to stop them from crossing and looked at the extended guard's hand. "What's going on here?"

"We surprise a lot of people," Frank said in a most pleasing tone. "Most people don't know we live in harmony with the Dinkies. There is no separation here in Patagonia."

McQueen looked at Frank's face, but tried not to look at his crazy eyes. "Can you take us to your chief earth officer?"

"No problem," Frank said. "He sees people all the time. Auger and the CEO are in a conference as we speak."

Relief spread through McQueen's tense body. He took the guard's outstretched hand. "Well let's get going." He pulled himself to his feet. "We have a revolt to stop."

"I can see why," Frank said. "We had one heck of a revolt a while back. A lot of Dinkies got eliminated."

"A lot of warriors,, too," the other guard said. "It wasn't a pleasant sight. But Augur and the CEO fixed all that. We'all live together now."

Frank motioned with his arm. "Come on down to the road. We have called an OvalCar for you."

As soon as McQueen's feet touched the edge of the road, an OvalCar pulled up. McQueen and Tommy stepped in. The female driver shot an appealing look at McQueen. He looked back. She wore the same kind of uniform that Danielle wore, neat and crisp; and it clung to her vibrant sensual body. For a moment his blood thrilled with excitement. He did not want to think about Danielle, but he couldn't help it. He wagged his head from side to side and wondered what Danielle was doing now.

He looked in the rearview mirror. The driver smiled back at him like Danielle had done. His breath caught in his throat for a moment. He recovered and turned away. He did not want to encourage this driver's friendship. He wanted to be true to Danielle, but if she didn't want him, maybe someday he would consider another woman. But before he could even hope to enjoy the new sunshine of anyone's heart, he had to stop the revolt.

He stared out the window. Outside the moving OvalCar, beams of silver sunlight strafed the peaks of a range of bald-headed mountains. Just over a ridge and along the side of a dry lifeless hill, a stone-lined trail zigzagged up out of a huge garden that blanketed the valley below. In single file, Dinkies hunched under the terrible weight of huge crates of produce strapped on their backs and labored up the side of the steep hill. Dragging their feet as if they didn't have the strength or the energy to lift them, they created puffs of dust that grew into a continuous cloud that hovered around their knees like an endless filthy hedge. Strips of rags covered their mouths and noses and they didn't look happy.

"McQueen tapped Frank on the shoulder. "Those Dinkies are doing all the work. I don't see one pig person doing a thing to help them."

"That's right, you don't. That is the Dinkies' own personal garden. The pig people have their own gardens just on the other side of that hill."

"That isn't fair," Tommy said. "If the Dinkies and the pig people live in harmony then why are there two different gardens?"

"There doesn't have to be two different

284

gardens. The pig people can grow enough for everyone, but the Dinkies have farmed that garden so long they don't want to change."

Concern shown in Tommy's face. "Maybe it's because they know something the pig people don't know."

"Not really," Frank said, exhaling like he had said it all before. "There is not one bit of difference in the food the Dinkies grow and the food the pig people grow, but the Dinkies say their garden grows better food."

McQueen knew that when people became accustom to a certain way of doing things, no matter how much better or easier it would be for them to change, they always clung to ignorance and resisted. The Dinkies refusal to accept a better way of doing things that caused them unnecessary labor seemed to be true. As he watched the trains of unhappy Dinkies waggle up the hill, the OvalCar traveled down the long road. After the unpleasant parade of plodding Dinkies had faded from view, the sadness didn't fade from his heart.

When the car stopped, McQueen and Tommy stepped out and were escorted into Patagonia's main city building. At the front doors, McQueen turned to Frank. "Is this where Augur and the CEO are?"

They will be here any moment," Frank said, and his one eye slanted to the right. "Go on in. We'll get you cleaned up to meet them."

Tommy and McQueen were led down a long hallway and put into an offset space with no door and no windows. Two little reclining armchairs were arranged against the walls with an opened bathroom door between them.

McQueen pointed to a little wash up sink in the bathroom. "Do your people use water here?"

"Oh yes," Frank said. "After the revolt, that virus farce was done away with. Nobody uses dry clay anymore." He gestured to the sink. "Go ahead, wash up if you want."

"Thanks," McQueen said. "I need to get this mud off my face."

One of Frank's eyes looked toward the ceiling; and the other looked at the floor; but he gestured toward the reclining armchairs with his hand. "Have a seat while we check on the CEO's progress."

Looking at Frank's twisted eyes caused McQueen's eyes to cross, again. He shook his head to get rid of the cross-eyed effect, sat in a reclining armchair, leaned back, and motioned to Tommy. "I could use a wash up, but you can go first. I need a break."

"That mud pit just about did me in," Tommy said, and walked into the bathroom.

McQueen listened for the sound of water on Tommy's hands.

Tommy leaned out the doorway. "Somebody turned the water off."

Frank returned to the offset and stood three meters away from McQueen and Tommy. His face looked different, almost menacing. "There has been a change in plans. You won't get to see the CEO or Augur until after you have been quarantined for the specified period of time."

McQueen leaped up from the chair. "What are you talking about?"

Frank's mouth stretched into a smile so big it

seemed to be hurting his face. "It's just normal operating procedure. You two have to stay here until everything is checked out by the CEO."

McQueen wasn't going to waste time with typical, stretched out, governmental regulations and bureaucracy. "Come on, Tommy," he said. "We're outa' this no-water-stand." He walked toward Frank.

Frank held up his hand in a halting gesture. With one eye looking up and the other looking down, he shouted, "Stop! Right there!"

McQueen kept walking. Ziiiit! An electric shock jolted his body. His feet jumped off the floor and he flew backwards. Bam! He slammed into the reclining armchair. It shot across the floor and crashed against the wall. Tommy threw both hands into the air and yelled at Frank. "What are you trying to do? Kill him?"

"It's for your own good," Frank said, and one of his eyes twitched with upward movement. "Your friend just ran into the sanitizing shield. We can't let infected outsiders run around without being quarantined for a few weeks."

"We're not infected," Tommy said.

Frank held a piece of paper in front of his chest. With his eye twitching, he looked down at it. "CEO Nelson has just sent a message," he said, and his eye quit twitching. "It reads that you have been infected with a new strain of virus."

"You can't believe him," McQueen objected.

One of Frank's eyes looked toward the ceiling. "Nelson said you'd say something like that." His other eye looked down. "There is no need to be angry because you two have had a little spat with

287

Nelson."

"We didn't have a spat," McQueen said, shaking his head to uncross his own eyes. "Nelson tried to kill us."

"If that's true, why would Nelson be so concerned with your safety?"

McQueen didn't want to, but he couldn't quit looking at Frank's lopsided eyes. "He only wants to save me so he can kill me on national TV."

"No one wants to kill you," Frank assured him. "To me, it looks like your brain is showing signs of infection."

McQueen felt his eyes crossing again. He jerked his head and looked away from Frank's crooked eyes. "I have no infection."

Frank turned his head and assumed an arrogant posture. "The way you keep jerking your head makes me think you could be wrong."

McQueen didn't want to get Frank angry, but he wanted to speak out loud. He wanted to say: If you didn't have one eye that looks up like you're hunting squirrels and another eye looking down like you're hunting rabbits, I wouldn't have to keep shaking my head to keep from going cross-eyed. But he didn't.

"Frank continued. "CEO Nelson also sent information that many Blue Town warriors have been infected. We have been ordered to keep Blue Town warriors outside the containment border fence."

"Good luck on that one," Tommy said.

"We won't need luck. If they get through, they'll start an epidemic. We have been ordered to shoot them on sight."

288

"Tell it like it is," Tommy said." The only thing that's contaminated is Nelson's brain."

Frank jerked his finger toward them. "Look! You two," he said with a demanding voice. "Don't be troublemakers. We're on your side. We can't take a chance and spread the new virus into Patagonia."

"But we have to get out of here," McQueen pleaded. "A revolt is in the making. If we're not back in three days many lives will be lost."

"Rest assured, CEO Nelson would never allow that to happen."

"He won't allow it to happen because he doesn't know about it."

"Calm down, McQueen. If you have a legitimate reason to see the CEO, you'll see him."

"Send for him now," McQueen demanded. "Life and death is a legitimate reason."

"The CEO is in conference at the moment, but he and Augur will be down here first thing in the morning. He'll talk to you through the sanitizing shield."

"If he can't come, then get someone down here that can make a decision."

"Don't get excited," Frank said and lowered his head. "There is no need to panic. The CEO and Augur have everything under control."

McQueen stepped away from the shield, turned, and then turned back again. "They think they have everything under control." He jerked his hand sideways. "I'm trying to tell you, they don't know a revolt is about to take place."

Frank lifted his head and turned it to the right. "Oh, that," he said and smiled. "Danielle and

Freddy told us all about the revolt. They're on their way here."

Tommy jerked his head in Frank's direction. "Freddy can't be alive. I saw the bullet go right through his head."

Frank's crossed eyes opened wide for an instant, then he looked groggy, like a fighter that had taken too many punches. They couldn't have." He smiled. "That's our new scare bullet. It creates a bloody illusion, and it looks like the target's bones have shattered."

"It looked real to me."

"That's what the corporation designed the bullets to do."

Tommy lifted his hands and looked at them. "I had blood and bone fragments on my face and hands." He dropped his hands. "I don't see how anything could fake that."

Frank leaned against the concrete wall and crossed his legs. "Don't worry, Tommy, Freddy's alive. He'll tell you all about it. We have made arrangements for him to travel back to Blue Town with you. I'm sure you'll enjoy the ride."

"What about something to eat?" Tommy asked.

"Frank stepped away from the wall and smiled like a clown with goofy eyes. "Sorry, quarantine subjects are not allowed food for four hours."

Frank left.

McQueen paced the floor. "I hope he was telling the truth. We're running out of time."

"That's for sure," Tommy said. "Sludge won't wait for anything."

McQueen watched the evening shift of guards walking past the offset. They turned into a room next to the offset. Muffled voices came from just beyond the offset's wall.

McQueen pointed to the wall and whispered to Tommy, "Do you hear that?"

Tommy pointed to the bathroom. McQueen walked inside and Tommy walked in behind him. Tommy bent over and held his ear to the wall.

"Good idea," McQueen said, and leaned his ear to the wall, too. The guards talked about what they had done on their days off, who was screwing who, and who would be scheduled for midnight turn. It was the usual relief talk until Frank's voice hovered over all the rest. "We really pulled one off this time," he said.

Sounding like he really didn't want to know, a guard said, "What did you do this time, Frank?"

"Those two prisoners think Augur and the CEO share leadership."

The guard laughed. "Augur's still on the most wanted list. Who's stupid enough to believe anything like that?"

Frank giggled. "McQueen and his dumb Dinky believe it. We have strict orders to turn them over to Nelson alive. We fed them a cock-and-bull story and they walked right into the offset."

"You're getting so good at lying," the guard said, "that you're going to start believing your own lies."

Frank laughed a tee-hee laugh and caught his breath. "When they saw those dumb Dinkies hauling food up that trail they almost had me, but I lied right out of it."

"McQueen almost had the all-time capture record," the guard said. "What's Nelson want him for?"

"He's spreading the truth about the virus."

"Whoa!" the guard said with surprise. That's no good at all. The Dinkies in Blue Town are already causing Nelson trouble."

"It's a touchy situation," Frank said. "If the truth gets out, it'll upset the whole balance of the system."

"We can't let that happen," the guard said. "I don't want those dirty Dinkies demanding equal rights."

"We'll just have to kill a few more," Frank said, and they laughed and joked amongst themselves.

The guard quit laughing long enough to say, "That finger of death works wonders. It brings them right back in line."

McQueen wondered what twisted part of their human nature fed itself on the sufferings of defenseless Dinkies. He pulled his ear from the wall and walked out of the bathroom. Tommy straightened up, walked out, and looked at McQueen. "Now what?"

Hate and revenge filled McQueen's mind. But if he were going to escape, he had to keep a level head. "The plan's still the same," he said. "We have to find Augur and get the antitoxin. We'll play their little game until we can figure a way out of here."

Tommy crossed his eyes and looked directly at McQueen. "But first we'll have to learn not to look at Frank so we can keep our eyes uncrossed long enough to see straight."

CHAPTER 27

Under the surface of the pool in the secret cave, Danielle didn't have a facemask to provide air for her to breathe. For the first time in her life she was being forced to hold her breath, and for a long time.

Down, down, she sank, deeper and deeper. She glanced upward. The orange lantern light reflecting on the surface of the water was a distant glow. She wanted to turn back and rush for the surface. But if she did, Parry and Sludge would be up there waiting — waiting with their rotten breaths. Her first breath of air would be their stinking air. She didn't want to do that.

Sinking deeper, she felt for the tunnel opening, found it, and swished her body in. Pulling herself though the dark water tunnel, she told herself, that she could hold her breath just as long as any man. If Sludge closed the water tunnel gates, she would just have to drown. It would be better than being in that cave with that stinking Sludge and that sleazy pervert.

Danielle felt the dull edge of the slide gate at her ankles. It did not come down. She was almost out of the tunnel. But she began to panic. Maybe the lever had slipped away from Sludge's greasy hand. She told herself not to make jokes now. Maybe Sludge had deliberately let her go. Maybe he thought the warriors would take care of her for him. She needed air. She wanted to breathe. But no matter how difficult it was, she had to hold her breath. As she was about breathe in water she realized that it made no difference if she died from holding her breath or she breathed in water and drowned. She would be just as dead.

With her lungs painfully begging for air, she glided out of the tunnel. Light shone down from above. She placed her feet on the edge of the tunnel and pushed. She rushed for the surface. Just as she was about to stop holding her breath, she swished through the top of the water house pool and gasped in great gulps of much needed air.

After she caught her breath, she realized just how close she had come to dying. Shivering, she came to the conclusion that it had been worth it. She was out of that dirty stinking cave. But she began to have second thoughts about Sludge. He has been around a long time. He should know a lot of things. Maybe he was right. Maybe she was just a resistant gene carrier. If she was, then McQueen and she had an obligation to the world to reproduce. Their offspring will be virus free. They could save the world.

She looked around the water house. It was empty, no warriors.

If she didn't make some kind of arrangement with Nelson, McQueen was going to be executed. His death could mean that the future of the world would be as empty as the water house she was standing in. She really didn't have a choice. Walking out the water house door, she was so angry at McQueen for making her do something she did not want to do that she walked right into the poison ivy vine.

"Damn," she said out loud and swept the clinging vine away from her arm. McQueen should have never hooked up with the Dinkies in the first place. All he had to do was catch one more Dinky.

If he would have done that, at this moment they would be the talk of the corporation. They would have been granted the privilege of reproduction. Maybe they still would. When they bring McQueen back, he'll be on TV. If the virus is real like Nelson claims, then McQueen has a natural resistant gene that could be farmed. At the very least, McQueen and she should be allowed to reproduce for the good of the corporation.

She stepped onto the road and walked toward Blue Town. An OvalCar zoomed past and sent a cloud of dust into her face. She waved her poison ivy hand at the dust. It made it itch. Brushing the dust away with her other hand, she continued to walk and argue with herself. If Nelson was serious about saving the world, McQueen and her reproducing a superior race would be a good thing to announce in front of the whole world. But if the antidote kills, their virus resistant children would never be born. It would be a great loss to future generations. If McQueen was allowed to die, all would be lost. The virus would continue to control the world.

She stopped and sighed. I will surrender. It is the only way to save McQueen's future, my future, and the world's future. I'll tell Nelson about the revolt. For the good of the corporation, I'll tell all.

CHAPTER 28

There were no windows In the setoff where McQueen and Tommy were being held prisoner. The early Patagonia sun could not be seen. But when McQueen awoke, he knew it was morning. He had only two days to get back to Blue Town and stop the revolt. He jumped up off the reclining armchair, walked to the invisible, sanitizing-shield, and stopped.

Frank stepped up to the barrier. Like a jack-in-the-box, he bobbled his head and smiled like he had stolen a clown's smile and pasted it on his face. "Going somewhere?"

McQueen didn't look at his weird eyes. "Just waiting for Augur and the CEO," he said, and stared at the floor.

"Augur will be along any minute." Frank cupped his hand to his ear. "I think I hear him now."

Two guards walked into view. One carried two metal trays with covers in one hand, and the other guard carried a long rubber coated pole.

Tommy pointed to the pole. "What's that?"

"I'm sorry," Frank said with phony concern in his voice. "It's not Augur. It's your breakfast. If you stand back against the wall, we'll turn off the sanitizing barrier."

McQueen and Tommy stood back against the wall. Frank reached up and pulled down the handle to the switch that turned off the shield. But he kept his hand on it. One guard placed a tray on the floor. Using the long pole, he pushed the tray onto the invisible, sanitizing-shield. McQueen saw his chance to get outside the shield. He lifted his back from the wall and stepped toward the escape opening. Frank pushed the switch lever up. The tray sparked, flashed, and sizzled black.

Frank took his hand off the switch. Shaking his head, he giggled. "How did I know you'd do that?" He nodded his head with short jerks of taunting laughter.

McQueen glared at him. Frank's clown smile faded and his happy face changed to one of blatant arrogance and total authority, but his crazy eyes broadcasted some kind of weakness or a hidden flaw. McQueen searched them trying to find what it was, but Frank's crazy-crossed eyes caused McQueen's own eyes to cross. He looked away.

Frank raised his voice. "Way to go, McQueen. You just fried your food. If you don't want your buddy's breakfast well-done, keep your back against that wall."

Frank reached up on the side of the wall and pulled the handle to the shield's switch to off. The guard continued pushing McQueen's burnt tray. When he had pushed it past the invisible, sanitizing-shield, the other guard held the pole and pushed Tommy's tray into the offset. After he pulled the pole back, he leaned it against the wall. Frank turned the shield back on. McQueen looked at the burnt cover on his tray and then he looked at the clean silver cover on Tommy's tray.

"Enjoy your meals," Frank said, and he and the two guards left.

"You can have half of mine," Tommy said, and lifted the lid on his tray. It was empty.

With the toe of his boot, McQueen lifted the

cover on his burnt tray. Black bits of wood charcoal were scattered around the tray. "This isn't food," he said. "What's Frank trying to pull?"

Tommy tapped McQueen on the shoulder and pointed to the edge of the setoff wall. McQueen turned and looked. Frank was peeking around the corner. His head was shaking with suppressed laughter. When he saw McQueen looking, he jerked his head back.

"Looks like the old mind game," Tommy said. "The guards use it on the prison Dinkies all the time. They lie to them until they believe they are going to get something."

"Why would they mess with your food?" McQueen asked. "It isn't anything great."

"It doesn't have to be anything elaborate. They'll mess with food, pee in the drinking water, or change anything a prisoner needs or wants. It makes it impossible for a person to maintain a normal existence."

McQueen looked at the sanitizing-shield switch and at the waterless bathroom. "We couldn't maintain a normal existence if we wanted to. This whole damn place isn't normal."

"They're trying to work us back and forth," Tommy said. "If we let them, they'll make us feel extremes of despair and then extremes of hope."

McQueen slumped against the wall and dropped to a squatting position. "One little thing shouldn't make that much difference."

"It may take a while, but after time when you have nothing, one little thing could help you keep your sanity."

McQueen put his hands over his face and talked

into his hands. "I'm going crazy already."

Tommy put his hand on McQueen's shoulder. "You're not even close. When the guards have you believing that you are actually going to get something, and your hopes are high, then, and only then, they will take it away."

McQueen felt ignorant. Tommy had just told him something he should have already known. His mind went from puzzled disbelief to sudden comprehension. He dropped his hands from his face and looked up. "How could anyone be so rotten?"

"If they're up to their usual tricks, you haven't seen anything yet. If it goes on long enough, it reduces a prisoner to a level where his only function is a total struggle for survival."

"It looks like this is another world."

As if greeting an important visitor, Tommy smiled and lifted his hand into the air. "Welcome to the Dinky world." He dropped his hand and frowned. "Just don't expect anything. You'll be better off."

McQueen stood up and kicked the burnt tray of charcoal into the corner. It rattled and the top banged off. Pieces of charcoal flew across the white floor and skidded tiny black trails.

Then he sat on the edge of his reclining armchair and stared at the charcoal trails. He knew they had to escape, but he didn't know how. He looked straight ahead. They couldn't get through the walls. He looked up. The ceiling's was solid cement. The little hole for the light wires was the only opening there. He looked at the bathroom. Those walls were solid steel. The water was off in there. He had a little water in his squirt gun, but it wasn't enough to short the electric in the sanitizing shield. The only way out, was through the shield. He needed to find a way to turn it off.

He looked at the charcoal marks again.

As if he were announcing a supreme being, Frank's rugged voice boomed down the hall. "The Great Augur has entered the building."

McQueen stood up with a start and turned toward Tommy. "What's Augur doing here? Isn't he's still wanted?"

"Maybe they captured him?"

Frank appeared in front of the sanitizing shield with his hands behind his back. "Gentleman may I present the great Augur." Smiling his clown smile, Frank pulled his hands from behind his back. Like an offering to a God, he held an auger, a large spiral tool used to drill holes in wood.

Tommy's jaw dropped and his eyes widened.

With confusion and disbelief, McQueen asked Frank, "What the hell's the matter with you?"

Frank tilted his head to one side and shifted his weight to one foot. "Isn't this the great Augur?" He let out a big hee-haw laugh that rebounded around the set.

"Don't be a clown," McQueen said. "What kind of game are you playing?"

"It's the Dinky game," Frank said, and his smile faded. "This auger is just like the real outlawed Augur. This auger drills holes in wood. Augur drill holes in our orderly society. As a warrior, you should know that if the pig people and Dinkies are not controlled they will ruin our elite society."

A loud voice echoed down the hallway. "Frank, they're here."

Frank smiled extra big. "Your friends have arrived."

"Don't tell me," Tommy said. "You got some guy named Dan Nail and some Dinky named Freddy, right?"

Frank's forehead wrinkled and his one eye went wild. "No," he said. As if he had been caught in a lie, his face reddened. He recovered and forced a phony smile. "That's a good idea. Remind me to pull that on you tomorrow."

"What are you some kind of an idiot?" McQueen wanted to know. "Why would you want to tell someone his dead friend is not dead? Have you no feelings for you fellow man?"

Frank beamed triumphantly and laughed. "I have feelings." He spread his hands apart. "If I feel like doing something, I do it."

Tommy flashed Frank a look of disgust. "We already know that, Frank."

Frank leaned back and looked down at Tommy. "And just what makes you think you're someone special?"

"I'm not special. I'm only a man who feels sorry for you because you can only do what you're told to do."

Frank thought for a minute. Then, as if he didn't want the thought in his mind, he growled and turned to leave but turned back. "We shoot idiots like you every day." He jerked his finger at McQueen. "And, you! Please be more tidy. Clean up your breakfast. I don't know why you scattered it all over the floor."

Frank left.

McQueen sat on the end of the reclining armchair and placed his elbows on his knees. As he bent over and stared at the charcoal marks on the floor, Tommy walked over and stood next to him. "Got any ideas?"

"What if the current in that shield could be shorted out?"

"Better yet," Tommy said. "What if we could make Frank think it's shorted."

Maybe," McQueen said, reached over, and picked up a piece of charcoal. He dragged the charcoal across the white floor and drew a little black line. "That's it."

"What's it?"

"Just in front of the shield, we'll draw a line on the floor."

"That won't stop a thing. They'll just use that long pole and push the trays over it."

"It won't matter. We'll make the line just beyond the pole's reach."

"Then what?"

"We won't cross it. When they push the trays in, we won't pick them up. We'll say there is a short or something. And that every time we go over the charcoal line to get the trays, we get shocked."

A hungry look shone in Tommy's eyes. "What if it's real food?"

"We don't have time to eat. Even if we have to let the trays sit there for days, we've got to do it."

"Tommy rubbed his little stomach. "But I'm already hungry."

"Me too, but we'll just have to starve until we can convince Frank that the shield has a short in it.

When we get out, we'll have all the food we can handle."

Frank walked around the corner carrying a food try. "Here you go, boys, breakfast is served."

Tommy held out his hands. "I'm hungry. If it's real, bring it on over."

"Sure it's real," Frank assured him. "Why would you think any different?"

"I thought you were just here. But I guess I was dreaming."

Frank waved his hand in a shooing motion. "Stand back against the wall. I'll push it to you."

He pulled down the handle on the switch and stepped away. Then he took the pole from the wall and pushed the try as far as he could. "Enjoy your meal." He stepped toward the sanitizing shield switch, pushed it up, and left.

"What's he bringing us breakfast again for?" Tommy asked.

"It's like you said. Don't expect anything. There are no windows in this place and no clock. He's trying to make us lose track of how much time has passed."

"That's right," Tommy said, and looked at the solid walls. "With no windows, we won't know if they are feeding us three times a day or six times a day."

McQueen ripped a piece of cloth from his undershirt. "If we count the days by the number of meals they serve us, we'll never know what day it is." He picked up a piece of charcoal and blackened the piece of cloth. He pulled his reclining armchair until it was under the light. Then he stood on it and placed the cloth over the light tube. The light shined dim.

Tommy took a piece of charcoal; and just behind the trays, he drew a long black line across the floor. Then he held his hand over the tray cover, poised to lift it, and looked at McQueen. "Can't we take a few bites and put the cover back on?"

"Let's not chance it," McQueen said. "There may not be food under it at all. If there isn't, Frank will want us to lift the tray just so he can get his jollies off."

"I guess you're right." Tommy pulled his squirt gun out of his pocket. "I'm thirsty and I don't have any water left."

McQueen reached under his shirt and felt his squirt gun. "I'd let you have some of mine, but we got to save it for the line."

"Too bad Frank doesn't know about the squirt guns, he'd try to make a stupid mind game out of them."

"He can make all the games he wants," McQueen said. "We only have to win one."

The guards changed shifts. Time passed. Frank pushed more trays past the sanitizing shield. He peeked around the edge of the setoff wall a few times. In front of the black line, the trays piled up and sat on the floor, untouched.

McQueen and Tommy waited.

After a while, Frank's voice ranged down the hall. "McQueen! Tommy! Wake up!"

He appeared at the edge of the shield with another tray of food. "Here you go, boys. Lunchtime! I hope you enjoyed that last try of happiness I brought you."

"We would have," Tommy said, "but we can't

304

get near it."

"What are you talking about? All you have to do is bend over and pick it up."

"We tried," McQueen said and shrugged. "Every time we get close, we get shocked."

Frank's face twisted grotesquely. "You're crazy. Nothing like that's ever happened."

Tommy pointed to the charcoal line on the white floor in front of the pile of trays. "Well it's happening to us. We had to draw that line to show us where not to walk."

Frank studied the line. "There is no way you could be getting shocked."

"I'm no electrician," McQueen said and pointed up, "but this light looks dim to me."

"Even if we could get to the food," Tommy said, "we don't have enough light to see what we're eating."

Frank wrinkled his forehead and squinted at the light. "Maybe there's a short in the shield jumping power to the light."

Tommy gestured toward the pole. "Well, shove that food across the line so we can eat."

Frank held his hand on the handle of the shield switch. "You're going to love what I brought you this time."

"Push it over," Tommy said. "I'm hungry."

"Get back against the wall," Frank snapped. Keeping a wary on McQueen, he pulled the handle to the shield switch down. He stepped away from the switch, took the pole, and pushed a tray toward Tommy. The tray stopped just in front of the charcoal line, again.

Tommy stepped away from the wall and

stepped toward the line. Frank stepped sideways back to the switch, and without looking, he reached up, grabbed the handle, and turned the switch on. "Ah, haw! Too fast for you,"

Tommy stepped back against the wall.

Holding onto the pole with one hand, Frank used his other hand and pulled the switch handle down. Then he pushed another try. When the tray neared the charcoal line, Tommy waved his hands like he was cheering for a turtle in a turtle race. "Come on, Frank, push. You can do it, just one little push."

Frank didn't push the tray. He pulled the pole back. The tray was still not over the line. He stepped sideways to the switch, and again, without looking; he reached up, grabbed the handle, and turned the shield back on. "Sorry, boys, I'm not buying your great short story. I know you can reach those trays."

Tommy bowed his head in submission. "Thanks anyway, Frank." He slumped into his reclining armchair.

Shaking his hand next to his ear, Frank said, "Any time," and left.

McQueen turned toward Tommy. "What are you doing? You act like he's your best friend."

Tommy cast a bewildered stare toward McQueen. "Didn't they teach you anything in warrior school?"

"Not these games you're playing."

"If I get Frank used to a certain pattern, he'll let his guard down. And I can't get him used to anything if he thinks I hate him."

"Love thine enemies," McQueen said. "That is

something I may have seen on the stones of life."

"I don't know about that. But the next time he comes, follow my lead."

"You want me to cheer him on?"

"Sure, those kinds of people are suckers for attention. The more they get, the more important they feel."

"If it'll help get us out of here, I'll feed him attention until he swells up and explodes."

Tommy reached up and scratched his right ear. "It's eight o'clock."

"How do you know that?"

"Every night at eight o'clock, my right ear itches."

McQueen glanced around the room. "We only got a day and a half to get back."

Tommy looked into McQueen's cold calculating eyes. "Maybe Sludge canceled the revolt."

"I doubt it." McQueen looked toward the hallway. "I wonder when Frank will be back."

"It shouldn't take long. He must have something under those trays that he wants us to see."

McQueen lay back on his reclining armchair. "He reminds me of a kid who likes to pull the wings off of insects and poke them with a needle just to see them jump." He looked at the charcoal line and at his feet. "Hey, Tommy, you think it's time to move the line?"

"Frank probably doesn't know a thing about depth perception. Let's try it."

McQueen watched the edge of the setoff wall to see if Frank was peeking. He wasn't. Tommy squatted down on the floor and rubbed the line. It smeared all over the white floor. McQueen reached into his shirt and took out his squirt gun. "Here, Tommy, use this."

Tommy took the squirt gun, squirted the end of his shirttail, and used it to wash off the charcoal line. McQueen bent over, redrew a new line, further back, and moved the trays in front of it.

Brushing the charcoal off his hands he winked at Tommy. "All we have to do now, is wait."

Tommy lay down on the seat of his reclining armchair and curled into a ball. McQueen leaned back in his reclining armchair and they both went to sleep.

Zzziit! The sanitizing shield zapped something. McQueen woke up. Frank stood on the other side of the shield with another tray. If you boys don't eat up, I'm going to stop bringing your food."

"We'll eat anything you have," Tommy said. "Just push it to us."

"Get against the wall," Frank ordered.

McQueen and Tommy stood against the wall. Frank turned off the sanitizing shield, stepped away, put the tray on the floor, and pushed it with the pole. The tray stopped short of the other two trays. It wasn't even close to the new line. Frank pulled the pole back and turned on the shield switch. "Enjoy your lunch," he said, and turned to go.

McQueen lay back in the reclining armchair and nonchalantly laced his hands behind his head. "If we don't get something to eat," he said loud enough for Frank to hear, we'll be in no shape to go on TV with Chief Earth Officer Nelson."

Frank turned back and faced them.

"Yeah," Tommy said. "It'll look pretty fishy when we show our starving faces on the big national TV screen."

"Yes, but that will be okay," McQueen said. "It'll show Nelson and the world how we were treated."

Tommy looked at Frank with pleading eyes. "Yes, and I'll tell the whole world, that our good buddy, Frank, was afraid to give us a decent meal."

Frank turned around and looked into the offset room. "You're not bringing my name into this."

"Gee, Frank," Tommy said. "It's not our fault you can't stretch far enough to push a single tray to us. You must be tired. You didn't even push this one as far as the others."

"The least you could do is push one tray so we could get it," McQueen said, and waved his hand in the air. "But it doesn't matter. Nelson will take care of everything."

Frank reached up and held his hand on the handle of the switch. "All right, all right," he said. "Get up against that wall."

Tommy and McQueen leaned against wall.

Frank smiled a mischievous grin, pulled the shield switch down, stepped away, and pushed the pole toward the tray.

McQueen figured Frank was going to push the tray next to the other trays. And that he knew there was no short and that he has enough time to get back to the switch. He was just trying to pull off another mind trick.

Watching the pile of trays, Frank pushed the lone tray toward it. He stepped over the sanitizing shield line. Tommy started to cheer. "Come on, old buddy, you can do it."

McQueen joined in. "Come on, Frank, we're hungry."

Frank pushed the tray next to the pile, stopped and began to laugh. McQueen flew from the wall. Frank jumped sideways. Without looking, he reached up for the handle of the switch. It wasn't there. His depth perception was off. He had stepped too far into the offset. The switch was behind him. Before he could back up and pull the switch, in one swift motion, McQueen tackled him around the legs. Then he rammed his shoulder into Frank's stomach. Hurumph! Frank let out a painful gush of air. Using his shoulder, McQueen picked him up.

Tommy ran past the sanitizing shield and held his hand on the switch. With Frank gasping for breath, McQueen held him on his shoulder and looked back at Tommy. "You ready?"

"If you got a second," Tommy said, with a hungry look in his eyes, "let's find out what's under those trays."

McQueen looked at Tommy with disbelief. Holding Frank, he kicked over the trays. More charcoal spilled across the floor. Frank grunted for air, waved his arms, and tried to kick his legs free. McQueen staggered, but he held onto Frank's jerking legs and looked at Tommy. "Can we go now?"

Tommy held his empty stomach with disappointment. "Come on." He placed his hand on the handle of the switch. "I'll throw it."

McQueen threw Frank on the reclining armchair and ran across the sanitizing shield. Frank jumped up and staggered after him. Just as McQueen cleared the shield, Tommy pointed at Frank. In abject disbelief, Frank tried to skid to a halt, but his jaw dropped and his eyes widened.

"Ah, haw!" Tommy jeered. "Too fast for you." He pushed the switch handle up. Zzziit! Frank flew back against the wall and fell flat on the charcoal-covered white floor.

Tommy stopped at the edge of the setoff wall, peeked back at Frank, and waved at him. "Enjoy your meal."

McQueen grabbed Tommy by the shirt and pulled him away from the wall. They ran down the hall. A guard at the door was absent from his post, but he had left a sandwich on his little desk. Tommy stopped and picked it up. McQueen turned back, grabbed Tommy by the seat of the pants, pointed him to the exit, and they ran out the doors.

CHAPTER 29

Somewhere in Patagonia, up ahead, military OvalCars prowled along the murky road. Tommy and McQueen leaped off opposite sides of the road and burrowed deep onto the cover of the dark foliage. Long scythes of light danced over Tommy's head and cut away the concealing nocturnal night. Watching the lights behind him, Tommy crawled further into the dark. Clunk! His head banged into the trunk of a small tree. He grunted in pain, grabbed his head, and rolled onto his back. Rubbing his head, he looked up. For a brief moment the branches of the tree shook and rustled. Out on the road, the OvalCars stopped. Their spotlights fixated on the tree he had banged into. Tommy jumped up and ran from the light. His shoulder crashed into another tree. He stepped to the side, went around it, and tripped. He hit the ground with a dull thud.

He stopped breathing and listened. Doors opened. He raised his head up just enough to see. With sidearms drawn, border guards jumped out of OvalCars and ran along the shoulders of the road. Like it was a training exercise, each one stopped at a predetermined place and formed a firing line. With itchy fingers on triggers, they aimed in Tommy's direction.

Tommy breathed slow and silent. A spotlight crept closer. He stood up and ran. A revealing slice of light nipped his shoulder. He stopped running and ducked down. He hoped they hadn't seen him. If they had, he wouldn't have time to escape the barrage of poison antidote bullets they would dispatch his way. He scanned the dark area just in front of him. More lights danced closer. A tingling edge of fear swept over him. From his crouched position, he leaped to an island of high dew-covered grass, flattened out, and waited.

The border guards in the OvalCars continued working the lights. Just over his head, white beams danced along the tops of the green grass. He knew they were searching for something the guards could shoot. He was glad he was a small target.

Without warning, a series of shots cracked the silent night. Sparkling yellow incendiary bullets went whizzing into the night. Like fabulous fire-spitting candles, they spun and sent down showers of orange sparks that landed all around him and fizzed out in the wet grass. Somewhere from the road, as if it were some kind of great show, someone went, "Awww!"

Tommy didn't move. The concealing dark returned. Then another sparkling series disrupted the dark. He waited and watched.

The shooting stopped. Silence filled the air. Muffled voices wafted through the night.

"It won't burn."

"It's too wet."

"If they're in there, we'll never burn them out."

Tommy breathed a sigh of relief. The wet grass had stopped the incendiary bullets form setting the grass on fire. He wanted to see what the border guards would do next, but he didn't dare poke his head up over the grass. He was shivering. He didn't know if it was from the wet or from the fear. It didn't matter. He waited and he listened.

From the line of border guards, more bursts of

bullets flashed and streaked new orange trails into the black night. Then one border guard yelled, "Shift change, we're outta here."

Amidst a roar of laughter, the searchlights went out. The military OvalCars hummed away.

Tommy couldn't believe how lazy the border guards were. Instead of staying and looking for him and McQueen, they felt it was more important to quit and let the next shift take over. He stood up, walked out of the grass and onto the road. Now, he couldn't find McQueen. He hoped they hadn't shot him.

With time nibbling the night away, he trotted across the road and searched the darkness. The tops of the tall grass that lined the road all looked the same. If McQueen was in there, he could be anywhere. Suddenly, in one little spot, the tops of the grass jerked. Tommy stepped off the road and walked toward the movement. When he parted the grass, McQueen was in front of him, squatting as if he were a hunted animal hoping the bloodhounds wouldn't find him.

Tommy crouched down beside him. McQueen let out a sigh of relief and patted him on the shoulder. "When those border guards blasted everything in the dark I thought they had you."

They walked out of the wet grass and down the dry road. Up ahead, set back on well-manicured yard of blue grass, a blue light lit the porch of a little stone house.

"Time's running out," McQueen said. As soon as we catch our breath, we'll go to that house and talk to the Dinkies."

"What do you mean?" Tommy said and

stopped. He was surprised that his voice was almost whining. He regrouped himself and repeated, "What do you mean, *we'll* go to that house?"

McQueen didn't pause or miss a beat. "You're a Dinky. With you by my side we should be able to find out where they're hiding. We have to find Augur before Sludge starts the revolt."

Tommy looked up at him. "You'll have to stay here."

"What do you mean, I have to stay here?" McQueen asked. "This is it! If we have to check every house we see, we're going to find Augur." He waved his arm and took a step toward the house. "Let's go!"

Tommy didn't move. He knew, with McQueen's big tall body standing next him, there wouldn't be a Dinky in Patagonia who would come near him. He wouldn't be able to get a scrap of information. He reached up and grabbed McQueen's elbow. "Wait," he said. "Your warrior reputation is known everywhere."

McQueen pulled his elbow away from Tommy's hand. "So what? We still have to find Augur."

"If the Dinkies see you, we won't find out a thing."

McQueen stopped walking. "I guess you're right." He let his hands drop to his sides. "But I don't want to stand here and do nothing."

"Do a mental hide and seek like we used to do when we were kids."

"Like we used to think of places each other would be hiding before we went looking?"

"It might save a lot of leg work."

"It was just kid stuff," McQueen said, paused, and reconsidered. "But sometimes it worked." He turned toward the grass at the side of the road. "Maybe Augur's hiding in a cave protected with water, or maybe in a wooden cabin." He lifted his hand with one finger in the air. "Or in a place surrounded with poison ivy."

Tommy turned toward the little stone house across the road. "Stay here and watch for the next shift of border guards. I'll go knock on the door."

McQueen crouched down in the grass. Tommy walked across the road and into the blue light of the house. He rapped on the plastic door. The blue light shone down on him and dimmed his vision, but he could still see a wink of movement behind the house. He turned his back to the light and searched the darkness. Like a fleeing rain cloud, the shadow of a Dinky raced across the blue grass and vanished into the night.

A Dinky with dirty ripped shirt opened the door. "Yes?"

Hello," Tommy said, and extended his hand. "I'm Tommy. I'm looking for Augur."

The Dinky stood in the doorway and wrung his hands. "There is no one who lives here by that name." He shifted his feet. "You must have the wrong house."

"Augur is the king of the Dinkies. Maybe you know of him by another name."

"I have lived here for years," the Dinky said, and looked back over his shoulder. "I have never heard of any king Dinky."

"Are you sure?" Tommy asked. "It is

important that I see him. Many lives are at risk."

The Dinky quit wringing his hands and stood still. His eyes narrowed into a frigid stare. "Don't tell me how many lives are at risk." He stepped toward Tommy and raised his voice. "My brother and all his friends were killed in that last revolt."

"I understand how you feel. But couldn't you give me at least a scrap of information."

The Dinky put his hand on the door and reared back to slam it. He hesitated, exhaled and closed it halfway. "You don't understand how it is," he sobbed. "We just don't need your kind coming around here starting trouble."

"But I'm trying to prevent trouble."

The Dinky's voice took on a cautious sound, and he whispered, "I can't give you something I don't have."

Tommy knew the little Dinky behind the door wanted to tell him something, but he was afraid. "You can talk to me," Tommy said. "I'm not with the corporation."

The Dinky closed the door until it was only open a small crack. "We have to work the fields early in the morning. If you don't get away from me, I'll call the border guards."

Tommy thought about getting McQueen to come out of the grass. He could tell this guy he's hunting for an escaped Dinky. He could threaten to capture him if he didn't talk. "If you call the border guards," Tommy said, "I go get a warrior and make you talk."

The Dinky squinted. "Go right ahead."

A voice from inside the house called out. "The border guards are on their way."

"You didn't have to do that," Tommy said, and ran away from the house.

CHAPTER 30

McQueen stood in the shadows along the edge of the road and watched Tommy. Tommy scampered across the blue lawn of the Dinkies' stone house, crossed the road, and stopped in front of McQueen. McQueen looked down at him. "What did you find out?"

"Nothing. They're afraid of something. They called the border guards. Let's get out of here."

Tommy started to walk away from the road and into the tall grass. McQueen reached out and grabbed him by the shoulder. "Don't be in such a big hurry."

Tommy shrugged McQueen's hand off his shoulder. "I don't know about you, but I don't need any more of Frank's food service."

"Don't get excited," McQueen said and smiled. "The border guards are not coming.

Tommy put his hands on his hips. "And just how would you know that?"

McQueen let out a giggle. "All phones are controlled by the corporation. Warriors, pig people, and Dinkies are not allowed to have phones."

Tommy hit his own head with his palm. "I must be losing my mind. I knew that. And if they were allowed to have phones, it wouldn't matter. Those things never work anyway."

McQueen looked toward the grass in front of the house. "Did you see that Dinky run across the grass just before you knocked on the door?"

"Just for a second. That blue light from the house took my night vision away."

"Why do you think he was in such a hurry?"

"He's a Dinky," Tommy said in hushed tones. "Maybe he saw you and didn't want to be your five-hundredth capture."

"Maybe, but he ran into that thicket off to the right. Let's check it out."

McQueen stepped off the road. Oncoming lights flashed in the distance. "Something's coming."

Tommy jumped into the tall grass. McQueen stepped next to him and crouched down. A military OvalCar with bright lights zinged past and was gone.

McQueen stood up and looked at Tommy. "You still think they called the border guards?"

"Don't rub it in," Tommy said, and they walked down the road until they were out of the blue shadows of the stone house.

The moon slid out from behind a cloud and lit the area with gray-night light. Tommy and McQueen stood at the edge of the road and looked at field of green grass.

"Those people in that house must know something," McQueen said. "That Dinky that ran across the blue grass didn't even slow down when he ran into this green stuff."

Tommy crashed through the tall weeds at the side of the road and onto the field of green. "Let's see where he went."

"Not so fast," McQueen said, and Tommy sloshed his foot right into a soft mud hole.

"Ahh, man!" Tommy held out his hand. "Pull me out."

McQueen grabbed his hand and pulled. Tommy's little foot sucked free and came up out of the mud. McQueen looked across the field. Moonlight brightened little imprints of mud holes scattered all over the field. "It looks like these things were dug for a reason.

"Maybe someone with a higher intelligence than pig people?"

"No necessarily. Maybe it was just someone trying to keep people away."

"Maybe they invented a fake mud-virus."

"I wouldn't doubt it," McQueen said, and walked into the tall grass. "Where there's mud, there's water."

"That's true, and by the way," Tommy said and mischievously giggled.

Splat! McQueen stepped into a small stream of water.

Tommy laughed. "There's water right in front of you,"

McQueen let out a little laugh. "Thanks for telling me before I stepped in it." He lifted his foot and started walking upstream. "Come on, Tommy, we go to quit foolin' around. Let's follow this thing."

Sloshing in and out of the twists and turns of the little stream, Tommy followed. "The way this thing curves," he said, "it looks like a barrier to keep the water-virus-believers out."

They kept walking. The little stream grew into a creek and then branched off into a full-fledged fast-flowing river.

"Talk about a water barrier," Tommy said, "this is the granddaddy of them all."

McQueen pointed to a stretch of soft mud along the riverbank. "Look! Dinky footprints."

"Must be that guy who ran from the house."

They kept walking. The river widened and flowed slow and easy. They stopped and looked up. In the silver moonlight, an old bridge spanned across the quiet river. At the other side, it was blocked with a big, avalanched mountain of yellow dirt.

Looking at the bridge, Tommy shook his head. "No OvalCars are going to drive across that thing."

McQueen looked at the washed out road leading to the old bridge. "They wouldn't even get close. This is no longer a road."

Tommy pointed at the bridge. "Look at those old rivets. They run all the way up the side of that slanted I beam."

"The way the paint's worn smooth," McQueen said. "It looks like someone uses them for toe-holds."

Tommy stepped to the slanted I beam and ran his finger across one of the humped rivets. He held his finger up and looked at McQueen. "Looks like yellow dirt."

"I think someone just climbed up there."

Looking up, McQueen shielded his eyes with his hand as if he were saluting. "That moon is dim, all I can see from here is a mountain of dirt, and it's the same color as the dirt on your finger."

Tommy placed his hands under the I beam. "Maybe we can get a closer look." Using the rivets for toe-holds, he climbed to the top where he turned and shouted down at McQueen. "Come on up you big dummy."

McQueen smiled, shook his head, and climbed up the I beam. Together, on the top beam of the bridge, they balanced-walked to the other side of the span and stopped at a big stone on a little ledge.

McQueen scraped his foot across the dirt. "This stuff's packed pretty solid and it leads under that rock."

Tommy ran his foot across the dirt. It didn't move. "This is a heavy traffic area, but how do we get behind that rock?"

"Maybe you don't."

"Maybe it's just a bluff to throw the border guards off."

McQueen studied the ledge. Look here," he said, and bent over. He brushed the ledge with the side of his hand. "This rock is solid and there's no dirt or dust on this one little spot." He looked down into the water below. "It looks like it's kept that way to keep little feet from slipping when someone dives into the river."

"Tommy walked to the edge of the ledge and looked down. "This might part of a good ploy. When the border guards chase someone, they can taunt them into coming up here."

"But if they did," McQueen said, "they could just dive into the river after them."

"Those big border guards are gutless. They would never do that."

McQueen looked down into the dark water below. "You're probably right. It's too high."

"Looks okay to me," Tommy said. "You going in?"

"Ahh, come on, Tommy, we don't know what's in that river. It could be a trap. There could be a big sharp rock just below the surface."

"You said we didn't have much time. I think

it's pretty obvious that they use this for a diving off spot. Maybe there is a water tunnel just below the surface."

"Don't be stupid. If you dive in, you'll be no good dead."

Tommy stepped to the edge and looked back at McQueen. "Have a little faith." He flexed his knees. "Dying's not an activity I'm ready to try. And anyway, I'm not diving. I'm jumping."

McQueen reached out to catch Tommy. Tommy jerked away from his swishing hand and jumped off the ledge.

McQueen watched Tommy's little Dinky body sail downward. It blurred and crashed into the moonlit gray river below. A mushroom of white water exploded up out of the river.

"Damn it, Tommy," McQueen yelled. "If you're still alive I'll going to come down there and drown your little ass."

Tommy's little round head bobbed up and he looked up at McQueen. "Come on in, you big dummy. Let's look for a tunnel."

McQueen shook his head in disbelief. "Oh well, if he can do it, I can too."

He stood on the ledge and flexed his knees to jump. Behind him, the stone screeched. He turned and stepped back from the edge of the ledge. The stone moved again. He looked through the opening and into the black behind the stone. Two little gold eyes glowed.

When he took a step toward the stone, it screeched shut. Leaning over the ledge, he yelled down to Tommy, "Come on back up, you little dummy. It's up here."

324

"It figures," Tommy said, sloshed next to the shore, and looked down. A little wooden penny whistle with little finger holes, stuck up out of the mud. Tommy picked it up, put it into the water, and swished the mud off. Tweet! He blew on it once, put it in his pocket, and climbed up the I beam. At the stone, he stood next to McQueen.

McQueen gestured to the stone. "Okay, how do we open it?"

"Maybe we could get a stick and pry it open."

"I think it's too heavy for that. There has to be another way. Those Dinkies aren't that big, and this thing is too heavy for twenty warriors to move."

"Are you sure it opened?"

"I'm positive." McQueen pointed to the ground just beneath the stone. "Look here."

Tommy looked.

McQueen waved his hand over the spot. "See, the dirt has just been moved away at the bottom."

"That doesn't prove anything."

"There's something behind that rock. I saw its little eyes."

Tommy sat down on the ground next to the ledge and crossed his little legs. "Let's think about it for a moment." He took the penny whistle out of his pocket. "This whistle had to be down there for a reason. Maybe there's a code."

"Morse code?"

"Maybe," Tommy said, and held the whistle next to his lips. "We don't know how far your father's teachings traveled."

"If it's Morse code, you got the key right in your hands."

Tommy put the penny whistle to his mouth and

stopped.

"Go ahead," McQueen said. "Try the name Augur."

Tommy blew Morse code on the whistle. "Di-dah, A. Di-di-dah, U. Dah-dah-dit, G. Di-di-dah, U. Di-dah-dit, R."

McQueen stared at the stone. It didn't move. "That's not it. Try something else."

"Let's keep it simple," Tommy said. "I'll try open." He high-noted the Morse code for open. "Dah-dah-dah, O. Dit-dah-dah-dit, P. Dit, E. Dah-dit, N."

The stone moved a centimeter and stopped.

"Try another word," McQueen said.

"This is crazy," Tommy said, and blew, "Cuck-oo."

The stone opened a half-meter and stopped. McQueen dropped to his knees and squeezed in behind the rock. Tommy stood up and followed. Inside, five meters from the stone door, a little lantern burned. McQueen's eyes followed ropes that were attached to the stone door and ran down the side of the wall. Pulleys and gears, set in the stone wall, screeched and groaned. Behind them, the stone door screeched shut.

The patter of little feet thudded in the air. A herd of Dinkies rushed out of the darkness and surrounded them. McQueen placed his feet under himself, switch to a crouching position, and threw up his hands up to surrender. Blap! His hands smacked against the low stone ceiling. He jerked them in front of himself. With his palms toward the Dinkies, he said, "We come in peace."

One Dinky stood above the rest. His thin

326

reddish-blond hair was filthy. His watery brown eyes crinkled at the corners. His skin, that wasn't caked with dirt, had the look of aged leather. Except for a yellow ring around his neck, his hard body was covered with wrinkles and carved lines that revealed he had spent many years in the sun. And even though his muscular back was bowed, he walked with the air of boyish ignorance.

Tommy pulled on McQueen's shirtsleeve and whispered, "He looks like Sludge's twin brother, but he's black."

Sludge's twin spoke up. "How can a warrior come in peace?"

McQueen didn't answer. He was amazed. Just like Sludge, when this Dinky talked, his mouth looked like it had a fat night-crawler hanging down the side of his mustached mouth; and it moved and jerked with each word.

Another Dinky spoke up. "I never heard a warrior tell the truth yet."

Sludge's black twin held his fist in the air and faced the crowd. "Throw the chains on them."

Like working ants, the Dinkies overwhelmed McQueen and Tommy and clanked chains around their hands and necks. Sledge's twin slammed a shackle around Tommy's ankle. Tommy grimaced in pain. "Take it easy, Sludge. I'm one of you."

Sludge's twin brother looked up and scowled. "My name ain't Sludge. It's Yellow Neck."

Tommy flashed Yellow Neck a mocking big grin as bright as sunshine. "You could have fooled me."

Staring at Tommy, Yellow Neck's face took on a puzzled look. "You tryin' to be funny?"

"We're not trying to be anything," McQueen said, and held his chained hands in front of himself. "Take us to Augur. We have important information for him."

A Dinky cried out from amongst the crowd. "It's another warrior lie. Watch out for a trap."

Yellow Neck turned his back to McQueen and pointed down a long mineshaft. "Take them to the chamber," he ordered, and McQueen saw the back of his neck. It had a roll of yellow fat that looked like a mouth.

The Dinkies tugged on the chains like dogs pulling a sled. "Take it easy," Tommy said. "We'll go anywhere you want."

Yellow Neck walked behind McQueen, kicked him in the back of the calf muscle and laughed. "How do you like me now?"

From his crouching position, McQueen dug his heels into the dirt and yanked on the chains. The tugging Dinkies stumbled and fell backwards onto the dirt floor. McQueen turned toward Yellow Neck. "Don't push it, Sludge. I'm trying to like you."

Yellow Neck backed off, but managed to blurt out. "I tole you before, my name ain't Sludge. It's Yellow Neck."

The Dinkies picked up the lead chains again, allowed for a reasonable amount of slack, and trudged forward.

At a little offset room, next to a little door, the Dinkies stopped. Yellow Neck expanded his chest and pointed. "Go in there and wait."

McQueen dropped out of his crouching position and dropped to his hands and knees and stared into

328

Yellow Neck's eyes. "Tell Augur we're here."

"I'm not tellin' him nothin'."

That's right," another Dinky said. "We can't trust you, Warrior McQueen."

Tommy pointed to himself with his little thumb. "What about me?"

"You neither," Yellow Neck growled. "You guys are only after a record capture."

"How can we be after a capture?" McQueen asked. "The corporation has wanted posters all over the land with our pictures on them."

Yellow Neck patted his pockets. "I had a poster right here. But it's just some kinda trick you guys cooked up with Nelson." He rubbed the back of his yellow neck. "The only-est thing you're gonna do is try and make Augur your five-hundredth capture."

"That's right," another Dinky said. "You two probably have border guards and reporters with cam-fingers waiting nearby."

McQueen pushed himself back to a kneeling position. "Why don't you let Augur decide?"

"We've heard all about you guys," Yellow Neck said and his eyes suspiciously slanted. "You guys will stab us in the back just to get credits so you can live like kings." Yellow neck took a hard look at McQueen; and as if he were the judge and the jury, he talked right into McQueen's face. "And we ain't buyin' a damn thing you say." He jerked his hand toward the little offset room. "You guys can git in there and rot."

McQueen nudged Tommy in the elbow. "Weren't we just in a place like this?"

Tommy pleaded with Yellow Neck. "We're of

the same race. Why can't you let me see Augur?"

"You ain't goin' nowhere."

"All right then," Tommy said with indifference. "Just let me stay here. When Augur asks me why I didn't give him the information sooner, I'll tell him you wouldn't let me."

"Nice try," Yellow Neck said and grinned a night-crawler lipped grin. "But you ain't never saw Augur."

"I've seen and talked with him many times," Tommy lied. "But don't take my word for it." He pointed to the little door. "Just go in there and ask him."

"I ain't askin' him nothin'."

McQueen knee-walked to a little cot at the side of the room. "Don't argue with Sludge's brother, Tommy," he said, and sat down.

"My name ain't Sludge," Yellow Neck growled. "I ain't tellin' you again. It's Yellow Neck."

McQueen waved his hand as if he were chasing a bothersome fly. "Whatever, Sludge. When Augur finds out we're here and you wouldn't let us see him, we'll be off the hook."

Tommy walked over to a little cot, lay down, and laced his fingers behind his head. "Have it your way, Sludge. I needed a break anyway." He rolled over and turned his back to Yellow Neck.

"My name ain't—" Yellow Neck started to say, but another Dinky whispered in his ear. Yellow Neck shook his head and glared at Tommy. "Git up, you little creep. We're gonna find out if you know Augur."

McQueen lay on his side and plopped his head

330

on the pillow. "Wake me up when you guys get back."

CHAPTER 31

Yellow Neck jerked on Tommy's chains. Tommy stood up and was led through the door. On the other side, Yellow Neck escorted him down a tunnel until they stopped at a steel-bared wooden door. Yellow Neck yanked at the chain around Tommy's neck. "You sure you talked to Augur before?"

"Tommy reached up and pulled the tight chain away from his neck. "Heck yeah. We practically grew up together."

Yellow Neck stepped in front of Tommy. A Dinky guard, in an official looking uniform, walked up to the door and stood at attention. "Is this the one who wishes to see Augur?"

"Yes," Yellow Neck said, "he says him and Augur are old friends."

The guard stood aside and held the door open. "You may go in."

Tommy went in. An old Dinky with a staff stood next to a wooden sink. Tommy wasn't impressed. The great Augur didn't look so great. But Tommy had to make himself look good. If this guy was as important as they said he was, he would never remember everyone he had ever met.

Tommy walked up to the old Dinky and extended his hand. "Augur, you old coot. How have you been?"

The old Dinky turned his back. Yellow Neck walked in with the guard by his side. "Take 'em back. He don't know Auger."

"Maybe he just doesn't recognize me," Tommy said, and tugged on the old Dinky's shirtsleeve.

"Augur, it's me, Tommy. Don't you remember me?"

The old man turned and looked into Tommy's face. "I'm not Augur."

Yellow Neck grinned from one big Dinky ear to another. "Nice try, dummy." He looked to the guard. "See, I told you he's a spy."

Yellow Neck pushed Tommy toward the door and yanked on the chain. Tommy held the chain and planted his little feet in the dirt.

"If I have to," Yellow Neck said and jerked him backwards, "I'll jerk you all the way back to that other spy."

Tommy lifted his hand in surrender. "All right," he said. "I don't know Augur. But we must see him."

As if speaking louder would make his statement perfectly clear, Yellow Neck raised his voice. "The only-est thing you're gonna to see is the bottom of the river."

The chain around Tommy's drooped down onto his shoulders and caused his muscles to bunch and ache. Tommy didn't know what to do. He was in pain, but didn't want Yellow Neck to interpret it as a sign of weakness. However, if he sounded like he was in pain, he might be able to get Yellow Neck to fall for the sympathy angle.

He contorted his face. "I don't blame you for wanting to throw me into the river." He rubbed the muscles around his neck. "It's hard for me to believe that my own people are against me." He turned his shoulder to rub it and the chain rode up around his neck.

Yellow Neck's eyes took on a faint look of

333

concern.

Tommy put his fingers under the chain and lifted it away from his neck. "But you just don't have any other choice. I guess you have been betrayed so many times you can't trust anyone."

Yellow Neck hesitated for a moment. Then, he yanked on the chain, turned, and led Tommy down another tunnel. At a little door, he stopped and dropped the chain.

The door opened. Yellow Neck stood as if he were before a god.

Tommy looked up and gasped. "Augur?"

Augur was a little taller than the other Dinkies. Loose fitting clothes, a faded light-yellow shirt, and a cloud-gray cloth vest covered his upper body. The typical Dinky dirt stains on the knees of his jade-green pants were not there. Having a complexion darker than the other Dinkies and a slender body with sharp facial features suggested an ancient intellectual ancestry. Under his little white garrison cap, he looked like a highly educated man.

Augur held up his hand. "Remove the chains and escort this man and Warrior McQueen to the hall of knowledge."

CHAPTER 32

McQueen looked up from his little cot. Tommy walked into the room with two guards by his sides. The chain was gone from around his neck.

McQueen sat up. "Did you see Augur?"

"I think so, and I believe we're going to get educated."

"Now what did you do?"

Two more guards entered the room. "Sergeant McQueen," one guard said. "You have been summoned by Augur. Please come with us to the hall of knowledge."

While the guards removed his chains, McQueen shook his head at Tommy. "Hall of knowledge?" he muttered under his breath.

Tommy smiled a sly smile and waved his arm in a follow-me gesture. "Come on, you big dummy."

The guards escorted them down the long tunnel and stopped at the steel-bared door.

Another guard opened the door. Tommy walked into the room. The arch above the door was too low for McQueen to walk under on his knees. He dropped down to his hands and knees and walked, knee-to-hand into the room.

The room had a high ceiling. McQueen stood up. From a mysterious place above, a shaft of magnified moonlight beamed down. Like powder blue cathedral light, it softened and flowed from the center of the room, spreading out and sending light where there was none. To the right, a small room with Dinkies, wearing white uniforms, scurried up and down long silver tables and only stopped for brief moments to measure ingredients and tip test tubes full of colorful liquids into some kind of processing machine. In the corner, piles of human bones and a few skulls were stacked high. Next to that, piles of green ferns, yellow reeds, and piles of plants with purple flowers sat like little haystacks. To the left, various colors of leaves on thick branches leaned against a wall.

Four guards stood at Tommy's and McQueen's sides. Tommy looked up at McQueen. "Now what?"

The guard on his right poked him in the back with a metal bar. "Don't show disrespect."

"Yes, sir," Tommy snapped back, and the guard pushed him toward the shaft of moonlight.

McQueen followed and they were stopped just before a strange light from above touched their foreheads.

Augur walked out of the side room where the little white-coated Dinkies were working and stepped into the light. "Gentleman." He clasped his hands together. "My friends tell me you have something to tell me."

McQueen placed his hands behind his back in a position of strict parade rest. "Yes, sir," he said. "We need your help."

"Why would a great warrior, like yourself, need the help of a lowly Dinky?"

"You're not a lowly Dinky," McQueen said with great haste. "The Dinkies of Blue Town are about to revolt. We need your antitoxin to keep the warriors from killing them."

"And," Tommy butted in, "the corporation is about to break into our tunnel system."

336

"We are very close to an antitoxin," Augur said, "but we haven't perfected one yet. He held out his arm and motioned toward the little laboratory on his left. "As you can see, we are still trying."

McQueen relaxed his parade rest position and lowered his head. "The antitoxin was our only hope. The Dinkies of Blue Town are going to revolt. They agreed to wait seven days for us to return. If we're not back by tomorrow they are going to revolt. Without the protection of an antitoxin many will be killed."

Augur's high forehead wrinkled with worry. "I hope they can wait. If they do not, it will be a worse slaughter than we had here in Patagonia."

McQueen felt useless. "Is there any way you can stop it?"

"Suppose we did have a serum," Augur said. "How do we know you are not just trying to seize it for the corporation?"

McQueen felt a surge of resentment. "That's Impossible. I'm a wanted man."

Augur's eyebrows arched. "I've seen the posters. They could be part of a ploy."

Yellow Neck jerked his fist in the air and started to speak. Augur waved his hand at him. He stood quiet.

Augur continued. "Sergeant McQueen, how can we be sure you are not looking to add one more outstanding achievement to your record?"

"You and I know, when you get the antitoxin, we will have nothing to fear from the corporation."

"And?"

"You and I, and all the others will take our

rightful place in society."

Augur lifted his finger and held it toward McQueen. "Some would say that as a warrior, you are in your rightful place in society."

McQueen shook his head sadly. "What can I say? I didn't mean to capture all those Dinkies, but now I realize, I wasn't in my right mind."

"Are you using that for an excuse?"

McQueen looked directly into Augur's eyes. "I'm not looking for any excuses. We all have done things we'd rather not have done." He turned his gaze toward the dirt floor. "I'm not proud of every day of my life. No one can be." He looked back into Augur's face. "No one can really judge until he has done what I have done, seen what I have seen, suffered what I have suffered."

"You are no different than others warriors," Augur said and looked to the others. "Under the corporation, these people have suffered more than any warrior."

McQueen nodded. "I know that." In an almost begging gesture, he hunched his shoulders and lifted his hands. "But Tommy and I are different."

"Yes, we are," Tommy added. "We grew up together on his father's farm."

Augur gave Tommy a curt wave of dismissal. "Just because you grow up with someone, it doesn't mean you haven't been brainwashed into believing evil is necessary and essential for the well-being of the pig people and the corporation."

"That's true," Tommy said and gave him one of his famous crooked smiles. "But, McQueen has touched the stones of life."

As he jerked his head toward McQueen,

Augur's eyes widened. "Are you the son of the man who was in possession of the stones of life?"

"He was my father, McQueen Senior. "I was just a child then. My father lifted me up and I touched the stones."

Augur hesitated. Then: "Are you in possession of the stones now?"

"No, but I know they have to be somewhere near our old farm."

Augur looked to the guards. "That might be worth perusing. Bring in the others."

A guard opened the steel-bared door, stood in the opening, and waved his hand. A stream of little Dinkies flowed into the big hall of knowledge.

When they were gathered around, the atmosphere became like a church. Auger spoke. "It is well known that the survivors of the time after the stones of life had to begin again. Like children with almost no memory of what had happened before they came into being, many wanted to know what had went wrong with the previous society, and they wanted to know how to prevent it from happening again." He gestured to Tommy and McQueen. "We have reason to believe that these men can be of help in finding the stones of life."

As a murmur of excitement waved through the crowd, Yellow Neck stepped forward. "How do we know they ain't lyin'?"

"That's right!" someone yelled from the back of the crowd. "How do we know they're not just after the reward that's on your head?"

Augur raised his hand. The crowd became silent. "It is true," he said and nodded. "I have a great reward on my head."

Yellow Neck thrust his finger at McQueen and Tommy. "They know you're wanted dead or alive." As if he had a knife clutched in his hand, he forcefully swung it down. "They'll kill you and git rich."

Staying calm, Augur gave Yellow Neck a disapproving look. "I do not believe Warrior McQueen or Tommy have it in their hearts to do anything like that."

Yellow Neck cast a scathing look in McQueen's direction. "Why not?"

"I have faith in these two men."

"We ain't got no faith in them at all." Yellow Neck turned and waved his fist at the crowd behind him. With the roll of fat on the back of his neck moving like it was talking, he yelled at the crowd, "Ain't that right?"

The crowd moaned in unison, "Yeah!"

Yellow Neck turned toward Augur for approval.

Augur waved his hand across the air in front of Yellow Neck's face. All was silent. "Does this man speak for all of you?"

As Yellow Neck slunk into the crowd, most of the Dinkies bowed their heads in shame and didn't answer.

"Then it is to be."

Yellow Neck raised his fist above the crowd. "McQueen's no God."

"Perhaps Sergeant McQueen is one of the new breed," Augur flatly said and nodded for emphasis. "Warrior McQueen has already proven he is superior to most men."

Dinkies moved away from Yellow Neck and

340

gave him space to be seen. The mouth in the back of his neck moved. "That's why we gotta keep pig-people-lovin' Dinkies and people like McQueen in chains."

In spite of the threat of having the chain put back around his neck, and being called a pig-people-lovin' Dinky, Tommy must have thought Yellow Neck's mouth was funny. He let out a little giggle. McQueen lifted his foot and tapped him in the shin. Tommy suppressed his laughter.

"That's right," someone murmured. "Put them in chains, then throw them in the river."

Augur held up his hand and gazed into the crowd. It was quiet again. He began:

"Years ago, we chased the promise of freedom and hope. We came to Patagonia to build a new vision. Leaders were supposed to serve the country. They babbled about law and order, but it's was just an echo of what they had been told before. Law and order became a monster on the loose that would not obey. The Friends of the Earth Corporation hunted us and made us weary. Then they bullied us and stole from us. When there was nothing left to steal, they turned us into slaves to serve their every need. Now Dinkies in Blue Town will be fighting a war. No matter who's the winner, Dinkies can't pay the cost. He looked to McQueen and Tommy. "We can't let them fight alone against any monster."

McQueen and Augur exchanged glances.

Augur continued. "Many lives are at stake. I will sacrifice my own safety and well-being. I will go with these two men and try to delay the uprising until we find the antitoxin."

Yellow Neck's eyebrows shot up. "But, you

341

can't. We need you here."

Augur's face took on a look of compassion. "Thank you for the concern, Yellow Neck." He stepped forward and placed his hand on his shoulder. "These two people have risked their lives to get here. I must help."

Pain showed on Yellow Neck's face. "But you ain't gotta risk your life."

"I feel in my heart these men are telling the truth." He held up one finger. "And, we may also find the stones of life."

A Dinky with a dirty-red baseball cap with a frayed bill spoke out. "But how do you know they're not lying?"

Augur looked in the Dinky's direction. "What good is mankind if one cannot trust his fellow man?"

Yellow Neck turned toward Augur. This time the mouth in the back of his neck moved toward the crowd. "But what if you git killed?"

"Years ago, the pig people came to our pristine land of great forest, rolling plains, and crystal lakes. During their quest for God, glory, and gold, we suffered, but we have survived. I will also survive." He turned to McQueen. "Do you have anything to add?"

"We can promise nothing," McQueen said. "I hope and pray that you will not regret your decision."

Augur raised his voice and spoke to the crowd. "It is settled. I will go with them."

"If you're gonna go," Yellow Neck said, "then we're all gonna go."

Augur shook his head. "He travels fastest who

travels alone. We don't want to draw attention to an already volatile situation. Until we have the antitoxin, my fellow Dinkies will stay here, safe. It is so ordered."

CHAPTER 33

Danielle walked out of the water house and down the mustard-colored road. A speeding OvalCar zoomed past, slid sideways, and stopped in a cloud of yellow dust. Trying to wave the dust away from her mouth, she fanned her hand in front of her face. Two warriors jumped out of the car and put their hands on their sidearms. "Driver! Stop!"

Twisting her slender body into a seductive pose, she put her hands into the air. "I'm sure glad to see you warriors are on the job."

The warriors relaxed their stance, but stood back. The one with a defiant grin spoke first. "You have the virus," he said, his sky blue eyes staring. "Soon you will be an infected Dinky."

Flexing his muscular arm, the other warrior ran his hand through his blond hair and walked toward her. "Prepare to be quarantined."

Danielle held out her hands. "Look, I don't have a virus. It's poison ivy. The Dinkies are curing it."

"Don't try to trick us," the blond said.

She held her hands close to his face. "No really. Look, it's not virus. The Dinkies have a cure."

The blond tensed his tremendous neck muscles and backed away. "Don't lie to us. You're wanted."

"I know that. Why do you think I'm out here on the open road waiting for you?"

The blue-eyed warrior removed his hand from his sidearm. "She may have a point there."

"Maybe she does," the blond said. "But I'm

not taking any chances." He pointed to the OvalCar. "I don't want to get what she has and turn into some kind of Dinky creep."

The blue-eyed warrior reached into the car and pulled out a full facemask with filtered ends over a breathing apparatus. "You're right," he said. "Her virus could be in remission." He gripped the mask with two fingers. As if it were contaminated, he held it at arm's length and presented it to Danielle. "Here, put this on."

Danielle put on the mask. The blond threw a pair of virus resistant gloves on the ground and pointed to them. "Put those on and cover up that rash."

Then both warriors unfolded a virus-barrier blanket in front of her and wrapped it around her body until only her face-masked head was visible. Her muffled voice sang from under the facemask. "You know this isn't necessary?"

"Maybe not," the blond said. "But until we get you to the decontamination chamber, we're not touching you."

As if she were some kind of living fecal matter that he didn't want to get on himself, the blond picked her bundled body up. Holding his head to one side, he carried her to the OvalCar. The blue-eyed warrior opened the door, and the blond placed her inside.

Traveling down the road, Danielle tried to spark a conversation, but neither warrior would talk. It seemed like they were afraid to breathe.

At the main base, the blond warrior carried Danielle to the entrance of the barracks. He stood her up and they stood in front of the scanner. The computer scanned their bodies and a voice announced: "Warriors and driver recognized. Please advance to next stage."

The blond warrior carried her through the doors, and stood her up at the next scanner. Standing next to her, the blue-eyed warrior held her head and turned it until the lens of the facemask was in front of the pupil scanner. It clicked. Then he held her ear next to a radar reflection recognition lock. Holding her up, both warriors scanned their own eyes and ears. The computer voice announced: "Warriors and driver cleared to enter chamber."

They all walked into the decontamination chamber. The blue-eyed warrior pulled the lever that activated the ultraviolet laser's excited glow.

Looking out the glass door, the blue-eyed warrior relaxed and finally talked to her. "Where have you been?"

She talked through the facemask. "I've been with McQueen and that little Dinky, Tommy."

He turned toward her. "You mean McQueen and the Dinky aren't dead?"

"They're still alive, and healthy as ever."

A puzzled look came over the blue-eyed warrior's face. "That's not normal."

"That's why I came back," Danielle said through the mask. "I want to tell the world that there might be a cure for the virus, or at least a chance that Sergeant McQueen has a virus-resistant immune system."

The "virus contained" light flashed and the computer voice spoke. "Warriors and driver clear to continue to live and fight for the chief earth officer."

346

"You can take off the mask now," the blond warrior said, and held out his hand. She pulled the mask off and placed it in his hand. The glass door opened automatically. Outside, leaning on the hall wall, Burke stood with his feet crossed and his arms folded across his steroidal chest.

"Well here he goes," Danielle said to herself. "This will be a good day for Burke. It should make his manipulating mind happy."

She stepped out of the chamber. The two warriors stepped out and walked away. Burke stood in front of her and blocked her path. "Welcome back, honey." He laughed with delight. "We've been waiting for you."

"Then you know?"

"Yes, we know." He smiled his big cheesy smile.

Danielle hadn't seen his sickening smile for a while and it was worse than ever. She hated the thought of being nice to him, but if she wanted to save McQueen, she knew she would have to at least try. "You mean you already know about the virus?"

As if he hadn't heard her question, Burke continued. "They caught McQueen and his Dinky friend in Patagonia. They threw them in an escape-proof jail. They'll be bringing them back any time now."

Danielle stared at him. "That's not what I asked you. I want to know if you really know about the virus."

With an arrogant tone to his voice, Burke answered, "We know that you have been told that old Dinky story that there is a cure for the virus."

"I have been told that," she said sensing his

lack of enthusiasm. "But I'm not sure it's a cure. I was exposed a long time ago, and you can see that I haven't mutated into a Dinky."

Burke looked away from her. "So What?"

"I believe that I have a virus-immune system. Sergeant McQueen has not mutated either. If he and I are granted the right to reproduce, the corporation could farm our genes and make a virus-free society."

Burke looked back at her. That sounds like a pretty tall order." He jerked his thumb toward his cadre quarters. "What do you have to offer in return?" He stood there with his arms crossed, waiting for an answer; and to make it worse, he flashed his best ear-to-ear cheese-face smile.

There was no way she was going to spend time with Burke in his quarters, and she knew she shouldn't tell him about the revolt; but it was the only real bargaining chip she had. And the cure for the virus was for the good of the world. If a person discovered something to improve the world that person had a patriotic duty to sacrifice themselves for the good of all. She knew McQueen and Tommy would be angry at first, but when they realized that there was no other way to save a lot of people, they would understand. But right now, the big problem was that she couldn't tell anything to a creep like Burke.

She turned toward him. A rotten feeling crawled up her back and eased into her stomach. She shuddered and shook it off. "Look, sweetie," she said. "I know you like to transfer information directly to Chief Earth Officer Nelson, but this time I have information much too important for you to

348

transfer."

Burke's cheese-face smile turned to mold. "Who do you think you are?" he wanted to know. "You're just a wanted driver with a Dinky virus."

"That may be so. But if you want the real information, you'll have to let me speak to CEO Nelson."

For a brief moment, Burke's face took on a disappointed look, but he recovered in an instant. "Why sure," he said, and smiled a little sneaky smile. "I'll take you to him right now."

Burke escorted Danielle to the door outside of Nelson's office. He tapped out some kind of code on a single red button on the door, but Danielle didn't understand what he was doing.

Dits and dahs tapped back from the other side of the door. Burke put his eye to the pupil scanner. After his eye was scanned, he grabbed Danielle by the back of the neck and pushed her head until her eye was in front of the scanner. The door opened.

Chief Earth Officer Nelson's bodyguards came forward and scanned Danielle's body with handheld scanners. "Never can be too safe," McQueen's old bodyguard friend, Judd, said to her. Danielle wanted to ask him if he had a chance to change the virus bullets. She threw him a questioning look. He didn't respond.

If he didn't have a chance to change the bullets, it wouldn't matter. If her plan worked there would be no revolt. There would be no virus, and there would be no need to change the bullets.

Blocking her path and flashing her a stone face, Judd stated: "Chief Earth Officer Nelson's time if very valuable. Your meeting will be restricted to just so many minutes. If Chief Earth Officer Nelson has said what he has wanted to say or heard what he wanted to hear your meeting with him will be over." He stepped aside. "Proceed."

Danielle stepped to the end of the long marble table, crossed her hands behind her back, and stood at parade rest. The seamless wall at the far end of the table cracked open. Seated Chief Earth Officer Nelson rotated around on a half-moon platform and stopped at a height just high enough that Danielle had to look up at him. She dropped her hands from behind her back and snapped to attention.

Chief Earth Officer Nelson picked up a metal wand and pointed it at Danielle. "Driver! State your business."

"Chief Earth Officer Nelson," she said, "I have information that could save the world."

Nelson leaned back and propped his feet up on the table. "I haven't been amused today." He waved the wand as if he were sweeping air. "Continue."

"I believe I have found a cure for the virus rash."

"We've heard all that that before. Our scientists have put the so-called magic powder through clinical trials. All it did was put the virus into remission. It always came back with much more vigor than before."

Danielle looked at her gloved hands. She could feel that the rash was almost gone, but she didn't want to take off the gloves. "If it comes back," she said, "then why is Warrior McQueen still alive?"

"He's just lucky. If he was exposed, and we have reason to believe he was, eventually the virus will catch up to him. He may be a Dinky as we speak."

"But if he doesn't die or turn into a Dinky, that means that he has virus resistant genes."

Nelson's voice became friendly. "So what if he does have those genes?"

Danielle felt her voice fill with hope. "If McQueen and I were granted the privilege to reproduce, we could start a race of virus resistant people and save the world."

Nelson let out a big belly laugh. "Thanks for showing me how ignorant you are."

Instant disappointment stabbed Danielle in her heart.

She wondered if she had come to Nelson for nothing. Was she going to turn into a Dinky after all? She hung her head in shame. "Have you tried making a race of virus resistant people before?"

"Do you think the corporation is a mom-and-pop organization run by uneducated Dinkies? We have scientists and men of supreme learning working on the virus cure every hour of the day and night."

The guard on the left brought out a silver reading pad and presented it to Nelson. Nelson glanced at the pad and looked at Danielle. "Your great virus-free warrior has escaped, but we have warriors in place. We will have him surrounded again."

"Oh please don't shoot him," Danielle pleaded.

Nelson was almost sneering when he said, "Oh, we won't do that. He's a hero. We want him and his little Dinky friend alive." Nelson snapped his fingers and glanced at Judd. Judd reached into his

351

vest pocket, slipped out a wanted poster, and flung it across the table.   Above McQueen's and Tommy's pictures, it read:

CAUTION

WANTED ALIVE ONLY

RUNAWAY VIRUS VICTIMS

"See, we won't hurt them," Nelson said with assurance in his voice. "We need them alive. We are going to give them the antidote on TV."

Danielle gave out a little yelp of surprise. "But don't most people die when they're given the antidote?"

"Many exposed people have died, but that was because they waited too long to take the antidote."

Danielle felt McQueen had been sentenced to death. She couldn't help it, but when she spoke her voice took on a whining pitch. "McQueen has gone way beyond the time period."

"That is quite possible," Nelson said as if it were an everyday occurrence. "But it won't be a total loss. Sergeant McQueen's death will remind the pig people just how dangerous the virus is. He will die a hero, and it will put a stop to this foolishness."

Danville's voice returned to a less whining, more serious tone. "But I don't believe it is foolishness."

"What do you know about foolishness?" Nelson said with a defiant grin. "You were trained to be a driver for the corporation. If you had performed your obligation, we wouldn't have this problem with renegade Dinkies and a virus-brain-infected warrior running around the country terrorizing people."

"But, Chief Earth Officer Nelson," she begged. "I'm only trying to help you save the world from the virus."

Nelson slapped the metal wand on the steel table. Danielle jumped back. The sharp sound smacked into her ears. They began to ring. He raised his voice. "Don't come in here whining to me. You're not my mentor. Since you failed to perform your obligation, you will have the honor of getting the antidote with your boyfriend, McQueen."

Danielle wanted to cry, but she held back the tears. "But I think I'm cured," she said loud and clear.

Nelson raised his voice and octave. "Don't fool yourself." With a satisfied look in his eyes, he smiled. "I can see it now. McQueen and his Queen."

Danielle shook her head and thought of what would have happened if she had just stayed in the secret cave. But she was here. She didn't want to tell Nelson about the revolt, but she had to do something to change his mind. She had to save McQueen.

Nelson took his feet from the table and slammed his wand again. He pointed it at Danielle and waved it toward the door. "I have said what I wanted to say, and I have heard what I wanted to hear. Driver you may leave."

Danielle stepped out of attention, shifted her weight to one foot, and put her hand on her hip. Ignoring his title of Chief Earth Officer and the respect she was obliged to show, she yelled, "Look here, Nelson! I think it will be advantageous to the corporation if you permit Sergeant McQueen to live."

Nelson talked in a cocky whisper. "Driver, why do you raise your voice, and why do you even think to say that?"

Danielle hesitated and lowered her voice. "Without Sergeant McQueen's leadership, the Dinkies will revolt."

"Let them revolt. Our warriors have taken care of revolts in the past. They can do it again."

"But, Chief Earth Officer Nelson," she begged. "The Dinkies are important to the world." She paused and breathed in hard. "It would do the corporation no good if they are slaughtered in a useless revolt."

"That's right, driver. We need every live Dinky we can get."

She breathed a sigh of relief. "Then you understand?"

Nelson stood up. "I understand that all corporation life requires energy and sufficient power to maintain the lifestyle you and I are accustomed to."

"I understand that, Chief Earth Officer Nelson."

Nelson banged his fist on the marble table. "If you understood anything, you would have turned in Warrior McQueen before he got out of hand."

Danielle slouched forward.

Nelson turned his back to her and spoke to Judd. "It will be a pleasure to see this driver and McQueen get the antidote. She doesn't even have enough respect to stand at attention. Get that incompetent Dinky lover out of here."

Judd yelled at Danielle, "Attention!"

Danielle didn't snap to attention. She didn't salute.

Nelson waved his hand at her as if he were shooing an insect.

"Driver dismissed," Judd said.

Danielle turned and slowly shuffled toward the door.

Suddenly, she turned back. "But, Chief Earth Officer Nelson, what if I can tell you where Augur is?"

Nelson's eyes widened. "We may be able to make a deal."

CHAPTER 34

Under the cover of darkness, McQueen, Tommy, and Augur slipped out of the cave by the river and followed an indistinct trail. They were on their way back to Blue Town.

Walking along, McQueen watched the faint glow of the new day's light creep into the eastern sky. On each side of him, tree leaves, grass, and bushes along the path began to turn from the blue-gray of night to early morning green. He began to feel a strange animosity toward the sun. When it was down, it provided the protection of darkness. When it was up, he could travel faster. But when it came up today, it meant that they had less time to get back. He pushed forward.

The silver morning sun turned to chrome, shone out of the sky, and ignited the new day. McQueen felt it was an omen, a sign that once the virus farce was exposed there would be a new awakening, a new life of freedom for everyone on the earth; and he wanted the Dinkies of Blue Town to be part of it. He wanted them to stay alive.

And, he was beginning to understand why Sludge and the other Dinkies were willing to die for their freedom. When he had thought he was going to die from virus exposure; and he was sure he was close to death, it had made him want to have died for something. It seemed the Dinkies felt the same way. Even if they died and wouldn't be here to see it, someday their deaths would have gone toward accomplishing something worthwhile.

In the past, McQueen's capture record had made him feel good. But now that he knew the virus was not real, he realized he had been just like the pig people, working in the make-nothing factories. After years of dedication to the corporation, they had looked back at their lives, and they regretted that the only thing they had accomplished was to work in a factory. The pig people believed McQueen was a hero. Now he knew they were wrong. All he had done in his life was capture four hundred ninety-nine harmless Dinkies. He was going to change that. He wasn't going to let the lies of the corporation squander his life or anyone's life any longer.

He looked back over his shoulder. Tommy and the other Dinkies were following. They made him feel like he had felt when his father was alive. He was part of a family again. It made everything different. Now, if he saved the Dinkies and exposed the virus, but got killed in the process, he would have lived for something. Now, he had a good feeling in his heart, and it penetrated into his very soul.

Coming down a steep grade, he scanned the trees and rocks for signs of an ambush. Even though he knew there would be danger ahead, he was at peace with himself.

He turned and looked at Augur. "The sun's already up. I don't know if we'll have time to make it back before Sludge starts the revolt."

"No problem," Augur said. "We'll have just enough time if we go by way of the safe path."

McQueen stopped walking. "How do we do that?"

Augur stepped around a little bush at the side of the path and passed him. He motioned with his arm. "Just follow me."

McQueen and Tommy followed. When Augur stopped at a big tree, they stopped too. Rays of the sun reached through the dark trees and illuminated black and white wanted posters stapled to the trunk of the tree.

WANTED DEAD OR ALIVE
AUGUR
KING OF THE DINKIES

Below that was a fresh poster. Tommy pointed to it. "Look, McQueen, we're both wanted alive, and only alive, by order of Nelson"

Augur looked at the posters and leaned back. "That's strange."

Tommy put his hand against the tree and leaned on it. "What did we do to be wanted alive?"

McQueen searched his mind trying to think of something Nelson or Burke could have accused them of doing that would make them want them alive. "I not sure," he said. "But I'd say they still want to give us the antidote on live TV."

"That's okay," Augur said. "We'll find out when we get there."

Still leaning on the tree, Tommy let out a laugh. "Just think," he said. "If we had enough of the antitoxin we could go on TV and let them inject us. Nothing would happen. I wonder how Nelson would explain that."

McQueen smiled at the idea and looked down the long path. If Augur were wrong about the secret path being quicker, it would take a long time to get back. He looked at Augur. "I just hope Sludge and his crew didn't revolt already."

Augur gave McQueen a concerned look. "If

they revolted, and it's anything like the one we had in Patagonia, we'll have a big mess to clean up."

"We'll worry about that when we get there," McQueen said. "Right now we have to make sure no one tries to collect the reward on your head."

Tommy took his hand from the tree and turned toward Augur. "All the scum of the earth will be out to get that reward."

"We'll try to keep you between us," McQueen said. "Since they're not allowed to kill us, they won't shoot if there's a chance they'll hit us."

McQueen turned from the tree and crashed through the brush and into the tall grass.

Tommy followed behind Augur. "Be careful up ahead," he said. "That's the place they caught us the last time."

McQueen turned and looked back at Augur. Salump! A bullet whizzed past McQueen's elbow. Augur fell to the ground.

McQueen turned and yelled at Tommy, "Get Down!"

Tommy dove into the tall grass. McQueen knelt down and cradled Augur's head in his arms. Pulling the syringed bullet from Augur's side, he looked toward Tommy and whispered, "It's an antidote-bullet."

On his hands and knees, Tommy crawled back to Augur. With a look of hope, he looked into McQueen's eyes.

"Sorry, Tommy," McQueen said. "He's dying. No one has ever lived after being shot with an antidote-bullet."

Tommy opened his mouth to speak but nothing came out.

"I know you feel bad," McQueen said. "But we should leave him here and escape."

Tommy wiped his eyes with the back of his hand. "The border guards will find him. They'll hang his body up for all to see."

McQueen gently lowered Augur's head to the ground. "Let's go," he said, stood up, and paused.

"What's the matter?" Tommy said with a face full of tears.

"We might as well give up the fight. We can't stop the revolt without Augur. We don't know the fast way back. We just ran out of time."

"But we still have time to escape."

McQueen knelt back down and held Augur's head in the crook of his arm. "We must take Augur back to the hall of knowledge. He is a man of great importance. The least we can do is make sure he gets a proper burial."

Tommy looked across an expanse of tall green grass, tapped McQueen on the shoulder, and pointed.

McQueen looked to his left. Tops of the grass waved and jerked.

"The border guards are coming." Tommy gasp. "What should we do?"

McQueen looked down at Augur and then toward the moving grass. "We can't just leave him here. Before they hang him up, the corporation will drag his body through the streets and display it on TV for all to see. They'll use him to show the people what happens to a Dinky who disobeys the laws of the corporation."

"But we still have to try and get back," Tommy said. "We still have to stop the revolt."

"I know that," McQueen said, and put his hand to his forehead as if he were in pain. "If we don't stop the revolt, a lot of Dinkies will be killed."

Tommy stared at Augur. Augur's head tilted to one side, and his eyes rolled back into his head. Movement in the grass intensified.

McQueen looked up at Tommy. "We can't leave him here on the trail."

Tommy wiped the tears from his face. "Let's take him back."

McQueen nodded and slipped his arms under Augur's back to pick him up. With pain in his face, Augur's eyes rolled to normal. Then slowly raised his arm and pointed to a big red-leafed bush. "Take me to the burning bush. There is a hidden tunnel."

McQueen carried Augur behind the red bush and stopped. Holding Augur, he searched for a tunnel in the yellow dirt embankment with his foot. It was solid. "I think his mind is going, Tommy. There's no tunnel here."

Augur pointed to the bush with the toe of his foot. Tommy grabbed a branch on the bush and shook it. "This thing's dead."

"Pull it out," Augur said.

Tommy pulled out the bush. A wooden trap door appeared beneath the roots.

McQueen opened the door. Carrying Augur on his back, he stepped down the ladder. Tommy stood at the top of the ladder and looked out across the grass. Ten meters in front of him, the tops of the tall grass jerked. He placed the bush back on the trap door. Holding it in place, he closed the door over his head.

McQueen carried Augur in his arms; and on his

361

knees, he walked through the semi-dark tunnel.

Tommy followed. "I hope this thing goes all the way to the hall of knowledge."

"I doubt it," McQueen said. "There's the end of it right up ahead."

Augur raised his head. "The tunnel only goes under the fence," he said, and dropped his head back down into McQueen's arms.

Tommy ran to end of the tunnel and looked outside.

"How's it look?" McQueen asked.

"I don't see anything."

McQueen switched to a crouching position and repositioned Augur in his arms. "Good. Let's travel." He duck-walked out the small exit.

At the river in front of the secret tunnel, morning rain fell from the sky, and lightening cracked on the surface of the wet metal bridge.

Tommy stopped and blocked McQueen's path. "We can't climb that bridge. Lightning will strike us."

The rain beat in McQueen's face, and lightning flashed all around the steel bridge. McQueen was scared, but he didn't want to let his fear infect Tommy. Smiling an assuring smile in Tommy's direction, he talked over the noise of the storm. "I don't know why, but I have never been afraid of lightning. I have always felt it was my friend."

Tommy looked at him as if he were crazy. McQueen gave him a knowing wink, adjusted Augur on his back, got a better grip; and using one hand, he climbed up the bridge's slanted I beam.

At the top, lightening flashed in front of his face and struck the entrance stone. A purple fizzle of smoke jumped into the dark rainy air. McQueen carried Augur to the stone and whistled the Morse code for open.

The stone opened. Little eyes appeared and waved them inside. McQueen carried Augur into the cave. Holding him in his arms, he duck-walked down the tunnel toward the hall of knowledge.

Yellow Neck lagged behind him shouting to other Dinkies. "Augur's been shot," he yelled. "See that? They tricked him so the guards could ambush him."

McQueen stopped at the entrance to the hall of knowledge. Yellow Neck pointed and jeered at him.

McQueen held Augur with one hand, and with his other hand he reached out and grabbed Yellow Neck by the throat. "Look, you little asshole. If we wanted the reward we wouldn't have come back."

"That's right," an older Dinky said, and opened the door to the hall of knowledge. McQueen laid Augur down on the dirt floor. Four Dinkies gently lifted him and carried him into the big hall. McQueen duck-walked into the hall, stood up, and walked behind them.

"A Dinky medic, in a white coat, rushed over from the little laboratory room and looked into Augur's eyes. "He's about gone. "We have discovered a new antitoxin, but we do not know if it will work."

McQueen rolled his fist into balls and held them at his sides. Clinching his teeth, he yelled, "He'll die anyway. Just give it to him."

"The medic rushed into the little lab, picked up a hypodermic needle, and sucked purple serum from a little test tube. He rushed back, inserted the needle into Augur's arm and pushed the plunger.

McQueen paced back and forth. Tommy took off his little floppy hat, rolled it in his hands, and waited.

McQueen stopped pacing and turned toward Augur. The scene looked familiar. His father had tried to teach him what to say at times like this. He wished he had paid more attention. But the words had been outlawed. They were in a special order. He should have memorized them, but they couldn't even be written down. He remembered the words were called a prayer.

He closed his eyes and stood over Augur. Then, he reached down and took his hand in his. He closed his eyes and tried to remember the words. Before a single word came to mind, he felt the finger of Augur's right hand move. He opened his eyes and looked into Augur's face. Like a clean new spring that had sprung back to life after a long rain, Augur's eyes opened.

Still holding the syringe, the medic breathed a sigh of relief. "It's working."

Augur closed his eyes and his hand went limp. McQueen dropped Augur's hand from his and turned to the medic. "I'm sorry."

But Augur opened his eyes and spoke. "I'm sorry, too. You had to carry me back in all that rain. Now I'll have to get out of these wet clothes." He sat up and smiled to the crowd. Everyone cheered and patted McQueen and Tommy on their backs.

Yellow Neck walked up to McQueen with his head hung low. "I'm sorry," he said, and looked up. "Now we know you won't harm us."

"We were not sure of your intentions," the medic said. "I guess Augur is a better judge of people than all of us. Your actions have shown us that you are on the right side."

Yellow Neck raised both his hands above his head and held them there. "We got the antitoxin. Nothin's gonna stop us now."

"It's about time," Augur said and sat up. "We have nothing to fear."

Like a little kid asking for candy, Yellow Neck looked up at Augur. "Can I go with you to Blue Town and help?"

Augur dropped his feet off the side of the table and stood up. "I see no reason why we all can't go."

Tommy balled his fists, bent his elbows into a running position, and excitedly churned his arms. "Well, what are we waiting on?"

The medic stepped up and held up his hand signaling time out. "Wait a moment," he said. "The antitoxin will take a while to reproduce in enough quantity for a revolt."

"But we don't have time," McQueen said in haste. "Sludge will start the revolt in a few hours."

With his brow furrowed, Augur went silent for a moment. Then he looked up. "We will take what little antitoxin we have and try to delay the revolt."

"That's right," Yellow Neck said and snapped erect. "If we have to, we'll fight them with sticks."

Tommy put his arm around Yellow Neck. "Come with us and I'll show you your irreverent brother."

"What are you talkin' about?" Yellow Neck asked.

"That's a surprise."

CHAPTER 35

Augur led McQueen, Tommy, and thirty Dinkies through the secret tunnel. This time, McQueen and Tommy didn't have to climb over the chain-link fence. With the concealing dirt and solid rock above their heads, they walked right under that fence. And they walked right under the warrior-booted feet of the border guards, too.

Walking behind Yellow Neck, Tommy asked. "What if they're waiting for us again at the same spot?"

"It ain't nothin' to worry about," Yellow Neck said. "I sent a gang out by the fence. They're gonna keep the guards busy long enough for us to git through."

In the tunnel, under the trap door, and below the red-leafed bush, McQueen held up his hand and signaled for the others to stop. "We don't need two people getting shot with one bullet. Try to keep in single file and leave space between yourselves."

"We shouldn't have much trouble," Augur said. "I feel that this land was created for us, and we are small targets."

McQueen reached up and pushed the trap door open. He eased his head above ground. Coiled on the ground with all three heads reared back, a three-headed snake hissed, ready to strike. Six gold eyes glowed and stared McQueen right in the face. Like little skinny razors, the snake's red forked tongues fluttered and cut the air. McQueen jerked back.

"What is it?" Augur asked.

"Damn snake, and it has three heads."

"It's harmless," Augur said. "Push it out of the

way."

McQueen pushed the snake away. The others filed up the ladder and onto the trail toward Blue Town. McQueen looked back over his shoulder and searched the tall grass for creeping movements of sneaky border guards. He saw none, but suddenly voices and the faint sound of antidote bullets zinging through the air, filtered through the trees.

"Keep movin'," Yellow Neck said. "We ain't never been able to trick those border guards for long." He ran down the path. Tommy and the others ran right behind him.

The sound of antidote bullets faded in the distance. A sense of safety hung in the silent air. Yellow Neck tripped. His stomach hit a large stump of grass. Humph! Air gushed from his lungs. Poomph! He let out a big loud fart.

"That's it, Yellow Neck," Tommy said, "call them right to us."

Yellow Neck jumped up, wrinkled his forehead as if he had been gassed. Then he cut in front of Tommy and farted with gusto.

"The way you stink," Tommy said. "Your farts act like air fresheners."

"Quit tryin' to make me laugh me," Yellow Neck said and chuckled. "This is important business."

"You don't sound too—" Tommy started to answer but McQueen butted in.

"He's right, Tommy. You should pay attention to what's up ahead."

Through the trees, the outline of a huge body of water loomed. An orphan breeze passed through the trees and caused the branches to bow and the leaves to flutter. McQueen walked forward and looked between the moving leaves.

In the distance, misty mountains sat on the long arm of a peninsula. Being three kilometers long and a maybe a kilometer wide, it looked like a good place to capture people who were afraid of water.

The wind calmed and they walked out from under the trees. Directly in front of them, like a watching god, a lone pine tree grew amongst a small mountain of jagged gray boulders. Off to the left, white waves of water rolled along a bare sand-washed beach that stretched to the peninsula. McQueen pointed to the beach. "There's not even a tiny scrub of a plant for cover." He looked to the right. On top of a stone church, a crocked cross shone bright in a silver afternoon sun. "That might be a safe way to go."

Augur's face clouded. "I wouldn't go that way," he said and stared at the ground. "That church has been taken over by border guards. They turned it into a military barracks."

"But we can't go along the beach," McQueen said. "It's just how the border guards like it. Every place to run, but no place to hide."

Tommy looked toward Augur and pointed to the water. "Is that the ocean? We didn't run into anything that big a few days ago."

Augur lifted his head. "It's a cove of the great lake. Most border guards are afraid of it."

Tommy edged around McQueen and scanned the shore around the cove. "What's there to be afraid of? All we have to do is walk around it."

"We could," Augur said. "But the border guards are always waiting in that notch just around

369

the bend. And if you go that way, it will take you three days."

McQueen looked back over his shoulder. Movement juggled the leaves. He held up his hand. "Listen."

The voices of excited border guards thundered through the air.

"Whatever we're going to do, we had better get at it."

Augur's eyes darted from side to side. Faint footsteps pounded in the distance. "They're running," he said. "We have about one minute to get into the water."

Tommy looked at the trees and then looked at the water. "Are they afraid of water?"

Augur shook his head. "Not in Patagonia."

The sound of an antidote bullet zinging through the air pierced McQueen's ears. "They're shooting at us," he shouted, and broke into a sprint. The others followed. Like little kids rushing to see who would be the last one in, thirty Dinkies splashed into the water.

When they were in deep enough to swim, they stroked toward the lifesaving arm of the peninsula.

The border guards ran up to the water, took off their helmets, and aimed their sidearms. Antidote bullets snapped and cracked. Like the jagged teeth of thousand-toothed sharks, they slashed at the top of the water. In the biting barrage, one lagging Dinky was shot. He struggled for life and went under. The border guard that shot him, cheered as if he had just scored the game winning point in a sports competition.

McQueen was amazed how rotten a person

could be. That border guard had no feelings for human life at all. He was amazed that people like that were permitted to live on the earth.

The current grabbed McQueen and the others, and drew them out toward the wide-open water. McQueen stroked harder. Tommy stroked next to him. They looked at Augur. Augur stroked away from them, parallel to the shore, and into deeper water.

"What are you doing?" McQueen asked. "If you go that way it's four times a far."

"Augur smiled. "There is a rip tide here. Don't swim for shore. Swim along it until the current stops, then we'll paddle to shore."

Tommy stroked his little arms and struggled to keep afloat. In-between labored breathes he blurted out, "I think you're nuts."

Yellow Neck paddled past Tommy like he was swimming on a quiet pond. "Go ahead, keep fightin' the rip tide. When your arms fall off from paddling, it ain't gonna bother me one bit."

"Okay Mister-know-it-all," Tommy said, and dog paddled after Yellow Neck.

McQueen took a powerful stroke and glided next to Augur. "Do the border guards know about the rip tide?"

"Let's hope not." Augur dog paddled some more.

McQueen rolled to his back. Leisurely paddling with his hands and feet, he looked back at the border guards swimming after them.

Tommy swam next to McQueen, rolled over onto his back, and motioned to the border guards with his arm. "Come on, you big dummies. We're over here."

The leader of the border guards pointed to the shoreline and shouted. "Don't follow them. Cut them off at the shoreline."

The border guards turned and stroked for shore. They went nowhere. They kept stroking and fighting the rip tide.

Following in the wake of McQueen and the others, three pursuing border guards stroked slow and easy.

McQueen tilted his head to the side and looked at Augur. "Why don't those border guards follow orders and swim for shore?"

"They're not border guards. They're bounty hunters."

McQueen rolled to his stomach. "Let's step it up." He stroked for the opposite shore and the others followed.

When they all sloshed up on to the distant shore, the bounty hunters were still following.

"Come on," Augur said, "we'll try our luck at the pass."

Tommy shot Augur a stunned look. "Now what?"

"Quit whining," Yellow Neck said. "Just follow him."

When the sun was half a disk, evening clouds folded on the horizon and reflected silver and purple. Augur stopped and looked at a long vegetated stretch of land. McQueen stood next to him and examined the land like a surveyor. Beneath the bent-over grasses and weeds, a little foot-trail hid. It led inland, and then ran up a dirty-gray mountain of dry shale that was interspersed with baldheaded boulders. And, one dead tree limb stuck out of a spot of lifeless cream-colored dirt.

McQueen looked to Augur. "Are we going up that?"

Augur thoughtfully nodded. "That is the way we must go." He sighed. "It's a shortcut."

McQueen stepped forward. The trail showed no signs of recent travel. At one place, it ran along the crest of a ridge that looked like the sharp edge of a knife. In most places, the trail was only meter wide on the crest; and on both sides it fell away and dropped a thousand meters.

It was getting dark. A tinge of fear shot up McQueen's back. "Are you sure this thing is safe?"

"Just do what I do," Augur said with calm assurance. "It's safe, but it would be safer if we had just one man with plenty of ammunition."

That's right," Yellow Neck said. "Why, with ammunition, we could hold off those stupid border guards for a long time."

"You might," Tommy said and idly kicked a loose rock, "if you had a gun to put the ammunition into."

Yellow Neck watched the rock roll past his feet, then stopped walking for an instant. "Oh, I never thought about dat."

The sun sank lower. McQueen looked down the mountain and watched twenty-nine Dinkies trailing behind. A bounty hunter caught up and cornered a straggling Dinky on the knife-edge. The bounty hunter swung. The Dinky ducked. The bounty hunter wobbled and fell over the edge.

The Dinky watched the bounty hunter fall into the abyss below. Another bounty hunter crept up behind him and pushed him. The Dinky tripped and fell over the knife-edge of the trail, but he reached out and clung onto the old dead tree limb that jutted out into the life ending open space.

The bounty hunter raised his foot to tramp on the Dinky's fingers. The Dinky's buddy ran down and plowed the top of his head into the back of the bounty hunter. The bounty hunter jolted down the trail and bowled into the third bounty hunter. They both windmilled their arms and tumbled over the edge. The Dinky's buddy pulled his friend up over the knife-edge, and they continued up the trail.

As the sun blinked below the horizon, border guards marched out from the trees. Dots of orange light from the torches they held above their heads flickered and nibbled at the semi-darkness. Along the steep side of the cliff, long cylindrical shafts of light beamed out from the dark forest and stretched out like white columns. From the intensity of the beams, McQueen figured the lights had to be carbide gas lights. The border guards aimed the lights and bathed a Dinky's little body in a strong beam, signaling the Dinky out as an easy target. The Dinky stepped on the edge of the trail. It crumbled under his little foot and gave way. Tumbling, he somersaulted, and kicked up a cloud of thick dust. His little hand flew out of the cloud and grabbed onto a crease in a loose rock. He ended up with his feet hanging over the gorge, running in midair, looking for lifesaving footing. There was none. His feet stopped. In the dusty air, he held on, gasping for breath.

McQueen tugged on Augur's shirt sleeve. "Let's go back and get him off that ridge."

Augur looked at the revealing columns of lights. "We must not attract more attention. We must sacrifice a few lives for many."

McQueen turned. "Maybe you're right." He took one step. Tommy tugged at the back of his shirt. McQueen turned back. "Maybe we can get him anyway."

"Do what you want, Yellow Neck said. "I'm not goin' back."

"What's the matter?" Tommy said, taunting him. "Is Ssssy-baby-goo-goo afraid of a little cliff?"

Yellow Neck stopped in his tracks and turned back. "I'll go any place you go."

McQueen and Tommy balanced down the darkening trail, and Yellow Neck ran ahead of them. McQueen looked back. All the other Dinkies were right behind them. Below, all along the skinny trail, lines of border guards with steel nets, lights, and sidearms, filed upward and toward them.

When Yellow Neck got to the Dinky, the Dinky was still hanging on to the crease in the rock. Yellow Neck lay on the ground, reached over the ridge, and grabbed onto the Dinky's wrists, but they were slipping fast.

Running down the trail, McQueen held up his fists and signaled to the Yellow Neck. "Hang on," he shouted. "We're coming."

When McQueen was next to Yellow Neck, he stopped and knelt down. When he reached out to grab the slipping little Dinky by the back of his shirt, the column of light beamed out of the dark and illuminated their efforts. The border guards fired their sidearms. A barrage of antidote-bullets whizzed into the air and over McQueen's head. He ducked down. Yellow Neck's outstretched body slid toward the edge, but he held onto the little Dinky. Tommy leaned over the ridge and tried to grab the Dinky's slipping wrists, but his arms were too short. Another Dinky lay down in front of Tommy. Tommy grabbed his feet. With Tommy holding tight, the Dinky slid down over the ridge. With loose dirt and stones raining down on him, the Dinky hung in midair and snagged the dangling Dinky by the back of the collar of his shirt. He pulled. Tommy pulled. Yellow neck pulled, too. At the end of this Dinky chain, the slipping Dinky kicked his feet in the air; but still, there was no footing. A bullet zinged past McQueen's ear and over Tommy's head. With torches in their hands and the bright lights scything the semi-darkness, the border guards trooped up the trail.

McQueen turned his face toward the Dinkins standing on the hill. "We need to put those carbide lights out."

From the dangling Dinky chain, Yellow Neck turned his head back toward McQueen. "We need a diversion."

A band of Dinkies ran down the trail. With no thought of their own safety, they gathered rocks and rained them down on the bright carbide lights. The thick glass lens broke, and the white carbide gas flames went black. The orange light from the torches continued to flicker and blaze, but the Dinkies didn't stop. They ran right up to the torchlight-bathed border guards. Like hungry ants, the Dinkies tackled them around the legs, grabbed them by the arms, hung on, and mauled them to the ground.   The other border guards continued shooting, but the Dinkies came out of the dark and kept on attacking.

In the orange glow of more oncoming torches, it looked as if the little Dinkies would attack until they were all shot. McQueen bent down, grabbed Tommy by the waist, and pulled. He dragged the chain of Dinkies, with the Dinky dangling on its end, up over the edge of the ridge. More bounty hunters attacked. Another wave of Dinkies suicide-charged the border guards.

The brave little Dinkies' deaths seemed unnecessary. In his heart, McQueen couldn't let them get killed, especially when he had a way to stop it. He figured that if he gave up, just went through the simple act of surrendering, then the Dinkies' lives would be spared. Tommy and he had escaped before. They could do it again. And it would be safe to surrender. They were wanted alive. They could return and fight another day. With a new column of revealing light glinting on his face, McQueen held up his hands in a sign of surrender.

CHAPTER 36

Inside the main base headquarters, Burke escorted Danielle to a room. He politely opened the door and said, "Go on in. I hear you have a hot date with your sweetie at the water house. We'll be by later to pick you up."

Danielle glared at Burke. "Thanks for reminding me what an understanding asshole you are."

Burke smiled a big mocking smile. "No problem. We aim to please," he said, stepped into the hall, and slammed the door.

Danielle wondered what McQueen would think of her now. Maybe she had made a mistake telling Nelson that Augur would be coming to the water house. But then again, she had Nelson's word. They had made a deal. After Augur was captured, McQueen would have his five-hundredth capture. Nelson would have to reinstate him and give him back his stripes. Best of all, he would have the right to reproduce. McQueen and she could be married, live in the big house on the blue grass, and fill it with children. This was a beautiful dream, and she was sure it would come true. But there was still a slight chance it wouldn't.

She walked across the room and looked out the thick-glassed window. A few reporters began bunching up at the end of the street, and more were driving past in their OvalCars.

There were so many reporters that is would be no problem telling them about Nelson's promises and how she and McQueen could save the Dinkies. But what if she was interviewed on live TV and had

378

gotten the wrong reporter? See scanned the gathering reporters. And he was there. The reporter with only one finger left. If he interviewed her, she would risk it all, maybe she would make a fool of herself. That reporter didn't want to lose his last finger. He would lash out at her. Somehow he would make her look like a liar. He would embarrass and humiliate her with a line of no-win questions. He could be brutal and relentless. He could make her say things she didn't want to say. He was very good at his job.

She turned from the window. "So what," she said out loud. "A life with McQueen is worth taking a chance. I'll do it."

She stepped to the door and turned the knob. It was locked.

She walked to the bunk and sat down. Trying to think, she placed her elbow on her knee and propped her chin up with her hand. Maybe Judd has switched the bullets. But if he found out she didn't tell him about the secret tunnel, maybe he would switch them back.

She told herself that it didn't matter. She was not just an ex-driver. She had virus resistant genes. With McQueen, she could save the world. She decided to take Nelson and Burke to the water house. She would show them the secret entrance to the mine complex. She would expose the whole system. The revolt will never happen. She would save McQueen and Tommy, too. She would save the Dinkies. She would even save stinking Sludge and Parry the pervert. Then the world would return to the way it was. McQueen and she would have virus free children.

CHAPTER 37

Amidst the bullets zinging in the air and the horrible screams from the throats of men being scathed, McQueen raised his hands and walked toward the border guards shouting, "Stop! Stop shooting! I surrender."

Ahead of him, two little Dinkies slowed their attack. With disappointment in their faces, they turned toward McQueen, and started to walk away from the fight.

A lone border guard ran up behind one Dinky, shot him in the back, and kicked him over the ridge.

Wondering what kind of a person would do such a thing, McQueen looked into the guard's face. There was no remorse or even a small hint that he had made a mistake. His face beamed with satisfaction. The border guard had no feelings for his fellow man. He was inhuman. All these border guards and bounty hunters were inhuman. McQueen dropped his hands. The needless death of a Dinky had shown him that surrender was not an option.

The surviving Dinkies turned into the fray, and attacked with more fury. A border guard held a torch and aimed his sidearm. A Dinky grabbed him at the knees. The guard whipped the fiery torch at the Dinky and tried to shake free. With hot sparks flying around his little body, and like a fly on a roll of flapping flypaper, the Dinky hung on to the guard's legs. The guard couldn't shake him.

The Dinky dug his little heels into the hard dirt and lifted the guard into the air. Holding on, he back-arched over the knife-edge; and still holding on to the guard's knees, he kamikazed off the edge. With a long flaming orange streak of fire following them, they both plummeted to a deep dark death.

McQueen had never seen anything like that. That Dinky sacrificed himself so that others could escape. McQueen reached down and grabbed the old dead tree limb that was jutting out of the edge of the knife-edge trail. He pulled. It didn't budge. He bent his knees, straightened his arms and pulled again. The heavy tree limb broke free. He lifted the limb; and like it was a set of barbells, he held it on the top of his chest. "Screw this surrender crap," he said, and walked toward the remaining border guards.

A border guard jumped behind McQueen. McQueen felt the guard's hand on his long hair. Before he could turn around, the guard ripped the purple-sheened feather from his hair. McQueen turned. The guard smiled and held the feather in his hand. "Come and get it, low-breed."

McQueen threw the tree limb into the guard's chest. The guard tumbled backwards. McQueen reached for the feather. It flew out of the guard's hand. McQueen bent over to catch it, but it had floated too far over the edge.

His father had given him that feather. With a great sense of loss, he watched it: Winking its purple sheen in the faint flickers of the yellow-orange torchlight, it floated down into the black abyss and was gone.

The guard rolled to his hands and knees, jumped up, and rushed toward McQueen. McQueen stepped aside and kicked him in the rear. The guard tried to stop his forward momentum, but couldn't.

His body jerked forward. Yelling in fright, he sailed out over the edge.

More guards with torches rushed toward McQueen. Anger from losing the feather erupted in his very soul. Adrenaline flowed into his veins. It fueled a newborn strength. He picked up the log again. Like a whirling destruction machine, he swung the log and knocked the warriors and their torches over the ridge. Screaming into the black night, they left long lines of trailing fire all the way to the bottom.

Tommy snuck behind a border guard and knelt down on all fours. Yellow Neck ran up and plowed into the guard with his head; and with both arms, he pushed. The guard tripped backwards over Tommy's back. Flapping his arms, he fluttered over the ridge.

McQueen whacked two more border guards and got ready to whack another. The guard held up his hand in defeat and ran back down the trail. McQueen wound up again. All the other guards ran.

"They're going for reinforcements, "Augur said. "Let's get off this ridge before they come back."

CHAPTER 38

Tommy ran up the trail and stopped at the top of the ridge. He looked down. Dropped torches burned in the dirt casting orange light and streams of stringy black smoke over bodies of Dinkies strewn along the bloody knife-edge trail.

Tommy wondered if the dinkies were crazy. How could anyone be so dedicated to one man? Tommy always thought Augur was no different than himself. Just because Augur had been in the right place at the right time, the Patagonia Dinkies looked up to him. The Dinkies of Blue Town always liked Tommy's antics and tricks, and he was sure that was the best way to fight the corporation. It has worked for years, but now that Sludge had convinced his fellow Dinkies to give up their lives in a no win situation, Tommy wondered if he should change his nonviolent ways of fighting.

He looked at a dying torch. Its flame flickered, sputtered, and went black. If the Dinkies on the ridge had used tricks and relied on nonviolence, today, they would all be like the torch. They would be dead.

Sludge had gotten the Dinkies of Blue Town stirred up and ready to fight, but he didn't have all of them united. Tommy figured he should change his ways and get the Dinkies of Blue Town to unite like the Dinkies of Patagonia.

CHAPTER 39

Just before the orange warning sign at the edge of Forbidden Forest, Augur held up his hand. The Dinkies behind him stopped. "Wait here," McQueen said. "We'll see if it's safe."

McQueen, Augur, Tommy, and Yellow Neck walked out of the forest, stopped next to the orange sign, and looked toward the water house. Silver light from the space-junk-lit sky bathed the water house in a foggy gray light. Its door was opened, just a crack. A slight breeze jerked at the poison ivy vine and caused its dark brown leaves to dance in and out of the opening.

Tommy stepped next to McQueen. "See any warriors?"

With a cautious eye, McQueen looked around. "I don't see anyone." He took a few steps in silence and stopped. "It doesn't look natural. Something's not right."

Tommy tilted his chin upward and surveyed the area. "Looks the same to me."

Turning his head from left to right and back again, McQueen continued to scan the area. "It looks deserted, dead, no life." His eyes fixated on the water house door. "Even that poison ivy vine is dead."

"Are we goin' in?" Yellow Neck asked, and his lips tightened in determination. "Or are we gonna be a bunch of candy-asses and stand under these trees all night?"

"Don't get excited, Yellow Neck," Tommy said. "We never know who's sneaking around."

Yellow Neck stepped away from the orange

sign and started toward the water house. "The only-est thing sneakin' around here is your stupid shadow."

Augur reached out and grabbed Yellow Neck by the shoulder. "We can't risk all our lives. You and the others stay here and watch."

Yellow Neck nodded in agreement, turned, and slipped back into the cover of the forest.

McQueen looked for signs of aggression in the darkness. No warriors were visible. No searchlights went on. "Maybe they gave up," he said, and they walked into the water house.

Tommy pulled out the squirt gun he had hidden in his belt and began to fill it in the water house pool. "No telling when we might need this."

Augur smiled. "It's been a long time since I saw one of those outlawed guns."

"They come in handy," McQueen said, pulled out his squirt gun and filled it, too. Just as he pulled it from the water a Dinky's little head popped up out of the water.

Tommy recognized him immediately. "Parry, what are you doing?"

Parry pulled himself over the edge of the pool and shook the water from his face. "Everyone has gone to the revolt." He looked back at the pool. "I'm supposed to guard the cave. If anyone pulls the lever, I'm supposed to pump the air pump, but I can't help myself. It's my duty to help with the revolt."

Placing the squirt gun into his belt, McQueen looked down at Parry. "You mean the revolt has already started?"

"Yes, it has," Parry said with excitement in his

voice. "Sludge will need all the help he can get."
He flopped his feet over the pool's wall. "I'm
going. You can too." He stood up and shook the
water from his body. "If you hurry, you should be
able to catch them." He ran toward the door.

"Wait!" Tommy said, but Parry had already run
out the door.

McQueen turned to follow. Bam! The back of
the water house door banged against the stone wall.
It had been kicked open. Burke, Danielle, two
warriors, and three, cam-fingered reporters walked
through the opening.

Tommy thrust his squirt gun behind his back
and faced the intruders.

McQueen looked into Danielle's face. Tears of
fear shone in her eyes. Silence grabbed his mind.
He wondered why she hadn't stayed in the cave
where it was safe, and what was she doing with
Burke? Did he trick her into becoming a spy? She
could have been tricked, but McQueen wondered
why he was doubting Danielle's loyalty. He always
had a good feeling about her. But Burke was a pro.
He could trick just about anyone. Especially when
he knew they had something someone he wanted.
Danielle must have taken a chance and sacrificed
her freedom to save them. She only wanted things
to be back to normal. In warrior school, Burke
wasn't really a bad fellow. Maybe Danielle got
through to him. Maybe they're here to let the
Dinkies go free.

Burke stepped forward. The three reporters
thrust their cam-fingers in front of his face. He
spoke. "My fellow distinguished associates of the
Friends of the Earth Corporation. We are pleased to

386

announce the capture of the hero Sergeant John McQueen and what would have been his five-hundredth capture." He pointed to Augur. "Here he is, Augur, the king of the Dinkies."

McQueen glared at Burke. "What are you going to do, Burke, tell the whole world what an asshole you are?"

Burke frowned for a second and continued talking into the cam-finger. "You'll have to excuse Sergeant McQueen, as you can see from his vulgar language, his brain has been ruined by the virus."

"There is no virus," McQueen countered.

"You heard it, Burke said into the cam-finger. "Sergeant McQueen's brain is so far gone he is having delusions. He believes there is no virus."

"What do you plan to do with McQueen?" a reporter asked as if McQueen weren't in his right mind.

"After we have taken McQueen and his Dinky friends into custody, we will have live coverage of the Dinky revolt and the resulting consequences."

Burke turned toward McQueen. The reporters held their cam-fingers in front of both of them. "Too bad, old buddy," Burke said. "You have finally attained your five-hundredth capture. I'm sorry you have contacted the virus and will no longer be of value to the Friends of the Earth Corporation."

"But wait," Danielle said. "That's not what we agreed on."

Burke grabbed Danielle's arms. Cam-fingers were thrust into Burke's face. He pointed to Danielle. "Here is another example of what the virus will do to a person."

387

The reporters pointed their cam-fingers at Danielle. She didn't speak.

Burke stepped close to the cam-fingers and continued. "This person is already turning into a Dinky." He turned toward Danielle and smiled his cheesy smile. "She is just an ex-driver letting her virus infected mind drive too fast for existing conditions."

Burke laughed at his attempted humor; and with the cam-fingers pointing at his face, he pushed Danielle toward the pool. Her elbow painfully hit the edge. She grabbed it and tumbled into the water. McQueen reared back and lifted his fist to strike Burke. The two warriors lunged forward. McQueen dropped his fist. Holding their cam-fingers in front of them like defensive weapons, the reporters backed away.

"Time to come home, Johnny," Burke said, and threw a sneak punch at McQueen's throat.

Unlike before, when Burke had sucker punched him in the chest, McQueen was ready this time. He jerked to the right and batted Burke's arm to the side. Burke's best clandestine punch became a harmless glancing blow to McQueen's belt. McQueen's squirt gun fell from his belt and landed on the floor. Augur picked it up.

Tommy pulled his squirt gun from behind his back and squirted the warriors in the face.

Augur did the same.

In unison, the two warriors screamed, "Virus-water!" and ran out the door.

Tommy and Augur turned the squirt guns on Burke. Augur sprayed him in the face, and Tommy sprayed him in the crotch. Burke smiled, "I'm not

388

afraid of a little water."

Tommy pointed to Burke's crotch. "And you're not afraid to pee your pants."

Burke stared at his crotch. It was soaked with squirt gun water.

The cam-fingers followed his stare and focused on his wet crotch. It looked like he had peed his pants.

Burke sneered at Tommy. "Shut up, you little creep."

McQueen looked toward the reporters. "I hope you got that on TV."

"Yes," Danielle said, and treaded water in the center of the pool. "Even Burke knows the virus is fake. He's not afraid of water."

The reporters looked at each other and walked closer with the cam-fingers. "Sergeant Burke, why are you not afraid of virus-water?"

"Is she right?" the other reporter said before Burke could answer. "Is the water-virus fake?"

"It's just another trick of McQueen's," Burke said, took out a white handkerchief, and wiped the water from his face. "I know I have been exposed to the virus water," he said. "But I have an obligation to the Friends of the Earth Corporation. Sergeant McQueen and I will take the antidote together on National TV."

"He turned toward McQueen. "Come on, old buddy, walk in with me."

"I'm not your buddy, and there is no virus."

"Come on, McQueen," Burke pleaded. "Don't make me take my boots off."

McQueen turned slowly and glared at Burke. He knew that sometimes, a warrior took off his boots just before a battle. It showed that the warrior was not afraid to fight to the death. It could be a psychological edge, and sometimes it would cause the warrior's opponents to back down without a fight. He knew Burke didn't have enough courage to do something as desperate or heroic as that.

"Take off whatever you want," McQueen said.

Burke took a whistle out of his breast pocket. "Okay, have it your way." He put the whistle to his mouth and blew three loud bursts. A hoard of warriors rushed into the water house. Holding their hands on their sidearms, they advanced toward the water pool.

Suddenly, everything happened all at once. McQueen threw Danielle a quick glance. "Go under."

She paddled to the center of the pool and treaded water. Warriors reached over the pool wall and tried to grab her. She stayed in the center. "I can't use my arm," she whispered, treading water with her feet and one arm. "I won't be able to swim through the tunnel without the air mask."

Tommy ducked under a warrior's outstretched hand and handed her the facemask. While he splashed water toward the warriors, she pulled the mask over her face. Muffled words came through the mask. "All the Dinkies have gone to fight," she said. "No one is on the other side to operate the air pump."

Tommy splashed a big wave of water toward the warriors. They jumped back. He looked toward Danielle. With the facemask in his hand he whispered, "Put this on and go under. Hold your breath as long as you can. I'll swim to the other

390

side and run the pump."

Danielle put the mask over her face and dove for the bottom. Tommy looked up at Augur.

Augur quickly nodded. "I'm right behind you."

Tommy dove down.

Augur dove in after him.

McQueen turned to dive. Burke grabbed him around the neck. McQueen reached up, grabbed Burke's head in the crock of his elbow, and squeezed tight. Burke loosened his grip but hung on. McQueen turned to the side, pulled Burke's head toward the floor, and lifted his wide-shouldered body over his back. Burke scissored his feet. McQueen back-stepped, lost his balance. They both fell into the pool. Burke released his grip. McQueen swam for the bottom of the pool and the tunnel. Burke dove after him. Just as he was about to enter the tunnel, McQueen felt Burke's feet. He didn't know how, but Burke must have glided past and gotten into the tunnel first.

McQueen figured Burke would never be able to hold his breath for a second dive. He decided to go back up. That way Burke would come out of the tunnel and follow him.

To let Burke know that he had not gone into the tunnel, McQueen grabbed Burk's feet and shook them. Burke began to back out of the tunnel. McQueen swam to the surface. With cam-fingered reporters holding their fingers at him, he breathed in deep breaths of air, and watched for Burke to come up. Air bubbled up from deep down, but Burke did not surface.

A reporter cautiously held his cam-finger over the edge of the pool and pointed it at McQueen.

"Sergeant McQueen, what happen to Sergeant Burke?"

"I don't know," McQueen said into the cam-finger. But he remembered that the tunnel was too narrow for Burke. McQueen barely fit. He hoped Burke didn't try to swim through the narrow tunnel. His shoulders were too wide. He'd jam himself in there. He'd drown.

McQueen glanced up at the reporter. "I think he's caught on a rock," he lied and dove back down.

At the tunnel, Burke's feet were kicking out the entrance. McQueen tried to grab them and pull, but Burke kicked his hands away. Running out of air, he tried again and again. Finally, he caught one foot and pulled. Burke kicked his hand off with the other foot. Out of air, McQueen swam for the surface.

On the surface, the same reporter was still there. McQueen spoke into the cam-finger. "He's drowning." He took a deep breath and dove back down. This time, Burke's feet were motionless. McQueen grabbed them and pulled, and pulled again. Burke did not move. He released his grip and placed his feet on the stones around the entrance to the tunnel. He grabbed Burke's feet again. When he pulled with the strength in his legs he pushed against the stones. Burke came out to his knees. But McQueen needed more air. He swam for the surface. On top, he breathed in three breaths and swam back down. This time, when he pulled, Burke came out, limp and lifeless. He reached around Burke's head and arm and towed him upward to the surface.

While the reporters aimed their cam-fingers at

McQueen and Burke, the warriors stood next to the pool and watched. McQueen dragged Burke's body over the pool wall and laid him on the floor of the water house.

"Are you going to take his boots off?" a reporter asked.

McQueen stood over Burke's body and looked down. A good warrior never died with his boots on. But because of Burke it was too late to stop the revolt. Why should he take Burk's boots off?

He looked at Burke's lifeless face. He looked like he did when they were in warrior school. They were best friends, and Burke was trying to be a warrior then. No matter what the injury or what the pain, a real warrior would have a last reserve of strength to take his own boots off. It was the mark of a true warrior. But Burke couldn't get to his boots. His arms and shoulders had been trapped in that tunnel. Maybe he changed at the moment of death. The greatest tribute a fellow warrior could do for a fallen comrade was to take his boots off.

The reporter repeated the question. "Are you going to take his boots off?"

McQueen turned away from Burke and looked into the pool. His mind raced. He didn't want to take Burke's boots off. But maybe the way Burke had turned out was his fault. Maybe he created him using the wrong image. He had showed him the corporation ways to get through the warrior school training. It had always been, do to others and get ahead. There was never compassion for the other man. That was how a warrior got through the training. But most warriors knew the training was only a game to be won. They knew it was a means

393

to a great future, but McQueen had failed to show Burke it wasn't a way of life. Maybe that was why he never changed back to a normal person like the other warriors had done. Burke had never had a father like McQueen had had. He never learned the real meaning of life: friends and the love of the fellow man. He was only a brainwashed product of the corporation.

McQueen bent down and slipped Burke's boots off. Burke lifted his head as if he were going to rise. He opened his watery eyes, looked at McQueen, and smiled like the friend he used to be. And then he ceased to be.

A reporter whispered into his cam-finger. "You have seen it here. Sergeant John McQueen has just paid the highest last respects to his longtime friend and fellow warrior."

The other reporter thrust his cam-finger into McQueen's face. "What are you going to do now?"

"We have to stop the revolt."

"Sorry, McQueen," the reporter said. "But you're not stopping anything. The housing authority is coming in plastic suits and they're wearing antidote fingers."

A great sense of immediacy filled McQueen's chest. "Those are fingers of death." He dove into the pool.

CHAPTER 40

McQueen broke through the surface of the water on the inside of the hidden cave pool and treaded water. He looked up at Augur. "We have to go to Blue Town and stop the revolt. But the housing authority is waiting on the other side of the pool with fingers of death."

Augur looked around the tiny room. "How do we get out?"

McQueen stepped from the water. "It might be too late, but we can go out the old secret tunnel in my father's cellar."

"I'll get a shovel," Tommy said, opened the cave-room stone door, and walked into the mine-tunnel complex.

Duck-walking, McQueen and Danielle lagged behind upright walking Tommy and Augur. When they arrived at the wall blocking the cellar tunnel, Tommy and Augur had the wall dug out big enough to crawl out.

McQueen patted Tommy on the back. "Way to go, Tommy."

Tommy wiped his sweaty brow. "Yellow Neck's just like Sludge. He's never around when you need him?"

"He'll show up outside," McQueen said, and crawled through the tunnel.

Outside, Yellow Neck and his crew joined up with McQueen, and the others. They stood at the dark dirt road. "It will take too long to walk to town," McQueen said. "We need an OvalCar."

Yellow Neck walked up to McQueen. "Show us one. We'll get it."

"I would, but I don't work for the motor pool," McQueen said, and started down the road. "Let's get moving.

As they walked down the road, not a car was in sight.

"They must have all went to the revolt," Tommy said.

Yellow Neck kicked a stone at the side of the road. "Those stupid pigs think it's some kinda holiday," he said, and the lights of an OvalCar flashed in the dark.

As if he had just dropped dead, Yellow Neck flopped down in the middle of the road. He lay perfectly still. The only thing that moved was his hand motioning toward the side of the road. "Get into the weeds."

McQueen and the others jumped into the weeds and crouched down. The OvalCar pulled up to Yellow Neck's outstretched body and stopped. He didn't move. The driver got out of the car, walked over to him and knelt down. Yellow Neck moaned a long loud moan. With the distraction of his moaning, the other Dinkies tiptoed behind the OvalCar and quietly pushed it toward the green weeds at the side of the road.

Yellow Neck stopped moaning. The OvalCar's back tires rolled into the weeds and made a swooshing sound. The driver jumped up and ran for the moving OvalCar. Before she could get to it, the Dinkies had pushed it off the road and into the tall green grass.

The driver stopped at the edge of the road, put her hands on her hips, and looked at the Dinkies standing in the grass. "You think that's funny?" she said. "I'll bet that little smart-ass Tommy put you up to this."

Another OvalCar hummed down the road, pulled up, and stopped. Yellow Neck edged toward the back of it. The driver powered down the side window. "Everything okay?"

"Tommy must be up to his old tricks," the standing driver said. "They pushed my OvalCar into the virus-grass."

"It doesn't matter," the driver in the other OvalCar said. "Hop in. After the revolt, we'll have the housing authority pull it out."

Before Yellow Neck could try to push the second OvalCar into the grass, the first driver stepped into it and they drove away.

"We only got one car," Yellow Neck said. "We gotta git some more."

"We don't have time to wait until you get more cars," McQueen said in haste. "If the revolt hasn't already started, we have to stop it."

"Augur stepped to the OvalCar and pointed to Yellow Neck. "We'll go to town. Get more OvalCars and get there as fast as you can."

McQueen stepped next to the car and turned toward Yellow Neck. "Don't take too long," he said. "We'll need all the help we can get."

Yellow Neck talked out the side of his mouth as if he were thinking. "Are those Blue Town warriors a-scared of the green grass?"

"They were afraid of it when we left," McQueen said, grabbed Augur's arm, and pulled him toward the OvalCar. "Come on, get in."

"Wait," Yellow Neck said. "If we gotta fight, how we gonna know when to start?"

Augur lifted his hand and turned his palm down. "Wait for this signal. If you see it, it's time to fight."

CHAPTER 41

Danielle jumped behind the steering wheel of the OvalCar. McQueen, Tommy, and Augur slipped into the back. Danielle drove the stolen OvalCar into Blue Town and stopped.

McQueen looked out the widow and studied the street. Blue vapor streetlamps drenched Blue Town in a chalky lilac light. The pavement looked dark blue. A few empty OvalCars decorated the streets next to the sidewalks. Three and four-story stores that had been built with cement and plastic, with apartments on top, stood next to the canopy covered sidewalks. All of the stores were of the same design. All conformed to the Friends of the Earth Corporation's building codes.

McQueen had never thought of it before, but then every building in the town had been built the same. There was no creativity here. He looked up at the orange-lighted apartment windows. People were poised as if they were waiting for something to happen; or it had already happened, and they were mad because they missed it. McQueen figured that might be a good thing. If the TV went out or Nelson cut it off the air, at least the world would have some witnesses in the windows to the battle that was about to happen.

McQueen looked along the sides of the street. Here and there, pig people stood as if they were trying to hide behind the few scrawny, blue spruce trees at the edges of the canopy covered sidewalks. The blue trees were all the plant life Blue Town could boast about. Beyond the boundaries of Nelson's Blue Grass Park, all of the trees were stunted and skeletal. Their branches drooped to the ground like dirty-blue bones reaching for the peace of the earth.

A wandering gust of wind pushed a scrap of thin plastic along one side of the sidewalk and out into the street. A Dinky slave scurried out of a store and stopped at the intersection.

Being careful to stay on the blue asphalt, a warrior drove an OvalCar through the park. If he drove onto the dew-covered grass, the car would have to be sanitized for water virus exposure. The car stopped next to the Dinky who was trying to cross the street. The warrior stepped out of the car and blocked his path. As if he were showing reverence to a divine being, the Dinky bowed down to the warrior. The warrior bent over and held his finger a centimeter away from the scrap piece of plastic. "Pick that up!"

Staying in the bent over position, the Dinky reached down and picked up the plastic paper. The warrior stood with his legs apart and his hands on his hips. The Dinky tilted his head upward and looked at the Warrior.

"Don't let that happen again," the warrior bellowed. Then, in a God-like motion, the arrogant warrior waved the Dinky away.

The Dinky straightened up and ran into dew-covered safety of Nelson's Park. Running along the blue grass, he reached up and deliberately ran his hand along the dead branches of the trees. They chattered like sticks on a bamboo wind chime.

As if he were too lazy to do anything about it, the warrior shook his head, slipped back into the car, and drove down an alleyway.

The pig people that had been behind the scrawny trees, pulled back and faded into the shadows. Now the street and sidewalks were empty.

McQueen, Danielle, Tommy, and Augur got out of the stolen OvalCar.

Tommy's face set in a grim expression. "I hope we don't get killed."

"We should be okay," Danielle said, and looked to McQueen. "Judd should have switched the bullets by now."

Augur shook his head with understanding. "If he has done this, everything will be fine."

"We should have an easy go of it," Danielle said but flashed a nervous look. "The Dinkies will only be disabled for a few minutes. They won't die."

McQueen gently patted her back. "Even if we have the edge, we have to try to stop the fight."

"Yes," Augur agreed, "we must try to reason with both sides."

"They never listened to anything we tried to tell them before," Tommy said, his eyes skeptical. "What if they won't listen now?"

"If they won't," Augur said without emotion. "We can at least try to stall for time so the Patagonia Dinkies can get back with the antitoxin."

McQueen stared into the street where the revolt was about to happen. "If they do, it still won't be a fair fight. Man against Dinky, brute force against brute force, hand-to-hand combat, just won't be enough."

"I heard that," Sludge said, and walked out of a dark, side alleyway.

401

A mob of Dinkies, armed with fresh-cut wooden two-by-fours, followed him. He stopped at the edge of the OvalCar. "I didn't think you guys had it in ya," he said, and looked to McQueen and Tommy. "But it looks like you guys finally came to your senses."

"We don't want to fight," McQueen said. "We want to settle this once and for all."

"We got 'em outnumbered," Sludge said. "We're gonna settle it." He held the two-by-four like he was a baseball player waiting for the first pitch. A big confident smile spread across his face, and he waggled the two-by-four. "I got your problem solver right here."

"A revolt won't solve a thing," Augur said. "We just had one in Patagonia. Now things are worse."

"Sludge waved the two-by-four around in little circles. "We ain't in Patagonia."

"That's right," a Dinky behind him said, and raised his two-by-four. "We have wood-virus clubs. If we can't scare the gutless cowards, we'll conk them over their stupid heads."

"I don't think they'll be gutless," McQueen said. "It's senseless to bring two-by-fours to a gun fight."

"So what," Sludge said. "Doze antidote-bullets are ah-sposed to be changed to sleeping bullets."

"We don't know if that has happened," Danielle said.

The threat of an oncoming battle caused McQueen's stomach to churn with butterflies. He searched his mind for something that would increase their odds of winning. "Maybe if we tell

402

the pig people about the virus, they will help."

"I doubt it," Tommy said. "Those pig people don't expect you or Augur to show up for a revolt. You're supposed to be in custody."

McQueen looked up at the shadows of the people in the orange-lighted windows. "There are enough pig people to stop any revolt."

"That's true," Tommy said and tilted his head toward the windows. "But they are only waiting to watch you be given the antidote on TV. They sense that something is wrong, but we'll never get any help from them. They never do anything but watch."

"It's a shame," Augur said. "But they just don't understand."

A Dinky behind Sludge spoke up. "We're tired being treated like inferior people. We want our equal rights."

"That's right!" Sludge said. "Let them stay in their stupid windows and watch us. We'll git our rights back by our selfs."

Augur held up his hand. His eyes looked as if they were focused on an object beyond the streets of Blue Town. "In the name of equality you will destroy equality." He paused. "The truth of the matter is that the victor is always superior and looks down on the people he defeated. Some day the world will figure out that all battles are stupid."

Sludge gripped his two-by-four and lifted it slightly. "You callin' us stupid?"

"I'm not calling you anything. You may call yourselves individualists. You may say victory is to the swift, the battle to the strong, you may believe that is the lesson you have learned from your history."

Sludge wrinkled his forehead as if he were confused. "So what?"

Another Dinky spoke up. "That's the way it has always been."

Sludge continued. "That's the way it will always be."

"But couldn't you just give us a little time," Augur pleaded. "What have you got to lose?"

The other Dinkies mumbled and took a few steps backward. Augur put his arm around Sludge and whispered in his ear. "Don't get excited, but we have an antitoxin."

Sludge's eyes widened with anticipation. "Well let's git this revolt a started."

"We don't have the antitoxin here. It's on the way. But we need more time."

Sludge moved away from Augur and raised his voice. "What do you mean, an antitoxin is on the way?"

"Keep it down," McQueen whispered. "With the new antitoxin, the antidote bullets are harmless."

"How do you guys know that?"

McQueen placed his hand on Augur's shoulder. "This man was shot with the corporation's poison bullets and he didn't die."

"He's living proof," Tommy added. "He was on the brink of death. Patagonia's new antitoxin brought him back. When enough antitoxin is made, the Dinkies of Patagonia will bring it here in force."

With a mischievous expression on his face, Sludge turned to his followers. "Let's go back. We kin fight another day and win for sure."

Augur stepped next to Sludge. "Thanks to you.

404

There will be no bloodshed tonight."

Everyone breathed a breath of relief. The Dinkies lowered their two-by-fours for just a second and . . .

A dark OvalCar hummed to the center of the street. Nelson jumped out and fired the first shot, right at Augur. Augur dropped to his knees. The bullet zinged over his head and stuck in the protective molding on the door of the OvalCar. Sludge and the other Dinkies scattered back into the dark alleyways.

Nelson's bodyguard, Judd, stepped out of the car. Danielle stepped out from behind the car next to the sidewalk and held her palms up. She jerked them signaling toward Judd. Judd seemed like he didn't understand what she was doing. Danielle yelled to him, "Did you do it?"

Jud shook his head and signaled that he did not change the bullets. Danielle yelled into the alleyway where Sludge had run. "The bullets are still live."

A line of Warriors, three deep, appeared, and loomed at the end of the street. McQueen turned toward the Dinkies and lifted his fist into the air. "Fight for your lives.

CHAPTER 42

The Dinkies flowed out of the alleyway with their two-by-fours raised. Over the years, Tommy had seen many warriors practicing war games, and the ones standing at the end of the street were no different. They wore intimidating uniforms, all the same military color. And they wore hard helmets. Their feet were protected with thick warrior boots. With hands on their sidearms, they advanced with military precision.

The Dinkies wore loose fitting clothes. Their colors were dull, non-threatening, ragged, and dirty from long hours in the tunnels. They had no helmets to protect their small heads. Instead, they wore those floppy hats made of soft cloth. Thin leather, one-size-fits-all, Dinky moccasins offered little protection for their feet. One step from a thick warrior's boot could break a tiny foot. The dinkies carried two-by-fours, but this small group of Dinkies acted as if they didn't know what they were doing. They would be no match for the accuracy of the trained warrior marksmen, shooting sidearms.

Hoping that Sludge would see that they were outnumbered and change his mind, Tommy pointed to the mass of warriors and then pointed to the little group of Dinkies.

Sludge acted like it didn't matter. "This is it, Tommy," he said, and offered him a two-by-four. "Let's go."

Tommy took the two-by-four. Danielle stepped toward him. "Good luck," she said.

"We ain't gonna need any luck," Sledge said, and waved his two-by-four. "We got wood-virus."

Tommy looked to Danielle. "You don't have anything to fight with." He offered her his two-by-four. "Take this."

She lifted her hand to accept it.

Sludge showed a look of disapproval. "Don't be givin' her that. Woman ain't got enough strength to hit nothin'."

Danielle lowered her hand. "It's okay. You can keep it."

Tommy leaned the two-by-four against the OvalCar. "I'll set it here just in case you change your mind."

Tommy took one step toward the forming mob of Dinkies, and stopped. He didn't want to fight. He never did. He had always made a joke out of authority or thought of a better way around it. He had never fought, except the wrestling matches McQueen's father had them do on the foam mat in the cellar. The old, underwear-wedged-up-the-butt-crack move won't work here. This fight was to expose the phony virus. It was a fight for the future of the world. He could die, but had no choice. He would fight.

He stepped next to Sludge. Sludge held up his arm. "Wait!" he said, and pointed to the street.

Military OvalCars hummed in from every direction and blocked the street exits. More warriors, with mean faces, stepped out of the military OvalCars, and more oozed out of the dark with antidote rifles slung low like guitars. Above the storefronts, pig people rushed to their orange-lighted windows and looked out.

Tommy turned to Sludge. "We were outnumbered before. Now we don't stand a chance."

Sludge shook his head with defiance. "Don't worry about it." He shook his two-by-four. "We got wood virus, and we got virus water, too."

Tommy wanted to turn and run. But every avenue of escape was blocked. The night became still, like before a storm. Out of that stillness, the patter of Dinkies' feet hitting the blue asphalt echoed in the dark. Tommy looked in front of him. Like rifle toting soldiers marching in a parade, a stream of Dinkies carrying two-by-fours, at shoulder arms, flowed into the street and formed attack lines. Sludge raised his two-by-four. "Wood-virus!" he shouted. "Get your red-hot wood virus right here!"

Jerking their two-by-fours into the night air, the little mob of Dinkies in front of him, formed a line and chanted, "Wood-virus! Wood-virus! Wood-virus!"

Tommy smiled inwardly. He no longer worried about how he would unite the Dinkies of Blue Town as Augur had done in Patagonia. His Dinky friends were united about as tight as they were going to ever be.

Tommy figured the Dinkies still had a few tricks in the old bag. He still believed that the best way to fight evil was to mock it. For a moment, he wished he had a two-by-four. But then, he realized he had something else that was better. He reached into his belt and pulled out his fully loaded squirt gun. The Dinkies next to him placed their hands on canteens of water.

CHAPTER 43

Standing next to the OvalCar, McQueen looked at Augur. "Are you ready?"

Augur put his hand on his canteen. "I hope your virus-water works here. It didn't scare anybody in Patagonia."

Danielle picked up the two-by-four Tommy had placed against the side of the car. "Sent them to me." With two hands she swung the two-by-four like it was a tennis racket. "I'm ready."

"We'll find out," McQueen said, and snapped his head to the right. "Look out!"

A warrior jumped out from behind the OvalCar and swung his fist toward Augur's head. Augur ducked, dropped to his knees, spun around, and leg tackled the lone warrior.

Surprised, the warrior tried to jerk his feet away, but Augur hung on tight. The warrior tumbled backwards and fell on the hard blue pavement. Augur pulled out his canteen and poured water onto the warrior's face.

Danielle stepped out from behind the OvalCar and pointed the two-by-four at the warrior.

The warrior jumped up. With water dripping from his face, he looked at Augur. "Water-virus?" he said as if he were asking a question and wanted someone to say it wasn't.

Augur smiled an evil smile and flicked a few more drops of water in his direction. The warrior jumped back, reached up, and grabbed his wet face. "Virus-water," he shrieked, and ran down the alleyway.

McQueen turned around. A warrior pulled out

his sidearm and aimed at him. "Give it up, McQueen."

The sharp light of a searchlight scythed the darkness and blasted into the warrior's face. Holding his sidearm, the warrior lifted his hand over his eyes. Before he could drop his hand from his face, McQueen was on him. He stepped to the left side of the warrior and rocketed his hand up and under the warrior's triceps. In one rotating motion, he slammed the back of his hand into the warrior's sidearm, making it spin downward. But it stayed on his finger.

McQueen reached around the warrior's neck and clamped it tight. Squeezing the warrior's neck below his helmeted head, he panted his feet firmly on the ground. In one smooth swinging motion, he pulled on the warrior's neck and arched downward. The warrior's legs soared up off the pavement. When McQueen released his neck and arm, the warrior went flying into the air. The sailing warrior held out his hands to break his fall. But when his body fell on the cement sidewalk, the bones in his arm cracked. His sidearm fell off his finger, clinked on the cement, bounced once, and skipped under the OvalCar.

Danielle stepped up and stood over him. Conk! She hit him on his helmeted head with the two-by-four. Instead of grabbing his head, the warrior held his arm, scrambled to his knees, stood up, lost his balance, and fell to the sidewalk. He rolled over and looked up. Augur stood over him and tipped a canteen of water until water dripped into the warrior's face. The warrior jumped to his feet. Holding his arm, he staggered down the sidewalk,

410

muttering, "Decontamination chamber! Decontamination chamber!"

Strong searchlights from the military OvalCars moved erratically, blasting blinding shafts of light into the line of Dinkies. Warriors ran in front of the lights and formed a defensive line. The Dinkies charged with their threatening two-by-fours, striking the air above their heads.

With their backs turned away from the brightness of the roving spotlights, the warriors stood their ground. When the Dinkies were ten meters from them, they pulled their sidearms and opened fire. Antidote bullets slammed into the Dinkies in the front line. They dropped to their knees. Their virus two-by-fours fell from their hands and clunked on the dark blue pavement. The next line of Dinkies pulled out their canteens and poured water on the two-by-fours.

"Water virus," they shouted.

The line of warriors jolted back like they were on the end of a snapping whip. Tramping over the fallen Dinkies, the second line of Dinkies charged. The warriors fired their sidearms again. A few Dinkies managed light hits with the two-by-fours, but fell before they could do any damage. The third wave of Dinkies charged. The fourth wave did not wait for the third line to fall. They charged, and all the Dinkies behind them charged.

McQueen felt a warrior at his back. He reached around, hooked the warrior's head in a headlock. The warrior struggled. McQueen threw his hip to the side, back stepped, pulled down on the warrior's head, and sent him into the air. Flapping his arms as if he were trying to fly, the warrior sailed toward the OvalCar. With a painful thump, he slammed onto its roof. Moaning, he grabbed his back, slid down the slanted window of the car, and fell to the pavement. McQueen turned and braced his body for another attack.

Four warriors stood in front of him, and ten more walked up behind. He saw a tiny gap in the wall of warriors. He lunged for it. He broke through. Looking in all directions, he tensed to run. With the spotlights flicking and cutting slices of darkness from the air, Judd appeared in front of him. Two massive warriors stood at his side.

"Come on, John," Judd pleaded. "Stop this nonsense. Come in peacefully."

McQueen looked on the other side of the car. Danielle was gone.

CHAPTER 44

While McQueen was fighting, a warrior had jumped up behind Danielle and grabbed her by both breast. Although she was trying to hit him with the two-by-four, he was dragging her far into the dark alleyway. He kicked at the two-by-four in her hands and shook her, but she held on to the two-by-four with both hands.

She knew that no warrior wanted a dead mate. So she played possum. She went limp. He stopped dragging her and let her fall. Whap! Her head hit the hard cement of the alleyway.

Pain flooded her brain. Everything began to go dark, but she managed to not black out. She figured that if she played dead he would go away. But he didn't. He took off his helmet and proceeded to have his way with her. When he reached down to unzip his pants, she jumped up and swung the two-by-four with all her might. It landed on the bridge of his nose. Blood splatted back and into her face. He lunged for her. She swung again. This time, the two-by-four thunked on the side of his head. He dropped to his knees. Reaching for his sidearm, he started to get up.

"Stay down," she said.

But he didn't. He lifted his sidearm. She wound up, swung the two-by-four around, and grand-slammed him. He buckled at the waist and fell forward. His head clunked on the alleyway cement.

Now the warrior laid there, blood oozing from his opened mouth. The smell of death hung in the dark air. It upset Danielle's mind and her balance of senses. She felt sick to her soul. She wanted things back the way they were. She had never wanted to fight. She didn't mean to kill anyone.

She turned away from the body. Her legs felt weak. She staggered, but caught her balance. After she took a deep breath and exhaled slowly, she used the two-by-four for a crutch. She forced her wobbly legs to step out of the alleyway. She hobbled next to the OvalCar, leaned on it, and cocked her head.

Hoping for a sign that McQueen was still alive, she turned her head toward the street. The fighting had waned. Spotlights from the military OvalCars no longer danced and made the night black and white. Waiting for death, Dinkies littered the street and the sidewalks. Warriors walked between them, kicking them in the ribs. If they groaned or cried out in pain, they were shot again. A few pig people stretched their necks and peeked out of the shadows.

From out of the dark, Nelson appeared right in front of Danielle. He stood erect and leaned toward her.

Huffing for air, she stood her ground.

She wondered what he wanted. Whatever it was, if she wanted to live, she would have to catch him off guard. She quickly regrouped her senses and surreptitiously set the two-by-four against the car.

Nelson relaxed his body movements. And, as if he wanted the whole world to know he had her under his power, he shouted loud and clear, "That's more like it."

Danielle blinked her eyes, swallowed, and vowed to perform the best acting job of her life. She swung her hips with a sensual sway, leaned against the car, unbuttoned the top of her uniform, and cast an inviting glance toward him.

"Good girl," Nelson said, and held his hand on his sidearm. He stepped closer, unbuttoned the front of her uniform, more, and slipped his free hand under the material. "Could this be felt?"

She closed her eyes and tried not to think about his ugly body. He moved closer.

He bent over, put his mouth next to her ear, and whispered, "This could be fun for you."

She arched back and drove her knee into his crotch.

He grimaced for a second and then smiled as if he enjoyed it.

Danielle grabbed the bloody two-by-four from the side of the car and swung. The two-by-four didn't land squarely. It hit Nelson in the kidney, twisted, then jerked from her hands and flew under the car. Nelson arched sideways, grabbed at his side, and staggered backward.

Danielle ran to the side of the street. A metal-handled broom leaned against the blue cement wall in front of a store. She grabbed it. Nelson lurched toward her. Using the broom handle as a spear, she tried to force it into his stomach. He grabbed the end of it and held on. She pulled back. Trying to take it off her, he pulled in. She pushed in and let go. Krr-oomf! The handle plunged into his stomach. She released the broom handle and ran behind the OvalCar.

Nelson sucked his breath in-between phrases. "So you want to play . . . I have a good . . . game for you."

Danielle's words dripped with venom. "Your

whole life is a game."

Nelson lunged for her. She jumped around the front of the car. He stood at the other end of the car. Trying to confuse her into running in the wrong direction, he jerked his body from side to side. She danced around the car. He couldn't catch her.

Standing at the side of the car, he leaned toward her and shouted, "Stand still, you low life driver."

Tommy stepped from the alleyway, wound up, and chunked a rock at Nelson. It ricocheted off the car and clunked on the side of Nelson's head.

Tommy ran close and waved his hands in front of him. "Hey, you big dummy," he taunted. "Do you think she actually wants you to catch her?"

It was a delayed effect. With his hand shaking, Nelson reached up and grabbed his head where the rock had hit him. He leaned over the front of the car and moaned.

Danielle relaxed her stance. Tommy walked up to her and gestured toward Nelson. "He's had it."

Danielle turned to look for McQueen.

"Hold it right there," Nelson shouted.

Danielle and Tommy turned toward Nelson. He stood with a sidearm in his hand. "Sorry, honey, you can't travel too fast for this road condition." He waved his hand in the air. Two warriors held McQueen by the arms and dragged him in front of the OvalCar.

Here's your honey," Nelson said, and presented McQueen to Danielle.

Danielle realized this was it. This time, there was no way out. If McQueen loved her, she would submit to death. But if things had turned out different, she needed to know if he would have married her.

Trying to escape, McQueen jerked and kicked. A warrior picked up Tommy and held him over his head. "Stop resisting or I'll slam your little friend into the pavement."

McQueen quit trying. The warrior lowered Tommy to the ground but kept a good hold on his little wrists.

Nelson smiled and motioned for the reporters. They came forward with their cam-fingers and stopped in front of him.

Talking into the cam-fingers, Nelson looked down at Danielle and McQueen. "You two have been infected with the water and wood-virus. "We will administer the antidote. However, you both know because of the time that has passed, you may not survive."

A young reporter, with a full set of fingers, gasp. Another reporter, with a single cam-finger, shoved the young reporter to the side and took his place. Nelson looked at McQueen and Danielle. "Do you two have any last words?"

McQueen struggled. The warriors subdued him, and he looked into the cam-finger. "There is no virus," he yelled. "It's all a lie."

Nelson motioned for the reporters to take their cam-fingers away from McQueen and focus on him. They hesitated but then turned and held their cam-fingers in front of Nelson.

In a most sincere tone of voice, Nelson said, "The Friends of the Earth Corporation are sorry that the great people of Blue Town had to see a great warrior like Sergeant John McQueen in such a state. But such is the state of anyone who ignores the warnings, goes off the blue grass, and contacts the virus."

In a low controlled voice, McQueen shouted, "I am not crazy."

As if he were sweeping McQueen's words away, Nelson waved his hand. He paused and shook his head sadly. "If the antidote works, we'll see the real Sergeant John McQueen return to his hero self."

"It's not going to work," McQueen said. "You already know that."

Nelson turned to Danielle. "Driver, do you understand the risks of taking the antidote?"

"Like a beaten dog, Danielle obediently shook her head. "I understand, Chief Earth Officer Nelson."

Nelson talked with an expressionless look on his face. "Do you have any last wishes or requests?"

Danielle felt embarrassed, but she had nothing to lose. She voiced her request. "My only hope in life was to marry and be granted the right to reproduce. Could the great Chief Earth Officer Nelson grant this one last privilege to a dying driver?"

Nelson immediately raised his voice and replied, "This is not a reproducing granting court. There is no way I could do that."

The reporter with a full set of fingers squeezed through the line of reporters. He popped his head up and held his cam-finger in Danielle's face. "You are about to die. Why do you think the great Chief Earth Officer will not grant you one last wish?"

Danielle let her hands drop to her sides. "I

have no idea. He has the power to marry people in combat situations. I don't see why he cannot do it now."

It started as a low murmur. Then, one lone pig person, in an orange window over the storefront, hung out and waved his hands in protest. "Perform your obligation, Nelson."

A voice beamed down from a far window. "Grant her a last request."

Pig people filtered out of buildings and formed a crowd on the fringes of the sidewalks. With their faces concealed in the shadows they chanted in protest. "Grant her the right! Grant her the right! Grant her the right!"

The little full-fingered reporter jammed his cam-finger in front of Nelson's face. "You are on function status. It is your obligation. Will you grant her the right?"

Judd nudged Nelson in the elbow and motioned for him to lean toward him. Nelson looked puzzled, but bent toward Judd. Judd whispered in his ear.

Nelson shook his head and stood erect. "I am the Chief Earth Officer with the authority," he said. "It is my obligation to go through the motions of a marriage ceremony."

Above the store fronts, pig people in the orange-lighted windows cheered and threw spirals of blue plastic out of the windows. Being careful not to step in water or on the pieces of splintered wooden two-by-fours, the pig people in the street danced amongst the dying Dinkies.

"Nelson glared at McQueen and then looked to Danielle. "Let's get this over with."

The warriors dragged McQueen over to

419

Danielle.

Tommy pulled on the arm of the warrior that was holding him. "I'm the best man," he said, and he led the warrior over to McQueen.

With Tommy standing next to him, McQueen relaxed and took her hand. Danielle looked puzzled.

"What's the matter?" McQueen asked.

"I just wanted you to ask me."

"Ask you—" McQueen started to say, but Tommy nudged him in the ribs.

"Ask her to marry you," Tommy whispered. "Drop to one knee, you big dummy."

"Please don't," Danielle said. "I want my last vision of you to be as you lived. Strong and proud."

McQueen nodded.

"Get on with it," Nelson barked.

McQueen lifted her hand to his chest. She felt the beating of his strong heart. The fact that they were going to die lay heavy in her very soul. They could have had wonderful children together. With children like McQueen, they would have changed the world.

McQueen held her hand tighter. She felt the fear. She knew he wanted to fight again. But he relaxed his hand and spoke. "Will you marry me and accept the privilege to reproduce?"

Danielle felt her face blush. "She managed her most seductive look. She looked into his dark eyes. "Yes."

Nelson raised his hand in the air as if he were saluting a higher God and proclaimed: "Under the laws of the Friends of The Earth Corporation, this driver and this warrior have been granted the privilege to reproduce."

With a disgusted look on his face, Nelson dropped his hand.

Tommy spoke up. "Tell him, 'You may kiss the bride.'"

Nelson scoffed at Tommy, raised his hand again and said, "It is so ordered."

Tommy spoke up. "You may kiss the bride."

McQueen embraced Danielle and held her like a delicate flower. She had never been held like this before. She wanted it to last forever.

Sludge yelled from far in the crowd. "Nelson may kiss my ass."

With his right hand behind his back, Nelson pointed into the crowd with his left hand. "Capture that Dinky," he ordered. He took his right hand from behind his back. Danielle felt a needle on her arm. Trying to repeat what had happened with the drunken medic, she jerked her arm sideways to make the antidote fly out the side of her skin, but she was too late. With his finger of death, Nelson had injected the full dose. She felt McQueen's body go limp. She knew he had been injected, too.

"I have now administered the antidote," Nelson said. "If it is successful, The Friends of The Earth Corporation will once again have to protection of a great warrior and the services of a reliable driver."

McQueen and Danielle unlocked from their embrace and slumped to the ground.

Nelson looked down at them. "This is a sad moment for the corporation," he said, and raised his head toward the cam-fingers. "However, we must be thankful for the warriors and the border guards of Patagonia. Because of their relentless efforts and dedication to the Friends of The Earth Corporation, infected Dinkies like this will never reproduce."

He looked at Tommy. "Bring that Dinky forward. "I've waited a long time to give this one the antidote."

Danielle lay next to McQueen and looked toward his dying body. A shaft of green light beamed down from the top of an orange-lighted window and cloaked them. She looked up. Two warriors held Tommy, but stood like attendants at a funeral. They weren't taking Tommy to Nelson. Something was wrong. She listened. Floosh! Floosh! Sounds of shoes dragging across wet grass drifted into the silent night. She looked down her body and past her feet. Ghost shapes emerged and silhouetted against the bony tree limbs of Nelson Park.

She hoped it was the Patagonia Dinkies coming with the antitoxin.

The silhouettes emerged from the velvety shadows and walked into the light, unafraid, laughing; and like miniature supermen, they were walking tall. They sauntered into the outer haze of the blue streetlights and into the orange window-lighted semi-darkness of the Dinky-littered street. The warriors with the antidote rifles slung low like guitars, stood before them.

"It's the same old circus," Nelson said into the cam-fingers. "We'll have these clowns taken care of in a few minutes."

McQueen gasped and tried to lift his head. "You can't kill them in cold blood."

Nelson smiled and held his hand high. He was ready to drop it down and signal the warriors to start

422

shooting, but he paused and said, "We'll build a monument to them. It will signify the ignorance of the former Dinkies of Patagonia."

McQueen started to speak. His head turned to the side and he was silent. Augur stepped out of the shadows. Nelson pointed at him and then at McQueen. He commanded, "Dinky, clean up this mess."

"Sorry," Augur said, lifted his hand and turned it palm down. "Your magnificent victory will never happen."

CHAPTER 45

McQueen was dying. This time he knew it was real. He rolled to his back and stared into the black sky. A strange wind blew. Lightning cracked, but it didn't crack one time and blink bright or fade like usual lightning. For a long time its bright pulsating veins reached down to the earth and sent a constant glow and the sky overflowed with purple velvet.

Because the poison antidote was working, McQueen's sight was not clear. At first he didn't recognize what the glow in the sky was. But then his eyes cleared. Amethyst light hovered in the low hanging clouds. He didn't know if he was dreaming or hallucinating, but what he was seeing was in the earth's heavens. It was a vision of an ancestral spirit.

Strong ancient lines of knowledge accented the spirit's face, but its forehead remained clear and untroubled. The spirit glowed with patience and wisdom. Beneath its Indian nose, a strong jaw and a closed mouth sent out a wordless expression of power. Its white hair flowed into the pale fringes of the lavender clouds and became one with the sky.

McQueen felt detached from his body. His mind was fading. He closed his eyes. When he tried to open them, only one eye would open. He squinted out of it. Below the purple velvet clouds and beneath the watchful eyes of the spirit, an Indian sat on a black and white pinto and held both arms out in a spread eagle position. In one hand he held a long spear, pointing it toward the sky. Just below its flint spearhead, two white feathers flickered in the wind. The other hand was extended with the palm turned up.

A small animal skin covered the Indian's midsection, and his chest was covered with a breastplate made of rows of little round bones. Moccasins of yellow, blue, red, and brown; with white fringe around the ankles, accented his feet. The lingering light from the amethyst veins of lightening bathed his smooth symmetric body and accented his purple and white full-feathered headdress.

The Indian looked upward and drew power from the spirit's lightning. Just in front of the horse's long flowing tail, a lone purple feather trailed in the wind. The lightning that had been frozen in time went black. The spirit and the Indian vanished.

McQueen couldn't move, but he could still see and he could listen. Thunder rumbled in the distance and the sky sent flashes of light down onto the blue town.

Like rats fleeing from a fire, the warriors rushed under the blue canopies; and as if they believed they were safe from a threatening virus rain, they patted each other on the back and congratulated themselves on the defeat of the Dinkies.

One warrior looked toward Nelson Park. "Halt!" he commanded. The other warriors turned their heads.

The Patagonia Dinkies were advancing. They carried syringes, and it looked like they had long stringy hair hanging out from under their floppy hats.

The warriors laughed until what was hanging

out from under the floppy hats was revealed under the lights. It was the feared green-virus grass. The warriors quit laughing, grumbled amongst themselves, lifted their sidearms, and began shooting the oncoming Patagonia Dinkies.

"That's more like it," Nelson said, and snorted a big satisfied laugh. "We'll show those little ingrates." He smiled at the warriors firing their sidearms. "Now, the world will know whose boss."

The one-fingered reporter looked away from McQueen's lifeless body and announced into his cam-finger: "The Corporation's great hero, Sergeant John McQueen, has just been killed by his own ignorance. The dangers of wood and water-virus should never be ignored."

A warrior next to McQueen whispered, "And it looks like Nelson is still in charge."

As the two warriors holding Tommy watched the Patagonia Dinkies, a Patagonia Dinky slipped through the line of distracted warriors and touched McQueen and Danielle with his Patagonia antitoxin fingers of life.

McQueen opened both eyes and looked down the street. More Patagonia Dinkies came out of the shadows. Yellow Neck, the black Dinky, stopped at Sludge's lifeless body. He bent over. When he looked at Sludge's face, he jerked back like he had seen a mirror image of himself lying dead. Then, as if he were checking to see if he was still alive, he felt Sludge's hands and arms. He stood up, nodded, bent back down, and administered the antitoxin.

McQueen wanted to walk over and watch the expression on Sludge's face when he woke up and saw that a black Dinky that looked just like him had

426

saved his life, but the warriors reloaded and shot more antidote-bullets. More little Patagonia Dinkies came out of the dark. Like ants tending to little precious grains of sugar, they touched the fallen Dinky bodies.

As if expecting a complete victory, Nelson paid no attention to what was happening. He placed one foot into his OvalCar, raised his hand in triumph, and turned toward the crowd. The crowd didn't respond. The reporters didn't focus their cam-fingers on him. They focused on the great rise from the dead.

Nelson commanded his warriors, "Fire! Kill them all."

Antidote bullets flew. They hit their targets. They stuck in the bodies of the Patagonia Dinkies. The Dinkies stopped for a moment, pulled out the now harmless antidote bullets and threw them into the street. Not one Dinky fell.

TV reporters held their outstretched cam-fingers in front of Nelson's face. In unison, they demanded, "Is the virus fake?"

Nelson didn't answer. Warriors quit firing and dropped their sidearms. The two warriors released Tommy from their grip. Turning toward McQueen, Tommy rubbed his wrists where the warriors had held him.

McQueen stood up and turned to Nelson. A cam-finger was thrust in front of McQueen's face, and the reporter asked, "Is the virus fake?"

"Of course the virus is fake," McQueen said. "The antidote bullets are filled with death serum."

"Then why haven't the Dinkies died?" the reporter asked.

"The Dinkies of Patagonia have discovered the antitoxin. The poison antidote bullets can no longer harm them."

Augur thankfully bowed his head. "It looks like we have won."

Nelson turned to the cam-fingered reporters. "The Dinky antitoxin is a fake. Someone switched the bullets."

Judd stepped forward. "Chief Earth Officer Nelson, no one has switched the bullets."

Nelson's face filled with rage. "I'll prove the antidote is not a death serum." He grabbed a warrior's finger of death and touched it to his neck. "I have not been infected with any virus. This antidote will not harm me." He started to say something else, but his words trailed off. He fell to the ground.

McQueen motioned to Augur. "Give him the antitoxin."

Lying on his back, Nelson coughed and held up his hand. "Stop," he said with strong authority, but it sounded like his throat was closing. "I'll show you all," he squeaked out. "The virus is real. The bullets have been switched." Suddenly, he looked up at McQueen. His eyes bulged wide and white. His voice constricted with pain. "Have I poisoned myself?"

McQueen looked down and nodded his head. "Yes, Chief Executing Officer, just like you poisoned many others."

"It is a fitting end," he said. "I'm tired of it all. Let me die."

Augur stepped close and knelt down. He reached over to administer the antitoxin. Nelson pushed the syringe away. McQueen knelt down to help. Nelson reached up and clung to McQueen's forearm. The strength of his grip seemed unreal. Gripping his forearm in return, McQueen realized it was the ancient warrior arm clasp. With a stern military face, Nelson looked to McQueen, and commanded, "Warrior McQueen! Take off my boots!"

McQueen bent down to oblige. Lightning flashed into the violet clouds. For an instant he saw the watchful spirit in the sky. It had a questionable look in its eyes. Below him, the Indian on the horse had his back turned. McQueen released the forearm grip. "Sorry." He stood up. "You never were a warrior."

CHAPTER 46

The reporters aimed their cam-fingers at the crowd of pig people who had watched McQueen and Danielle receive the antidote. When they realized they were going to be on the news, they disbanded and rushed home to watch themselves on TV.

The resurrected Dinkies eased back into the shadows. All was calm. Pieces of splintered two-by-four wood lay scattered in the street. The few pig people that had stayed in their apartments above the stores, left the safety of their orange-lighted windows, trickled down the apartment stairways, and eased onto the sidewalks. Milling around in the street, they tiptoed around the water spots; and they were extra careful not to touch the broken two-by-fours.

As if they had always been his friends, and as if nothing had happened, McQueen's former warrior friends patted him on the back.

Tommy looked up at the warriors and at McQueen. "I trust that everyone is enjoying their freedom."

"We most certainly are," McQueen said, took Danielle's hand, and they strolled down the liberated street.

Tommy ran ahead of them, jumped up and down, and made faces. "Hey, you big dummy," he joked. "Do you still want me" — he pointed to his own chest, and then pointed to McQueen — "to let you catch me?"

"That five-hundredth capture record is useless now," McQueen said. "Without the virus threat, everything's going to change."

Lightening snapped above. "Watch out!" blared from across the street.

Wrraammmm! A noise hummed down the street and headed toward McQueen. He looked up. Ten meters in front of him, a huge armored, metallic-green OvalCar stopped.

The pig people ran from the street, scooted up their apartment stairways, stood safely behind their orange-lighted windows, and stared. The warriors turned. Some half-walked, and some half-ran away from the threatening OvalCar.

As McQueen watched the OvalCar, bewilderment immobilized him for a moment. Then his warrior training took over. He turned and looked toward Augur. "I didn't know Blue Town was so far advanced."

"I didn't either," Augur said. "It looks like the corporation has brought out its big gun."

Tommy reached into his belt for his squirt gun. It was gone. "Here we go again." He scrambled into the street, and picked up a two-by-four.

Reporters ran behind buildings, squatted under apartment steps, and cowering in fear, they stuck out their cam-fingers.

The armored OvalCar hummed loud. On its sides, red, blue, and yellow lights — like old carnival lights — hung on dirty-gray wires. The lights fluttered, blinked, and went black. The car screeched once and the humming stopped. Its wide side doors cracked open just a few centimeters. For a moment, light radiated from inside and caused the car's doorframe to glow a hazy green. Then, the doors continued to move and revealed an inner shield. Like fat wings, the doors unfolded and spread across the canopy-covered sidewalks and almost touched the storefront buildings. Now, the huge vehicle blocked the deserted street and the sidewalks, too.

Danielle grabbed onto McQueen's arm and held tight. Auger checked his canteen for water. It was empty.

McQueen placed his hand on Danielle's and gently pulled it from his arm. "Say behind me."

Tommy swung the two-by-four as if he were in the batter's box at a Dinky baseball game. "At least it'll be a fair fight this time."

"I don't think so," Augur said. "I've heard of an army of superior mercury mutant warriors."

McQueen's body tensed for a battle. "Maybe they have come to take us out."

CHAPTER 47

The inner shield, inside the OvalCar opened. Strong yellowish green light emanated from inside. McQueen didn't know what was about to happen. He was ready to fight.

Something amorphous moved inside the car. The yellowish green light fluttered and formed a brilliant grass-green halo. As it intensified and spread out, its outer edges fogged to a blue haze. Then, a thin black figure stepped out of the car and silhouetted against the soft light. The figure stood about a meter tall. A long skinny tail that resembled a rat's knurled tail, curled down from its back and dragged on the blue pavement. It walked toward McQueen.

Watching the rat-like tail, *Snake!* Flashed in McQueen's mind. He drew back and shuddered. The little figure stopped walking and stood at attention. McQueen shook off the repulsive felling and walked toward the figure. It held up its hand and smiled. Its only two front teeth were white rectangles that stuck out like a goofy cartoon character's teeth. It swung its hand down and spoke. "Augur has summoned you." In a welcoming gesture, it pointed toward the OvalCar.

McQueen looked at Tommy. Tommy looked at McQueen. McQueen shrugged. "Let's go." He led the way.

Danielle, Tommy, and Augur followed McQueen into the green light and stopped.

With its tail dragging behind him, the skinny black figure stepped to the entrance of the OvalCar and stopped.

As if they were protective weapons, reporters held their cam-fingers out in front of them and ran toward the OvalCar. The black figure closed its lips over its cartoon front teeth and blew out a long threatening hiss. Then it lifted its tail up off the pavement, curled it into an S, and jerked it in a threatening snake-like manner. The reporters turned and ran.

From within the OvalCar, a deep voice called out. "Let them come forth."

The figure's tail dropped to the pavement and its hissing mouth turned to a sunny smile.

Glancing back over his shoulder, McQueen walked toward the car. Danielle and the others looked at each other for a second and shambled after him.

McQueen stopped into the outer fringes of the haze of the blue light and looked inside the car. A man with his back turned toward him sat in a wheelchair. He seemed to have a warrior's body, but McQueen was puzzled by the three head supports that stuck up behind the chair. And then, the man turned and faced him. The man was a mutant. He had three heads.

Tommy tugged at McQueen's arm. "Maybe he's related to that three-headed bass we saw at Hidden Lake."

McQueen didn't answer. He stared at the mutated man and wondered if he could be the real Augur, the mythical Augur.

A wheelchair ramp buzzed out from the under the rocker panel of the OvalCar. With the green light surrounding him, the big three-headed mutant steered his motorized wheelchair down the little ramp. When he rolled into the blue haze of light, he stopped.

The skinny black figure turned and stepped into the blue haze. The change in light didn't change the color of its body or accent any of its limbs, but its knurled rat tail thumped on the pavement. It stood tall and spoke like a machine. "Augur has one functioning head," it said, and thumped its tail once. "It draws power from the other two heads and creates a God-like intelligence."

Trying to get a better look, McQueen leaned toward the mutated man. "Can we talk to him?"

As if he were looking for a sign or a reaction, the little figure snarled and looked to the mutated man. Then it looked at McQueen. "You may be able to get through today. Augur has changed since we were rescued from the sideshow." The figure shuddered, but continued. "Augur's knowledge has gone beyond an intellectual level. Some of my fellow pygmies say he evolves in and out of the future."

Rescued from the sideshow gave McQueen doubts. This three-headed person couldn't be the real Augur. The rat-tailed pygmy must be some kind of freak who belongs in a carnival. He looked down at the pygmy and pointed to the three-head man. "What does he want with us?"

"You can ask him," the pygmy said. "But Augur has trouble talking to common people."

McQueen figured that if this mutant man could speak more than one language he might be intelligent. "What language does he speak?"

"Augur speaks all languages known to man and more. We mere humans are not on his usual communicating level." The pygmy's tail rose up and its end wagged like a begging dog's tail. "It is difficult for him to lower his intellectual level long enough to communicate with people with limited intelligence.

McQueen looked at Augur's three heads. The one on the left hung off to the side and rested on one of the three head supports. Clear mucus streamed from its weak opened mouth. The head on the right, sat solid on its support. Like lifeless wet stones, its big round eyes stared straight ahead and blinked as if they were on a timer; and its mouth was big and fixed in a permanent smile. The center head resembled a frog's head. The skin had a light green cast to it, and hints of yellow lines crisscrossed the face like a child's scribbling.

McQueen couldn't believe how ugly the man was. Knowing all those languages and being so smart that no one understood him must be horrible. He could be a very lonely man.

The head on the left, slobbered out of its mouth. The pygmy walked up, pulled a red sponge from a holder in the wheelchair, and wiped that head's mouth. The head on the right tilted and closed its eyes.

"If you have questions" — the pygmy looked at McQueen — "Augur will be able to talk in a few seconds."

The mutant motored his wheelchair into the fog of light and stopped at a place where it turned from green to blue. Like a motor beginning to run, but not up to full power, he spoke from his middle frog head. "Only a few men have the courage and imagination to lead the Dinkies out of the ruins."

436

From the tone of mutant's voice and a feeling in his own chest, McQueen knew that this mutant's intellectual abilities were far above those of any ordinary man. He was the Real Augur.

"I don't think it was courage," McQueen said. "I just had to convince the people that virus is not real."

Real Augur talked faster. "Why did you tell the pig people and the warriors there is no virus?"

"Because there is no virus. And it's wrong to force people to live in fear?"

The real Augur lifted his mutant hand, spread two fingers, and pointed to his heads. "Look at my heads."

"I see them."

Real Augur's speech sped up again. This time he talked with a mouse-like voice. "Do you think this is wrong?"

McQueen winced. "Well, yes, but—" he began to say, but the real Augur interrupted. The words came out of his mouth so fast that McQueen could scarcely understand them. The Pygmy lifted his tail and slowly rotated it in a circle.

The real Augur slowed his speech. "Perhaps you would like the whole of mankind to look like this?" He pointed to the pygmy's tail. "Or maybe you would like everyone on earth to have a tail."

McQueen glanced at the rotating end of the pygmy's tail, but he couldn't help watching the real Augur's head on the right. It bobbled around and its eyes crossed, making its big floppy ears seem larger. It looked like some kind of puppet, a humorous knucklehead.

McQueen knew he shouldn't laugh at

someone's misfortunes, but the sight of the knucklehead caused laughter to creep inside his chest. "No, I don't want mankind to look like that," he said with strained politeness. "But the virus is still fake."

The real Augur stared at McQueen. "The virus cannot be fake," he said, and the knucklehead stuck out its tongue and twirled its eyes. The real Augur must have known McQueen was about to laugh. He reached up and backhanded the knucklehead. It quit its antics.

McQueen looked at the pygmy's rat tail. It was lying on the ground. It was motionless and looked threatening. McQueen swallowed his laughter and took on a serious tone. "But the virus can be fake, and it is."

Tommy stepped closer. "We're living proof it's fake. We're alive."

"I can see that," the real Augur said. "The pig people must be so starved for a hero that they tell lies, make up stories, and promote anyone willing to lead. They have made a common man a hero."

"I don't care what the pig people say," McQueen said, and raised his voice. "The virus is fake. We fought to prove it. If we have to, we'll fight again."

As if it were getting ready to fight off aggression, the pygmy's tail rose up.

Patagonia Augur looked at the tail. It dropped to the pavement. Patagonia Augur hesitated, but stepped closer. "All my life I have wondered why people have told me of things I have not done." He slowly shook his head. "They have been praising me for things a real Augur has done."

Tommy's face creased with confusion. "So what?" He stiffened and raised his little fist. "The virus is still fake."

"I believed it was," Patagonia Augur said. "But now, I am not so sure." He looked to the real Augur. "Are you?"

The real Augur rolled his frog head once. "When a being changes the way it looks at things, the things he looks at change."

Tommy lowered his fist. "What are you talking about, sir?"

Real Augur stared into Tommy's eyes. "The inhabitants of the earth have not evolved past the simple tree."

McQueen let out a frustrated breath of air. "What do you mean? A tree just sits there. It doesn't do a thing."

The real Augur turned toward McQueen. "No tree has branches that fight amongst themselves," he said with a sharp tone to his voice. "Before the virus came to be, the pig people of this fragile earth were destroying everything the future would inherit."

Pecking the air like a chicken, the knucklehead crossed its eyes and dipped its skinny neck. Tommy grinned and caused an aura of comedy to creep into the conversation.

The real Augur reached up and smacked the knucklehead again. It quit. The aura turned back to serious. The real Augur continued, "The pig people forced The Friends of The Earth Corporation to create the virus."

"But it's not right to treat people like ignorant pigs," McQueen argued.

The pygmy's tail rose up and threatened.

McQueen ignored it. "People are individuals. They are important."

The real Augur's mouth turned downward. "The earth's atmosphere is more important." He jerked his hand toward the dirty-orange dome above Blue Town. "It is not right to fill the atmosphere with carbon dioxide and filth." He gestured to a pool of water next to the OvalCar's wheel. "The earth's water is important. Why should pig people be allowed to poison it?" He pointed to the pigmy. "The earth's animals are important. Why should chemicals lace the earth and mutate people into things like this?" He pointed to his own face. "And like this!"

McQueen nodded but didn't speak.

The sweat-matted hair on the head, on the real Augur's left open the lower side of its mouth. A stream of clear, thick slobber dripped onto the blue pavement. With its tail in an S curve, the pigmy ran up to it and sopped it up with the red sponge. The right head blinked, but didn't start its antics. The real Augur continued. "The pig people have already made most of the earth uninhabitable."

"We know that," McQueen said and jerked his hand in the air. "But if we expose the virus farce, we can go further. We can expose the lies about radiation."

"Radiation is the least of our problems," the real Augur said, and paused.

The pygmy stepped back to the entrance of the OvalCar and let his tail fall to the pavement.

Real Augur pointed to his knucklehead. "If man's ignorance is not controlled, the earth's

440

devastation will continue. The few remaining livable areas of the world will be destroyed. Man or animal will not survive."

The pygmy's tail stood up and wagged with a negative swish. The real Augur glanced at it. "It is not right to infect the air and land to the point of man's extinction for the sake of greed."

McQueen knew real Augur was making sense, but he had almost died proving the virus wasn't real. He didn't want his efforts to be for nothing. "But the pig people should know there is no virus."

The pygmy let out a whoosh of air. Its tail drooped.

The real Augur threw his hands into the air. The knucklehead turned and stared cross-eyed at the real Augur's frog head. "The wonderful pig people," the real Augur said and waved his hand in the air. "Oh, my yes, the wonderful pig people."

The knucklehead snapped his head in the direction of the pigmy. The real Augur waved his hand toward the pigmy and back toward himself. "We are examples of what the pig people have done for the human race."

Like a dog at feeding time, the pygmy's tail wagged happily.

The real Auger smiled at the pigmy. "Because the pig people considered the pygmies to be of little or no importance they destroyed their land and almost eliminated the whole race."

"Maybe they didn't know what they were doing," Tommy said.

The knucklehead crossed its eyes and grunted. The real Augur grimaced. "The pig people knew the effects their actions would have on the pygmies.

They knew about the effects of nitrogen and how it released ancient carbon into the air. They knew what would happen when they destroyed their rainforest. And worst of all, they knew what the nuclear tests would do."

McQueen shrugged. "The earth's a big place. Maybe they just didn't believe a little climate change would hurt."

The knucklehead's jaw dropped and it mouthed the word, "Duh!"

As if his head hurt, the real Augur's skin above his eye creased, but he continued. "For years scientists warned that the polar icecaps were melting. The pig people deliberately ignored the warnings. They killed the fragile gift of the earth."

"That's right," Tommy said with a hint of laughter in his voice.

The real Augur reached up and looked at the knucklehead. It was expressionless. The pygmy's tail stopped its happy movements. Then Augur glared at Tommy.

Tommy's face turned serious. "I'm not laughing at you," he said. "I'm laughing about the time the corporation tried to make us believe that large animals passing gas was the cause of global warming. Nobody believed it, but the corporation still claimed it would stop when the animals were eliminated?"

The real Augur's left head wobbled and hung over the side of its head support. The real Augur leaned back, reached over, and pushed the head back onto the support. "It may have been funny back then, but the truth is that the corporation killed all the large animals because they caused damage when they ran in front of their vehicles. And the ignorance goes on and on. Now you must have trained drivers to drive simple OvalCars."

McQueen looked the real Auger right in his frog eyes. "That maybe so, but why must the pig people fear water?"

The real Augur breathed in and cringed as if he had been stabbed in the chest. The knucklehead closed its eyes; and as if he were expecting pain, he squeezed them tight. The pygmy put its tail into an S and put the bottom half of the curve between its legs. The real Augur thrust his fist toward the sky and threw out his finger. As if he had caused it to happen, a zigzag of lightning scampered across the dark night. "Never permit the pig people to venture near the water."

Tommy glanced at the sky and then looked at the real Augur. "Why not?" he asked with a hint of fear.

The knucklehead relaxed its eyes. The real Augur lowered his hand and lifted his finger, but he did not jerk it toward the sky. "Every time the pig people are permitted to go near water they poison it."

"Your aid here," McQueen said and gestured toward the pygmy, "says your mind has ventured into the future. Couldn't you use your superior mind and let these people see what their actions will do to the future?"

The head's eyes on the left began to tear up. A thoughtful expression came over the real Augur's face and his frog head bent down. "The pig people have a destructive nature," he said. "They do not care about the future. "They cannot be trusted to live without fear."

With his tail still in an S curve and with the bottom half between his legs, the pigmy stepped up and wiped the left head's eyes.

Real Augur whipped his frog head into an upright position. "If we are to maintain an ordered social universe, we must use the power at hand and ensure all organizing principles stay in place."

Even if the man was the real Augur, McQueen believed he was wrong. "That's nonsense," he said. "We can pass laws that will make the pig people respect the land."

"That has been tired," the real Augur said, and cast McQueen an exhausted look. "The ignorant pig people have too much idle time. There are not enough warriors or border guards to enforce all the laws all the time."

McQueen turned his palms up and shrugged. "What else can we do?"

The pygmy stepped back to the doorway of the OvalCar. The real Augur straightened up in his chair and pointed at McQueen. "You, John McQueen, must marshal the collective energy of these self-destructive people."

McQueen raked his fingers through his hair. "The pig people have always been okay with me. We could let them off the blue grass, but keep them busy building something."

"Our ancestors tried that. They kept them busy building colossal pyramids. But history has shown us that when the pig people are given free rein over their lives, they ruin or destroy everything they touch."

"But we don't know if they'll still do that."

444

"Have you seen mutated life?"

Now, McQueen felt like saying, "Duh?" He was talking to a three-headed mutant. He had seen a three-headed frog and a three-headed bass. He had seen the three-headed snake that had wiggled its tongues in front of his face, and now a pygmy, with a rat tail and cartoon buck teeth, was standing right in front of him. "Yes, Augur." He sighed. "I have seen mutated life."

"Have you seen eagles fly with no chance of offspring?"

"I get your point," McQueen said. "But what do you expect me to do about it?"

"If your Indian ancestors would have put the pig people on the reservations, we would not have the problems we have today. You are going to correct the mistakes of your ancestors."

The knucklehead's eyes opened wide. The pygmy's tail wagged with anticipation.

"I can't correct anything," McQueen said, and looked down at his boots. "I'm no longer a warrior."

The real Augur raised his voice. "Don't lower your head in shame. You are a natural born leader."

The knucklehead squinted. The real Augur lifted his finger that had caused the lightning and jerked it at McQueen. "It's your job to create and to keep order against the powers of chaos."

McQueen lifted his head. "But I'm not qualified to do that."

The real Augur pointed his finger at McQueen and held it there. "Whether you like it or not," he said, "just like your ancestors, you were born qualified."

McQueen felt his forehead wrinkle with confusion. "Why me?"

"Someone must lead and organize the world's human energy around a central idea."

McQueen shook his head.

As if it sensed something had already been decided, the knucklehead's eyes relaxed.

In a show of finality, the real Augur swished his hand pointing-fingered hand down. "Don't shake your head. Now that Nelson is dead, you are that leader."

McQueen leaned back. "I can't. I don't even have a central idea."

The real Augur raised his hand. "You are not a pig person. Use your mind."

McQueen thought for a moment, and then said, "We did have a central idea, but it was lost in the stones of life."

"We are not talking about religion. We are talking about an established central idea that has controls the pig people. We are talking about staying on the blue grass."

McQueen looked down. The sight of the blue pavement beneath his feet burned in his mind. "When I was in the forest," he said, everything was clean and new. The green colors relaxed my mind. The world must be sick of blue things." He looked to the real Augur. "The stones of life are a stronger symbol. Why can't we use those?"

All three heads shook with negativity. The pygmy closed his mouth over his cartoon teeth and dropped his tail to the pavement. Real Augur stopped shaking his frog head and forced out a long, slow breath of air. "In a time long ago, the stones

446

of life caused the pig people's religious commitment to be strong."

"It can be strong again," McQueen said. "We can let the pig people go off the blue grass."

"The past has shown that the pig people retain an excessive desire for far more than they need or deserve. Because they refuse to change, it is impossible for them to understand total freedom."

"We could at least give them a chance," McQueen said with quiet urgency.

The real Augur's nose on his frog face wrinkled with disgust. "When the pig people had unlimited freedom they outlawed the stones of life. After that, they no longer had the desire to combine their energy and act as one to realize a common mission. They became weak and lazy."

McQueen held up his hand. "Now back up just a second," he said. "If they became so lazy, then why are they such a threat?"

"Laziness brings a complete and random disregard for right and wrong. No living being, plant, or water source is immune to the destructive greed a lawless society brings."

Tommy's little forehead wrinkled as if he were getting the drift of what was being said, but he couldn't keep up. "So what does that have to do with the blue grass?"

"If the—" the real Augur started to say, but the knucklehead wobbled and pecked the air. The real Augur reached up and threatened to smack it. It quit pecking the air and the real Auger continued. "If the pig people lose fear of the virus they will have nothing to follow. Their behavior will once again become random."

447

Tommy butted in. "That doesn't seem so bad."

"Whether you consider it good or bad, when nothing is controlled in some form or some way, the very ground you're standing on becomes prey to the forces of chaos."

Tommy lowered his head and looked at the ground under his feet.

McQueen was puzzled. "Why would anyone try to stop development of humanity?"

"Development causes population growth and the unchecked pollution that goes with it."

"Just as long as there are laws to stop the pollution, McQueen said. "There's nothing wrong with development."

Good point. But if you will remember, nearly seventy percent of the world's population used to live within fifty miles of the oceans. When the pig people were free to develop it, by proxy they were killers in an age when mankind had supposedly attained wisdom. Even with strict laws against pollution, they turned the oceans into dumping grounds for toxic waste, and they haven't recovered yet."

For a moment, as if he had just dropped dead, the real Augur stopped talking and his three heads flopped forward.

McQueen turned toward the pigmy. "Is he all right?"

Before the pigmy could answer, the real Auger's heads snapped upright. As if to make an important point, he held up one finger. "And worst of all, is the sad fact that there is less fresh water on the earth than there was three thousand years ago. Fracking companies shot it down deep wells.

Radiation is coming up but the water is not coming back up. A thousand years ago, the population was a small percentage of what it is now. Letting the pig people off the blue grass will kindle development. The fracking will flourish until every drop of water is used for profit. If mankind survives the radiation, the poison in the air will become so thick it will fill our lungs and cut off the very air we breathe."

As if he were reading something in the sky, the knucklehead looked off into the distance.

Following the knucklehead's lead, the real Augur looked to the sky. "If a civilization fails to live by laws, it is no longer a civilization."

The knucklehead squeezed his eyes once. Lightning arced across the dirty-orange dome of Blue Town and thunder cracked in the night.

Like a man who changes the subject when he doesn't understand what is being talked about, Tommy raised his arm and pointed to the lights strung around the car. "What are those lights for?"

The real Augur nodded his head in the direction of the pigmy. "We were sideshow freaks." The pigmy smiled and showed his cartoon teeth. The real Augur continued. "After our pigmy friends freed us, we were greeted by a world of filth, greed, and destruction from within. No safe rain fell from the filth-filled sky. On the ground, there was no fresh water to be found. Without fresh un-poisoned water to grow plants nothing is safe to eat. Without food the will to live will vanish." He reached up and turned his left head. It blinked its eyes in rapid succession and stared toward the lights. "Oh yes, those ancient sideshow-freak lights are a reminder that the pig people have become clowns in a million-ring circus. They have become clowns who cannot be trusted with water, plants, the air, or outer space."

McQueen knew real Augur was right. He shook his head and felt as if he were about to cry. "But what am I supposed to do?" he asked, and the knucklehead's face looked overwhelmed.

"Don't be confused," the real Augur said, and his voice filled with anxiety. The knucklehead squinted. The real Augur shook that lightning finger at McQueen. "Your ancestors gave you the key to the substance of the heavenly bodies which is dormant in all things."

McQueen shook his head. "I don't understand what you are telling me."

The knucklehead opened one eye, but kept the other one shut tight.

The real Augur's frog face tensed, and he wagged his head around. "You have the substance of the heavenly bodies. You have what is latent in all things. You have quintessence."

"What?" McQueen questioned.

The real augur paused and continued. "Like it or not, you have the fifth and highest essence after the four elements of Earth, Air, Fire, and Water. You are part of the true spirit of the earth."

"I don't care what I have," McQueen scoffed. "I'm not going to lie for you or anybody else."

The pygmy's rat tail stayed flat on the ground. The tone of the real Augur's voice showed that his patience was beginning to wane. "Will you ever learn? If you expose the secret of the virus, all the Blue Towns and Patagonia of the earth will wither

450

and die"

"How can that happen? Truth always prevails."

"The truth is that the pig people live for self-satisfaction and greed."

"Not everyone thinks like that."

"Think about it, McQueen," The real Augur snapped back. "Patagonia is a good example of what can happen."

"They had a riot," McQueen said, and a strong sense of grief entered his chest. He unconsciously lowered his voice. "Many people were killed."

The real Augur's face turned as hard stone. He spoke in a businesslike tone. "When the pig people of Patagonia learned the truth about the virus they began to go off the blue grass. They had to be killed."

Patagonia Augur lifted his hand and gasped. "I was in those riots. The Dinkies started them."

The knucklehead wobbled around, crossed its eyes, and stuck out its tongue. "Sure they did," the real Augur said, with sarcasm in his voice.

The knucklehead stuck out its tongue and crossed its eyes. McQueen tried not to look at it. "Are you saying the Friends of the Earth planned those riots?"

The real Augur reached up and smacked the knucklehead. It stopped its antics. The real Augur continued, again. "Because they are friends of the earth they had no choice."

"But that's murder."

"Call it what you want," the real Augur said with a strange look of regret on his face. "It is a necessary evil. Now, the people of Patagonia are being controlled. Now, you must get the people of

451

Blue Town back on the blue grass.

McQueen exhaled a long breath of air. He was tired of it all. He really didn't want to be responsible for the lives of so many people. "What if I can't?"

"If you can't get them back on the blue grass, your warriors will shoot them with poison antidote bullets. If that fails we'll engineer another riot. It'll be so awful they'll never forget why they have to stay on the blue grass."

Something familiar and strange struck deep in McQueen's heart. He did not fully agree with what the real Augur was telling him, but he was beginning to think it was going to be a bitter pill that he was going to have to swallow. He nodded his head with semi-understanding.

The real Augur relaxed his frog face. "For the pig people's own good, they must be forced to live with the earth, not on the earth. To do this, they must stay on blue grass reservations."

Tommy spoke up. "We have found an antitoxin. The antidote bullets are harmless."

The knucklehead opened its eyes in surprise. Real Augur shook his frog head once. "It will only be a short time before the housing authority has a new antidote bullet." He looked into the sky. "They may have it as we speak."

"So what," Tommy said. "We'll just find another antitoxin."

Like a frog stalking a fly, the real Augur stared in Tommy's direction. "You probably will," he said. "But the cycle will go on and on. It has to."

Patagonia Augur nodded. "The virus is the only way we can peacefully save the earth."

From what I have seen in the forbidden forest," McQueen said. "It looks like the earth has recovered."

Real Augur turned his frog head toward McQueen and spoke like a father to a son. "You know in your heart that it has only attained a small foothold. If the destructive pig people are allowed to go back into the green lands, the fragile earth will never recover."

As if he wanted to make his words perfectly clear, the real Augur talked with an agonizing snail-like pace. "For thousands of years your Indian ancestors observed nature. They discovered how and why nature had to be helped."

"What do you mean helped?" McQueen asked. "Nature can repair herself. Just leave her alone."

"Setting aside wilderness doesn't freeze it in a permanent state. A balance has to be maintained."

Tommy shifted his weight onto one foot. "There's not much left to balance."

The real Augur pointed to McQueen. "Your Indian ancestors knew old-growth forests needed to be periodically replaced with new growth. They made sure the forests burned down periodically, and they left little islands of old-growth forest in the midst of plains and meadows. They cultivated the forest."

McQueen felt a sudden burst of anger. He wanted equal treatment for all. "Indians changed their environment to suit their purpose. Why can't we let the pig people do that?"

Tears fell from the head on the left. The real Augur's tone became crisp and authoritative. "The pig people have slashed, burned, and poisoned

453

beyond balance," he said. "The only thing they understand is greed and wealth."

With his limp rat tail dragging behind him, the pigmy stepped up and wiped the left head's tears.

McQueen still wanted the truth about the virus to be known. "If the pig people can't live on the green land," he said. "Then why should the Dinkies be permitted to live there?"

The real Augur seemed surprised at McQueen's growing resentment. "The Dinkies didn't ruin the land. The pig people did. In its slow recovering state, it can only support a small population of the Dinky race." He looked toward the pygmy. "The Dinkies are much like my pygmy friend's ancestors of the ancient rain forest. They can come and go without harming the feeble forests. They live mostly underground. They weave their small bodies amongst the plants without disturbing the growing cycles."

McQueen objected. "But couldn't the pig people be taught to live like the Dinkies?"

A sour look spread across the real Augur's frog face. "You have seen it. I have seen it. Everyone here has seen it. When the pig people are allowed into the green world they destroy it and everything they touch. Why do you think they're called pig people?"

Tommy shook his head in agreement and looked at McQueen. "Maybe that is what your father was trying to show us when he told us the parable about the man who believed in the stones of life, but was killed because he trusted mankind?"

"But why so much fear?" McQueen asked. "Why so many lies? Couldn't we just educate them?"

The real Augur looked to Tommy. "If your Dinky friend has ever been accused of stealing, he knows the routine."

Tommy nodded. "If a Dinky takes something, it's stealing. When a pig person takes something, it's good business."

"When it is not for their personal gain," the real Augur said, and wagged his frog head to one side, "the pig people reject education. The earth can no longer survive in selfish ignorance." He clinched his hand into a fist and waved it in the air. "Lies that generate terror and fear are the only way to control the pig people."

"What about—" McQueen started to say.

But the real Augur held up his hand. "If the pig people are not controlled, this is the end of the earth as we know it."

Patagonia Augur spoke up. "What about the other outer space? Couldn't we inhabit another planet?"

The real Augur closed one eye. "Space travel is impossible. The satellite wars covered the earth's atmosphere with billions of pieces of shattered satellite metal. And even if pig people could go to another world, who would want them?"

McQueen looked back at Danielle and the others. They stood there, stunned. He realized that during the whole time with the real Augur, Danielle had not said a single word.

The real Augur dropped his hand. When he looked up, his frog face took on the look of a cautious creature. "You four have disrupted the earth's healing cycle." He motioned to all of them with his arm. "You have snatched the evil torch of necessary medicine from Chief Executing Officer Nelson." He pointed at McQueen. "You have begun to eliminate the fear of the virus. You must realize that people are just pigs. You have seen how they did not lift a finger to help you. They only take and destroy for their own good. They have no fear or knowledge of the black book, and they have never touched the stones of life."

The real Augur reached out and placed his wise hand on McQueen's shoulder. McQueen looked up, bewildered.

In a strange orator's voice that seemed to be coming from a tunnel, the real Augur talked like a father to a son. "It is now your obligation to save the earth. You must undo all that you have changed."

"What?"

"If the truth about the virus spreads, the remaining livable Blue Towns of the earth will be thrown into a state of panic. Fear of the virus is our tool of controlling terror. For it to continue to work, we must keep it sharp. Sergeant John McQueen, you have dulled the sharp edge of our tool."

"But," McQueen objected. "The pig people need to know the virus is fake."

The real Augur snapped back, "It is too dangerous."

"I have touched the stones of life," McQueen said. "What's so dangerous about the truth?"

As if he were being overwhelmed with something he didn't want to hear, the real Augur moved his frog head from side to side. "The stones of life only function," he said, and emphasized, "if,

456

and only if, all live within their rules. The second that money or credits become involved the pig people immediately disregard the rules or change them to suit their unnecessary pleasures. The pig people have not learned how to reconnect to the source from which they came."

"But they could," McQueen objected. "I'll find the stones of life and show them the way."

"A man on a cross tried that and then the pig people destroyed his black book." The real Augur looked up as if he were looking toward heaven. "At one time it worked for the good people of the earth and it still would, but the mighty hand of evil has taken over."

McQueen thought of all the trouble he had gone through to expose the virus farce. He still felt that the truth was the answer and that the pig people had the right to know the virus was not real. "But we could make the stones work."

"Maybe in the distant future," the real Augur said. "But if you continue your present quest, a handful of panic-stricken pig people and a few warriors will transmit their hysteria to the entire population. The world will end in a hellish mess."

McQueen turned to Danielle. "What do you think we should do?"

Danielle reached out and held onto McQueen's arm. "I just want everything to be like it used to be."

Augur of Patagonia, placed his hand on McQueen's shoulder. "You know she's right and you know Augur's right."

Confused, McQueen rubbed his forehead. "I just don't know."

Sludge and his band of Dinkies appeared at the edge of the blue light.

CHAPTER 48

Sludge and his band of Dinkies walked under the outer wing of the OvalCar and stopped at the fringes of the blue light. He held up his hand. "Stop."

His followers stopped. Red-faced and puffing, he waved his hand in the air and advanced toward McQueen. "Just 'cause you're too dumb to know the pig people hav'ta stay on the blue grass," he said." It don't mean we're ah-spose to."

The pygmy's tail rose up into its defensive S curve; and with his lips covering his cartoon teeth, he lifted his hand and signaled Sludge to stop.

Tommy looked at the Pygmy and gave him an approving nod. "It's all right," he said. "Let him speak."

The pygmy's tail drooped, but remained in the defensive S curve.

Before he could catch his breath, Sludge pointed to the orange-lighted windows. "We ain't gonna live with them pig people." He made a face and took a deep breath. "They stink, they're dumb and stupid. And there ain't no way you kin trust 'em."

"Take it easy, Sludge," Tommy said. "You don't have to actually live with them."

"Sludge let out a harsh grunt. "You wanna bet? When they find out the virus ain't real, they're gonna be everywhere." Sludge pointed to the real Augur. "You guys ain't been listen to him."

The real Augur nodded his frog head.

The redness in Sludge's face paled and he continued. "You ain't gonna be able to tramp down a forest path without stepping in their crap. You ain't gonna be able to take a bath or drink a single drop of water they ain't sellin'."

"But I want to be free," Tommy said. "When they find out the virus is not real, they'll be able to do their own labor, farm their own farms. We'll be free again."

"Don't be so stupid. You know the only-est thing those pig people do is cut down every tree and plant more than they can ever eat."

"What's wrong with that?"

"They clear out all the trees and the sun dries up the land. And then when they don't sell the food, they stack it up and let it rot. Let 'em do that, next thing you know, they'll be fillin' in our tunnels with it." Sludge waved his hands in the air. "We won't never be able to git away from dem pigs. We ain't gonna have no place to live, and when they poison the water, we ain't gonna be able to live."

McQueen looked toward Tommy. "I never thought of it that way."

Tommy tilted his head to one side. "You know, Sludge, for once in your life, you might be right."

Sludge puffed up his chest with self-importance. "Don't give me that crap. He raised his hand in a threatening manner. I'm always right. What are you gonna do about it?"

The tip of the pigmy's tail jerked toward Sludge. The pygmy raised his hand. "We have had enough fighting today."

Sludge glared at the pygmy, lowered his hand, and quit talking.

The real Augur pulled an eagle feather from his right breast pocket. "Perhaps I should remind you

460

of the words of your father." He held the feather and spoke directly at McQueen. "Although you and I are in different boats, you're in your canoe and I in my boat, we share the same river of life. What involves me, involves you. Downstream, in our river of life, our children will pay for our lack of vision."

McQueen knew the words had value and meaning, but had heard his father say them so many times that the words were stored away in the Indian backwashes of his mind.

Danielle jerked her head and looked into McQueen's face. "We have to do this for our children."

McQueen bowed his head in silence and looked at the feather. It was an eagle feather with a white tip, but the brown vanes shone with a rich purple-sheen more reflective than the feather his father had given him.

Real Augur turned the feather on an angle. The purple-sheen flashed deep into McQueen's brain. As if he were speaking out of a long tunnel of time, the real Augur pointed to McQueen with the feather. "What are the seven directions?"

Boyhood memories flashed in McQueen's mind, and he said, "North, South, East, West, up, down, and inside."

Real Augur turned the feather and presented it to McQueen. "And what is the color inside oneself?"

McQueen stared at the purple sheen on the feather. "North is white," he said. "East is yellow. South is red. Black is West, and purple is inside."

Urging McQueen to accept it, the real Augur

waved the feather at him. "Then you know in your heart that your ancestors should have put the pig people on the reservations."

Without warning, what McQueen had to do broke upon him with the radiance of a fresh sunrise; but it was cluttered with long uncertain shadows. He felt like he was at the end of a glorious sunset. He felt the light he had found when he exposed the virus was going out, and he would have to find a way to bring it back to light a different path.

He reached out, accepted the purple-sheened feather, and placed it in his breast pocket. The real Augur's middle frog head trembled, and its chin dropped to his chest. Mumbling, he said, "The pig people are trying to survive on the earth, they must be trained to survive with the earth." The head on the left fell off the head support, tilted sideways, and rested on Augur's shoulder.

Patagonia Augur looked deep into McQueen's eyes and spoke clear. "We cannot bring back the earth's fathers and mothers that greed has murdered. Regardless of the cost to mankind, we must get rid of the poison in the air, the carcinogens in the earth, and the water we drink. We all know what to do. Let's just do it."

McQueen slowly shook his head and stood in the blue light. "No wonder Nelson said he was tired of it all. The pig people are like mentally deficient dogs that can't make it through obedience school. They are not ready to go off the blue grass." He turned to the real Augur. "Fake or not, the virus has to be real."

The real Augur's face beamed with hope for the future, and when he smiled it resembled the

462

innocence of a happy baby smiling. As if he had come to the end of a long race, his expression relaxed. He sighed and slumped down in his wheelchair. His left head's mouth opened wide. A stream of slobber ran down the front of his arm. The head on the right wagged around. With its eyes rolling, it dipped its skinny neck; and like it was happily gulping huge gulps of water, it said, "Gunk! Gunk! Gunk!"

As if he were embarrassed by the knucklehead's antics, the pygmy stepped between McQueen and the real Augur. "You must depart now," he said. "Augur can no longer speak."

With the knucklehead gulping, the pigmy smiled his two-toothed cartoon smile, pushed the real Augur through the blue light, and into green emerald light of the OvalCar. And the pygmy's knurled rattail crawled after.

Sludge walked back to his band of Dinkies. "Come on, you guys. While these dummies are tryin' to figure out what to do, we got work to do."

Sludge and his band vanished into the dark.

With tears in his eyes, Patagonia Augur watched the OvalCar. The pigmy stepped inside, slid the inner shield across the opening, and the winged doors folded shut. But the fog of blue light remained, mysteriously hovering in the night air. McQueen turned his back and stood in the blue cloud. Tommy and Danielle stood alongside.

Tommy looked up at McQueen. "What are we going to do now?"

"We must go back to what we were before. I must be a warrior." McQueen's voice wavered. "I must take Nelson's place."

Danielle let out a gasp of surprise, but covered her mouth with her hand. As if she were waiting for an explanation, she looked over at McQueen.

McQueen looked off into the dark. "I will be the new Chief Executing Officer."

"But what about the fake virus?" Tommy asked. "I don't want to live in those mines for the rest of my life."

McQueen felt a tear well up in the corner of his eye. He didn't answer. He walked outside the fringes of the blue haze, stopped, and looked down at Tommy. "We have knowledge that we can never use."

"But I want to be free," Tommy said. "It is what we fought for."

"If we don't control the pig people they will destroy every place they populate. No one on earth will have a place to live."

Patagonia Augur wiped his eyes on the sleeve of his shirt and looked back at McQueen. "How can a man be free if he is not alive?"

"Have we come to the end of the earth?" Tommy asked.

"Without the virus," Patagonia Augur said, "it is the end of the earth." He held out his wrists toward McQueen. "You must arrest me."

McQueen looked down at Patagonia Augur's wrists. "I could let you go."

"You can't. The pig people need a valid reason to accept you as their new Chief Earth Officer. My arrest will be a sign of credence amongst them. It will give you a reason to modify your statements about the virus."

Modify was just another word for lying.

McQueen didn't know if he could do it.

Lightning boomed and then, Wrraammm! The sound of the real Augur's OvalCar faded into the dark. The reporters rushed forward. The pig people came down from their orange-lit apartments and gathered around McQueen.

"The pig people were always suckers for a hero," Tommy said.

McQueen turned from the crowd and whispered to Patagonia Augur, "I'll arrest you on national TV. I'll tell the world all this has been a farce. I planned it all. It was just a ploy. Now my five-hundredth capture would be the capture of the most feared Dinky of all, the great, the all-powerful Augur."

McQueen walked to the stolen OvalCar and looked down at Nelson's body. His warrior-booted feet stuck out of the plastic body covering. No one had taken them off. A one-fingered reporter rushed up to McQueen and held his cam-finger in his face. McQueen didn't speak. Patagonia Augur nudged him in the elbow. "Do it," he whispered.

McQueen stood above Nelson's body and talked into the cam-finger. "This man was a mental warrior," he said, and gestured toward Nelson's body. "He made the hard decisions. He suffered extreme sacrifices. To save the world, like the warrior he was, he performed his function."

McQueen turned from the cam-finger. Patagonia Augur nudged him again. McQueen bent down and removed Nelson's boots. From between the tongue of the boot, a pure purple feather fell.

He picked it up, placed it next to the new feather in his breast pocket and stood up. Jud stood in front of him, holding hybrid-spider restraint-bands. He took the bands and placed them around Augur's wrists.

Photographers rushed to set up cameras on tripods and cam-fingers avalanched in front of McQueen's face.

Before he could speak a reported announced, "This is John McQueen, the hero of the pig people. He has just captured his five-hundredth Dinky."

McQueen stepped up on to the roof of the stolen OvalCar and looked skyward. He held his opened palm up, saluted a higher being, and was photographed for a propaganda poster.

A TV monitor was placed on the hood of the OvalCar. McQueen could see a clear image of himself. His blue-spruce-blue hunting uniform showed the tears and scars of the battles of his quest. His coal-black hair hung rough and matted down his weary curved back. The eagle feather he once wore was gone, but now he had a two new feathers sticking out of his breast pocket. He lowered his arm. His three gold sergeant stripes faded in the darkness of the night. His jet-black eyes leveled a lingering gaze at Patagonia Augur. Patagonia Augur's hands and feet were bound with the hybrid-spider restraint-bands. People in the crowd pointed and jeered at him as if he were a sideshow freak.

The reporter continued, "John McQueen has just broken the all-time record." He pointed to Patagonia Augur. "The great Augur is his five-hundredth capture."

The pig people cheered and waved their hands in the air. McQueen looked down at Tommy. Tommy looked up with a hurt look on his face.

466

With a slight jerk of his head, McQueen gestured for his old friend to leave. Tommy nodded his head in understanding and ran into the alleyway. The other remaining Dinkies ran after him and disappeared into the shadows.

McQueen looked beyond the sea of the crowd. Under a blue streetlight, Sludge and his newfound black twin, Yellow Neck, stood together. With his fist raised in the air, Sludge yelled at Yellow Neck, "See, I told you, 'You couldn't trust a darkie.'"

Black Yellow Neck reared back to strike white Sludge. Warriors rushed toward them. Yellow Neck dropped his fist, and they both ran into the darkness of Nelson Park.

"Don't worry about those Dinkies," the reporter said. "Our warriors will capture them. We have breaking news. The Friends of the Earth Corporation have just proclaimed: "Sergeant John McQueen A Prince of Peace.""

The reporter looked up at McQueen and stretched his cam-finger until it was in front of his face. "You were married under stress. Will you keep Danielle as your reproduction mate?"

Pointing to Danielle, McQueen said, "She's still the one."

Reporters ran to her. "What will it be like to live in the safety of the blue grass?"

But she didn't get a chance to answer. Another reporter, with one finger, pushed the other reporters aside and spoke. "Sergeant John McQueen has just been promoted. The Friends of The Earth Corporation have just come out of emergency conference. Sergeant John McQueen is no more. He is now, Chief Earth Officer McQueen."

The Humpty-Dumpty-shaped pig people cheered and chanted. "CEO! CEO! CEO!"

McQueen shook his head with sudden realization. Fear of the virus would not always be the answer, but it was the only thing the ignorant pig people understood. He turned and raised his hand. "Attention good people of Blue Town. The virus has mutated. It is much worse. You have just seen that the new antidote may not stop the new strain. It has killed Chief Earth Officer Nelson. You must not venture onto the green. You must—" he said, but suddenly in the dirty-orange dome above Blue town, lightning twisted bold and bright. Tumbling thunder trumpeted the coming of virus rain. A sea of pig people huddled together and looked toward the protection of the blue canopies. When they looked back at McQueen, their usual puffy-faced phony smiles were gone. Fear and confusion beamed up at him. They waited for him to speak.

The new Chief Earth Officer John McQueen paused. He swallowed hard and forced the words from his mouth. "You must stay on the blue grass."

THE END

468

www.ingramcontent.com/pod-product-compliance
Lightning Source LLC
Chambersburg PA
CBHW011737010726
47496CB00010B/2973